STRONG MEDICINE

A flash of motion caught Small Elk's eye, and he turned curiously . . . *Aiee!* Here was a thing he had not foreseen. A wolf, one of the gray ghosts that follow the herds, was creeping through the short grass.

He had suddenly become the quarry. He must do something quickly. The hunter was so close that he could see the glitter of the yellow eyes as it crept forward on its belly. Any moment now, it would make its rush.

Then the idea came. He was pretending to be a calf . . . what would a calf do? There was no time to stop and consider. He raised his head toward the herd, let out a bleat of terror and began to scramble away.

Suddenly, six or seven cows charged forward. He turned toward the wolf, who now seemed confused. The cows thundered past Elk on each side, brushing close and kicking up dirt, but avoiding injury to him.

The wolf retreated.

"Aiee!" greeted his father, White Buffalo, his eyes bright with excitement. "You have done well. You will be a great medicine man!"

Books by Don Coldsmith

The Changing Wind

》》 》》 》》 》》 》》 》》 》》 》》 》》 》》

D O N   C O L D S M I T H

BANTAM BOOKS
NEW YORK · TORONTO · LONDON · SYDNEY · AUCKLAND

THE CHANGING WIND
A Bantam Book / March 1990

All Rights Reserved.
Copyright © 1990 by Don Coldsmith.
Cover art copyright © 1990 by Tom Hall.

ISBN 0-553-28334-0

Published simultaneously in the United States and Canada

Bantam Books are published by Bantam Books, a division of Random House, Inc.
Its trademark, consisting of the words "Bantam Books" and the portrayal of a
rooster, is Registered in U.S. Patent and Trademark Office and in other countries,
Marca Registrada, Bantam Books, 1540 Broadway, New York, New York 10036

PRINTED IN THE UNITED STATES OF AMERICA

OPM   14   13

Introduction

» » »

A year or two after the release of *Trail of the Spanish Bit*, one of my students approached me with a suggestion. Why not, she asked, write in more depth about the life and career of White Buffalo, the medicine man? This character appears only briefly in the first few books of the Spanish Bit Saga.

I considered at some length. In many ways, this man represents a pivotal character in one of the greatest cultural changes in the human race. His life spans the entire time period of this cultural change. The Stone Age hunter of the plains and mountains evolved, in a single generation, into the finest light cavalry the world has ever seen. The factor that made the difference was the acquisition of the horse. This must have been not only a profound change, but a major threat, to one in the priestly function of White Buffalo, holy man of the People. I tried to imagine his feelings, his thoughts and fears. I wrote a few chapters and a brief outline but then became preoccupied with other projects and shelved the idea.

In 1987, Greg Tobin, a senior editor at Bantam, suggested a spin-off novel to supplement the Spanish Bit Saga. Would it be possible, he asked, to select minor characters from the early series for an original novel, a "superedition," connected to but not a part of the series? I mailed a proposal the following day, with the material I had outlined.

So this is the story of one man's lifetime. We see him at first resist, then accept, and finally take part in the cultural shift. It will alter his civilization forever as the winds of change sweep across the prairie and the People advance into the centuries that mark the Golden Age of the Horse.

—Don Coldsmith
1989

Part I

The Vision

There was little about the childhood of Small Elk that foretold his place in the story of the People. Perhaps his mother, Dove Woman, anticipated that her son was destined for greatness, but such expectations are regarded as a mother's privilege. However, his father also suspected that here was a child with an unusual mission.

The two older children of Dove Woman and White Buffalo had grown, married, and had their own lodges before the coming of Small Elk to the lodge of the medicine man. That alone set him apart, but there were other things that his father noticed. There was his curiosity. The child would sit for long spaces of time, watching a column of ants going in and out of their underground lodge. There were those in the tribe, White Buffalo knew, who would regard this as useless activity. And, he had to admit, for some it may have been. But not for Small Elk. There was something about the *way* the child watched the creatures. His father was certain that Small Elk *understood* the apparently aimless scurrying around the anthill. He did not say so, but there was a look of wonder on the small face, the wonder of learning. White Buffalo saw in the shining dark eyes an understanding of the spirit of the ants.

It was, in a way, like the understanding that had been in the eyes of the infant the day of his birth. White Buffalo had seen many infants. Most were squalling in protest at the indignity of having been thrust from the warm and protective lodge which had been theirs for the past nine moons. True, it was a rude shock to enter a world that included cold and hunger. But occasionally there would be an infant whose approach to life seemed different. And this was such an infant. After the preliminary protest, and the cough to clear newly expanded lungs, this child was quiet.

The woman who had assisted Dove Woman with the birth had lifted the lodgeflap to allow the father to enter and see his son. White Buffalo paused a moment, allowing his eyes to become accustomed to the dim interior of the lodge. He smiled at his wife.

"Our son is here," Dove Woman said softly.

"It is well with you?" he asked.

"Of course. Come, look at him."

She lifted the corner of the robe that covered her. White Buffalo knelt and looked into the small red face. It was only then that he felt the impact of the tiny newcomer. The eyes, which in most infants are squinted tightly shut against the new experience of light and air, were wide open. They looked around the lodge and then directly into his own with a shocking intensity that startled White Buffalo.

It must be remembered that White Buffalo was no ordinary man. His medicine was considered strong, his vision accurate. His contact with things of the spirit was an ongoing vibrant thing. Even so, it was with something of a shock that he looked into the dark eyes of this newborn child. There was knowledge there, and an interest, a curiosity, that burned brightly in those eyes. Unaccountably, White Buffalo felt for an instant that he was the one under scrutiny, not the child. This small one seemed to already possess an understanding of the nature of the world and a desire to learn more about it.

"This is a strong spirit," he told his wife.

"Of course"—Dove Woman smiled. "He is ours, yours and mine."

White Buffalo nodded, still entranced by the strange feeling of communication he had had for a moment. The moment had passed now.

"Let us call him Small Elk," Dove Woman suggested.

White Buffalo knew that this was because of their experience the evening before. It was exceptionally fine weather, early in the Moon of Roses, and they had walked a little way from the lodges to be alone and enjoy the setting of the sun. Dove Woman had grown large and was impatient to bring forth her child. It was pleasant to walk with her husband and to admire the lavish colors of the western sky.

"Sun Boy chooses his paints well this evening," she observed.

"Yes," her husband agreed.

After all their years together, there was little need for talk. They communicated without it, each understanding what the other felt. This evening they were comfortable with each other and with the world. It was a time of waiting, of wondering about the new life in Dove Woman's belly.

"Oh, look," she exclaimed suddenly, pointing to an area near the stream.

A cow elk had come down to the water to drink. She raised her head and sniffed the breeze, catching the scent of the couple who watched. They were near enough to see the droplets of water that dribbled down the animal's lower lip. The cow fidgeted, uneasy but undecided.

It was unusual for elk to approach the village this closely. The cow was in no danger at this time, but she could hardly know that. The People had hunted well, with the greening of the prairie. White Buffalo had selected the time for the annual burning of the prairie to remove the winter's dead grass. The buffalo had appeared as expected, in the Moon of Greening. The spring hunt had been successful enough to add prestige to White Buffalo's reputation and respect for the power of his medicine, successful enough that there would be no interest in killing a thin cow elk during the calving season.

The cow turned nervously, sensing something wrong, and finally sprang away, clattering across the white gravel of the riffle toward the other bank. Only then, as she turned and made a quiet lowing sound over her shoulder, did they see the calf. It came scrambling up out of the tall grass beside the stream, a confused scramble of long legs, knobby knees, and floppy ears.

The mother paused to wait while the calf stumbled after her through the shallows. They quickly disappeared in the willows across the creek, and Dove Woman laughed softly.

"It is a sign, my husband."

"Your time is near?"

"Maybe so."

She smiled and leaned against him.

Looking into the face of his son the following day, White Buffalo realized that the incident by the stream *had* been significant. Dove Woman had felt it too and had chosen his name. He nodded in agreement.

" 'Small Elk.' It is good."

As the child grew, White Buffalo wondered sometimes if he had been mistaken. Small Elk seemed much like other children, no better or worse, no more or less mischievous. He participated in the games, dances, and instruction of the Rabbit Society with the other children. But no, there was that other quality, the desire of this child to be alone sometimes, to watch ants or silvery minnows in the stream, or the red-tailed hawk's lazy circles in the summer sky.

When Small Elk was in his fourth summer, he came to his father one afternoon with a small object in his closed hand, his face shining with excitement. White Buffalo was reclining on his willow backrest, enjoying a smoke during a moment of leisure.

"What do you have there, little one?"

"It is a stone," the child confided in hushed excitement. "Its spirit is good."

White Buffalo became more attentive. This was not the usual play of a three-year-old.

"May I hold it?"

Small Elk proudly placed the stone in his father's palm. It was white and rounded, polished by many lifetimes of tumbling in the rolling waters of the stream. White Buffalo closed his fingers around the smooth sphere, thinking as he did that it was much like an egg. The egg, perhaps, of one of the small ducks that sometimes nested in the reeds along the stream. It was warm, and the feeling was good.

"Yes," he told the child, "its spirit is good."

"Father, do all things have a spirit?"

"Yes. Some are stronger spirits than others."

"But this is a good spirit?"

White Buffalo felt the smooth surface in his palm, the warm, comforting sensation that was unmistakable.

"Yes," he said seriously, "this is good."

"I will keep it," Small Elk announced happily.

White Buffalo was still a little surprised that he was carrying on this conversation with a child of three. However, his expertise with things of the spirit told him not to ignore it. Small Elk was showing signs of spiritual awakening quite early. It might be that this child would be offered the power of a strong medicine when he was ready—if, of course, he chose to accept the responsibility of such a gift. The idea pleased the holy man, that a son of his might follow in his steps. But for now , , ,

"Come," he said to Small Elk, "let us make for you a medicine bag. Your stone will be its first spirit."

It would not do to try to influence the boy. However, it would do no harm to make the means available to him if and when he was offered the gift. After all, he could still refuse the responsibility if he wished.

2

Small Elk sat on the grassy slope with the other children of the Rabbit Society. One of the women was demonstrating the use of the throwing-stick. She was holding a stick not quite as long as her arm, the thickness of her wrist. A few steps away, slender willow twigs had been stuck in the mud to form a miniature fence as a target.

"Now, see!"

Bluebird suddenly whirled her arm and released the stick in a hard overhand throw. The missile whirled, end-over-end, at the willow target, knocking one of the slim twigs flat as it bounced beyond. The children laughed happily. One of the boys ran to retrieve her stick.

"Now, see again!" she called as she readied the stick for another throw.

This time the throw was a sidearm swing. The clublike stick spun horizontally, whirring toward the row of twigs. When it struck, the damage was apparent. Because of the flat spin, not one but several of the willow twigs were broken or knocked flat, in a path two handspans wide.

"So," Bluebird announced, "you will kill more rabbits with a sidethrow. Now, try it. Don't hit each other!"

"When can we try the bow?" asked Red Fox.

"Later. Soon, maybe, if you have one. But it is good to know the throwing-sticks."

"But I would rather eat buffalo than rabbit," one of the girls protested.

"So would everyone," Bluebird agreed. "But when meat is scarce, in the Moon of Hunger, it is good to know how to hunt with the stick. Or, when the hunters are unsuccessful. Then what?"

The children took their small throwing-sticks and began to play at hunting rabbits. Bluebird walked over to speak to her friend Dove Woman, who sat watching.

"I will stand clear now," she laughed. "They are reckless sometimes."

Dove Woman smiled.

"At least, the dance is not so dangerous."

Hers was the teaching of the first dance-steps to the smaller children of the Rabbit Society. From others they would learn the skills of hunting and the use of weapons, and compete in running, wrestling, and swimming. Both boys and girls learned all of these skills. It was not until later that their diversity of interests would sharpen the fine skills of the hunter-warriors and the domestic skills of the young women planning for their own lodges.

There was a yelp from one of the dogs, hit by an accidental bounce of a thrown stick.

"Be careful there!" called Bluebird.

Then she spoke aside to Dove Woman.

"Better a dog than each other. Now they will be more careful."

"Yes. There is no way to keep dogs away from throwing-sticks, I think."

"Your Small Elk seems good with the sticks."

"Thank you. Your daughter, also."

Dove Woman was pleased. These two children, Small Elk and Crow, were nearly the same age. Their mothers were friends and usually chose to set up their lodges near each other.

"They play well together," Bluebird observed.

"Yes, for children of five summers, they quarrel very little."

Both women laughed.

"Will your Small Elk become a medicine man?" Bluebird asked seriously.

"Who knows?" Dove Woman shrugged. "White Buffalo says he may. We will see if he has the gift."

The children were becoming tired of playing with the sticks now and were straying off to other pursuits. Small Elk and Crow were near the stream, sitting on a level rock. Between them were a number of miniature green lodges, made by rolling cottonwood leaves into cones and pinning the edges together with a grass stem.

"Let us make a whole village!" Crow suggested.

"Why? We need only one lodge, you and I."

Then they both giggled.

"Elk, do you know how to make a moccasin from a cottonwood leaf?"

"No. I have seen them. It is harder than making the little lodges."

"You could ask your father. He knows all things."

"Yes, but . . ."

Small Elk was a little uncertain whether a holy man's area of skills included the making of toy cottonwood-leaf moccasins.

"I will ask, sometime," he agreed cautiously.

The conversation was interrupted by the approach of one of the other boys.

"Want to go swimming?" asked Bull Roarer.

He stood there, whirling a noisemaker on a thong around and around his head in a wide circle. With each revolution, the flutter of the flattened stick at the thong's end made a deep whirring noise, like the distant bellow of a buffalo bull. It was a common toy, but this boy's affinity for the pastime had led to his being called by the name of the device, "bull roarer."

"Who is going?" Crow asked.

Bull Roarer continued to swing his noise maker.

"We three, Fox, Otter, Cattail, my sister Redwing."

"We will ask," Crow announced.

She jumped up and ran to her mother with the explanation and request. Bull Roarer's sister was a few summers older, a reliable supervisor, and both Bluebird and Dove Woman quickly agreed.

Most children of the People were strong swimmers. The bands must always camp near a water supply, and summer camp was frequently selected with an eye to its recreational possibilities. Of course, this went hand in hand with the more serious purpose of the selection, availability of game. Grass and water, essential to the buffalo, also make a campsite esthetically pleasing. In turn, the presence of a clear, cool stream in the heat of a prairie summer invites swimmers.

The summer camp this season was in a favorite area of the People. Sycamore River, trickling over white gravel bars and long level shelves of gray slate, was a favorite stream. Its deep pools were spaced at intervals along its course like beads on a thong.

The pool the children preferred was perhaps two long

bowshots below the camp. It was ringed with willows on the near side, except for a level strip of white gravelly sand, a perfect place to lie in the sun to dry after a swim. Across the pool, a stono's throw away, cattails formed a backdrop for the scene, as well as a site where ducks and smaller water-dwelling birds might build their lodges.

The memorable event of the day for Small Elk, however, was not the swimming party. It happened on the way back to the camp. He and Crow had lagged behind the others to watch a shiny green dung beetle roll an impossibly big ball of dung, larger than itself.

"What do they do with it?" asked Crow. "Where is he taking it?"

"To his lodge, maybe," Small Elk suggested.

He hated to admit that he had no idea what a dung beetle does with balls of dung. He would ask his father later. White Buffalo, who knew all things, could surely tell him about dung beetles.

The children rose to move on. It was just at that time that the rabbit sprang from a clump of grass beside the path and loped away ahead of them. Small Elk was startled for a moment but then reacted almost without thinking. He was still carrying his throwing-stick from the earlier lessons of the day. The missile leaped from his hand, whirling toward the retreating animal. His throw was wide and should have missed completely except for unforeseen circumstances. The whirling tip of the stick struck a sapling beside the path and was deflected, bouncing crazily end-over-end. Even so, the rabbit would have escaped harm if it had continued in a straight line. But rabbits do not run in straight lines as a custom. They sometimes zig and zag, taught to do so at the time of creation to escape the strike of the hawk or the lunge of the coyote. In this case, the escape trick proved the rabbit's undoing. It bobbed to the left just as the whirling stick bounced to the right. There was an audible crack as the hard wood met the skull of the animal.

"*Aiee!*" exclaimed Crow softly.

Small Elk rushed forward to grab the kicking creature, wriggling in its death throes. He picked it up and watched the large brown eye lose its luster and become dull with the mist of death. It was his first kill, and he should have felt good. It should have been a glad and proud moment, but that was not what he felt. There was a letdown, a disappointment. The rabbit had been more pleasing to look at in life than it was now, its eyes glazing and a single drop of blood at the tip of its nose. He was confused. Why had he wanted to kill the rabbit? For meat. Yes, for its flesh, he thought. That is the way of things. The rabbit eats grass and in turn is eaten by the hawk, the coyote, or man. That is the purpose of a rabbit. He watched as a flea crept into sight from the thick fur of the rabbit's cheek and burrowed into another tuft.

Then he remembered watching his father at a buffalo kill early in the spring. The medicine man had stood before the head of a massive bull . . . yes, of course. He would perform such a ceremony. He placed the rabbit on the ground, arranging it in a natural position. Then he stepped back, faced the head of the dead creature, and addressed it solemnly.

"I am sorry to kill you, my brother," he stated, trying to remember his father's words of apology, "but I am in need of your flesh to live."

He felt a little guilty for such a statement, because he was not hungry or in need at the moment. What had White Buffalo said next?

"Your flesh feeds us as the grass gives your life to you."

Yes, that was it. Small Elk felt better now, and forged ahead. How was it? . . .

"May your people be fat and happy, and be plentiful," he told the rabbit.

Feeling considerably better about the incident, he picked up his kill and moved on toward camp. In his preoccupation, he did not notice the expression in the eyes of the girl beside him. It was an intense look of surprise mixed with admiration and approval.

A similar expression might have been noted on the face of the man who had watched the whole scene from behind a thin screen of willows. White Buffalo waited, perfectly still, until the children had moved out of sight. Then he rose, a satisfied smile on his face. He must share this with Dove Woman.

"It is good," he said quietly to himself. "And Small Elk performed the apology well."

3

It was in their seventh summer that the Head Splitters came. Among the People, youngsters were warned against this threat from the time they were small.

"Don't go too far from the lodges. The Head Splitters will get you."

Sometimes, even, it became a tool for discipline.

"If you don't behave, the Head Splitters will get you!"

Usually that sort of threat was not used because it was not necessary. The loosely organized instruction of the Rabbit Society was carried on by nearly all adults. The shared parenting made all adults responsible for the welfare of all children, and after all, the future of any group lies in its children. On the other hand, such a system makes all children responsible to any adult, and misbehavior is difficult. So the threat of the Head Splitters was rarely used for discipline, except perhaps in a joking way.

Actually, the danger was quite real. For many lifetimes, past the memories of the oldest of the band, these enemies had staged sporadic raids against the People. Both tribes hunted buffalo, and both were partial to the Tallgrass Hills, so their paths occasionally crossed.

Small Elk had seen them, as the People moved from one camping area to another. They would encounter a similar band of travelers moving across the prairie, carrying their lodgecovers and baggage or dragging it on poledrags behind the dogs. There was a time-honored ritual for such a meeting. The two columns of travelers would halt, perhaps a long bowshot apart, and wait while two or three chiefs from each band approached one another in the no-man's-land between.

It was understood that there would be no fighting. It was too dangerous. Both groups were vulnerable, with women and children and all possessions exposed to the enemy. So the principal chiefs of the two groups would make small talk, using the universal handsigns of the prairie. They would discuss the weather, the quality of the summer's grass, and the success of the hunt. Sometimes there would be veiled threats and insults, but it was only talk. No chief would risk his family's safety by initiating a skirmish.

Even knowing this, the heart of Small Elk always beat fast when such a meeting occurred. He watched the confrontation from his mother's side, seeing the prominently displayed stone war clubs that were the trademark of the Head Splitters. Even at a distance, the suggestiveness of these weapons was a chilling thing.

"What do they talk about?" he whispered to his mother.

Dove Woman placed a hand on his shoulder reassuringly.

"Small things. The weather, the hunting, where we will camp this season."

Small Elk was alarmed.

"Broken Horn will tell them where to find us?"

Dove Woman smiled.

"Yes, and they will tell us. You see, if they mean us harm, they can find us anyway. And hunting will be better if we are not too close together. So, the chiefs exchange that knowledge."

The conversation was finished now, and the chiefs parted. The two columns resumed travel. It was a relief to have the meeting over. Looking back later, it had been an exciting diversion on the long trip to meet the other bands of the tribe for the annual Big Council.

A raid by the Head Splitters was a different matter. It would be carried out by a surprise attack, a ruthless strike by a force of strong, heavily armed warriors. They would quickly kill and plunder, taking supplies and robes, perhaps weapons, anything easy to carry.

And children. The threat of abduction by the Head Splitters was not an idle one.

"But what happens to the children?" Small Elk asked in wonder as he and his playmates discussed the situation.

"Maybe the Head Splitters *eat* them," Bull Roarer suggested with a horrible grimace.

"No, that's not true!" scolded Crow. "They just keep them forever. Besides, they want mostly girls."

"We will ask someone," suggested Small Elk. "There is Short Bow."

The children approached the subchief, who was reclining on his backrest nearby.

"Uncle," began Bull Roarer, using the customary term of respect for any adult male, "could you tell us of the Head Splitters?"

Short Bow puffed his pipe a moment.

"What of the Head Splitters?"

"Why do they steal children?"

"Don't they want mostly girls?" asked Crow.

Short Bow nodded seriously.

"Yes, that is true. Our women are prettier than theirs. They want them for wives."

"Aiee!" exclaimed Crow. "To be the wife of a Head Splitter!"

"You are safe," teased Bull Roarer. "They want only the pretty ones."

Crow made an obscene gesture, and the boys laughed. The girl had not yet started the spurt of adolescent growth that would make her long-legged and shapely like other women of the People. It had been known for generations that Head Splitters coveted these girls as wives. Their own racial stock was slightly different in bone structure, and the lanky athletic build of the women of the People was greatly admired.

On the day that the Head Splitters came, the three friends had been playing along the stream. It was a warm, sunny afternoon in the Moon of Growing. The children had been watching minnows and trying to catch the small spotted frogs that hid in the grass along the shore. They watched a muskrat pull himself out of the water and shuffle along the opposite shore. It was a narrow path that the creature followed, because a rocky bluff rose almost from the water's edge.

"Let's try to climb the bluff!" Bull Roarer suggested.

They made their way upstream to a point where they could cross and started back along the bluff's base.

"Look! A path!" Crow pointed.

It was a narrow ledge, rising from the water's edge and angling upward against the face of the bluff. It was far from being a path, but it did appear to have been used by small animals. The three crept upward, clinging closely to the rock. They were nearly back to the point where they had seen the muskrat when there was a sudden flash of motion ahead.

"A fox!" Small Elk pointed. "Look, there is his lodge!"

The fox had disappeared, but they found that the shelf widened to perhaps a pace across and several paces long. The opening to the fox's den showed evidence of recent use.

"Maybe there are pups inside!" Bull Roarer said excitedly.

The boys were trying to peer into the dark hole when there was a sudden gasp from Crow.

"*Aiee!* Head Splitters!"

The others whirled to look. They were about a long bowshot from the camp and high enough on the bluff to see over the tops of the newly leaved trees. A dozen warriors, painted for combat, slipped quickly among the lodges.

"They have not been seen!" Small Elk exclaimed. "Should we? . . ."

His question was interrupted by a scream of terror from the village, immediately answered by a chorus of yipping, falsetto war cries from the attackers. It was the first time any of the three had heard the terrifying war cry of the Head Splitters. Small Elk felt a chill up his spine, and the hairs on the back of his neck stood erect in his terror.

"Get down!" he mumbled.

The three crouched on the narrow ledge, watching in fascinated horror. There were few men in the camp; most of them were gone for the day on a spring buffalo hunt. It was decided later that the Head Splitters must have watched and waited for such an opportunity.

They saw Sits-in-the-Rain, who often told tales to the children around the story-fires, start up from his backrest in front of his lodge. The old man reached for his bow, but age had slowed his reflexes. The Head Splitter who struck him down hardly bothered to break stride as he moved on.

A lodge toppled, and greasy smoke began to billow out from under the collapsed lodgecover as its own cooking fire began to devour it. The invaders seemed everywhere. People were running in all directions, a few standing to fight and being clubbed down where they stood.

Bull Roarer was crying as he saw his mother's lodge fall.

They could not see whether she was trapped inside as it began to burn. His sister scrambled out under the edge of the lodgeskin and ran for the bushes, pursued by a yipping Head Splitter. This was too much for Bull Roarer. He jumped to his feet, the others trying to pull him back out of sight. The boy jerked away, lost his balance, and fell over the edge. His scream was unheard in the village because of all the noise, death, and destruction there, but it was heard by his friends on the ledge.

"We must help him!" Crow gasped.

They peered cautiously over the edge. Bull Roarer lay below, partly in the water, his left leg crumpled under him, jutting out at an unnatural angle. His big dark eyes, full of agony, looked up at them helplessly.

"Lie still; make no noise!" Small Elk used the handsign talk.

Bull Roarer nodded.

"We will help you as soon as we can," Small Elk continued.

There was another gasp from Crow. Directly across the stream, looking up at them, stood a Head Splitter. He moved a little to see what occupied their attention and discovered the injured Bull Roarer. Chuckling, the man took an arrow from his quiver and fitted it to his bowstring. Then he seemed to consider and lowered the weapon. Apparently he thought the crippled boy not worth an arrow; he would have to cross the creek to recover it. He looked up again at the two on the ledge and smiled as he pointed to them.

"I will get you next time!" the man signed.

He turned and trotted to join the others, who were withdrawing, laden with loot. Small Elk and Crow were already scrambling down the narrow path to help Bull Roarer. From the direction of the camp there now rose a mournful wail as the women began the Song of Mourning.

4

» » »

The children scrambled quickly down and along the ledge to where Bull Roarer lay, partly in the water.

"We will help you!" cried Crow. "Does it hurt much?"

"A little," said Bull Roarer between clenched teeth.

His face was pale and sweaty, his eyes wide and bordering on panic. Small Elk knelt in the water beside the injured boy. He had seen his father examine such injuries.

"Do not try to move yet," he advised. "Now where does it hurt? Only your leg?"

"Y—yes, I think so. Elk, it hurts a lot."

"Does it hurt in your belly?"

"No. I don't think so. My leg . . ."

Small Elk was looking at the twisted leg. Something was definitely wrong with it. There appeared to be an extra joint, like an extra knee, between the real knee and the hip. This gave an odd zig-zag appearance to the leg and accounted for the awkward position of the foot, which could never be used if it pointed in the present direction.

"Your leg is broken," Small Elk said professionally.

"I know that," snapped Bull Roarer irritably. "Help me!"

"It must be pulled straight," Small Elk stated, "and I do not know how."

The crying and the wailing sounds continued from the camp. There was an occasional scream as a new casualty was discovered. People called out names of missing loved ones.

"Bring your father," Bull Roarer demanded. "He can fix my leg."

"He is not here!" Small Elk reminded. "He went with the men."

"Maybe we can pull him out of the water," Crow suggested. "There is enough space here for him to lie more comfortably."

The two took Bull Roarer by the arms to drag him ashore. The injured boy screamed as the broken leg moved and bone grated on splintered bone.

"It looks straighter now," Elk observed.

He picked up a small stick and handed it to Bull Roarer.

"Here. Bite on this. We nearly have you out."

One more sustained pull, and they were able to drag the victim ashore to lie full length on the damp grass. Tears streamed down his face, but as the pain subsided, he removed the stick from his mouth, crushed and broken from the pressure of his teeth.

"Aiee!" he whispered, his face still pale. "It hurts less when you do not move it."

"This leg is shorter than the other," observed Crow.

"Yes, and the toe points backward," Small Elk noted. "Should we not turn it to the front?"

"No, no," Bull Roarer protested, "you will turn it the wrong way! Go and get help!"

"I will go," Crow suggested. "You can stay with him."

She jumped to her feet and ran nimbly along the bank to the point where they had crossed. Small Elk sat down near their suffering friend.

"Elk, I think I am going to die," said Bull Roarer weakly.

"No, you are not," Small Elk snapped. "I will not let you."

"All right. But can you stop the leg from moving?"

The damaged muscles, protesting this injury to their form and function, were twitching spasmodically. With each spasm, the uncontrolled motion created new waves of pain.

"I don't know," Small Elk admitted. "I will try."

He attempted to hold the foot still against the paroxysm of muscles. It seemed to help some, but his own muscles quickly tired.

"I am going to let go for a little while," he told Bull Roarer. "I will get some rocks to prop around your foot."

This appeared to be the best answer yet and seemed to comfort the injured leg. Crow came splashing back across the shallow riffle, carrying a small buffalo robe.

"No one can come yet," she announced as she spread the

warm cover over Bull Roarer. "Dove Woman says keep him warm. Someone will come soon."

"How bad is it for the others?" Small Elk asked.

"Bad. Some are dead. Several lodges burning."

"I saw mine burning," Bull Roarer said. "Is my mother alive?"

"Yes. She is looking for your sister. Elk, your lodge still stands. Mine is gone, but my mother is safe."

"But I saw my mother's lodge fall on her," Bull Roarer said.

"Yes," Crow explained. "She hid under it, hoping the Head Splitters would leave before the fire reached her."

"How did your mother and mine escape?" Small Elk asked.

"They were both in your lodge. The Head Splitters spared it because of its medicine, Dove Woman said."

The lodge of Dove Woman and White Buffalo was painted with designs and symbols that marked it as the dwelling of a holy man. To confront an unknown medicine could easily be hazardous, just as walking into a dark cave could be, without knowing what dangers lay inside. The attackers had simply chosen to avoid the risk.

"Who all was killed?" Bull Roarer asked.

"I did not ask about everyone," Crow said. "Sits-in-the-Rain is dead. I saw Otter's mother mourning, but I do not know for whom. Cattail's lodge is burned, but I saw her. Her family is safe."

"Is my mother coming over here?" asked Bull Roarer.

"Yes, she said she will, after she finds what happened to Redwing. Dove Woman will come, but she is helping some who are wounded first."

Before long, Dove Woman and Bluebird came across the stream. Dove Woman, who often helped her husband with his healing ceremonies, understood his work quite well.

"*Aiee!*" she exclaimed. "This is a bad injury, Bull Roarer, but we will fix it. White Buffalo will soon return. He will want to bind the leg here, before we carry you across the river."

Dove Woman had brought some strips of hide from an old robe and now began to cut splints from the willows along the shore. She was still occupied with this when the men returned, attracted by the plume of greasy black smoke from the burning village. Songs of mourning rose again.

"Elk, go and bring your father," Dove Woman instructed. "Tell him I have bandages and splints."

Small Elk darted away and soon found his father near their lodge. White Buffalo, concerned for his family, had already learned that their daughter was alive, though her lodge had been destroyed. The family of their older son was unscathed.

"Is your mother safe?" he asked.

"Yes. She wants you to come and help Bull Roarer."

"Where?"

"Across the river. He fell from the cliff."

They crossed, and White Buffalo knelt to examine the injury.

"Bull Roarer, I am going to move your leg," he warned. "Here, bite the stick."

With one quick motion, he twisted the injured leg into a more normal position. The grating of the bone was quite audible as it snapped into place, and the boy's scream was muffled by the stick in his teeth.

"There," the medicine man said. "It will feel better now."

He began to bind the strips of buffalo hide around the leg, incorporating the willow splints as he did so. Finally he rose.

"Now, I will carry you," he announced.

He picked up the boy, whose pain in motion was not nearly so great with the splints in place. As they stepped out of the water, Bull Roarer's mother met them.

"Is he all right?" she asked anxiously.

"A bad break, but it will heal," White Buffalo assured her. "Where will you stay, Pretty Robe?"

"My mother's lodge. Here, this way."

Those whose lodges were destroyed were salvaging what they could and moving in with relatives for the present. It appeared that there were only four fatalities, though several more people were wounded or had suffered burns from fighting the fires.

Three children were missing. One small girl escaped and made her way home a few days later, but Redwing, sister of Bull Roarer, was never seen again.

5

It had been seven winters now since the attack by the Head Splitters, and there had been no further trouble. As usual, they had encountered traveling bands of the enemy each season. There was no direct reference to the incident, beyond the smug demeanor of the Head Splitters.

Of course, the band they encountered that next summer may not have been the same band that carried out the attack. One Head Splitter looks much like another. Still, both Small Elk and Crow felt that they recognized one of the subchiefs who came forward to talk.

"That is the one!" Crow whispered. "The one who was about to shoot Bull Roarer."

"I think so too," Small Elk agreed, "but they all look alike. What do you think, Bull?"

"How would I know?" Bull Roarer asked, a trifle peevishly. "I was lying in the water below."

If the man recognized them, he gave no sign, but it was hard to forget the threat that day at the cliff. The Head Splitter had promised to return.

The stolen children were not seen, at this or any later encounter. It was assumed that they would be hidden, silent under threat of death if they made their presence known. Or, someone suggested, maybe they had been traded to some other band. Even some other tribe. Bull Roarer's mother had mourned the loss of her daughter, as if Redwing had died in the attack, and then resumed her usual activities. Life was hard, and losses were to be expected. The period of mourning allowed relief from the pressure of grief, and life went on.

Those events seemed long ago now. The seasons had passed, and the children grew. Bull Roarer's leg had healed, and in a few moons, he could walk again. But he would never walk properly. The leg was too short by nearly a hand's width. The boy walked with an odd rolling gait.

"Will it grow like the other?" he had asked White Buffalo.

"No," the medicine man answered. "It will always be different. But you are alive, and you can walk. Does it hurt?"

"No," Bull Roarer admitted, "but I am very slow."

"It was a very bad break."

It was difficult for the active youngster. Formerly one of the best, he could no longer compete in many of the games and contests. In such things as swimming he could still excel, but out of the water, his ability was limited. In time, even his swimming skills began to suffer. There was no way to keep his muscles in condition. He tried to remain cheerful, but it was difficult.

His problem had become even more apparent since the other boys had begun to hunt. Bull Roarer had participated in a few hunts, short forays near camp, carefully supervised by an older warrior. No one said anything, but it was not necessary. All could see that Bull Roarer could not keep up with the group. It was equally apparent that they could not wait for him while their quarry escaped. No, Bull Roarer would be unable to participate in the hunt.

It was even more frustrating for him because he was an excellent shot with the bow. But what good was that if he could not place himself in a spot from which to shoot? Often, he cried privately. He could hunt small game, of course, but one does not support a family on rabbits and squirrels. Neither can a lodge be made from rabbitskins. Bull Roarer feared that he was doomed to a life of poverty, unable to find a wife who would consent to share such a fate. He would always be dependent on the charity of those more fortunate, and when times were hard . . . He shuddered to think that in lean years, when the hunt had been less than successful, the Moon of Hunger took on an even more ominous meaning.

Supplies always ran low in the time just before the Moon of Awakening, when the earth began to green again. In the best of years, it was a time of hunger. In the worst, it became, instead, the Moon of Starvation. Some would not survive. Bull Roarer was aware that sometimes older members of the tribe walked off into the night at such times, to die in the silence of the prairie snows. It was a heroic gesture, one designed to save desperately needed food for the children, who represented the People's future. Regardless, those who would starve would be the poor and needy. Who could give them food when his own family was hungry?

Increasingly now, Bull Roarer felt that this would be his fate in life—existing on handouts from his friends or those who took pity on him. Eventually, he would come to the point where a hard winter or a scarcity of game would bring about his own starvation. Sometimes the young man had considered walking into the prairie as the old ones did, so as not to prolong the tragedy of his thwarted life.

It is probable that on these occasions, seldom though they had been, he had postponed the act because of his friends Small Elk and Crow. These three were almost inseparable as they grew. The others seemed to feel almost a responsibility for the accident that had made Bull Roarer a cripple. When he was dejected, one of the others was always near, to distract him and bring a smile to his face.

Now they had seen fourteen winters, and subtle changes were taking place in all their lives. As the other young men became more proficient at the hunt, Bull Roarer became more morose. Today, for instance. There had been a hunt, hastily organized, when someone reported a band of elk grazing a short distance north of the camp. The other young men, and some of the girls, seized their bows and ran to join the hunt.

Bull Roarer watched them go, lonely and dejected. It was not unusual for young unmarried women to participate in the hunt; after all, that was where the young unmarried men would be. Except, of course, for the lame and crippled, he reflected bitterly. He wandered along the creek, skipping stones and longing for the company of his friends. How useless I am, he thought. Small Elk and Crow were the only close friends he had left. The others had gradually drifted away as it became increasingly apparent that Bull Roarer could not keep up.

Now he felt completely abandoned. Even Crow had left him for the hunt. He resented this. Crow could have stayed behind with him. Probably, he decided, even she and Elk had remained loyal only out of pity. He could not blame her for preferring the company of one who was able-bodied. He wondered how the hunt was going.

Small Elk gripped his bow with sweating hands, an arrow ready on the string. He glanced to his left, where Crow returned his glance, her face alive with excitement. Their good fortune was incredible. The animals had moved into a small box canyon and were still inside. Short Bow, the organizer of the hunt, had quickly deployed the youngsters across the entrance. More experienced hunters were posted between them at intervals. Short Bow himself was beyond Crow. Now he motioned them forward, cautioning quiet. They moved into the canyon, crouching to stay in the concealment of clumps of sumac, dogwood, and bunches of real-grass.

Small Elk was aware that the animals were up ahead of them in the canyon. It was not that he heard or smelled them, as sometimes happened. It was more like a feeling, a knowing without the use of his other senses. He should soon be able to smell or hear them. By sheer good fortune, the hunters were downwind of the herd.

Then he heard a muffled snort and froze in his tracks like a rabbit. Between the tall stems of the real-grass ahead, he could see the shapes of large animals. Most were still grazing, but one old cow stood, alert and staring. Her ears flared wide, and Small Elk was sure she was looking straight at him. The cow snorted again, and the others raised their heads to look. Then everything seemed to happen at once. The wary old cow leaped aside and struck the ground, driving forward.

Short Bow had explained to the young hunters how it would happen. The elk, trapped in the box canyon, would rush to escape and in doing so, would run past the hunters into open prairie. There would be a moment, the space of a few heartbeats, when they must pass between two of the hunters, and someone, perhaps everyone, would have the opportunity for a shot.

"Try not to hit each other!" Short Bow had cautioned.

It was a joke, repeated since they were small, but this time there was no laughter.

Now, as the herd came charging down at him, Small Elk was sure that he would be lucky to survive, much less shoot. A great bull, his antlers as wide as a man's outstretched arms, thundered down on him. Small Elk stepped quickly aside. There was nothing graceful about it, he simply jumped to safety while the bull rushed past, its mind too only on escape. The animal brushed so close to him that Small Elk could see the thin strips of furry skin hanging and fluttering from the antlers. The bull would soon be polishing those antlers in preparation for the rutting season. Small Elk felt the patter of bits of dirt and grass thrown up by flying hooves, and the bull lunged on past him. He stood there in wonder, completely forgetting to shoot. There was another rush of hooves, and a young cow raced past, her eyes rolling wildly. Small Elk raised his bow and loosed an arrow as the animal passed. He thought that the shaft struck the cow's flank but could not be sure. In the space of another heartbeat, the animals had dashed through the brushy mouth of the canyon and into the open plain.

Now there were shouts and yells of triumph and disappointment as the hunters turned to pursue the retreating herd. Small Elk ran, dodging among the bushes toward the open where the animals were rapidly outdistancing their pursuers.

"Enough!" called Short Bow. "Now look for the wounded."

Small Elk now remembered to fit another arrow to his bow.

"Elk! Over here!" Crow shouted.

He turned and trotted toward the sound of her voice. There, her eyes shining, stood the girl, bow in hand, her smile wide in triumph. In front of her lay the carcass of a fat cow elk, an arrow protruding from just behind the ribs. The animal was still kicking feebly.

"Our kill!" Crow called. "That is your arrow. Mine is in the other flank."

"Are you sure? This is my arrow?"

"Of course! Look at it. I saw you shoot, and the cow turned away toward me. I shot too, and she went down."

"Good!" Short Bow observed as he passed. "You two have done well."

Crow was practically jumping up and down with excitement.

"I can hardly wait to tell Bull Roarer!" she exclaimed. "He will be so pleased."

6

Crow and Small Elk had excitedly described the hunt, repeatedly and in detail. It was only after the first flush of success had begun to fade that they noticed that their friend was not altogether pleased with their success. Actually, it was Crow who noticed. Bull Roarer listened politely, quietly congratulated them, and lapsed again into silence.

"Aiee, what a hunt!" Small Elk was still chortling. "My friend, this cow came rushing past; I shot, but could not see where the arrow struck. Then Crow placed her arrow too. You—"

He started to say, "You should have been there," but suddenly realized the problem. It was an uncomfortable moment, and there had been few such moments in the lifelong friendship of these three.

"Come, Elk," Crow interrupted the awkward silence. "We must help with the butchering."

Bull Roarer sat and watched them go. Normally he would have helped too. Normally, of course, the others would have good-naturedly demanded it.

Crow was silent and depressed. They had, in their excitement, failed to realize that their success would only hurt their friend, who could never accomplish such things. He could have helped with such chores as skinning and butchering, but that would only call attention again to his handicap. She could understand Bull Roarer's fears, and her heart went out to him. He would feel that he was good for nothing but menial tasks.

She could see that Small Elk felt it too, but neither of them spoke. It was an unpleasant thing, this obstacle that had come between them. She felt that they must find a way to help their friend, not from pity, but from friendship. They had had so many good times during their childhood that it must not be spoiled now. She thought of speaking to Small Elk about it but rejected the idea. She would think of something.

It was only a few days later that another hunt was planned. This would not be an urgent situation, as when the band of elk had suddenly become available. This was a carefully planned foray into the prairie, where a fragment of one of the migrating buffalo herds had wandered close. Small Elk's father, caped in the sacred white robe that gave the holy man his name, performed the buffalo-dance ceremony at the fire the night before. Hunters sat, meticulously putting finishing touches on their weapons, readying everything for the hunt. It was an important hunt, the first in which the youngsters would take part as fully eligible hunters, ready to prove themselves. There were still a few who had not yet made a kill of large game. Small Elk and Crow, of course, with their success in the elk hunt, carried some degree of prestige.

The morning dawned with a slight chill in the air, mist rising from the stream like a thin white veil of smoke. The hunters were already stirring.

"Come on, Crow," Small Elk called. "It is time to go. We must not keep Short Bow and the others waiting."

The girl stood in front of her parents' lodge, watching the hunters' preparations.

"You go ahead," she said. "I will stay here with Bull Roarer."

Small Elk stared at her for a moment, a mixture of emotions struggling within him. Then he turned on his heel.

"It is good," he snapped over his shoulder.

Crow knew that it was not. It was bad, all of it. She had been forced into a situation where she appeared to choose between her friends. She was not rejecting Small Elk, her lifelong friend and more recently her hunting companion, but Elk obviously felt her decision as a rejection. In his eyes, she supposed, her staying behind appeared to be a choice of the company of Bull Roarer. *It is not that way,* she wanted to shout at him. *Bull Roarer needs me more, needs us both. We cannot leave him now, in the time of his greatest need.*

The girl watched Small Elk stride away, the hurt and anger reflected in every motion of his body. She had never realized before that one can *walk* angrily. Tears came to her eyes as she realized that his hurt had come between them. It would never be the same again, the easy, happy friendship they had shared. She hurried to a secret place behind the lodges and dried her tears, then ran to the stream to wash her face. She rose, combed out her hair and replaited it, and then went looking for Bull Roarer. She walked along the stream, knowing that he often sought solitude there, away from the camp.

He was seated on the trunk of a fallen cottonwood, idly tossing pebbles into the pool. He looked up irritably.

"You should go," he said sharply. "The hunters will be leaving."

"They are gone," Crow said.

"You are not going?"

"No. What shall we do today?"

Bull Roarer stared at her, first with a puzzled look, then with hurt and anger. She had not been prepared for this.

"Go away!" Bull Roarer almost shouted. "I do not need your pity!"

Crow was silent, fighting back the tears. Now both of the young men were angry at her. She had tried only to help, and was completely misunderstood by her two best friends.

"Bull Roarer, I—"

"Do not deny it. You are here only because you feel sorrow for me." He struck the crippled leg with his hand. "I can do nothing, with this useless stick. I wish the Head Splitter had killed me that day."

Crow was angry.

"Of course I feel sorrow," she snapped at him, seating herself on the log, "because you are my friend. But mostly, you feel sorrow for yourself!"

He looked at her, fighting back the tears.

"Crow, you do not understand. My spirit wishes to do things that my body cannot."

She sat silent, unable to comment. *Everyone,* she thought, *experiences that sometimes.* But that would be little consolation to Bull Roarer. His limitation was more pronounced, more permanent.

There was a sound of someone approaching, and Crow

turned to see one of the older men of the band, following the path along the stream. She recognized Stone Breaker, who now noticed the two young people on the log. Ordinarily, unless he had something to tell them, he would simply nod and leave them alone. Privacy was always prized and respected. But Stone Breaker came over to sit near them, putting down the bundle he carried. Crow quickly brushed at her eyes, hoping there were no remaining tears. She resented the man's intrusion.

"*Ah-koh!*" he greeted. "May I join you?"

"*Ah-koh*, Uncle. Of course," Crow said politely.

She used the traditional term of address for any adult male older than one's self, even though she knew Stone Breaker only slightly. Bull Roarer said nothing.

"It is a pleasant day," the man observed. "Let me see . . . you are Crow Woman?"

Crow blushed, but the man seemed not to notice. She felt much less resentful now. It was the first time she had been called Crow *Woman,* and the attention was quite flattering. She had begun to notice changes in her body—a swelling and sensitivity in her breasts and the sprouting of hair in places that hinted at her coming womanhood. She was experiencing new emotions, new and strange urges. But she had thought no one noticed except herself. Her parents, maybe, but they had said nothing. Now it was an honor to have her maturity and coming womanhood acknowledged in this way. She sat up straighter, quite aware of the slight pressure of her enlarging breasts against the soft buckskin of her dress.

"Yes, Uncle," she said self-consciously.

"And Bull Roarer?" the old man asked.

Bull Roarer nodded. Crow wondered if the next question would be why the young man had not gone on the hunt, but it did not come. Stone Breaker seemed not to think of that obvious question but still seemed not to notice the crippled leg. Crow would have thought the man quite dull and nonobservant, except for his obvious powers of perception about her womanhood. He must have some purpose here, but what could it be?

Stone Breaker opened his little pack and took out some flakes of flint, a piece of heavy leather, and a tool made from the tip of an antler. It was fitted with a handle made by wrapping the shaft of the horn with rawhide. He spread the leather pad over his thighs and studied the flints. Finally, he selected one, a smooth blue-gray flake as wide as two fingers and twice as long. It seemed already partly shaped.

"This is a good place to work," Stone Breaker said conversationally. "The light is good, and my eyes are not what they once were. My legs, either"—he chuckled.

Crow glanced in concern at Bull Roarer, wondering if the remark had hurt him, but he was busily tossing pebbles into the stream. The girl was still a little surprised at Stone Breaker's disregard for their privacy. She was now willing to overlook it because of his flattering observation of her womanhood.

Stone Breaker placed the flint on the leather pad across his knee and held it tightly with his left hand. He pressed the antler-tip tool on the flint's surface, near the edge, and a tiny flake snapped off the stone. He moved the tool a little and repeated the chipping.

Crow was aware that this man had a reputation as a skillful worker of flint. This, of course, was the reason for his name. Some men made their own arrowheads and spear points, but one made by Stone Breaker was highly prized. Her mother used a skinning knife of his workmanship.

He worked rapidly, and an arrowpoint began to take shape. This would be a fairly large and heavy point, it appeared, a hunting tool, made from the blue native stone that appeared in veins in the softer white stone of the hills.

Now, Bull Roarer too was watching as the shape of the point continued to emerge. Stone Breaker paused to hold it up and examine it for balance and symmetry. He nodded to himself and continued to work. Finally he laid aside his leather pad and tools to stand and stretch.

"*Aiee,*" he said, "I become stiff from sitting."

"May I see the stone, Uncle?" Crow asked.

"Yes, of course," he said casually. "Would you like to see others?"

Without waiting for an answer, he reached into a small pouch at his waist and drew out a pair of buckskin-wrapped objects, which he unrolled and displayed on his palm. Both were of a stone that was plainly not native to the area, used as a display of Stone Breaker's craft. Crow knew that this man, like others of the tribe, traded extensively with anyone they contacted. Meat and robes to the Growers in exchange for corn, beans, and pumpkins. Sometimes people traded even with the Head Splitters during the occasional chance meetings. This trade, Small Elk had said, was the source of such things as the pipestone of his father's ceremonial red pipe, found far to the north somewhere, in only one place.

Now she saw the two objects in Stone Breaker's palm. Neither, she suspected, was intended for use, but only to demonstrate the skill of the maker. One was a miniature arrowhead, precise in every detail but so small that it was no bigger than Stone Breaker's thumbnail, of stone of a dark, lustrous red color, warm in character. The other was an amulet, slightly larger, of rosy pink stone. It was more intricate in shape and seemed to represent a bird in flight.

"They are beautiful!" exclaimed the girl.

Now even Bull Roarer was looking over her shoulder at the objects.

"These are my best work," Stone Breaker was saying proudly, as he began to rewrap them carefully. "*Aiee*, it is bad that I have no son to teach these skills!"

Crow glanced at Bull Roarer. It appeared that he had not yet figured out the reason for the old man's unorthodox behavior. She said nothing but resolved to let her friend think this out for himself. What good fortune, that this respected weaponsmaker of such great skill had practically invited Bull Roarer . . . She felt better than she had in many days, and her heart was not nearly so heavy.

7

Bull Roarer quickly became proficient in the skills being taught to him by Stone Breaker. At first, his arrowheads were rough and imperfect, though usable. His work was slow, painfully slow, and his right hand had become sore from the unaccustomed pressure of the flaking tool.

"Let it rest a few days," Stone Breaker advised. "Your hands will become hardened like mine, but slowly."

He showed the young man his own hands, strong and callused from many seasons of such work. Bull Roarer impatiently waited until his blisters had partially healed and the tenderness was receding. Then he resumed the practice of patiently chipping the flints. He could tell that his work was improving and was frustrated again when his hand became sore.

"*Aiee*, you still work too long at a sitting!" Stone Breaker reprimanded gently. "Now you will have to rest again."

"But my fingers will never be as skilled as yours, Uncle!" Bull Roarer protested.

"They will, my son, but you are too impatient. Someday, when you have worked the stone as long as I have, you will be even more skillful."

Bull Roarer, not convinced, sat depressed and frustrated, watching the work of his tutor.

"You could pick out some stones and examine them," Stone Breaker suggested. "Decide what you will do with them."

He pointed to a rawhide storage bag against the inside wall of the lodge. Bull Roarer dumped the contents on a level spot outside and spent an afternoon sorting stones while the old artisan worked nearby.

"Will this make a spear head, Uncle?"

"Yes," Stone Breaker decided, after examining the large

shard of flint, "but not a good one. See, the thin vein of another color? It will be a weak spot, and the spear will break easily. It would make two very good arrowpoints."

"Should I break it now?"

"If you wish. But if you leave it in one piece, it is easier to hold. You can rough out both ends, and then break it in the middle before you start the fine work."

The Moon of Ripening was at hand, and the hunters were pushing to harvest meat for the winter. This increased the demand for the skills of Stone Breaker, and his supply of flints was growing low.

"We need more stone," he told his apprentice one morning. "We will visit the quarry."

Bull Roarer knew that Stone Breaker occasionally went out into the prairie to obtain more material, but he had never wondered where.

"How far is it, Uncle?"

"Half a day's travel, maybe. We will sleep there. It is good that this summer camp is close."

"Are there other quarries?"

"Of course, but this is the best. See, this smooth blue-gray stone comes from there."

He held up the piece he was working. Stone Breaker seemed to have a preference for this type of material, though maybe it was just more available, Bull Roarer thought.

They set out the next day, traveling slowly because of Stone Breaker's age and his companion's disability. Bull Roarer carried his bow; Stone Breaker, no weapons except a knife. His dog, a massively built wolfish creature, pulled a pole-drag on which Stone Breaker tied their sleeping robes, a few supplies, and empty rawhide storage bags.

"We will carry our robes on the way back," he explained. "We can bring more stones that way."

The Blue Stone Quarry was very unimpressive to Bull Roarer. Stone Breaker led the way along a gametrail into the upper end of a small canyon. A clear spring came bubbling out from under a limestone ledge, and Stone Breaker knelt to drink.

"The quarry is just above," he said, pointing as he rose and wiped water from his lips. "There, behind that bush."

Bull Roarer saw nothing but knelt to drink, then followed the older man. Only a few steps away, Stone

Breaker stopped and pointed again to the shelf of stone opposite the spring.

"There," he said simply.

Bull Roarer looked. It looked exactly like a hundred other rocky ledges in the Tallgrass Hills. Many of them possessed a layer of blue-gray flint, and this one seemed no different at first. There was the horizontal blue stripe, but this one appeared darker and more uniform. It took a few more moments to realize that there was a marked indentation here in the rocky wall. Bull Roarer stepped forward for a closer look. Yes, this little cleft had certainly been formed by many generations of people who had come to obtain the finest of stone. Now he realized that around and below him on the slope lay discarded or useless fragments of stone. He was walking on shards of flint which had been rejected by centuries of workmen.

Here was one, he thought as he picked it up from beneath his feet. A fine flake of flint, clean and blue, just the size for a large arrowhead or small scraper. He turned it over and began to understand. The other side of the flat stone was white—the soft limestone unsuitable for their purpose. He tossed it aside, wondering even as he did so how many through the years had picked it up as he had, only to reject it as he had, and for the same reason.

"Do not bother with those," Stone Breaker was saying. "If they were usable, someone would have taken them before this."

Bull Roarer saw other flakes that had been partially worked and then discarded because of a hidden flaw or accidental fracture.

Stone Breaker was kneeling in the narrow cleft, his skilled fingers examining the face of the flint vein. He grunted to himself and finally spoke.

"Yes, others have been here since I was. Bull Roarer, bring one of the poles from the drag."

For the rest of the day, until it became too dark to see, they worked. The old man would select a protruding bulge of flint. By prying with the pole and striking with a heavy boulder, they would break loose a block of the fine blue stone. It would be set aside and a new chunk selected.

"That will be enough," Stone Breaker announced as the last pumpkin-sized chunk fell away. "We cannot carry more."

Bull Roarer was exhausted from the hard physical labor and fell asleep quickly. Stone Breaker smiled knowingly as he finished his pipe, knocked out the dottle, and rolled in his own sleeping robe. Yes, the boy would be good at this, he thought to himself. He had seen how Bull Roarer's hands touched the stone, with reverence for its spirit. He was glad for this opportunity for his apprentice to experience the spirit of the quarry. It was always an uplifting thing, to sleep here and commune with those who had come to this canyon for the same purpose, maybe since the time of creation. He thought his apprentice felt it too.

Stone Breaker's heart was full of satisfaction as he drifted off to sleep.

Though Bull Roarer was now showing more interest in life, the same influences were driving the three childhood friends apart. Crow continued to spend time with Bull Roarer, and he continued to tolerate her presence. It was, after all, pleasant to be able to share each small success with someone. Crow, in turn, was increasingly shut out by Small Elk. He had not been the same since the day she stayed behind while he went on the hunt. Crow's heart was heavy for this, but she did not know what to do. If she tried to rekindle her friendship with Elk, Bull Roarer might become depressed again. He was still a bit moody sometimes, especially when his fingers were sore.

It was some time before Crow, with her feminine instincts coming strongly to the fore, realized that it had become a matter of jealousy between the two young men. Bull Roarer had begun to call her Crow Woman, teasing at first, after Stone Breaker used the flattering term. Now, not only he but most of the band were using the name, and it had begun to fit her. Fit her, in fact, as well as her new buckskin dress, with the chest cut somewhat roomier to accommodate the changes in her body. It would have been an exciting time, a time of pride in her newfound maturity. It was unfortunate that it was happening at the same time as the rift between her two friends. It made things so much more complicated. *Aiee,* she thought, *things were so much simpler when we were children.*

As for Small Elk, he felt completely alone, abandoned by his friends. Bull Roarer resented his ability to run, walk, and hunt. Crow, now calling herself Crow Woman, had also abandoned him, preferring the company of Bull Roarer. It made his heart heavy, though he understood. Bull Roarer, people said, was rapidly becoming skilled in the craft he was learning from Stone Breaker. How could he, Small Elk, compete with such success? Of course, any woman would prefer the security that such a skilled artisan could provide. Why *should* Crow choose him, a young hunter with no special skill?

His heart was very heavy.

8

» » »

As Bull Roarer's prestige increased in the band and even as widely as the other bands of the People, the schism widened. Small Elk seemed intent on proving his worth as a hunter and doggedly pursued that elusive goal. Maybe he tried too hard, but ill fortune surely followed his efforts. Stubbornly, he continued.

Crow Woman, irked at his stubborn narrow-mindedness, spent more and more time with Bull Roarer, which seemed to push Small Elk more firmly into his self-defeating pattern.

By the time of their seventeenth summer, some were seeking the flintpoints of Bull Roarer, even in preference to those of Stone Breaker. There was much talk at the Sun Dance that year. Young Bull Roarer was surely destined for greatness as a weaponsmaker. People told one another this as the various bands gathered for the annual religious ceremonies in celebration of the return of Sun Boy, the grass, and the buffalo. Such skill was rarely found in one so young. Flintpoints and tools made by Bull Roarer were traded as objects of great value. It was no wonder that there were young men in all the bands who envied his success.

Yet another reason for envy was the beauty of his almost constant companion, Crow Woman. How fortunate can one man be? men asked each other, with much envious clucking of tongues.

All this did not go unnoticed by their former friend, Small Elk. As he became more embittered, his skills deteriorated. Before he realized what was happening, their roles had reversed. Bull Roarer, once avoided because of his handicap, now carried himself proudly, admired by others, while the embittered Small Elk sought solitude. His heart became heavy over the loss of the girl who had been the best friend of his childhood, the girl who had never really been his at all.

It was an evening late that summer when the southern band was beginning the fall hunt, that Stone Breaker called his apprentice to him. Bull Roarer crossed the open space from his parents' lodge, wondering what the older man might want at this time of day.

Stone Breaker watched him and the odd rolling gait that had resulted from the old injury as a child. It had prevented the youngster from participating in normal activities but was no handicap now. Stone Breaker was pleased that he had chosen to help the boy. There was no way that he could have foreseen the rapid progress his apprentice had made, and he was pleased to take some of the credit for Bull Roarer's success.

And how the boy had changed! The swing to his rolling stride, which had once appeared labored and difficult, now looked proud as the young man approached. Stone Breaker sat leaning on his backrest, smoking comfortably. He had come to an important decision.

"*Ah-koh*, Uncle," Bull Roarer said in greeting.

The old man nodded to acknowledge the greeting and pointed for him to sit. Bull Roarer settled himself on the ground before his tutor. After a suitable pause to satisfy custom, Stone Breaker began to speak. It was apparent from his tone that this was a matter of some importance.

"My son," he began, a dreamy look of nostalgia in his expression, "do you remember the day, there by the river, when you first watched me work flint?"

"Of course, Uncle." Bull Roarer smiled. "That seems long ago."

The old man nodded, and took a puff on his pipe.

"Yes. I hoped you would find an interest in such work. You have."

"Your instruction, Uncle," the young man began, "it has—"

Stone Breaker waved a hand to silence him.

"Hear me, Bull Roarer. I told you once that you would be as skillful as I."

"No, Uncle, I—"

"Be still," Stone Breaker admonished gently. "You are as

skilled as I am now. Maybe better. You will gain skill, while I will lose mine."

"No, you are still the best," Bull Roarer insisted.

"My eyes are failing," stated the old man. "You have not seen that I do not try the smaller, finer pieces that I once loved?"

"I . . . I had not noticed, Uncle."

"Yes, it is true. I can still get by, feeling the edges on the larger things. Spear points, scrapers, but . . ."

He spread his palms in frustration, then continued.

"Well, I have many winters. I will continue to work, but I have something to give you."

"Give me?" Bull Roarer was puzzled.

"Yes. I will give you my name. I will announce it at the next council."

Now the young man's head whirled. He had not expected such an honor, perhaps the greatest that could be given to a young person.

Since it was forbidden among the People to speak the name of the dead, it had become common to give away one's name. Usually it was passed to a grandson or other close relative. There had once been a problem over this, it was said. A popular young subchief had been killed, gored by a wounded buffalo. Since he was young and had never given his name, it could not be spoken. It was an unusual name, worn by no one else, but contained common words, that, now forbidden, were lost to the language. The People had devised new words to replace the old, and in a generation, the original words were forgotten.

This story ran through the mind of Bull Roarer as he sat dumbfounded before this respected man who had so changed his life. It made good sense, this gift of Stone Breaker's; in all the tribe, there was no other who carried this name. This gift would prevent the loss of the words *stone* and *breaker* at the old man's death.

But more important, of course, was the honor. Few men of the tribe were so respected. Besides the skill that had earned the name, Stone Breaker was respected for his kindness and charity. He had always had a reputation as a teacher in the Rabbit Society, freely giving advice to the young in the use of weapons and tools. It was overwhelming to Bull Roarer that he should be the one chosen to carry on the honor of so respected a name. He swallowed twice to clear the lump in his throat before he could speak. "I am honored, Uncle. I will wear it with pride."

"And you will bring honor to it, my son," said the old man.

There was no public announcement until the next council, but that was not far off. With the fall hunts beginning, frequent councils were held, and it was not half a moon when herds were sighted and the hunters met to prepare strategy.

It was then that Stone Breaker made his announcement, and young Bull Roarer stood to receive the approval of the band. It was given freely, because both Stone Breaker the Elder and the young man who now assumed the name and the prestige were quite popular and well respected. Several people made short speeches about the fine qualities of both men or complimented their workmanship. One suggested that now Stone Breaker the Younger would probably want to take a wife and establish his own lodge. Everyone laughed at the young man's embarrassment. Crow Woman blushed becomingly, her face shining in the firelight, glowing with excitement and pride.

The discussion quickly turned to the practical matters of the next day's hunt. It was a time of happiness and expectation, and everyone in the band felt that times were good. The buffalo were moving, it was said, into an area where they could easily be maneuvered and trapped. White Buffalo performed the Dance of the Buffalo in his ceremonial cape, and the council began to break up.

There would be little sleep tonight; excitement ran too high. Men would be talking and planning, checking bowstrings and the fletching on their arrows or the lashings of their spear heads if that was their preference in hunting buffalo.

It was a time of expectation for the entire band, and there was much happiness. Everyone looked forward to the coming day.

Everyone, that is, except one young hunter who had sat on the far periphery of the council circle. The firelight could barely push the shadows back that far, so no one noticed his glum countenance or that he slipped away early, before the council adjourned.

Small Elk wanted to be alone. His heart was very heavy,

and he could not find it in himself to appear pleased and excited over the events at the council. He had been especially hurt by the jokes about the taking of a wife by Bull Roarer, now Stone Breaker the Younger.

9

"**F**ather," said Small Elk, "I wish to go on my vision quest."

White Buffalo took time to think very carefully before he answered. The young man had weathered many disappointments in recent moons. His father had seen how the lack of success in the hunt had affected him. And in truth, there had seldom been such a persistent run of bad luck for anyone in the medicine man's memory. Small Elk had not made a kill worthy of the term for two seasons. That was odd, too. On their first hunt, Small Elk and Crow had achieved such success that their prestige had been high. Then, abruptly, there was no more success. It had crossed White Buffalo's mind that the strength of his son's personal medicine was helped by the presence of the girl, Crow Woman. This was not uncommon. However, it was also a matter that could not be helped. One could not interfere in such things.

He also suspected that part of his son's problem now related to the same matter. He noticed Small Elk's glum looks over the jokes about Stone Breaker's probable marriage. White Buffalo was probably the only one who saw Small Elk slip away into the darkness, alone and dejected. He wished that he could bear some of the young man's hurt.

Now Small Elk had come with talk of a vision quest. He must be very cautious in his counsel now. This was a turning point in the young man's life and must be handled carefully. It was unwise, of course, to enter the vision quest when one's heart was heavy. The dark thoughts of personal disappointment might easily interfere. One's mind and spirit must be free and open to receive the visions properly. Yet he had seen Small Elk's anger flare over disappointments. It was unlike the boy's basic nature, quiet and easygoing, but must be reckoned with at a time such as this.

"Why do you wish a vision quest now?" White Buffalo asked cautiously.

"It is time," Small Elk answered vaguely. "I am grown now."

It was difficult. White Buffalo wanted to answer something like "then why not behave like it?" but knew that the matter was more complex than that. Such a remark would only drive the young man away. That would not be good, because at this time, Small Elk needed all the help and kindness possible.

It was also difficult for White Buffalo, as holy man, to advise Small Elk in matters of the spirit. There was a certain conflict with his own feelings. Maybe, if he could maintain the purely detached approach of his office . . .

"My son," he began, "this is good, but there are things to consider."

He saw anger flare slightly in the eyes of his son, then come under control again.

"What do you mean?"

"Well, the season . . . that is probably all right. But you must be ready in your heart."

Small Elk said nothing, but at least he appeared to be thinking.

"You see, it is not just the fast and the visions that are important, but also the preparation for them."

He paused, trying to think of a way . . . ah, yes!

"Remember, now," he continued, "each spring, in the Moon of Greening, we burn the grass. This makes it come back greener, better for the buffalo. It makes the herds come back."

"But what has this to do with me?" Small Elk demanded.

"It is much the same, my son. The buffalo will not return without the greening of the grass. A vision quest is not a success unless the heart is ready."

"But my heart is ready, Father."

It would not have been nearly so difficult, the medicine man thought, if this were someone else's son. He could merely state "you are not ready," and his judgment would be accepted.

"Yes, your heart is ready," he acknowledged cautiously,

"but for what? No, wait . . . hear me out, my son. You have had bad luck in the hunt. *Again.* Your bowstring broke with the first shot today, I am told."

Small Elk nodded glumly.

"And you feel that you must escape this season of misfortune?"

"Yes. A vision quest . . ."

White Buffalo nodded.

"I can understand this need, Elk, but there are two needs here. One is the need to get away from the misfortune that follows you. The other is your quest. Now, what if the misfortune follows you, and your quest is spoiled?"

He paused and saw that Small Elk was beginning to understand. No one would wish to risk his vision quest.

"Maybe," he suggested carefully, "you could get away somewhere first, leave the bad luck behind, and then, when that has been overcome, it would be a better quest."

The young man nodded thoughtfully.

"Yes, maybe so," he agreed. "But where?"

"One of the other bands?" suggested White Buffalo innocently.

This was the important moment. Small Elk must think it his own idea.

"My mother's people!" Small Elk proclaimed triumphantly. "The Northern band!"

White Buffalo managed a look of surprise.

"Yes!" he exclaimed. "It is good, Elk. Your grandmother would welcome you!"

Now the young man was warming to the idea, showing more excitement for this than for anything since, *aiee*, how many moons!

"Their band is near the Big River this season?" Small Elk asked.

"Maybe so. But they said they will move to winter camp on the Salt River. You could meet them there, winter with them, and we will see you at the Sun Dance next summer. Then, that might be the time for your vision quest."

"Yes. It is good, Father!"

His mother's reaction was somewhat different.

"Of course not!" Dove Woman sputtered at her husband. "Have you gone mad, to think of letting him do this?"

"Be calm, Dove," he said soothingly. "Look at him. This

is the first interest he has shown. His spirit has been slowly dying."

"But how can he find them?"

"Ask the Growers, if he must. But we know they will camp on the Salt River this winter. He has visited your parents there before."

"He traveled with them, after the Sun Dance! This is different. He must not travel alone."

White Buffalo took her hand and looked seriously into her eyes.

"Dove," he said, "that is the important part. He *must* travel alone. He needs to find himself."

Dove Woman shook her head.

"It is too dangerous."

"I know, he is your youngest," he said gently. "But he is grown. That is part of his trouble. He wanted to go on a vision quest. This is no more dangerous."

"*Aiee,* a vision quest!" wailed Dove Woman.

"He can do this easily," White Buffalo assured her. "He needs to regain his spirit. We will see him again in a few moons."

Reluctantly, Dove Woman finally consented. Now Small Elk became eager, restless to be off. The change in his spirit did not go unnoticed among the People. Several remarked to his parents that Small Elk appeared heavier, or seemed to be growing nicely. They replied that yes, he was preparing to winter with his grandparents in the Northern band.

It was several days before his supplies were prepared and extra moccasins readied for the journey. By that time, everyone in the band was aware of his plan. Many of his peers stopped by to wish him a good journey, and many seemed a little envious. One even offered to accompany him, an old friend who had drifted away.

"No, Otter, I must go alone. My father has said so."

"Ah, it is a medicine thing, then?"

"Yes. A thing of the spirit. Like a vision quest, almost. But different."

White Buffalo, who happened to overhear, felt that he would be greatly pleased when his son actually departed. Small Elk was trying to gain too much prestige out of this. On the evening before his departure, Small Elk was surprised when Bull Roarer, now Stone Breaker the Younger, approached. The two stood, not speaking for a moment, both embarrassed.

"I wanted to wish you well," Stone Breaker mumbled.

"And you," agreed Small Elk, "though it seems you have already done well."

"Stone Breaker has been good to teach me," the young man said modestly.

He hesitated a moment.

"Elk, we should not have drifted apart."

"That is true," Elk agreed.

It was difficult to remain jealous of the success of a friend who was trying to make amends. They stood, both awkwardly silent, for a little longer, and Bull Roarer–Stone Breaker finally broke the quiet.

"May you have a good journey, Elk," he said, extending a hand.

Small Elk clasped the offered hand, still uncomfortable, and the other turned away. Elk watched him go with the rolling gait that now identified him. Now it seemed like a proud walk, this swing to the step of a successful young man. Elk found that he could not begrudge his former friend's success. Their differences were like ashes in his mouth, and he left the camp to wander in the deepening dusk, alone with his confused thoughts.

"Elk?" someone spoke from beside the dim trail.

It was Crow Woman, standing in partial concealment behind some dogwoods.

"I have seen you come here sometimes," she said. "I hoped you would come tonight."

A mixture of emotions now flooded over him. He was angry at her. Why did she want to seek him out tonight, to confuse further his already confused thoughts? He was also angry at himself. Crow Woman stood there in the dimness of the fading twilight, her large dark eyes looking straight into his. He had never seen a woman half so beautiful. Her long body had ripened into the fullness of womanhood. The gangly frame of adolescence had now been filled out, angles replaced by soft and graceful curves. He had not been this near her for many moons. They had avoided each other, and now all the old hurt came rushing back.

"Why?" he blurted roughly.

"I wanted to see you."

"You could have done that at any time."

She chose to ignore the accusation.

"I wish you a good journey."

Why would she do this? She had avoided him these past many moons; then, when finally he had nearly worked out a way to escape the hurt, she had gone out of her way to seek him out and hurt him again. Carefully, he held in his anger.

"I am sorry, Elk," she said softly. "I would not have hurt you."

It appeared for a moment that she would have come into his arms, but he turned away. It was partly from the darkness that he did not see the tears in the girl's dark eyes. Partly, too, because of the tears in his own.

10

It was early in the Moon of Greening when the traveler stopped at the winter camp of the Northern band. He inquired as to the location of the lodge of the chief, so that he might pay his respects according to proper protocol. There he visited, exchanging small talk about the weather, the mild winter just past, and the season to come.

He was traveling somewhat earlier than usual, the stranger said, to join the Eastern band before they broke winter camp. There was a girl there whom he had met at last year's Sun Dance. He had been unable to dismiss his constant thoughts of her and with favorable weather, had left his own Red Rocks band far to the southwest to go to her.

The old chief smiled. Ah, young romance! This young man had undertaken a dangerous journey in winter. But he had survived, and such a romantic effort would certainly impress the young woman of the Eastern band. Actually, the foolhardy journey would probably seem quite appropriate to the Eastern band. They had always had a reputation for foolish ways.

"And where did you winter?" the chief asked.

"I traveled some. I spent part of the Moon of Snows and the Moon of Hunger with the Southern band. Of course, I supplied my own food."

The chief nodded.

"And now you travel on?"

"Yes, my chief. I bear greetings from Broken Horn. He says they will meet you at the Sun Dance. Oh, yes . . . is there a young man, Small Elk, staying with your band? His parents wished me to bring him greetings. He stays here in the lodge of White Antelope?"

"Yes, of course. He is with his grandparents. He

wintered with us, you know. Is there any other news of the Southern band?"

"No, I . . . yes! Their weaponsmaker is dead. Stone Breaker. He gave his name away. He was very old, I heard."

"Yes. A good man."

The traveler left the chief's lodge to seek the lodge of Small Elk's grandparents. There he was welcomed as a long-lost relative since he brought greetings and news from White Buffalo and Dove Woman.

"*Aiee,* come inside, young man," Fox Woman invited. "Tell us everything."

"Thank you, Grandmother."

He sat and carefully related all the details he could recall while Fox Woman prepared food.

"That is all I remember," he said finally. "They and their other children are well. They sent special greetings to their son."

He nodded across the fire to Small Elk, who had said little.

"Is there other news of the band?" asked Small Elk.

"Yes, I just told the chief, your weaponsmaker is dead. Stone Breaker."

"The old man?" asked Small Elk, his voice tight.

"Yes. He had given his name to his apprentice. I heard he is quite skilled, too. A young man with a limp."

"Yes, I know him."

"Ah! And did you know he had married? Yes, a beautiful woman. She is with child, someone said. I cannot remember her name."

"Yes, I know her, too," Small Elk said, trying to choke back emotion.

"It is good!" their talkative guest chortled. "I am glad I remembered to tell you."

Small Elk was not quite so pleased but gradually decided that it was just as well. He began to realize that he had spent the winter without really coming to grips with his loss. Now it had been forced on him, and though it was a shock, maybe this was the only way to recover his sense of reality. Before, there had been the possibility that things could change. Now there was little hope. Crow Woman was not only married but pregnant and beyond reach for him.

He had made some progress during the winter, had done some growing up. It was possible, now, for him to think more calmly, almost objectively. He wished that he could rejoice in the happiness of his two friends. Maybe someday he could do so. For now, he would continue to try. It would not be easy.

The Sun Dance that year was to be held at Turkey Creek. It was customary to choose a central location for ease of travel. It was never satisfactory for all but was usually most difficult for the bands to the far west. Occasionally, the Red Rocks, or the Mountain band, farther north, would decide not to attend. Those seasons were rare, however, usually restricted to years when the location for the Sun Dance was too far east to allow for the journey to be practical. Of course, if the Big Council chose a site too far *west*, the Eastern band was sure to protest loudly.

It had been a tradition of the People to scatter widely each season. But likewise, their tradition of oneness, though they might be scattered, was strong. This and the strong sense of the sacred nature of the ceremony had made the Sun Dance their most important annual event.

That, of course, was not to deny its importance as a social event. It might take many sleeps to travel to the prearranged site. Upon arrival there, people were ready for celebration, so there would be feasting and dancing, renewing of friendships, the greeting of relatives, gambling, gaming, and smoking—all leading to the seven days of the Sun Dance.

The northern band would be the first to arrive. It was their responsibility to begin to prepare the open-sided arbor in which the Sun Dance would be held. It had been their task since the election of their popular young chief, Many Robes, as Real-chief of the entire tribe. With honor goes responsibility.

One facet of their preparation fell to the family of the chief—the selection and securing of a large buffalo bull for the ceremony. A magnificent animal was found, and the hunters—relatives and friends of Many Robes—were able to stalk and kill it successfully. It was good. The ease with which this preceremonial was carried out seemed a good omen for the year. The skin, with the head still attached, was stretched over a framework of poles at one end of the dance arbor to form an effigy in honor of the return of the buffalo.

Small Elk had never seen these early preparations before, since the office of Real-chief had not been in the Southern band for a number of years. He was fascinated by the size of the bull that the hunters had selected. He would have gladly taken part in the hunt if he had been invited. He was beginning to recover his confidence in his ability. But he was young and an outsider, and he knew that the chances for such an invitation were remote. It, the ceremonial hunt, was too important to risk the participation of amateurs.

Still, it was easy to become excited over these goings-on. Enthusiasm began to return, and Small Elk felt a thrill in the air over the coming festivities. This excitement and anticipation, of course, was an important part of the purpose of the celebration, the rejuvenation of the traditional urges that had led the People onto the plains for centuries.

The Red Rocks band was next to arrive at the site of the Sun Dance. This was unusual, in that they had the farthest to travel. But maybe not. This band held fiercely to tradition. Their very name told of their devoted preference for a specific place, a place long important to them. Sometimes they wintered elsewhere, but their favorite locale was in the Red Rocks.

Their other fierce loyalty, however, was to the rest of the tribe. It was very seldom, in the memory of anyone, that the Red Rocks missed a Sun Dance.

The helpers of Many Robes showed the Red Rocks the area assigned for their camp. This was only a matter of traditional welcome; they could have located their camping area themselves. It was always the same. The circle of the camp was open directly to the east, and all lodgedoors faced that direction to welcome Sun Boy's appearance each morning. The Northern and Southern bands would camp in their respective segments of the circle, and the Mountain band in the northwest. The Eastern band would erect their lodges just north of the symbolic gap left for Sun Boy.

For now, the Red Rocks proceeded to the southwest segment of the camp circle and began to establish their camp. It had always been so, from before the time of memory. Probably since Creation, it was said. The same arrangement was always carried out in seating of the bands around the council fire. That too went back into antiquity. There was even an empty space in the circle, reserved for a band that had occupied a southeast position. They had been exterminated long ago, killed by a warlike tribe who lived in the woodlands to the east. The empty spot in the camp and the empty seats in the Big Council had served as a grim reminder for many generations.

In another day or two the scouts reported the approach of the Mountain band, and again there were happy family reunions, the greetings of old friends, and the hustle and bustle of establishing camp. Excitement increased, and the festive atmosphere became stronger. It was a time of joyous celebration.

Small Elk, though he had mixed feelings, looked forward eagerly to the arrival of the Southern band. It would be good to see his parents, his brother and sister, and their families. His slightly uneasy feeling of apprehension revolved around greeting Stone Breaker and Crow Woman, now his wife. That would be difficult, at best. He would be expected to congratulate his friends and be happy with them in the happiness of their marriage. He was not certain that he could handle that in a convincing manner but knew that he must try. Eventually, he must overcome his jealousy and learn to live with the disappointment—either that or concede that he could not live with it and join a different band permanently.

There were eligible young women in the Northern band. Some had cast sidelong glances at him and smiled invitingly. He was certain that his grandparents would welcome a permanent move to their band. It was not uncommon. There was a constant shifting in the bands. Some families, in fact, seemed to change loyalties every two or three seasons, to follow the band whose chief seemed at the moment to carry the greatest prestige. He seriously considered such a move for a time.

No, he finally decided, he could not do it. His father had always looked with scorn upon those who instead of facing their problems, tried to avoid them by moving to a different band. Besides, he was not ready to become romantically involved with any of the beautiful daughters of the Northern band.

He was ready, he thought, to talk seriously with his father about his future. He believed that White Buffalo would approve a vision quest this season. That would certainly help to show him the right way. It had been a stupid thing, he realized, to consider a vision quest out of anger and disappointment. Those were the wrong reasons. Yes, he looked forward to the arrival of his parents and the expected talk with his father.

Even so, he was caught totally off guard when the day finally came. The scout who had been watching to the south came trotting into the camp.

"The Southern band comes!" he announced as he made the circuit of the area. "The Southern band has arrived!"

11

Small Elk found himself avoiding contact with anyone except his parents. He realized what he was doing. Everyone else was hurrying around, greeting friends or family, exchanging jokes, stories, and small talk. Although he had assured himself that he too must do so, he found it difficult to mix with the others. He stayed away from the gregarious happiness, only belatedly joining his parents to help set up their lodge. He studiously avoided even looking around at other families, as they too began to establish their campsites.

This was going to be more difficult than he had thought. He kept imagining Crow Woman in the arms of his friend Stone Breaker, now her husband. Despite his resolve, he now wondered if it would be possible for him to accept it. Maybe he should consider again the possibility of joining another band.

He was somewhat distracted for a time by the reunion with his parents and the tasks of setting up camp. He knew it would be a day or two before he could find an opportunity to talk to his father, and that too was worrisome. It was midafternoon when the Southern band arrived, so there was much to do before dark. That was both good and frustrating—good, because it postponed the inevitable meeting with Stone Breaker and Crow Woman; bad, because it also postponed his chance to talk with his father.

Without actually realizing that he was doing it, he spent the evening finding ways to keep busy and avoiding prolonged conversation with anyone. He did not want to spend the evening hearing about the marriage of Crow Woman or her pregnancy. Also, he was not ready for his mother's questions about the girls of the Northern band.

He rather suspected that a romance with a young woman of her own band would not be entirely unwelcome to Dove Woman.

Small Elk also found himself reluctant to go out and mix with the other young people, as would be the usual custom. There would be the risk of encountering Crow Woman, Stone Breaker, or both.

Never was a lodge so meticulously aligned, so carefully set, or the thongs which held the cover to the poles tied and retied so many times. At first Dove Woman attributed her son's overattentiveness to his happiness at the reunion. Gradually she began to see his preoccupation but was puzzled by it.

"Let him alone," advised White Buffalo. "He will work it out."

Reluctantly, Dove Woman did so. She tried to ignore the repetition of tasks, the meticulous tying and retying of the lashings, the readjusting of the laces over the door, and the interminable fussing with the smoke flaps.

Finally, it was apparent even to Small Elk that there was nothing more that he could do to help his parents establish the camp. He must settle down to make small talk, and the the subject of Crow Woman's marriage would surely come up. Another idea struck him.

"I will bring some fuel," he said, and was off like an arrow from the bow.

His mother shook her head.

"What is the matter with him?" his mother asked. "Why is he behaving so?"

"I am not sure," White Buffalo said slowly. "He will tell us, when he is ready."

"Is it about Stone Breaker's marriage?" Dove Woman wondered. "He should be happy about that."

"Maybe," his father answered. "He knows of it, because he told us that the traveler stopped with them."

Puzzled, they settled down in their new campsite to wait for Small Elk's return.

Shadows were lengthening, and Small Elk had gone far upstream to gather wood and buffalo chips. He had felt a need to escape the social pressures of the day. He wished there was some way he could leave the entire tribe for a few days—until after the Big Council and Sun Dance, maybe. A vision quest still seemed like a good idea, but he really wished to discuss that with his father. *Aiee,* growing up, assuming the duties of a man, was difficult.

He picked up a dead cottonwood limb and added it to the stack in the crook of his left arm. Already, he had almost more than he could carry. But it would soon be dusk, and if he waited a little longer, he could unobtrusively slip back to his parents' lodge. Now the sleepy sounds of the creatures of the day were becoming fewer as they settled for the night. A great blue heron beat his way overhead, hurrying to his lodge before darkness fell. There were sounds of some of the night-creatures, coming alive with the departure of Sun Boy and his torch.

Small Elk turned to start back and noticed a figure on the path ahead of him.

"*Ah-koh,* Elk," said Crow Woman.

For a moment, he felt that he had lived this before. The girl carried an armful of sticks, but somehow he doubted that an accident had brought them together. He remembered well their last, emotional meeting. He had a moment of anger. Why would she repeatedly torture him this way, seeking him out to imply things that never were and never could be? He could not stay angry, however. The look in her eyes would melt any but the coldest heart.

At their last meeting, he had thought that he had never seen her more beautiful. Even that was eclipsed now. She stood there, straight and tall, not moving, looking directly into his face, and her spirit reached out to touch his.

"I followed you," she admitted.

"I know. Crow, you should not have—"

Now anger flared in her face. He was distressed by it, but *aiee,* how it accentuated her dark beauty. Her eyes flashed, and she stamped her foot impatiently.

"Elk, what is the matter with you?" she demanded.

As she moved, the fringes at the bottom of her buckskin dress swayed, and the motion caught his attention. He looked at the attractive exposure of long tan legs, from above the knees downward. He should not be appreciating this, but he had always admired Crow's appearance, even before the advent of her womanhood. Now she was another man's wife, and it was wrong to look at her with the thoughts he was thinking. Forcibly, he tried to raise his eyes, trying not to stare at the womanly curves that he found so appealing. The willowy shape of her hips, the flat belly . . . wait! Even in the dim light . . . The traveler had told him, three moons ago, of her pregnancy. This was not . . .

"I heard you were pregnant!" he blurted.

Immediately he felt like an idiot, but it was too late. If she was angry before, now her face showed a rage that was frightening. For a moment, he thought she would hit him with her firewood. Instead, she threw it to the ground and stepped toward him.

"*What?*" she demanded. "Elk, I should walk away and never speak to you again!"

Now his anger rose. How could a woman for whom he had such high regard be acting so shamelessly?

"Yes, you should!" he snapped. "You shame your husband."

"My *husband?* Elk, you have gone mad!" she shouted at him. "You know I *have* no husband! I would not come here—"

She turned and started away.

"Wait!" he called.

He dropped his own firewood and ran to catch her.

"Crow! You and Bull . . . Stone Breaker. I was told . . . the Falling-Leaves Moon? You were not married?"

Slowly, a light began to dawn in her face.

"No!" she said flatly. "Stone Breaker and Cattail. You remember her? *She* is pregnant."

They stood, staring at each other in disbelief for a moment, and then both burst out laughing. In another moment, they were in each other's arms, both trying to talk at once, interrupting, and dissolving into laughter again.

"Elk," she whispered in his ear, "there has never been anyone but you in my heart."

"Or you, in mine!"

Now both were laughing and crying at once, holding tightly.

"I did not know what was wrong!" she murmured.

"Nothing is wrong, now!"

"We must tell Stone Breaker," she said, laughing. "He will be pleased for us."

"Our parents too," Elk agreed. "I am sure my mother thinks something is wrong with me."

"Mine too," she said. "We will go and tell them. But first, let us stay here a little while."

She snuggled closer in his arms, shivering a little, only partly against the chill of the prairie night.

12

» » »

The world was bright, happy, and exciting after the reunion of the two childhood sweethearts. They threw themselves wholeheartedly into the celebration of the Sun Dance and all that it stood for.

For Small Elk, the prayers of thanksgiving for the return of the sun and the renewing of the prairie would carry a broader meaning. His ritual prayers would also hold the gratitude for the return of Crow Woman. At first, he could hardly understand what had happened. How could he have been so wrong, have misinterpreted events for so long? Gradually, he came to understand. His jealousy had been one of the major obstacles. He had been unable to see objectively, to realize that the relationship between Crow and Bull Roarer had been one of friendship, not romance. Bull Roarer had badly needed a friend, and Crow had seen that need. Small Elk was now feeling a guilt that he had not been there to help. He had nearly destroyed himself with jealousy. First he had been jealous of Crow's attention to their friend, then jealous of Bull Roarer's success. *Aiee*, it was not pretty.

In his jealousy, he had completely overlooked the fact that Cattail, the quiet, sweet child who was their childhood playmate, had also matured. Now, with the clarity of hindsight, he realized that she had been around all along. Probably she too had been jealous, jealous of Crow's attention to the rising career of Stone Breaker. But Cattail had been persistent, patiently waiting. Small Elk would never know whether Stone Breaker had first asked Crow Woman to join him as his wife and been refused. He knew that Crow Woman would respect such a confidence, and for this he loved her even more.

Regardless, Stone Breaker, now the respected weapons-

maker of the Southern band, had now taken a wife. Small
Elk had gone to visit their lodge early in the morning after
his meeting with Crow Woman. His reception was cool.
Cattail, her belly large with the expectation of the child,
apologized for the disarray of the lodge.

"We only arrived yesterday," she explained.

"Yes, I know. And only last night I heard of your marriage. I wanted to wish you well, both of you."

Gradually, the atmosphere warmed as they began to
recall incidents from their childhood. Then Crow Woman
stopped by, and soon they were laughing together. The
intervening years were stripped away, and they were children again, giggling and reveling in the joy of one another's successes.

"You wintered with your grandparents?" Stone Breaker
asked.

"Yes."

Small Elk was reluctant to reveal the bitterness and jeal-
ously with which he had left the band last autumn.

"I needed some time away," he explained.

The others nodded in understanding. It was apparent
that for Small Elk, life had not been as kind. Privately, he
was just beginning to realize how his jealousy had nearly
devoured him from within. Much of his bad luck, it
seemed, had been self-inflicted.

The moment seemed good now, and he related the story
of the traveler's visit, when he learned of Stone Breaker's
marriage.

"He did not know the name of your wife," he finished,
"and I thought it was Crow Woman. I was very jealous."

"You thought . . . *aiee*, Elk, it is no wonder you avoided
me yesterday!"

Stone Breaker collapsed into laughter.

"When did you learn?" Cattail asked.

"Only last night. I encountered Crow Woman while we
were gathering wood. She did not seem very pregnant, so
. . . well, then she told me."

Now all four were laughing. Finally, Stone Breaker
paused, wiping the tears of laughter from his eyes.

"Ah, my friends, we have been apart too long. Now,
when will you two be married?"

There was a moment of embarrassed confusion. Crow

Woman blushed becomingly, but did nothing to help Small Elk answer.

"I . . . we . . . ah . . . there has not been time to talk of it," he mumbled.

"Of course!" Stone Breaker broke into laughter again. "Last night!"

Maybe a trifle too much laughter, Small Elk thought. Maybe he *had* been rejected by Crow Woman. No matter, now. Stone Breaker and Cattail obviously had a good marriage and were pleased and proud about the pregnancy.

"We will talk of these things," said Crow Woman, relieving some of the pressure that Small Elk was feeling.

The others nodded.

"I will speak with my father, also," Small Elk explained. "I have not seen him since last season."

"About your marriage?" Stone Breaker asked, puzzled.

"No, no. I may take a vision quest."

"Yes, you should do that first," advised Stone Breaker.

The women laughed.

"No, I—"

"We understand, Stone Breaker," Crow Woman said, teasing. "You have hardly been out of your lodge since last fall!"

"Will you follow your father's medicine?" asked Stone Breaker, attempting to change the subject.

"I do not know," Small Elk answered slowly. "I am not sure I have the gift."

He had been so preoccupied with his jealousies, he realized now, that he had given little thought to such things. He should be making these decisions. It was quite usual for the son of a holy man to follow his father as an apprentice. However, he must first have the gift, the visionary second sight, to make such a choice. Even then, some who were endowed with the gift refused it, unwilling to accept the responsibility and sacrifice required for such a career. Small Elk's older brother, Blue Owl, had not chosen such a path. Small Elk was not sure whether it was due to a refusal or whether Blue Owl had not received the gift. One did not ask such things. While it was permissible to ask whether such an apprenticeship was upcoming, the reasons for the decision were quite personal.

When he was younger, Small Elk had often imagined himself following his father's footsteps. In recent moons, the past two years, such thoughts had rarely occurred to him. He now regretted the wasted time.

"It is one of the things that my father can help me with, to find the answers," he explained to the others

The next afternoon, Small Elk went to talk to his father. White Buffalo was pleased with the change in his son. He and Dove Woman were not certain what had caused the change, but it was certainly for the better—something that had happened that first night, it seemed, when the Southern band arrived at the camp on Turkey Creek. Elk had spent the morning with his friends, and it was apparent that the reunion had been a happy one. Probably joy over the marriage of Stone Breaker and Cat Tail, they decided.

"Father, I would speak with you," Small Elk began.

White Buffalo remained silent, waiting.

"I asked of a vision quest, before," the young man went on.

His father only nodded.

"I was not ready, then. You told me, but I did not believe. Now I know I was not ready, but maybe I am now."

"Maybe," answered the medicine man cautiously. "Tell me more."

"Well, I . . . after the Sun Dance, of course . . . Crow Woman and I have spoken of marriage. But would it not be better to take the vision quest first?"

"Probably." White Buffalo's eyes twinkled. This was going well. "But, I am made to feel there is more?" he asked.

"Maybe so," Small Elk said cautiously. "I have wondered, Father. Do you suppose I might have the gift of medicine?"

Aiee, thought White Buffalo, *of course you have, my son, but you must discover it for yourself.*

"Why do you ask this?" he said aloud, trying to control his elation.

"No reason, but I wondered how one finds out such things."

"Oh. Well, no one can tell you that, my son. You must seek it."

"How?"

"There are many ways. Start to mention it in your Sun-Dance prayers. *Ask* for the gift, if you wish. That could do no harm. But, only if you wish it."

"I . . . I am not sure, Father."

White Buffalo nodded in understanding.

"Then what *do* you wish, that you are sure about?"

"I wish to marry Crow Woman, and to go on a vision quest."

"Ah, you are answering your own questions. Your vision quest may answer your doubts about the gift. But it might be difficult to think in the right spirit of the quest with a new wife at home." It would be hard enough, he added to himself, to concentrate on *anything*, with a new wife like young Crow Woman waiting for one's return. No, it would be better to postpone that distraction.

"Your quest should be first," he suggested. "It may provide some other answers. When you return, then you will be better able to plan."

"And the marriage?" Small Elk asked.

"It is good, Elk. But, you should wait. Wait until your vision quest is behind you. Who knows? Maybe the quest will help you decide when it should take place."

Small Elk nodded, looking a trifle disappointed.

"But before that, even," his father was saying, "comes the Sun Dance."

» » »

13

The Eastern band straggled in, almost on the appropriate day, in their usual state of disorder and disarray. The time-honored jokes were exchanged about the ineptness of the Eastern band. This opportunity for wry humor at the expense of one group was never overlooked. If anyone of another band made a mistake or suffered any accident or misfortune, someone was sure to comment on it.

"It is to be expected. His grandmother was of the Eastern band."

The origin of this good-natured ridicule was lost in antiquity but seemed to be self-perpetuating. Some of the members of that band even seemed to revel in the reputation and to behave foolishly just to produce laughs. And people with a more serious approach to life may have transferred their loyalties and their families to other bands through the generations, leaving the reputation of the Eastern band more accurate each season.

With the arrival of the last band, it was time to begin the announcement of the Sun Dance. For three days, the keeper of the Sun Doll danced ceremonially around the entire encampment, chanting his announcement to the People. Three circuits each morning he traveled, ending each time in the Sun-Dance lodge. Meanwhile, the medicine men from each band had tied their respective medicine bundles in place around the sides of the lodge. Excitement was building.

The Sun Dance proper would continue day and night for seven days. Exhausted dancers would drop out, and others would take their places. Those who beat the drums also traded off for a half-day's sleep, to return later. The throb of the drums and the chanting were continuous.

Dancers placed carefully planned sacrifices before the

buffalo effigy—a well-tanned robe, a choice otter skin, or a perfectly fletched and painted arrow; medicine sticks, carved, painted, and decorated with fur and feathers. One man sacrificed a favorite bow with which he had found spectacular success at the hunt in an effusion of thanksgiving.

There were also prayers of thanksgiving for the return of the sun after the long, dark nights of winter, when Sun Boy's torch had nearly gone out. There were also prayers that involved pledges and promises of patriotism, sometimes mixed with supplication. One might publicly pledge a specific sacrifice at the next Sun Dance in return for good health or good hunting this season. The aged and infirm attempted to dance and sing the chants of supplication for healing. As the excitement of the dance stirred their blood, arthritic old limbs actually seemed to take on a new and youthful vigor.

Small Elk participated, of course, with prayerful chants of thanks for his good fortune. He had nothing to sacrifice but pledged to do so when he was able. His supplication was that he be helped with his vision quest and with the decisions ahead. He also mentioned good health for himself, his family, and his intended wife.

It was not before the third day of the dance that Elk found occasion to talk with his father again. White Buffalo, occupied with his ceremonial responsibilities, finally decided that things were going well enough for him to take an interval of rest. He slept for part of an afternoon, ate sparingly, and drank deeply. When the medicine man stepped out to return to the Sun-Dance lodge, he encountered his son.

"*Ah-koh,* Father."

"*Ah-koh,* my son. You did well at the dance lodge. It brought me pride."

"Thank you, Father. But I must talk with you. When the Dance is over maybe?"

White Buffalo shrugged and spread his palms, secretly delighted at this overture.

"Of course, Elk. Why not now?"

They walked together, a little way from the camp, away from the clamor of drums and chanting.

"Yes, my son?"

"Father, you know that I . . . Crow Woman and I . . . we wish to marry!" he finally blurted.

"Yes . . . you have talked with her parents?"

"No, but I think they will agree."

"Probably," White Buffalo observed. He was actually quite certain. He and Dove Woman had already discussed the matter, and the two mothers of the couple had long hoped for this.

"But I also wish to take my vision quest, as we spoke before."

White Buffalo nodded understandingly. "It is good. Do that first."

"There is more. Do you think I might have the gift of spirit, to follow you?"

White Buffalo's heart leapt for joy. He managed to control his delight, for such a decision must not be based on the wishes of others.

"Maybe," he said calmly. "Your vision quest should tell."

Then he saw the young man's dilemma. Elk was afraid that his thoughts of the coming marriage would interfere with the spiritual nature of his quest. It was something to consider. It would be possible to marry now and seek his vision next year. But no, that would postpone the decision about his career. Not only that, but by that time there might be the distractions of a family. And the longer the quest was postponed, the more difficult it would be. He took a long breath.

"My son," he said slowly, "my heart tells me that the sooner you seek the visions, the better. I will cast the bones, but I am already sure."

"As soon as the Sun Dance is over?" Small Elk asked.

"Yes! Have you thought where you will go?"

"Some. There is a hill above Sycamore Creek, above the place we camp sometimes."

"Yes, I know the place. You knew we are to camp there this year?"

"No! I had not heard. It is good!"

Elk paused a few moments, then spoke again. "Father, I could leave tomorrow, to go and begin my fast. When you arrive there for the summer camp, I will already have my quest behind me."

White Buffalo considered that proposal. Yes, that would give the boy time alone to think. It would be dangerous

. . . *aiee,* a vision quest always held a certain amount of danger. Alone on the prairie . . . but that was the purpose, to be alone, to experience the things of the spirit. Elk would arrive in the selected area a few sleeps before the rest of the band and would be undisturbed. He had proved himself able to travel alone last season.

"Yes," the medicine man agreed. "Yes, Elk, I think maybe this is good. Then, when we arrive, you will be ready to begin whatever your heart tells you. When will you start?"

Small Elk shrugged. "Tomorrow?"

"Good! Now go, make your preparations. I must go back to the Dance now."

"Your vision quest? Now?" Crow Woman's eyes were wide with wonder. "We have just found each other again," she protested.

"This is one reason why," he told her. "It will help me know what I must do, and we can be together sooner."

"Yes," she agreed reluctantly, "but I wish I could go with you."

"But then it would not be a vision quest," he reminded her playfully.

"I know."

She snuggled against him, her body warm in the cool prairie twilight. "Elk, when you return, I will be waiting."

"Good," he agreed. "Then we will start another quest, we two, together."

She smiled at him in the gathering dusk. "You start tomorrow?"

"Yes. At daylight. Have you told your parents? About us, I mean?"

"A little. Only that you thought I was married to Stone Breaker."

They laughed together quietly.

"Not that I was pleased to be wrong?" he teased.

"Well, yes, that too."

"Good! Then they will not be surprised!"

"You will talk with them now?"

"No, not until after my quest. I must keep my spirit free to receive the visions."

She nodded, understanding.

"My heart will be with you," she said.

Dove Woman again protested a lone journey of this type, but not so long or so strongly. He had proved his ability already, and she knew she could not keep him a child forever.

"Take care, my son," she told him as she wrapped a small pack of dried meat and a little pemmican for his journey. "If the weather is hot, eat the pemmican first, before it becomes bitter. Save something to eat when your fast is over."

"Yes, Mother," he answered her, smiling. "I know this."

"I know you do, but mothers say such things. It is our privilege."

She hugged him and smiled, pretending that the tears were not welling up. *Aiee,* her youngest, on his vision quest! It seemed only yesterday he was a babe at her breast.

She watched him until his long strides carried him to the crest of the little rise. The rays of the rising sun struck his face as he turned to wave, then crossed over.

Dove Woman turned back toward her lodge. *I have never noticed before,* she thought, *how much Small Elk walks like his father.* From beyond the lodges, the rhythmic cadence of the drums and the chanting went on.

14

» » »

Small Elk sat by his fire, uncertain what to expect. From time to time, he felt the sharp spasm of a hunger pang. Sometimes his belly rumbled loudly in protest against the indignity of emptiness. This was a disappointment. He did not know how a fast was supposed to proceed, but surely there must be more to it than this.

He had reached the hilltop on a pleasant evening a little before dark. There had been time to gather fuel and to establish his camp. He broke a stick of dried meat in half and chewed one portion while he gathered wood. He would begin his fast immediately after lighting his fire. That was always an important step, the symbolic lighting of the fire. He used rubbing sticks, the yucca spindle whirling in the little depression of the fireboard as he drew the bow back and forth. Smoke began to pour forth, and a black powdery ash gathered below the notch in the flat board. Soon smoke seemed to be issuing from the little pile of powder itself. Elk laid aside the sticks and the firebow, and picked up the precious spark on its tuft of shredded cedar bark. Carefully, he breathed on the spark, watching it glow and recede with each breath. Smoke became more dense, pouring from the tinder. He blew a trifle harder. He was ready when the cedar bark burst into flame, and he thrust the blazing tuft into a little opening in the pile of sticks he had prepared. The smallest sticks began to ignite, and the yellow tongues licked upward, the fire growing rapidly. He added a few larger sticks and sat back to chant the Song of Fire.

It was a time-honored ceremony, this song, performed as a ritual whenever a new fire was kindled. It was in two parts, the first a prayer of thanks for the gift of fire. The second, perhaps more pertinent to each new fire, was a statement. "Here," it said, "I intend to camp. The fire indicates my intention to live here a little while." The fire was a public gesture to whatever spirits might live in this place, a request for permission to stay here, and a marker of the site. Ceremoniously, he placed the other half of his stick of dried meat on the fire to appease the spirits of the place.

Small Elk finished the ritual and spread his robe to prepare for the night. There would be little sleep; he was too excited. He was actually beginning his vision quest, that most important of lifetime experiences. How could one sleep?

That had been a day ago. Nothing had happened, except that he was hungry, and his belly was growling aloud in protest. He was bored. Since his Song for Morning, there had been very little to do. He had watched a circling hawk for a while, and observed a band of antelope on a distant hilltop. He assembled a supply of firewood and a stack of chips of buffalo dung, which would burn slowly and long, with little flame.

Beyond that, there was nothing to do but wait. He took a sip from his water skin and settled himself to watch the setting of the sun. Sun Boy had chosen his paints well tonight. The reds and purples, made more brilliant by the presence of a few clouds to the west, had never been more intense. He watched the bright disk slide beyond earth's rim, and twilight began to settle across the prairie. Far below him, in the giant oaks along the stream, *Kookooskoos*, the great hunting owl, sounded his hollow rendition of his own name. A cautious doe and her fawn made their way out of a thicket of dogwood on the slope below him and ventured into the open to browse. Far to the north, across the river, a coyote called, and another answered. Stars began to appear, one by one, and Small Elk tried to guess the location of the next one he would see. He abandoned that pastime when suddenly it seemed the sky was full of the tiny points of light, and the background had faded from gray to the deepest blue-black.

Something at the edge of his vision made him turn to see the fiery circle of the rising moon sliding into sight in the east. *How odd,* he wondered, *the size and color is so different when it first rises.* He had always noticed this, but tonight it seemed especially so—the glowing red, with the markings in purple on its surface. So plain tonight . . . a face, a rabbit, or a woman combing out her long hair, depending on how one chose to perceive it. He watched with fascination while the disk became smaller and brighter. Soon its light was silvering all of the prairie in a ghostly splendor. He was no longer bored. He felt that he dared not sleep because he might miss something on this night of beauty and enchantment. Surely it was a night of strong medicine.

Even so, the moon, now tiny and white, was directly overhead before Small Elk began to realize that perhaps this was a part of his fast. The sharpness of the senses, the intensity of color, the distances that he could see across the silvery prairie . . . were these the early effects of the fast?

He was a little startled when he suddenly awoke with the sun shining in his face. It was morning, and he had not expected to sleep. There was no mistaking it now. He felt a sense of exhilaration and well-being that he had never known before. The hunger pangs had ceased, replaced by a calm confidence, a clarity of understanding. That made such things as an empty belly completely unimportant. The joy of this new sense of perception made the day pass rapidly. He observed the world with new insight, from the hugeness of the clouds in the distance to the smallness of the tiny creatures in the grass at his feet. All seemed to have their place in the world.

That night he began to dream, but the dreams were not materially different from the things he had observed while awake. This in turn led to a strange trancelike state when he woke in which he could no longer decide what was dream and what reality. He felt that there was nothing that he could not do. He could fly from the top of his hill if he wished, to soar high among the clouds with the eagles. He could burrow into the earth with the lesser creatures if he wished.

From that point on, it became impossible for him to distinguish . . . no, not impossible, but *unnecessary* to distinguish even night and day. His existence seemed above and beyond such mundane things as days, or even moons, so he was never certain afterward when the visions began.

They were not actually visions—in the sense he had

expected, anyway. He had thought of them as . . . well, maybe bizarre night-dreams of exceptional clarity. If he actually had an expectation that could be defined, that was it. So he was confused, even in his dream-state, when it began. It was, at first, merely an understanding. He was looking at a distant antelope (or at a vision of one, he was never certain) when he suddenly realized that he was thinking the creature's thoughts. They were shy, timid thoughts, yet curious. He knew that the creature could see far greater distances then he and that the ability to do so was part of the fear that the antelope felt. Fear of some distant, as yet unseen predator. The animal now raised its head, flashed white rump-patches, and disappeared over the hill.

He lifted his attention to the red-tailed hawk that soared above. Its attention was focused on a tuft of grass as it hovered, watching for any suggestion of motion. Small Elk's spirit now seemed to enter that grassy clump, to feel the terror of the white-footed mouse which crouched there, afraid to run, yet afraid of the terrible strike of the hunter's talons.

The hawk decided that the clump held no food and lifted a wing to catch a rising air current and soar away. Small Elk diverted his attention closer, where a bird sat on a stem of sumac and scolded. It was an urgent tone, and his searching spirit entered the head of the bird to experience its alarm at the approach of a great blue snake. He transferred his thoughts there and found that the snake was hunting, looking for a nest. It had actually been attracted by the bird's protest. It could not find the bird's lodge, however, and moved on. So did Small Elk, or at least his spirit. He experienced the dull awareness of a large fish that lay under the roots of a sycamore, waiting for prey to drift past.

He enjoyed a mud slide with the spirits of a family of playful otters as they plummeted down a steep bank into the pool below.

The process of getting "inside the head" of these creatures was becoming easier, more rational. He spent a little while with the thoughts of a coyote as she hunted. There was not an urgency to the hunt as there had once been. Her pups were grown and were hunting for themselves now.

He moved among a herd of buffalo and felt the calm reliance on the herd for protection, a group spirit. A large bull grazed quietly, and for some reason, the spirit of Small Elk moved toward it.

Welcome, my son. I have expected you.

It was not a spoken statement, only a thought, but it came to him with shocking clarity.

You are my medicine animal? My spirit guide? he asked.

There was no direct answer, but he felt that it was true. There was a feel, somehow, of humor, as if his surprise had been mildly amusing.

What am I to do now? Small Elk thought to himself.

Continue your visions, the thought came.

He was not certain whether it was an answer to his question or merely a coincidence. The buffalo grazed on, and now he felt a sort of oneness with them a part of the herd-feeling.

It was then that the visions began which were to prove so puzzling. He was traveling, in spirit, over great bodies of water and large areas of land. There were plains and forests and great areas of snow and ice, but he did not feel the cold. He saw wondrous things, the stuff of dreams and unreality. There was a real-bear, which prowled across endless snow when it should have been hibernating. It was not the color of a real-bear either as it stood on its hind legs to see farther across the snowpack. It was pure white.

He moved on, and saw great cats like the long-tailed cougar, but with heavy manes like the buffalo. There were strange, ugly creatures like large deer with a deformity, a hump on the back, that did not seem to bother them at all. A huge creature with great flapping ears appeared to have a tail at both ends, but one proved to be an extension of the nose with which it pulled down trees to browse. There were little men with tails who appeared to live in the tops of trees. All of these things were seen in rapid sequence. They seemed quite believable in the dream-state, as even ridiculous dreams will. Most of them were quickly forgotten, as dreams usually are when confronted with reality in the clear light of day.

One of his visions, however, persisted. In later days, even years later, it would somehow recur unexpectedly. It was as nonsensical as the other visions but was certainly more persistent. In this vision or dream, he watched from a hilltop over a vast expanse of grassland. Below him grazed a scattered herd of animals, moving slowly across the prairie, like buffalo. But they were not buffalo. They were long and lean like elk, but they had no antlers or horns. They were all colors—black, white, gray, red, and spotted. Yet all were formed alike and appeared to be the same species.

One came running, fast as the wind, across the plain and up the slope toward him. He was frozen with fear, but the creature may not even have seen him because it paused nearby and rose on its hind legs to give a long wavering call. In its eye was a proud, confident look, like the look of eagles. It gave the cry again, a sort of challenge like the bellow of a bull elk at rutting season. But different . . . there was no question that this creature was different from any others he had ever seen. And his heart was made to feel that it was real. The other fanciful creatures of his vision might be purely dreams, but this one was significant in some way.

After he woke, he tried to remember all he could about the creature. An elk without horns, but . . . *aiee*, it made no sense at all! When it had stood on its hind feet to thunder its challenge across the plain, it had pawed the air with its front feet, directly in front of him. He had seen the feet plainly. That was the thing that assured him that it was either a bit of madness or a creature of the supernatural. Still, he was certain what he had seen, as clearly as if he were awake: The creature had worn a turtle on each foot!

15
» » »

"**A** turtle? On each foot?" White Buffalo was incredulous.

"Yes, Father, it seemed so. Can this be?"

The medicine man pondered a moment. "Who knows what can be?" he answered thoughtfully. "And this seemed to be your medicine-guide?"

"What? No, no, Father, I think not. It—"

White Buffalo held up a hand to stop him. "Wait. You need not reveal your guide to me . . . to anyone."

"But I may?"

"Of course."

"It seemed to be a buffalo."

White Buffalo was pleased. That would seem to say that Small Elk's medicine inclined him toward the buffalo medicine of his father. He nodded.

"We will talk more of that, but now, tell me of the strange creatures."

"It is as I have said, Father. There were many strange creatures. Some I have forgotten. The visions did not last. But this one is still quite clear in my head. It was as big as an elk . . . bigger, maybe. They were of different colors, but the one I saw closely was gray."

"And it wore a turtle on each foot?"

"Yes, Father? What does this mean?"

"It could mean many things, my son. But I did not see it. Tell me, what did *you* see as its meaning?"

Small Elk shook his head. "I do not understand it all. I saw many things, but this one . . . I am made to think it is more important than all the other visions."

"Yet this is not your spirit-guide, your medicine animal?"

"No. That is the buffalo. But this one . . . with the turtles . . . is of great importance, somehow. *Aiee*, I do not know!" He shook his head in despair.

"Do not be concerned, my son," the holy man advised. "Some things we understand now, some later. Some, never, maybe, because they are not *meant* to be understood. But now, about the buffalo. You think that is your medicine?"

"Yes, Father, I am sure of it now. And I am made to think that I should follow you. Can it be so?"

White Buffalo nodded, pleased and proud. "Of course, my son, it is good that you wish to learn the duties of the medicine man. But it is hard. You must accept much responsibility."

"Yes, I know. I am ready."

"Good. What about your marriage?"

"I cannot do both?"

"It would not be best. Either would demand your complete attention for a while. But why not start your instruction and plan for the marriage later?"

Disappointed as he was, Small Elk managed to control his feelings, at least in part. After so long a time, when he felt he had lost Crow Woman forever, it had been such a thrilling discovery to find her again. Their reunion had been partly marred by the necessity to part again, even for a little while. Now he had the vision quest behind him and was looking forward to planning their own lodge.

But he could see the difficulties in a marriage at this time. It would be very hard to turn aside from the company of Crow Woman in their own lodge to devote time away from her to learning. *Aiee*, there should not be such a thing, the necessity to make such a choice. But it must be. He should not postpone his apprenticeship now that the trail lay plainly before him with his quest behind. And now that he and Crow Woman had resolved their misunderstandings, they would be able to share each other's company. What little time he was able to spend away from his duties as the medicine man's apprentice they could share.

He dreaded telling Crow Woman of his decision. He was certain that she had her heart set on an immediate marriage, as he had. Now he must explain. . . .

"It does not matter," she assured him. "We were apart for a long time. Now we can be together when we can, when your duties allow. And later, together always."

She snuggled next to him in a suggestive way that implied that the rewards would be worth whatever delay was necessary. *Aiee,* this could become more and more frustrating!

He also told her of his vision quest, omitting the part in which he identified his spirit-animal, the buffalo. Later, perhaps, it would be good for her to know that too; he felt a closeness in their spirits that said so. But he wished to share now the visions of the strange creatures, especially that of the hornless elk with the turtles on its feet.

"You are joking," she accused, eyes wide with wonder. "You are teasing me."

"No, no, it is as I told you. It came close to me, rose on its hind legs, and pawed the air!"

"Like the real-bear?" she asked. "The bear-that-walks-like-a-man?"

"No, not like that. It is hard to tell, but it was different."

"And it seemed something special? Your spirit-guide?"

"No. White Buffalo asked me that. That was another . . . I will tell you some day. But this . . . Crow, you know my spirit well. What could it mean?"

"*Aiee,* I know nothing of vision quests, Elk. It must be something of meaning. If it is for you to know, someday it will be shown to you. You have dreamed of it since?"

"Yes, twice. It was the same both times. The strange animal came and stopped on a hill near me, to stand and cry out. Its cry was frightening and loud, a roar almost, but there seemed little danger."

"Then it must be a good sign. I do not know, Elk."

There was little time to wonder. Now that the decision had been made, White Buffalo was anxious to proceed with his son's education. Elk was only too willing. The sooner he began, the sooner he and Crow Woman could establish their own lodge. However, he had not counted on the immense quantity of information that his father was eager to give him.

It was nearing the Moon of Ripening, when all things that grow are completing the year's cycle and preparing for the winter's sleep. It would be a while before that process would be completed. But already, the bluish stems of the big grasses were pushing upward, sometimes taller than a large man before the seedheads opened.

In the giant oaks along the streams and in the canyons,

busy squirrels hurried to gather and store acorns. Sometime soon, the restless herds of buffalo would be migrating, drifting south for the winter. It would be a time for the People to hunt, to store as much food as possible for the winter. It was the responsibility of White Buffalo, possessor of the buffalo medicine, to predict their arrival. He would also assist with the plans for the hunt, sometimes using his calfskin cape to mingle with the herd and gently maneuver them to an area favorable to the hunters.

"But how do you tell when the buffalo will come?" asked Small Elk.

"Patience!" White Buffalo said impatiently. "You have much to learn before that."

They walked the prairie together. White Buffalo sniffed the air, seeming to study the maturing grasses, the stage of development of the nuts and acorns along the timbered streams, the profusion of golden flowers of different types.

"At this moon, most of the flowers are yellow or purple," he pointed out.

"Why, Father?"

"To tell that it is the Moon of Ripening!" White Buffalo said.

Small Elk wanted to ask about the buffalo but sensed that it would not be advisable.

"Now, at about this season," his father was saying, "there will come a change in the weather. Rain Maker has been resting, and the land becomes hot and dry. Then comes the change, and that tells the buffalo to move. One day we notice that the prairie smells different, *feels* different. We must be able to tell, just a little while before it happens."

Elk started to ask why, but realized his own answer. The holy man must be ready to tell the others, so that they could be ready for the hunt.

"There are many things to watch for," White Buffalo explained. "Hear how the insects in the trees sing at evening? It is their time."

Small Elk remained quiet, sensing that more was coming.

"The change sometimes comes with rain, sometimes not. The summer wind is from the south. When it begins to change—but look! There is a sign!"

He pointed across a little meadow. Elk saw nothing except some swallows, apparently from nests in a nearby cliff. The birds were swooping low, crisscrossing the meadow, darting after an occasional insect.

"But, I—" Elk began, but his father held up a hand.

"When birds fly low, the weather is about to change. Rain, maybe."

"Why, Father?"

"Aiee, Elk, you have asked such things since you were small! Maybe they are hunting insects, and *they* fly low. Yes, *'why?'* I suppose. There is a difference in the air . . . do you not feel it?"

Elk nodded. It was something that could not be described, but it was there. A different *spirit.* The wind, which had been blowing steadily from the south for many days, was now quiet. The air was still and heavy.

"The South Wind," said White Buffalo. "It is resting. A change is coming."

Strange, thought Small Elk. This had been happening each autumn since he was born. No, since Creation maybe. He had never noticed before—well, that the wind usually came from the south. That was a recognized fact and gave the area one of its names. There was even a tribe who called themselves South Wind People. Small Elk had noticed that the wind sometimes changed and that the change often meant rain, but he had not even begun to realize the intricate connection here, the thing his father was teaching him. This change, this time in the late summer, was a signal. At least, it seemed so.

There was a stirring in the air now, a breathlike movement that seemed to come from nowhere and everywhere, and to have no direction. White Buffalo pointed to a distant line of timber to the north. The trees were writhing in the grip of the changing wind, like a great green snake, their tops twisting to show the silvery undersides of the leaves.

"It comes," he said softly. "The changing wind."

He turned back down the ridge toward the camp.

"Come," he said over his shoulder. "I will make the announcement."

Small Elk was puzzled.

"That it will rain?"

"No. They can tell that, and it is coming soon. I will tell them of the buffalo."

"But Father! We saw no buffalo!"

"No. But things are right. All the signs. This is the season. I will dance the Buffalo Dance and bring them."

"But . . . what if they do not come?"

"Ah!" said White Buffalo. "Sometimes they do not, and the dance does not work. Then the People will say someone broke a taboo, or the buffalo are displeased with where we camped—or maybe, even, White Buffalo is getting old, and his medicine is weak."

He paused a moment to catch his breath and continued. "But most of the time, Elk, they will come this way. Then, the People say, 'Aiee! White Buffalo's medicine is strong. He has brought the herds back again!'"

Small Elk was astonished at this revelation.

"Then your medicine does not really? . . ."

"Ah, did I say that? Who knows, my son, why they come. When I see that everything is right, I say, 'the herds may come.' It would be foolish to say that when things are *not* ready. The medicine is strong, but I must help it, by knowing when to use it. Now, I am made to think, is the time to do the Buffalo Dance. Maybe they come, maybe not."

"But more likely than not?" Small Elk persisted.

"Of course. If the herds were more likely *not* to come, I would not try the dance."

"And in the springtime?"

"Ah, you will learn that later. That is a matter of firing the grass at the right time. You have much to learn before then. Come, we must hurry."

They approached the medicine man's lodge, and he called to Dove Woman. She unrolled the bundle and shook out the white buffalo cape with horns attached, the symbol of office. White Buffalo swung it across his shoulders and tied the thongs under his chin and across the chest. He settled the horned headdress portion on his head and nodded to Dove Woman. She began a rhythmic beat on the small dance-drum as White Buffalo picked up his rattles and eagle-fan and began to dance.

Small Elk had watched this ceremony all his life, but now he seemed to see it for the first time.

"Watch the cadence," Dove Woman whispered. "Next time maybe he will let you try it."

People were coming to watch the ceremony, and in the distance came the mutter of Rain Maker's drum in answer to the one held by Dove Woman.

16

» » »

The buffalo did come, and the People were loud in praise of the medicine man's skill. Small Elk was mildly confused. He was not certain whether the skills included *causing* the herds to return or skillfully *predicting* the event.

"Does it matter?" his father asked with a quiet smile. "They are here. Either way, it was successful. Maybe both are true."

On one point White Buffalo was absolutely correct. Either way, it was a successful season. After a day of rain, which freshened the prairie and brightened the green of the grasses, the sky cleared to a bright autumn blue. Days were warm, nights cool. On the third day, the scouts spotted the first of a large herd, grazing as they came and moving slowly southward. It was soon enough after the ceremony for White Buffalo to take credit for the herd's appearance. He modestly accepted the praise and the attention that fell to his office and his buffalo medicine. He conducted a ceremony for the hunt, and it too was an outstanding success. White Buffalo was riding high on a crest of prestige.

"Will you use the calfskin to move the herd, Father?" Small Elk asked.

"No, it is not necessary. The buffalo already come where we want them. Anyway, that works better in the spring hunt."

White Buffalo and his apprentice watched this hunt from a low ridge overlooking an isolated meadow. A few animals, some twenty in number, had detached themselves from the main herd and grazed into this meadow. It was formed by a loop of the stream which meandered past, partly enclosing this level spot of choice grass. It was a long bowshot in diameter, making it ideal for the hunters, hidden in the brush, trees, and rocks around the perimeter. Short Bow would loose the first arrow.

This was the first time that Small Elk had had the opportunity to watch a hunt as an observer. He could see the entire sequence unfold. The animals moved, unhurried, into the loop of the stream, past the narrowest part of the opening. Short Bow waited until they were well into the meadow and chose a fat yearling as his quarry. The animal jumped as the arrow struck, staggered a few steps, and stopped, sagging slowly to the ground. The others milled around nervously, now catching the scent of the hunters. Another animal stumbled and fell.

This could go on only a few moments before the herd began to panic and run, but now there were at least three kills. A fourth animal was struggling along, probably with a fatal wound. A hunter, unable to restrain himself further, let out a yell of triumph, and the buffalo started to run. They were deterred on three sides by the creek and its screen of timber; it was by no means a barrier, but by nature the buffalo saw the open plain as their path to safety. They turned to rush back to the plain, where they had come from.

Now came a crucial and dangerous part of the hunt. A few men, the bravest and most daring, would jump out from concealment among the trees to try to turn at least some of the animals back toward the other hunters. Small Elk saw Short Bow leap from behind a clump of willows, flapping a robe and yelling at the top of his lungs. This signaled the others, who seemed to appear like magic to confront the running herd. The leading buffalo paused and shied away from the noise and the threat of danger. Some tried to turn back uncertainly; others dashed ahead toward the blockers, who leapt nimbly out of the way. One man, Elk thought it was Bluejay, was tossed high in the air by a large bull as it thundered to safety. That unusual sight itself seemed to turn back some of the herd.

Now those remaining in the meadow seemed to feel trapped. In a panic, they crashed through the brush and small trees to reach the streambed. There they were met by another rain of arrows from the hidden bowmen as they clattered and splashed across the stream to safety. In a short while it was all over. Dead or dying buffalo were

scattered across the meadow. Men poured out of concealment to identify their kills and congratulate each other.

"Come, White Buffalo, make the apology for us," someone called.

The medicine man and his assistant made their way
down the hillside. The hunters had already selected the
largest bull of the day, and one was busily chopping off the
head. Then two men carried the massive trophy aside,
placing it in the spot indicated by White Buffalo.

"There," he said, pointing. "The nose to the east."

The head was propped in a more lifelike position with
stones, and White Buffalo took a pinch of some powdered
plant material from a pouch to sprinkle over it. He sang:

> We are sorry to kill you, my brother
> but your flesh is our life, as the grass is yours.
> May your people be numerous and prosper.

The women were now beginning to straggle over the
hill, preparing to start the butchering. They were chat-
tering over the success of the hunt. *Aiee,* the medicine of
White Buffalo is powerful!" Elk heard one say.

As the butchering began, Bluejay came hobbling up. His
left arm hung limp, and pain lined his face.

"Ah, Bluejay!" one of the other hunters exclaimed. "You
will do anything to avoid the butchering!"

There was general laughter, even as several helped the
injured man to lie down and White Buffalo came to help
with the broken arm, a mixture of concern and relief that
the injury was no worse. The man could have been killed,
and fatal injuries were not unusual in such a hunt. That
Bluejay's was the only injury and not a life-threatening one
was a cause for joy and laughter. An arm would heal. In the
importance of things, anyone would prefer a broken arm
to being gored in the belly, would he not?

The band moved into winter quarters, choosing a favorite
area in the southern portion of their range. There were
thickets of scrubby oaks, which would hold their dead
leaves for most of the winter, to provide an effective wind-
break. The campsite itself was bordered by such a thicket
on the north and west, leaving the east ceremonially open
to the sun. This location also had a major advantage in that

there were no trees to the south for perhaps a hundred paces or more. The rays of Sun Boy's dying winter torch would strike the camp unimpeded. Beyond that open space was the river, clear and swift over white gravel. Their water supply would be convenient and reliable.

Another advantage to this location was the presence of numerous squirrels. In a hard winter, a few of these could make the difference between survival and death. There were also signs of deer in the thickets, drawn by the same acorns that sustained the large population of squirrels. In the dark moons of winter, a change to fresh meat might prove a refreshing diversion. Not that there was any threat of starvation this year; the fall hunt had gone well. *Aiee,* how well! Every lodge had a store of dried meat and pemmican, stored in rawhide packs behind the lodge-linings. Even the arm of Bluejay, the only casualty of the fall hunt, was healing well.

The People utilized the long still days of the Moon of Falling Leaves to prepare their lodges against the onslaught of Cold Maker. Some, whose locations gave more exposure, carried brush and sticks to build a small snow fence directly northwest of their own lodges. Everyone cut and carried armfuls of dry grasses to stuff in the space around the bottom of the lodge. Between the outside cover and the lodge-lining, which hung like a vertical curtain of skins, was a dead space for storage. Supplies would keep well, away from the heated inside of the lodge. But in winter, stuffed with dried grasses, any remaining space became an important part of the winter preparation; it was insulation against Cold Maker's howling winds.

By the first frosts, late in the Moon of Falling Leaves, most of the lodges were ready. Even then, there would be a period of perhaps half a moon of fine open weather, cool at night and pleasantly warm by day, the Second Summer. Some called it Spirit Summer. It was a happy time, a time of excitement but no urgency, a time to enjoy the pungent smells of autumn and rejoice in the beauty of Earth.

Long lines of geese trumpeted their way south, and in the distance, the challenge of the young bull elk resounded across the prairie. It was the rutting time for the deer in the thickets, and the clash and rattle of their antlers in the battle for a harem of does was frequently heard. It was a good time to hunt, the bucks more concerned with rutting than with caution, but few men bothered to hunt. There was enough stored already.

It was discovered that a half-day's travel downstream, there was a village of Growers. This led to an increase in hunting for a short while. Surplus meat and hides could be traded for corn, beans, and dried pumpkins. There was brisk trade for half a moon before Cold Maker put a virtual stop to travel.

During the pleasant time of Spirit Summer, Small Elk worked and studied as never before. It seemed that his father would never finish with the gathering of plants, seeds, and flowers. Bunches and bundles of herbs hung from the lodgepoles to dry, bringing the pungent smells that Elk's memory always associated with autumn. As they gathered the plants, Elk received instruction in identification and habitat.

Once, they spent an entire day lying on the ground, painstakingly scraping and brushing dirt from the roots of a gourd vine. The root was branched and convoluted, and when it was exposed, it was apparent that it could be interpreted as the likeness of a human figure. This, said White Buffalo, was especially good, but even more dangerous.

He explained as he scraped and brushed. This gourd, whose dried fruits were used for rattles and whose root was powerful medicine, was different from many plants. It would die each autumn but come to life again in the spring and so live forever. The silvery blue color of its vine and leaves identified it. The danger in digging the root was accidentally breaking it. That would be very bad medicine. No one but a medicine man would ordinarily even attempt this dig, and even he was in jeopardy. White Buffalo told as he worked of a medicine man who broke such a root and returned to his lodge to find that his son had been bitten by a real-snake. Another had broken a root such as this human-shaped one, destroying one of the legs. On the way home, he had fallen among the rocks, badly shattering his own leg, which never healed properly.

By this time, Small Elk was having second thoughts about his apprenticeship. His father read his face and chuckled.

"Is the responsibility too heavy?" he asked teasingly.

Small Elk was more serious. "I think not, Father. Are there many who are offered the gift but refuse it?"

White Buffalo wanted to laugh aloud, but saw that his son was serious. "There is no way to know," he answered. "I am made to think that in some generations there are many who are offered the gifts of the spirit, and sometimes only a few."

He scraped a few moments in silence.

"Elk," he said seriously, "if you have doubts, if you want to refuse, it is no disgrace."

Small Elk took a deep breath. "No, Father, it is not that," he said slowly. "I was only wondering if I am worthy of such responsibility."

Ah, thought White Buffalo, pleased beyond measure. What better evidence that this boy *is* worthy? Again, he felt the strong suggestion that Small Elk would somehow become very important to the People. Just how, he was unsure. But there was much to suggest it. Those strange visions at the time of his quest . . .

"Here, Elk," he said, handing him the slender digging tool, "you scrape a little while. But be very careful."

The shadows were growing long when they returned to the lodge, but Small Elk proudly carried the root of the gourd-that-lives-forever. More importantly, the root was unscathed. Small Elk's pride was well justified but was no greater than that of his father. It had been a day well spent

17

"We have hardly seen you this fall!" Stone Breaker protested.

It was the Moon of Long Nights, when Sun Boy's torch nearly goes out. There had been no extreme weather yet. Cold Maker had blustered and bluffed occasionally, and several times the grasses had been powdered with frost when the sun rose. Once there had been a light dusting of snow, which soon disappeared.

"I have been busy with White Buffalo," Elk explained.

"Yes, we know," Stone Breaker said. "But now, you are here, and welcome to our lodge! Both of you."

It was a chilly overcast day, and White Buffalo had decided that it was a poor day for instruction. Elk was quite willing to take a day's respite from his learning to be with his friends. Such a day was good for socializing. Many of the people were visiting in one another's lodges, smoking, visiting, or gambling with the plum-stones or the stick game. Crow and Small Elk had decided to call on their friends, and were warmly welcomed to Stone Breaker's lodge. Crow Woman was holding the baby, a fat, happy child that Cattail called Little Bear. The name seemed to fit quite well. Crow Woman was thoroughly enjoying cuddling and rocking the infant.

"How motherly she looks!" Cattail teased. "Elk, could you not do something about this?"

Everyone but Small Elk was amused; he knew there was no answer for the present. At that moment the infant, rousing, turned his head and attempted to nurse at the buckskin-covered breast of Crow Woman. Disappointed, he wrinkled his small face and stuck out his tongue in disgust.

"Aiee!" shouted Stone Breaker with glee. "He is used to better food than leather!"

"Here, you take him!" Crow Woman handed the child to his mother. "I cannot help him."

Cattail loosened the front of her dress to uncover a breast, and Little Bear began to nuzzle hungrily.

"Your learning goes well, Elk?" asked Stone Breaker.

"Yes, but there is much to learn. Sometimes I think my head cannot hold it all."

Stone Breaker nodded understandingly.

"I think it would be very hard."

Small Elk shrugged. "Maybe. But, I could not do your work."

"Oh, you could." Stone Breaker held up his work-hard hands. "But it takes a long time to grow such calluses. *Aiee*, my blisters were so sore when I started!"

"But now, my friend, I hear people speak very highly of your work."

"Thank you, Elk. What are you working on this winter?"

"Many things. Plants, preparing them for use; also the rituals and dances. When the Moon of Greening comes, I suspect that White Buffalo will have much to show me about the grasses."

"Is that not when the burning takes place?" Stone Breaker asked.

"Yes, but I have not yet learned how to tell when the time is right."

"What if you choose the wrong time?" Cattail asked.

"Maybe the buffalo would not come back."

"Then everyone would starve," suggested Stone Breaker. "What a responsibility!"

"Except for Little Bear," said Crow Woman, pointing at the noisily feeding infant.

Everyone laughed.

"But seriously, Elk," Stone Breaker said, "you are learning the dances and chants?"

"Yes, but what—"

"And your mother beats the cadence, as she does for White Buffalo?"

"Yes. Sometimes I do, for my father."

"Ah, yes! I have a thought. Would it not be well to have your own assistant, to beat your cadence? Someday, Elk, it

will be so. Would it not be better to have her learn as you
do?"

He pointed to Crow Woman. There was a long silence.

"I . . . I do not think it is done, Stone Breaker. I do not
know of a medicine man whose cadence is set by other
than his wife or assistant."

"That should be no problem!" insisted Stone Breaker.
"She would be a better wife *and* assistant later if she learns
now, while you do."

"It sounds good to me," laughed Cattail. "You could be
together more!"

It sounded so sensible, so reasonable, that surely there
was something wrong with the idea. Finally, the other
three teased and cajoled until Small Elk's temper flared.

"All right," he snapped. "I will ask, now!"

He rose and left the lodge. The wind was cold as he
crossed the camp to the lodge of his parents. White Buffalo
was sitting against his willow backrest, enjoying a smoke.

"*Ah-koh*, my son," he said. "Back so soon?"

Elk nodded, speechless.

"Does it look like snow?" Dove Woman asked.

"Maybe tonight," Elk guessed. "It grows colder."

Cold, however, was hardly the word for the reception
that his question brought. White Buffalo stared at his son
with an expression of righteous indignation that left a chill
hanging in the air.

"Of course not!" he sputtered. "Elk, have I not taught
you better?"

"But, Father, if Crow could learn while I do—"

"No," White Buffalo stated positively. "It is not good.
Elk, you are not taking this seriously."

There was no use arguing, and Small Elk left the lodge,
angry and frustrated. It was not easy to return to his
friends' lodge and face the others. He told them very
tersely that White Buffalo would not consider such a thing
and sat again by the fire. In a little while, the antics of the
baby and the bright conversation had lifted his spirits a
little.

When Crow Woman rose a little later and left the lodge,
no one attached any particular importance to it. She
threaded her way among the lodges and slapped on the
lodgecover of the medicine man.

"It is Crow Woman," she called. "May I come in?"

Dove Woman lifted the doorskin, and the girl stooped to enter.

"*Ah-kuh*, Uncle, Mother," she said. "I wished to tell you, do not be angry with Small Elk. We urged him to ask you about the drum."

Crow Woman was in no way provocative, but she was an exceedingly attractive and straightforward young woman. White Buffalo had to admire her bold approach.

"It is nothing," he smiled. "It is forgotten."

"It is good," Crow Woman said. "Uncle, may I ask a question?"

"Of course, my child. What is it?"

"How did Dove Woman learn the cadence and the beat to accompany the dances?"

If White Buffalo had chanced to look, he might have seen that there was a twinkle in the eye of his wife.

"Why, I taught her," he said proudly.

"Ah, yes, then Elk can teach me."

"No, no, child. This was after our marriage. It is not proper for a woman to be the helper of a medicine man unless they are married."

He appeared suspicious, realizing that something was happening that he did not quite understand.

"It is good!" exclaimed Crow Woman. "He can teach me later."

She paused to think for a moment.

"But, Uncle, I will keep the drum cadence for him for many years. I would hope to be the best help that I am able. Would it not be best for me to learn it directly from you?"

Few men can resist flattery from a beautiful young woman. White Buffalo looked at his prospective daughter-in-law sympathetically.

"Possibly," he agreed, "but that cannot be until you and Elk are married."

Crow Woman gave him a quick hug and jumped to her feet.

"Oh, thank you, Uncle," she said brightly. "We will talk of when."

She vanished through the doorway, and the skin swung back into place. White Buffalo looked at his wife, bewildered.

"What? What was that . . ."

Dove Woman was laughing, her eyes squinting closed until the tears of laughter could scarcely escape from beneath the lids.

"My husband," she was finally able to say, "I think you just gave permission for your apprentice to marry! *Aiee*, she will make a good wife for a holy man!"

She collapsed into laughter again.

Crow Woman and Small Elk, the medicine man's apprentice, were married soon after. They sat together by the fire in the lodge of the girl's parents, and their fathers united them in marriage by placing a robe around the shoulders of the two, making them one. It would have been usual for them to live in the lodge of Crow Woman's parents until they had their own. In this case, however, one of the reasons for marriage at this time was that they could be instructed together in the duties that would be theirs. Crow Woman moved into the lodge of Small Elk's parents, to observe and learn from White Buffalo and Dove Woman. It was not the best arrangement, but it would be temporary.

People immediately began to contribute skins toward the lodge of the newlyweds. There would be no honeymoon, because Cold Maker had descended with a vengeance; it was a hard winter, and it was well that the People had supplies. Even so, they were together. There would be other disadvantages to marriage at this time. Even after they had established their lodge, there would be little time together. When warm weather came, there would still be no honeymoon, for that would be the time for the most demanding part of Small Elk's instruction.

But at least they were together.

Stone Breaker and Cattail were delighted, of course, for the happiness of their friends. The two girls had long conversations about establishing a lodge, the feeding of babies, and the care of husbands. Crow Woman's time was necessarily limited by the fact that she must live up to her part of the instructions. There were times when it seemed to her that White Buffalo was intent on punishing her for her part in contriving the early marriage. But probably, she decided, it was only that the life she had chosen *was* difficult and demanding, one of responsibility. She watched her husband's parents, how Dove Woman was an important part of the medicine man's skills, and reveled in her own learning. There was much of importance in the way a wife could help a medicine man.

By the time they had worked together through the Moon of Snows and the Moon of Hunger, which was not especially hungry this year, even White Buffalo agreed that the marriage had been an excellent idea. By the Moon of Awakening, the medicine man half believed it had been his idea all along. He could never have hoped for a finer assistant for Small Elk than this delightful young woman. She intuitively perceived many things of the spirit and seemed to put them into practice without thinking. In her hands, the dance-drum spoke with authority and meaning. *Aiee*, the world was good. White Buffalo had an apt pupil to carry on his work, and Elk had a wife-assistant second to none.

Now winter was nearly over. Long lines of geese honked their way back north. Here and there, as a snowbank began to melt, small sprigs of green appeared. The upper twigs on the willows began to show a bright yellow color as their buds swelled. Little rivulets of snowmelt trickled and joined together to swell the prairie streams.

It would soon be the Moon of Greening and another great step in the instruction of Small Elk. White Buffalo called his son to him.

"Elk, you have done well so far."

"Thank you, Father."

"No, no, it is nothing. But you are now ready to begin *serious* instruction. So far, it is all just preparation."

Elk did not answer.

"Now, my son, this is where we begin to talk of the medicine of the buffalo. It is like a vision quest, and no one can help you, not even your wife. What you start now is far more dangerous. Not at first, but soon. Are you ready?"

Small Elk paused only a moment.

"Of course, Father."

"Good. Then let us go out on the prairie. The greening has begun, and you have much to learn before the buffalo come."

18

» » »

"There are seven or more kinds of grasses here," White Buffalo said, pointing to the tiny green sprigs among last year's growth. "All are different, though they look much alike now. This one," he knelt to touch the new growth, "is the tall real-grass. At the time of awakening it looks much like the other tall one, the plume-grass, but it does not matter. They, together, give the sign that it is time to burn."

"Is it time, Father?" Elk asked.

"No. Another few days. It should be about this tall." He indicated with thumb and forefinger. "Then we must have a day when the wind is right, both in direction and strength. If we send smoke through the camp, we lose some respect."

"And then the buffalo will come?"

"It is to be hoped for. Usually, it happens. This is all very much intertwined, Elk. The herds are now far to the south, who knows where? Something happens to start them moving north. Maybe nothing but a few warm days, Sun Boy's torch warming again. Probably, they are already moving. Now, we burn the old grass to prepare a good feeding-ground. The new, tender grasses entice them into this area, instead of somewhere else."

"This always brings them?"

"Almost. If the season is bad somewhere else—or good, maybe—they take a different trail. A few always come. But now, let us talk of the calfskin."

Elk had never seen his father actually work a herd with the calfskin. He knew it was one of the most important parts of the medicine man's art, and also one of the most dangerous.

"I have not used this often in the past few seasons,"

White Buffalo admitted. "It takes agility and quickness, and my bones are old and slow. You have that now. Sometimes it is almost necessary to work the herd in this way. Now, first, you must begin to practice the movements of a calf."

He watched critically while Small Elk, feeling somewhat foolish, stooped to mimic the motion of a buffalo calf.

"You can observe them, and do better, when the herds come," White Buffalo said. "No, a little more stiff-legged. That is better. We will let you wear the skin, and that will help."

The calfskin was a soft-tanned hide, with the wooly, yellowish hair of the young animal still intact. It held none of the sacred medicine of the white cape, but was merely a tool. A very useful tool, it was true.

"I once would wear out a calfskin in a season or two," the medicine man recalled. "It is a good method to handle the herds."

Small Elk continued to practice, away from the camp and under the watchful eye of his father. Never, it seemed, could he do quite well enough to please White Buffalo. He began to resent the discipline. His muscles were sore, his legs aching, from the unnatural position.

"I do not see the importance," he complained to Crow Woman one evening under the stars. "White Buffalo has not even used the calfskin for two or three seasons."

"But he is very wise," the girl reminded him. "There is surely a reason."

At the next instruction session, White Buffalo attempted further explanation. It was as if he had sensed the unrest in his apprentice.

"You do well, Elk," he stated, "but I am made to think that your heart is not in it."

Small Elk started to speak, but his father waved him to silence.

"No matter. More important," White Buffalo continued, "is that the ceremony of the calf helps you to understand the buffalo. You must feel their feelings, get inside their heads. Only then can you move the herds and put the buffalo where you want them."

Small Elk was still in doubt. It seemed to make little sense that it was possible to do without the calfskin ritual, but that his father insisted on it. It seemed unfair that he was required to develop this uncomfortable, tedious, and dangerous skill. He made the mistake of mentioning this one evening after a grueling day. White Buffalo flared in anger.

"When you have been a medicine man for forty winters," he said hotly, "then you will know enough to question this!"

"But Father, I—"

"Enough! There may come a time when your ability with the calfskin ceremony makes the difference whether the whole band lives or starves. Now, we will speak no more of it!"

The day came when White Buffalo declared that it was time for the burning ceremony. There was great excitement. He chose several young men as helpers and stationed them along the edge of a wide expanse of open prairie. A gentle breeze rustled the dried grasses of the winter. In some areas the tough seedstems of the real-grass and plume-grass still stood taller than a man's head. The burn would remove these tough, dry stems to expose succulent new growth.

White Buffalo chanted a prayer of thanks for return of the grass, while Dove Woman kept the cadence on the drum. Then he stooped to place a few carefully protected coals in a clump of curly, pink-colored little-grass. Flames licked upward, and the puff of smoke signaled the waiting helpers to begin. The fires grew like living things, expanding and merging. Soon the appearance was that of a fiery snake, crawling across the low hills, with blackened prairie on one side and the ragged remnants of last season's growth on the other. It was always fascinating to watch, to smell, and to listen to the sounds of the fire. The People did little else that day. In some areas, the breeze fanned flames into a roaring inferno, racing ahead of the advancing line only to die down and fall behind when it encountered an area with less fuel to sustain its advance. In the places where the taller grasses stood in abundance, the crack of the exploding stems was like the popping of corn. Then the flames swept on, leaving blackened prairie that would be lush and green again in a few days.

Night fell, and from any slight rise, the crawling line of flames could still be seen snaking over hills a day's journey

away. They would burn out when they encountered a
stream too wide to jump or when the next of the frequent
spring showers occurred.

"It is good!" declared White Buffalo.

Now, there was only the waiting for the arrival of the
herds.

White Buffalo was confident, but when the scouts reported that the first animals had been sighted, it came as a
great relief to Small Elk. This season, he had a more personal affinity for the event. However, all things seemed
timed perfectly. The grass was lush and green, the buffalo
calm and unexcited.

This would not be a big, heavily organized hunt. There
was no need to store a large quantity of meat until preparation for the next winter. Besides, the hot season was ahead,
and meat does not keep well in hot weather. This was a
season to procure some fresh meat, to revel in the life-
giving juices of the raw liver, a delicacy enjoyed a bite at a
time during the butchering. After the nutritional depriva-
tion of the winter, even with good supplies, there was a
craving. There are some things that dried meat and pemmican simply cannot supply.

White Buffalo, after the appropriate ceremonies for the
first kill of the season, turned his attention again to Small
Elk's instruction. They spent an entire day on a rise near a
calmly grazing herd. There were many calves, their yellowish color quite obvious among the darker coats of the
older animals.

"It is a good season!" White Buffalo spoke with approval.
"A good season for you to learn the calfskin. Now, watch
the calves. See, a calf is never far from its mother. But
sometimes several will lie down together. One cow
watches over them. See, to the left there? The others
graze, and then return."

Small Elk nodded.

"Now, watch when they play," White Buffalo continued.
"You must make your motions look like theirs. And *think!*
Your thoughts must be theirs. Here, put on the skin. Tie it
well. Now, practice a little before you go down. Ah, that is
good! That little kick, yes!"

Small Elk's heart was beating fast. This was a climactic
day, one he had long been preparing for. White Buffalo
seemed every bit as tense.

"Remember," he cautioned, "do not place yourself between a cow and her calf. And do not panic. They can
smell the fear. Above all, do not try to run."

With his palms sweating, Small Elk made his way toward
the herd. He was certain that they would run, but none of
the buffalo seemed to notice him. He moved among the
first animals, trying to mimic the stiff-legged walk of the
young calves. He must think like the buffalo, now, react as
they would. He passed near a grazing cow, and she lifted
her head to threaten him. For a moment, he felt the grip of
fear. The horns—so black and shiny and sharp, the broad
forehead so big—*no*, he told himself, *she is not threatening
Small Elk. She threatens a calf that is not hers, lest it try to
suckle.* In that way, he slipped "inside the head" of the
cow. As he had seen the calves do, he made a move toward
the cow's flank, pretending to try to nurse. She swung her
head again, and he dodged playfully aside to trot on a few
steps.

A large bull grazed peacefully, and Elk approached it.
Bulls, he had noticed, paid almost no attention to a small
calf. Their minds were on other things. Boldly, he approached the huge animal, who continued to crop grass. As
he had expected, there was no reaction. As he had seen
calves do, he nosed curiously, and actually brushed against
the massive shoulder. Then he moved on.

He felt, rather than saw, a calf approach him to play. The
creature loped around him, playfully made a make-believe
charge at him, and then approached to try the head-push-
ing game. Trying to behave like a normal calf, he pushed
back, but the calf was persistent. Besides, it was stronger
than he and had a weight advantage; he was handicapped
by his stooped-over stance. He could not stand without
revealing his true identity. Finally, in desperation, he
slapped the calf boldly across the nose. The startled youngster retreated, and Elk glanced around to look for reac-
tions from other animals. There were none. Apparently
the adults had ignored the episode as the play of the
young. In retrospect, he realized that it would have been
more in character if he had retreated to end the game. But
no matter . . . he moved among the herd, with growing
confidence now. A cow swung a threatening horn his way,
and he stepped aside without a thought.

White Buffalo had advised that the first time or two in

the herd, he should merely get the feel. The skill of moving them would come later. For now, he found that despite the uncomfortable position, he was actually beginning to enjoy this experience. It was a spiritual uplift, a feeling of power, to be able to move through a herd of the great animals at will. If he was perceived as a human, he could be in great danger instantly. But the smell of the calfskin, as well as the scent-killing herbs that White Buffalo had rubbed on him, seemed to prevent identification.

He skirted around the edges of the herd, pleased at his success and looking forward to the time when he could advance to the next step, trying to manipulate the herd's movement.

A flash of motion caught his eye on the side *away* from the herd, and he turned curiously. *Aiee!* Here was a thing he had not foreseen. A wolf, one of the gray ghosts that follow the herds, was creeping through the short grass. Always ready to pull down a sick or crippled animal, a straggler or a stray calf, the great wolves were always circling and ready. It took a moment to realize that while the calfskin might fool the buffalo with their poor eyesight, the wolf would perceive it quite differently. Here was a calf which was not quite right, which appeared misshapen, which moved oddly—*aiee*, he had suddenly become the quarry!

It was tempting simply to stand up, jerk the calfskin aside, and flap it at the wolf to drive it away. Surely, it would not attack a man standing upright. But there were some doubts. What effect would this action have on the buffalo? He must do something quickly. The hunter was so close that he could see the glitter of the yellow eyes as it crept forward on its belly. At any moment now, it would make its rush.

Then the idea came. He was pretending to be a calf . . . what would a calf do? There was no time to stop and consider. He raised his head toward the herd and let out a bleat of terror as he began to scramble away.

The effect was, to say the least, startling. At least six or seven cows answered his bleat with a protective motherly call, even as they charged forward. For a moment, Elk was sure he had made a fatal error. Even if he escaped the wolf's rush, he seemed in danger of being trampled by the defensive action. He turned toward the wolf, who now seemed confused. It appeared about tò rush at him but seemed to reconsider, then turned to retreat. The cows thundered past Elk on each side, brushing close and kicking up dirt in his face but avoiding injury to him.

The confused wolf barely made its escape, turning on an extra burst of speed to elude the horns of the leading cow. Elk watched it retreat over the hill, tail between its legs. He in turn retreated, before the return of the cows, to rejoin his father on the rise.

"*Aiee!*" greeted White Buffalo, his eyes bright with excitement. "Elk, you have done well. You will be a great medicine man!"

Small Elk untied the thongs, removed the calfskin, and stood erect, working the stiffness out of his back.

"Thank you, Father!"

It was the greatest compliment his father had ever given him.

"Of course," White Buffalo added as they turned toward home, "you take too many chances."

Part II

The Winds of Change

19

In later years, it would be referred to as the Year-of-No-Rain. There was no apparent reason, though there were many theories. The older members of the band were only too ready with accusatory explanations, with much clucking of tongues and wagging of heads. No one was certain exactly what taboo had been broken. As far as could be determined, no one had committed such a blatant transgression as eating bear meat. Surely the breaking of personal, private vows would not bring misfortune on the entire band, though that was a possibility.

The greening was not satisfactory. White Buffalo studied the sparse growth day after day, shaking his head and muttering to himself. The People grew restless and complained against the holy man. The prairie burned, though White Buffalo warned that it was not good. It was never determined how the fire started. It may have been from natural causes. It was possible, some pointed out, for sparks from the stones in the grass to ignite the grass. However, that usually occurred only under the trampling hooves of running animals, and there had been few. More commonly, spears of real-fire would ignite the dry prairie grasses, but again, Rain Maker had not come, with or without his spears of real-fire.

There was one frightening theory that Rain Maker was dead and would never come again. This was discussed only in whispers because it was apparent that without rain, the grass would not grow, and the buffalo would have nothing to eat, would disappear. Then the People would die.

Regarding the fires, most people suspected that someone, tired of waiting for the holy man's proclamation, had fired the dead grass on his own. That too was seldom discussed publicly. It was a serious infraction, if true, and the council must decide punishment. It would be far preferable if the rains would come, greening the prairie and restoring the season to normal. That would remove the problem and the council's need to act.

But the rains did not come. Neither did the buffalo. The People were reduced to hunting rabbits and squirrels. They had already made great inroads on the dogs, having eaten far more than would have normally been consumed by the Moon of Growing. There were barely enough dogs left to carry or drag the baggage when the time arrived to move the camp.

There was an increasing mutter of discontent against the medicine men for their inaction. It was tempting to perform the rain ceremony, but White Buffalo was quite definite in his stand: It was not the time to do so.

"Tell me, Elk," he asked his assistant privately, "have you seen any of the signs of rain?"

"No, Father, but maybe . . ."

"Ah, this is one of the hardest things," White Buffalo said sadly, "to wait until the right time. Look, Elk, we burn only when the signs are right?"

"That is true, Father."

"You would not dance the ceremony for the buffalo when there is snow on the ground?"

"Of course not."

"Ah, and we do not dance for rain when there is no chance at all. Our ceremonies must be within possibility, or we fail and lose our respect."

"But, Father, we are losing it now."

"Yes, my son, but when the rains do come, it is restored. If we say now, 'It will not rain,' the People will be angry, but they will know we are right. Then, when times are good again, they will say *'Aiee*, the medicine of White Buffalo is good! He was right about the rain!' "

Small Elk nodded, not totally convinced.

"Our visions," White Buffalo continued, "must tell things as they *are*, not as we wish them to be."

Early in the Moon of Roses, the council decided not to attend the Sun Dance and the Big Council. The Southern band was tired, frustrated, and weak from lack of supplies. It was doubtful that they could make the journey. A runner was sent to take the message to the other bands, and returned in due course, tired and thin. There would be no

Sun Dance, he reported. All the bands were in trouble because the drought was widespread. The Mountain band had not been heard from, but it was assumed that they too were experiencing problems. It seemed likely that their solution would be to pull back farther into the mountains instead of coming onto the plain as usual.

Later, many of the People tried to blame the problems of the Year-of-No-Rain on the fact that there was no Sun Dance. That, of course, confused cause and effect. There was no Sun Dance *because* the People were already suffering from the worst season in the memory of the oldest of the band. Still, in later years, the story became confused with the retelling.

There was one puzzling question that was never really resolved. Where had the buffalo gone? If they were not here or in the areas of the other bands, then *where?* Again, fanciful explanations suggested that they had gone back down the hole in the earth, from where they came at the time of Creation.

The Southern band did move, in the Moon of Thunder, though in truth there was no thunder. There was no rain, and the water dried up in the stream on which they were camped. Despite the fact that the People were really too weak to make the move, they must find water or die.

There were several favorite springs in the Sacred Hills, but it was unsure whether they would remain productive in a year that was worse then any other in memory. White Buffalo studied the yearly paintings on the old Story Skins, and found no record of a worse year. He recommended that rather than risk the reliability of the springs, it would be safer to travel in the other direction, a bit farther, to reach one of the larger rivers. Though he said nothing at the time, he confided later to Small Elk that in part, he had considered the possibility that the People could eat fish.

"Aiee! Fish?" Small Elk exclaimed.

It was known that some of the tribes who lived along the streams ate fish regularly, but it was not an acceptable thing for the People.

"We may not have to," White Buffalo explained, "but it would be good to be where they can be found. People can eat many strange things if they are starving."

Even the river ran low before the end of the summer. There was much sickness, especially of the stomach and bowels. Thick green scum formed around the edges of stagnant pools as the stream's flow slowed to a trickle. There were many who despaired that times would ever return to normal. For the first time, Small Elk saw the beginning of a change in his father.

The holy man had always been vigorous and cheerful, kind and gentle, though a strict teacher. He had always been noted for his intelligent, quiet good humor and his optimism. When times were hard, White Buffalo could always be counted on to furnish calm reassurance. "Of course things will be better," he always advised. "Has it ever been otherwise?" He was the solid footing on which the Southern band relied for reassurance. That help, and the traditional habit of taking one day's problems at a time, had served the People well for many seasons.

"Of course it will rain again," White Buffalo assured the first serious questioners in the Moon of Thunder, which held no thunder. "It always has."

The Red Moon, always parched and dry, was even more so this year. The muttering and rumor increased, and there were whispers. Even though Rain Maker might not be dead but only sulking, there was certainly something wrong with the medicine man. Maybe his power was weakening. White Buffalo seemed tired, discouraged, and unconvincing when he gave his predictions that Rain Maker would return. Something seemed to be drawing the strength from his body, and this too became a topic for rumor and whispered suspicion.

There was a great sense of dread. Already, the People were hungry. Seldom was there hunger in summer. That was bad enough, but the implications that it carried were terrifying. It was time for the coming of the herds, time to be preparing and drying the supplies for the winter. Yet there were none to prepare. The Growers had few crops and none to barter, even if the People had had meat and skins to offer.

"The Moon of Starvation will come early," someone observed.

"Hush! Do not talk so," an older woman warned.

Small Elk sought out his father to discuss the possibilities.

"Of course it will rain," White Buffalo repeated his long-standing advice.

Now it seemed that he only half believed it himself.

"It will rain," he went on, "but it may be too late."

"What do you mean, Father?"

"Elk, we must say nothing of this. It would cause great alarm. But look at the lateness of the season. The wind has not changed yet. There is no sign of rain, and it is late. Soon, Cold Maker brings frost, and there will be no growth."

Small Elk began to understand. There was presently nothing for the buffalo to eat, and that was why they had gone elsewhere. The People longed for the rain that would make the grass grow and bring back the buffalo, but now . . . The time for growing was becoming short. If there was no growth, there would still be no grazing for the herds, and they would not come.

As alarming to Small Elk as this threat was, it was no worse than the change in his father. In his dejected state, White Buffalo seemed to shrink, to lose stature, and to become indecisive. His posture, his walk, and his attitude became hesitant.

Some of the People began to seek out Small Elk for advice and counsel. Elk was unprepared for this; he was not yet skilled enough in the ways of the holy man.

"But you *are* skilled," insisted Crow Woman as they talked one night. "You have studied with White Buffalo for four winters now. Did you not make the decision when to burn last season?"

Their baby girl stirred restlessly, and Crow Woman rose to pick up the child and put her to breast.

"I made the decision, that is true," Elk answered. "But, Crow, it was with his approval."

"Of course. But your choice was right. You always choose as your father would."

Small Elk was still uneasy. Even after the years of instruction, with Crow Woman by his side, he relied on the thinking, the experience, of the older man. Sometimes he wondered when his status as apprentice would change. Maybe this was how it would happen. The People would gradually come more to Small Elk for their spiritual counsel and less to White Buffalo as the strength of his medicine ebbed with the strength of his body. Elk was not ready to see this happen. He wondered if his father had ever suffered from this sort of insecurity about his medicine.

Elk had gained confidence through the years of instruction, but there was always the knowledge of White Buffalo to sustain him in indecision.

"But you never rely on it," Crow Woman reminded.

"True, but I could if I needed it."

Crow smiled and touched his arm, showing her confidence.

"Ask your spirit-guide," she suggested.

Small Elk was embarrassed. He should have thought to do so before, should have been trying to make that contact. He had been preoccupied with the troubles of the People and with a new baby in the lodge. Three years they had tried without success, while Stone Breaker and Cattail had produced two more children, now three in all.

Elk looked at the sleeping infant, now cuddled in Crow's arms. White Moon they called her, after the full moon which shone at the time of her birth. It had been the Moon of Awakening, just before the onset of the Never-rain season. It had been a happy time, a time of beginnings. The child began to grow and thrive. She was doing so even now, though it was proving a drain on the strength of Crow to nurture the child.

"It is nothing," Crow had said as she adjusted her dress over hipbones that had become more prominent. "I will be fat when the buffalo come."

His preoccupation with all these things had prevented Elk from seeing the obvious: He should be in touch with his spirit-guide in this season of emergency. Now that Crow had brought the matter to his attention, he wondered why White Buffalo had not mentioned it. Could it be that his father was failing more rapidly than he realized?

The next morning he declined to eat, informing Crow Woman that he would fast for a few days while he attempted to make contact with his guide.

"I will be back," he assured her. "Three, four sleeps, maybe."

He kissed her, cuddled White Moon for a moment, and left the lodge. This would not be as intense a search as his vision quest. He need not remove himself as far from the camp. He carried only a water skin and stopped to fill it at a clear spot in the stream above the camp. There were a couple of women gathering nuts among the trees, and they nodded to him. Normally, the People gathered few nuts, and those only for variety and flavor. This year, every possible source of food was being utilized, even the acorns from the giant oaks along the river. Though they were bitter and inedible, they could be leached in water to remove part of the bitter taste. He waved at the gatherers and moved on up the slope and away from the village.

By noon he had reached the hilltop that he sought and settled down by the symbolic fire that marked his camp. His belly was beginning to protest, and he took a sip of water. The pangs would pass. Now there was nothing to do but wait.

20

T he fasting experience was difficult to describe, as always. There were the initial pangs of hunger, but that was a familiar sensation this year. After the first day, his discomfort was forgotten as the brilliant clarity of all the senses began to dominate. It seemed to happen rapidly this time, and Elk wondered about the effect. The People had been virtually fasting from time to time all summer. Did that make it quicker?

One feature of the clarification process that Small Elk now noted was that his thinking became clear. He sat on his hilltop and watched the sun rise over the parched tallgrass prairie with a new understanding. It was almost as if he were a disinterested party, an outside observer with no real contact with the situation. What did it matter, he was now able to wonder. The People lived or died, and if they lived, their descendants would live in the Tallgrass Hills. If they died, someone else would live here. It did not matter. He thought of the Death Song:

The grass and the sky go on forever . . .

He considered chanting the song to himself to indicate his understanding but decided against it. After all, the next line carries a different connotation:

. . . but today is a good day to die . . .

That was a thought he was not prepared to approach. Not yet, at any rate. His purpose was to try to find a way to help his people. Besides, he reminded himself, the Death Song was used only when it had become certain that death was imminent.

He retreated from thoughts of death. He had an increased clarity of understanding about death's place in the scheme of things but must not dwell on it. It was not appropriate now, and he moved his thoughts away from thoughts of death, almost reluctantly.

Little else happened that day. Elk's distant vision seemed improved, and he watched a doe and her fawn in the far distance, so far that he could barely have seen them at all without the clarity of the fasting. They tiptoed along a distant stream, searching for pools which still held water. Another doe joined them. The deer were better off in such a season, he noted, than buffalo. Deer were normally browsers, preferring brushy areas to grass. The buffalo were more dependent on the grasses.

Even so, he noted, the deer he watched now had only one fawn between them. In a good growing year, each of these does might easily have two fawns. How useful is their medicine, he thought, to tell them these things. This year you should have only one, for it is a poor season, or this is a year of plenty, so all deer should have twins. His clarity of thought seemed to make him understand all these things. It was a thrill, an excitement beyond description, to know of these things, part of the plan of Creation, if even for a short time.

He watched the smooth circle of a buzzard, riding on fixed wings high above him—searching, searching. *Ah, my brother,* he thought, *your hunting must be good this year. But do not look at me; it is not my time yet.* As if the bird understood, it suddenly lifted a wing and shot away to the northwest on a puff of air known only to itself. Elk watched it go. Ah, to have such vision and such power to fly high above and see the distances. He recalled his vision quest, its sensation of flight, and all the strange creatures he had seen a few seasons before. That had been odd. He had seen the strange creatures, had dreamed of the turtle-footed one twice more over the ensuing moons, and had then forgotten them. *Aiee,* much had happened. With a sort of surprise, he recalled how vigorous and domineering his father had seemed then. Now the medicine man seemed old and tired. When had it happened? How had he failed to notice?

Small Elk slept that night and dreamed—not the mystical, exotic dreams of his vision quest but real and believable nonetheless. He found himself walking through a herd of buffalo, not in his calfskin disguise, but upright, as a man, and the animals did not react to his presence. He recognized the visionary nature of the dream, because he was inside the heads of the animals, feeling the collective thoughts of the herd. It came to him as a low, comfortable hum, like distant conversation, without individual words. Yet the thoughts were clear, comfortable and comforting. They grazed calmly, and it was good, the way of things as they should be. A calf approached to butt playfully at him, and Small Elk laughed and patted its head.

"Run and play, Little Brother," he murmured quietly. He was aware even as he did so that the youngster perceived his thoughts, though not his words.

Ahead of him loomed a giant bull, and it took Elk only a moment to recognize it.

Ah-koh, Grandfather, he thought at the creature, wordlessly.

The bull raised its head, fixed understanding eyes on him, and stood quietly.

Ah-koh, my son, the thought came quietly back at him.

The large dark eyes shone with intelligence and understanding. And calm . . . Elk had never experienced such a feeling of calm confidence.

Grandfather, he began in the strange, wordless conversation that seemed perfectly reasonable. *We have seen none of your people. It is a season of no rain.*

Yes, that is true, his spirit-guide acknowledged.

Small Elk waited a moment, but there was no further message.

We . . . we will die, unless . . .

Yes, came the answer, before Elk had even finished, *some of you. Some of my people too. But some will live. It is the way of things.*

But . . . but how? *What can I do?*

The great shaggy head now turned and lowered to crop grass again.

You will know, the thought came as a parting farewell. *Watch for the signs that you know.*

The dream vanished, and Small Elk was awake, standing alone on the top of his hill. He was sweating profusely, and his body was cold in the chill of the night breeze. He picked up his robe and drew it around him. The black of the sky was dotted with an endless number of tiny points of light, like the campfires of a mighty tribe. There was beauty in it, and a calm reassurance. *But what am I supposed to do?* he asked silently, *I have no answer. The children are hungry.*

From somewhere out in the vastness of the dark prairie came a thought, wordless, a mere awareness of an idea.

You will know.

Small Elk was still at a loss, but more confident now. *You will know.* He had received the same thought in two ways, both in the dream and in reality, though he was not always certain which was which.

Now he watched the sun rise and realized that his present mission was finished. He had contacted his spirit-guide and had received a most frustrating answer to his question regarding what he should do: nothing. Nothing but wait. At least he had been assured that he would know when the time came. He picked up his water skin, tossed the robe over his shoulder, and set out for the camp of the Southern band.

Though it had been chilly when he started, by midmorning the sun's rays were causing sweat to run in rivulets from his face and body. He paused to rest on the top of a low ridge, hoping to catch a stirring of air. The prevailing breeze from the south should be present. Its breath had been hot this season, blistering the skin and sucking moisture from the lips as it dried the whole world of the prairie. But, Elk reasoned, he was wet with sweat, and in the drying, he would cool a little. He faced south, and lifted his sweating face to catch any stirring of the air. But, it was still.

Too still. It took him a little while to realize that. There was a heavy, muggy stillness. What . . . were the signs present? He looked to see how the insect-hunting birds were behaving. No, that was no good. The swallows were gone, having moved south for the winter already, so their flight could not be observed. He looked around again. It was nothing he could identify specifically, but something . . . in the stillness there was expectation. The sky was a brilliant clear blue, beyond all reality. It appeared that he could reach his hand upward and thrust it into the blue of the sky, as one could thrust it into water. He reached but could not touch the brilliance that was there. Still, there was something . . . an air of expectancy. There must be . . . yes, there *was* a change of some sort in the air. And with the expectation of change, should he not dance the ceremonial dances for rain, and . . .

Elk was already tossing the robe aside and reaching for his fire-sticks. He had no drum, but the cadence of the chant would suffice to set the tempo of the dance. He had prepared his tinder and readied the fire-sticks when a thought came to him. White Buffalo had often said that much of the effect of a ceremonial was through the spirits of the observers. Elk had sometimes suspected that part of the task was to impress those observers and increase the prestige of the medicine man. But no matter—there was no question that there was more excitement, more suspense, and emotional uplift where people were gathered together to participate. Was that not the purpose of the gathering of all bands to celebrate the Sun Dance?

Quickly, Elk put away the fire-sticks and picked up his robe and water skin. He glanced at the sky. There was nothing apparent yet, other than the feel of impending change. Yes, he should be able to reach the camp before anything remarkable occurred. He started off at an easy trot, pausing frequently to walk, to rest and conserve his strength. By midday, he jogged into the village and paused at his own lodge to speak to Crow Woman before continuing to the lodge of his parents.

"Father," he called, "it is time. The change is coming, and the buffalo will return."

His mother lifted the doorskin and held it aside for White Buffalo. Elk was startled at his father's appearance. The old medicine man was stooped and bent, and appeared to have aged in the few days they had been apart.

His spirit is dying, thought Elk. *He has given up.*

"Father!" Small Elk began excitedly. "The change is coming! I feel it. We must dance the Rain Dance, and the Dance of the Buffalo!"

"No, my son, it is not time. Look, do you see clouds? Has the wind changed?"

It seemed that White Buffalo considered the conversation at an end. He started to turn away.

"Father!" Small Elk spoke sharply. "You must listen to

me. I have fasted, have seen visions, and I am made to feel that it is time!"

There was not the least spark of interest in the old man's eyes.

"No," he said wearily. "It will happen, sometime, maybe. Not now. Go back to your lodge."

Small Elk took a deep breath. He had never defied his father before, but White Buffalo was refusing to listen to his own medicine.

"Father," he said with a voice tight with emotion. "I am going to dance the Rain Dance."

The old man stood, his mouth open in astonishment for a moment. Elk stood transfixed, afraid that his father would challenge his right to do so. A few curious onlookers waited expectantly. Was this to be a clash of the medicines of the two? A contest, to see whose gift had greater strength?

Finally, White Buffalo threw up his hands in resignation. He turned and shuffled feebly into his lodge, jerking the doorskin closed behind him. Small Elk turned to speak to his wife.

"Crow, this is our most important ceremony. Are you ready?"

She nodded. "I have your paints ready. Come, we will prepare you for the dance."

It was quickly done, the face-paint that would honor Rain Maker and draw him closer. The two proceeded to the center of the village, the council area, and Crow Woman began to tap softly on the drum. Elk danced a few tentative steps, and Crow steadied the cadence. The voice of the drum began to speak with authority, and the People began to assemble.

"Small Elk does the Rain Dance!" The excited murmur ran through the crowd. "The Dance for Rain!"

21

When Small Elk began his ceremony, there were many doubters—this despite the fact that there had been grumblings all summer because the medicine men would *not* perform the Dance for Rain. Now there were grumblings that the young apprentice did not know what he was doing.

Word had spread quickly that the two medicine men had quarreled. Or at the very least, there had been a disagreement. It had been a public thing, right in front of the lodge of White Buffalo, and a number of people had seen and heard it. As the story spread, it grew, and the seriousness of the quarrel was exaggerated.

"I thought White Buffalo would strike him," reported one witness.

There was a gasp of disbelief, but before long, the rapidly moving tale related that Small Elk *had* been slapped across the face by his father. This was a very serious breach of custom. To strike another was practically unknown among the People. Such an act would be reserved for, perhaps, a captured enemy. A Head Splitter, for instance, might be subjected to such an act as part of the ridicule and demeaning treatment that he must suffer before he was killed. But to strike one's own son . . . *aiee!* There were those who suggested this as evidence that White Buffalo's mind was gone, that he was insane. Others insisted he could do nothing else in the face of open revolt by his apprentice.

But, countered the other faction, Small Elk has studied the skills of their craft for four, maybe five seasons now. He has the knowledge, the *right* to disagree. The argument became partly a generation- or age-related split, but not entirely. There were young people who supported the authority of White Buffalo and oldsters who supported Small Elk's right to challenge.

There were a substantial number who took neither side but took great glee in observing the clash of power and prestige. There were bets within this group on whose medicine would prove the stronger.

Small Elk was largely unaware of all this as he began the ceremony. He concentrated only on the drum cadence and the song. The sun's rays beat down, and soon sweat was pouring from his body. He was still in his fasting state, not having taken time to eat. Consequently, he was still experiencing a bright clarity of the senses and of the mind. This was a great advantage in the spiritual part of the ceremony. However, it led to a disregard of reality. Elk was largely unaware of the gathering tension in the crowd that quickly assembled to watch the ceremony.

"He does do the steps well," admitted an old woman who had watched a lifetime of Rain Songs.

"Yes, but he has no authority to do so!" snapped her friend who sat beside her.

The ceremony continued. From time to time, Small Elk looked to the heavens. Clear bright blue still pervaded the entire expanse. He would have been discouraged, except that the very brightness held excitement and promise. His energy continued to flow. He finished the cycle of the ceremony once, then repeated it. Crow Woman appeared tired. The physical strain of maintaining the cadence as the afternoon dragged on was wearing at her strength. Additionally, the excitement of the ceremony itself lent added stress, he knew. Cattail was caring for Crow's baby, but . . . he hated to put her through this, but it might mean survival for the desperate band, now heading into winter unprepared. He nodded to her, and the drum cadence began again.

A mutter went through the crowd, a quiet ripple. It was apparent that there was a restlessness. There was a look of triumph beginning to show on the faces of those who had wagered against the success of Small Elk. Some of those not wagering were beginning to change loyalties. After all, had not White Buffalo been a wise leader in things of the spirit? Maybe it was unwise to side with the apprentice in this test of strength.

Small Elk danced on. He was tiring now, beginning to be

discouraged. Had he been wrong? Was it only the exhilaration of his fast that had led him mistakenly to expect the wind's change? He began to doubt, to wonder. What would be his father's reaction? Would he now abandon his son? When this was over and Elk had failed, would his father refuse to teach him more, deny the validity of Small Elk's gift?

It was the first that he had thought of failure. Now he realized that success too could drive them apart. White Buffalo might easily hold anger against the son who had shown his medicine to be stronger than his own. But that seemed unlikely now. He was nearing the end of the third repeated cycle of the chant, and nothing had changed. Surely his spirit-guide would not mislead him. There was only one explanation: He had misread the signs. In doing so, he had failed. He had failed his guide, his father's teaching—yes, even his calling.

Elk finished the cadence, and the drum ceased to speak. He stood, swaying, defeated, his defeat like ashes in his mouth. He was exhausted, ready to drop. Three times he had completed the ceremony and . . . nothing.

His paint was dissolving in sweat, running down his face. The crowd shifted a little in embarrassment, and a few people, their eyes averted, began to move away from the scene of failure.

Small Elk's older brother, who had had his own lodge before Elk was born, now approached angrily. They had never been close because of the difference in their ages.

"Let it go, Elk!" the older man hissed. "You dishonor your father."

Elk looked around him for support. No one seemed willing to look at him. Across the circle he encountered the gaze of Stone Breaker. It was a look of friendship, of understanding, and he held and treasured it for a moment. But it was not right. It was a look not of confidence but pity. It promised friendship despite failure, and that was not what Small Elk needed. He needed the support that would come with the belief that he was *right,* faith in his skill and knowledge. He looked to Crow Woman. She sat, tired and discouraged, her hands limp on the skin of the silent drum. But in her eyes shone love and confidence. At least Crow was still with him in spirit.

"Come on, Elk," his brother urged angrily.

Small Elk drew himself up proudly. He looked at the sky, the parched hills, and the trees on the opposite bend of the river a few hundred paces away. Their leaves hung limply in the afternoon heat. He must keep confidence in himself, in his ability to interpret the signs. He focused his eyes on those distant trees, and the wilted leaves seemed to shimmer in the heat. He wiped the sweat away to clear his vision, and looked again. Yes! There—the tired leaves in the tops of the giant sycamores were stirring. A stray puff of wind had put them into shimmering motion. Now it increased, bending the tops of the branches. Small Elk smiled and turned to his brother.

"You must get out of my way, Antelope," he said gently. "I have work to do."

"Look!" someone cried. "The wind changes!"

The cool breeze swept across the open meadow, stirring the seedheads of the grasses. The People watched it come like a flood of water sweeping across the level space toward them.

"The wind has changed!"

"Look! It comes from the northeast!"

There was no hint of rain, but as the breeze swept through the village, there was a feel, a smell, a *spirit* of change. An old woman gave a joyful shout.

Small Elk turned to Crow Woman. She sat, smiling her approval.

"Now is the time," he said softly to her. "Can you beat one more cadence?"

"Of course!"

She did not look so tired now. Elk's blood was racing as Crow began her measured strokes and the drum began to sing with authority. People cheered and danced, and those who had departed began to drift back.

Then there was a sudden silence. Someone pointed with a gasp of amazement. White Buffalo had emerged from his lodge and was standing there, observing the dance. His face was stern, but even the most unobservant among them could not fail to notice one fact. The holy man was wearing his ceremonial paint. A gasp ran through the crowd. Was White Buffalo going to challenge the authority of his son?

He strode over to the council ring, and it seemed to the onlookers that he had grown taller, more sturdy. There was a confidence, a strength, that no one had seen in a long time. He nodded to Crow Woman, whose beat never faltered as she nodded back. Now the old medicine man strode forward and fell into step with his son, dancing the cadences of the Rain Dance.

For a moment Small Elk seemed not to notice. Then he turned and came face-to-face with White Buffalo. Neither broke step, but Small Elk smiled and shook his gourd-rattle high for a moment. His father was more dignified, merely nodding a greeting as they passed.

"All bets are no good!" cried one of the wagerers.

The crowd roared with laughter.

It was during the night that the rain came. Small Elk heard the dull plop of the first fat drops as they struck the lodge-skin. He was already awake, waiting. He had been sleeping the well-earned sleep of exhaustion when the distant mutter of Rain Maker's drum roused him.

"Listen!" said Crow Woman softly. "Do you hear it?"

"Yes," Elk whispered. "My vision . . . it was true!"

"Your heart was good," Crow stated simply, "and you made a good decision."

"I am glad that my father is not still angry."

"Your father is proud, Elk. Did you see how tall he stood as he danced?"

"Maybe so, Crow, it hurt my heart to go against him."

"I know. But you were right, and he knows it too now."

"About the change in the wind," he agreed, "some rain, maybe. But Crow, I do not know if the buffalo will come."

"One thing at a time," said Crow Woman soothingly. "Listen. The rain comes."

At first there was only an occasional drop, plunking on the taut, dry lodgecover, but soon there were more, and then a constant drumming as Rain Maker seemed intent on making up for his summer absence. Real-fire flashed, illuminating the doorway and the smokehole. Then, a few counts later, the boom of the thunder-drum would shake the earth. Elk and Crow Woman snuggled together, reveling in the smell of rain and the storm's cooling effect.

The height of the booming thunderstorm moved on, leaving behind only the rain, a steady quiet patter that lulled the senses, soaking into the thirsty ground. In some seasons a storm of this kind in early autumn would bring the threat of a flash flood, sending the People scrambling to move the camp to higher ground. Not this time. The water would be quickly swallowed up by the great cracks in the earth. They had opened through the hot moons of the summer, widening as the hot winds dried and cracked the prairie. In some areas the yawning fissures were large enough to thrust an arm into or to present a hazard to walking. Now, with the moistening effect of the rain, soon there would be no wounds in Earth's skin to remind them of the dreadful Year-of-No-Rain.

By morning, the main part of the storm had passed. For a little while after daylight, the thinning patter continued. Then there was only the occasional drip of water from the trees. Children ran, shouting and splashing happily in the puddles, while adults spread their belongings to dry. The river was beginning to stir, the small rivulets between stagnant pools widening in a promise of normal flow to come.

As the sun broke through clouds to the east, the medicine men stood on the hill behind the camp, evaluating the scene.

"It is good," pronounced White Buffalo.

At no time did he ever mention their quarrel.

In the glorious feel of this moist autumn morning, it was possible to see the change in the prairie—mostly a change in color. From the stark, sun-baked yellow-brown that had become so familiar, the general tone was now of green. Not the lush green of spring, but a mature green that would soon ripen into the yellows, pinks, and muted reds of autumn grasses. Here and there were autumn flowers, already striving for blooms to re-create before the dying of winter. Their golds and purples had seemed wilted and pointless. Now they blazed in all their glory, heralding the season.

"It is good," White Buffalo repeated.

"Yes," Small Elk agreed.

"Now," White Buffalo continued, "comes the greatest question. Will the buffalo come?"

22

When the scouts reported the approach of buffalo, the People accepted it almost as a foregone conclusion. There was very little surprise, only delight, at the good fortune that had come their way. It was seven days since the rain and the weather change that had broken the drought. Small Elk, in the minds of the Southern band, was responsible. He knew that his major part in the event had been to announce the change, not to cause it. In truth, the People might realize this too. But there was much of the spirit about the medicine man, secrets not revealed to ordinary mortals. This gave him the ability to foresee the future. This time, the young medicine man had boldly announced the coming of rain when there seemed no signs. He had even challenged his teacher. More importantly, he had been right. Small Elk's prestige soared. Quiet discussions among the lodges suggested that possibly White Buffalo was past his prime, that he would soon step aside in favor of the young holy man. Had Small Elk not performed the ceremonies to bring rain? *Aiee,* the Southern band was fortunate to have reared such a man!

By the time the buffalo came, morale was high. There was no longer any question whether the herds would come, only *when.* From hopeless despair to open optimism had been a matter of only a night's rain, a few cool days, and a hint of green on the hills.

There would be no individual hunting, at least at first. In a time when the survival of the entire band would depend on success, no individual had the right to threaten the success of the others. No one would disturb the herd until the council decided that the time was right, based on the advice and counsel of the medicine men. The kill must include enough animals for the entire band.

. Small Elk and White Buffalo went out together to view the approaching herd. Since the rain, the older man had undergone a great change. He no longer appeared so weak and frail. Much of his strength had returned with the life-giving moisture that had given a new strength to the world. With White Buffalo's returning confidence, however, was a new respect for his apprentice. He now treated Elk almost as an equal. It may have been, in part, an effort to convince the People that there had been no real quarrel between them, only a professional disagreement. Regardless, the People saw their two medicine men as seers of great skill whose medicine was strong, and it was good.

The two men crouched in a sumac thicket and surveyed the herd. It was half a day's travel away, and at the slow rate at which the grazing animals usually moved, they would not approach for a day or two. One thing was immediately obvious. This was not a great seasonal herd of many thousands.

"There are only a few hundred animals," Small Elk observed.

"Yes, but we had none before," his father reminded him.

They watched for a little while the excruciatingly slow movement of the leading edge of the herd. It was like pouring honey from a gourd on a cold morning, a motion barely perceptible.

"They move in the valleys," Small Elk observed.

"Yes. It will be wetter there, and the grass will be better."

They studied the direction of the buffalo's progress. It would be necessary to surround the herd partially, so that the hunters, all shooting at once, could bring down several animals. Small Elk studied the roll of the land and the herd's movement. This herd, a group which had split off from the main herd during the migration, would move steadily southward. It would reach a suitable place to winter and stop there, much as the People did to establish winter camp.

A long line of geese went honking past high overhead, sounding much like barking dogs in the distance. Elk wondered if they too made a kind of winter camp somewhere far to the south. He turned his attention again to the buffalo, trying to estimate their direction of movement. It would be basically south, with some variation, depending on the gently rolling hills. Tomorrow they would be on an open flat, there to the northwest. It was wide and level, with no places to hide a hunter. Certainly, the grass was not tall enough this season to be a practical concealment. Another day south would bring the herd to rougher country, approaching the river west of the camp. At that point was an abrupt bluff, a cliff that dropped away from the flat grassland to jumbled rocks below. It was too steep to descend, so the herd would move in one direction or the other to find an easier slope.

They would probably not move in the direction of the village. The scent of man was there. The herd would shift to the west to avoid the precipice. In that direction was rocky broken ground with many hiding-places. Even better, the slight breeze, if it held, was from the northeast, carrying the scent of the hidden hunters away from the herd. It was good, except for a problem or two. The hunters could easily be in position by that time, but the first animals to enter the rocky ravine would be alarmed by the man-scent. They would retreat back into the open prairie and be lost. There should be a way to put the herd where it would be easy to approach and yet ensure that there would be no flight. How to use the man-scent, and yet not cause a stampede . . . or maybe stampede into the ravine, where they would be slowed in their flight, long enough to shoot, and shoot again.

He studied the distant terrain with this in mind. Yes, if the herd was gently moved, by careful use of men showing themselves upwind . . . if they could be made to approach the cliff at about the gray boulder near the rim, and then turned west into the ravine . . . How, he wondered, could they be made to approach the right spot to turn?

"Father," he said suddenly, "do you think the calfskin will work now?"

"Maybe," answered the old man cautiously. "It is better in spring, when there are calves. Why?"

Quickly, Small Elk outlined his idea. His father's eyes widened.

"*Aiee!* It is very dangerous, Elk."

"Not really, Father. And if it is successful, our kill will be great."

"But if they run in the wrong direction?"

"A few will still have a chance at a shot. Will you help me? Dance the Buffalo Dance?"

White Buffalo paused only a little while.

"Yes," he said simply. "But we must hurry. Come, we will talk to Short Bow and Broken Horn."

It was a busy night. Men, women, and children were kept from sleep to accomplish the tasks that must be ready by daylight. When the sun rose, all was ready, the hunters in position in the ravine. A few men had spent most of the night circling far to the north, to approach the herd from that side. They would show themselves from time to time at a distance, just to remind the buffalo of their presence and keep the animals moving in their generally southern direction.

The day dawned crisp and clear, bright golden sunlight streaking the prairie. Dense plumes of mist rose from the surface of the river below to hang like a furry white robe over the water. The creatures of the day were beginning to stir. An owl, who had stayed out too long, made his way across the grassy flat, pursued by a trio of noisy crows. A great blue heron sailed majestically toward the river and glided out of sight below the bluff. Small Elk had always marveled that a creature so ungainly and awkward-appearing on land could be full of grace and beauty on the wing.

He turned to watch the approaching herd from behind the boulder where he crouched. He carried no weapon but wore the calfskin, firmly tied in place with its thongs. The skin of the animal's head covered his own, and the legs were fastened to his wrists and ankles. Now, as the herd approached, he must concentrate. It was time to get inside the heads of the herd.

He focused his attention on one old cow in the forefront of the advancing animals. She appeared to be the leader, picking out the path. She was nervous, probably from the knowledge of something behind. Yes, now he began to feel the cow's concern. The hunters who had circled behind had shown themselves, and the entire herd was aware and alert, moving a little faster, but not yet alarmed. The leading animals were now approaching the critical point, where the plan would depend on Small Elk's ability to feel their thoughts. At any moment, they should smell the smoke and man-scent from the village. Yes . . . *now!* The wary old lead cow stopped suddenly and raised her head for an instant. Elk knew that she had caught the scent—also that it was not an immediate threat but a matter for caution. Nervously, the cow shifted direction, moving a trifle toward the west and the ravine.

To keep the main body of the herd moving in that direction, the People had spent a good part of the night carrying and placing objects from their lodges in a long line. Several hundred paces the line stretched, from open prairie, angling toward the bluff. It consisted of old robes, rawhide packs, worn-out buckskin garments too useful to discard. Anything long-used that would carry the scent. This assortment of items would not, of course, stop the buffalo. That was not the intent. When they became excited, there would be no stopping the rush. The immediate goal was to shift their direction ever so slightly, to place the herd's leaders precisely at the right point when the moment came.

Now the lead cow and her companions felt better, having angled away from the man-smell. They moved on, into the ever-narrowing trap, even pausing to graze a little. A long bowshot from the cliff's edge, Elk felt a sense of unrest among the leaders. Something was not quite right. They stared southward and sniffed the air, trying to make up for limited eyesight with their keen sense of smell. But the breeze continued to favor Elk's undertaking. What little stirring there was had continued to move from the northeast, pushing the herd almost unconsciously to the southwest, toward the angle where the ravine met the cliff's edge. His main concern was whether they would come close enough.

The lead cow now decided that something was wrong. She circled, snorting nervously, turning back toward the prairie. *No,* Elk thought, *she must not do that!* Tense and sweating, even in the chill autumn air, Elk stepped from behind his boulder and assumed the position of the calf whose skin he now wore. A few steps into the open . . . *now!* He voiced the bleat of a calf in trouble, the tremulous scream for help that would strike to the heart of every mother in the herd. In an instant, a dozen alarmed cows came thundering toward him. It was an alarming thing, seeing that charge and knowing that the edge of the cliff was only a step or two behind him. He bleated in terror again, and the rush came on. He hoped that the hunters in the north end of the ravine understood their part in this scheme.

At the last possible moment, Small Elk dodged out of the path of the thundering animals and took refuge behind his boulder. The confused animals slid to a stop, almost at the rim, and milled uncertainly, unsure at the calf's sudden disappearance. Elk crouched there, wondering what they would do if they discovered him. But the great shaggy heads turned this way and that in confusion. The notoriously poor eyesight of the buffalo was helping him. In addition, his scent was obscured, not only by the herbs he had used to anoint himself but by the cloud of dust raised by pounding hooves.

What was wrong? The moments dragged past. The hunters to the north should have acted by now.

Then he heard it. A chorus of yells in the distance, followed by a low rumble as the herd began to run. Ah, finally! He could visualize the men, jumping from concealment to startle the herd. Shouting, flapping robes, swinging their arms, and rushing forward as if in attack. The buffalo, if they behaved as he expected, would come crowding down upon the ones near the rim. Their course as they ran would be somewhat limited by the man-smell of the carefully placed objects on the east and on the west, by the ravine where bowmen lay hidden. The crushing force of the herd would push down the narrowing course. . . .

The thunder was louder now. The animals that he could see were milling in panic. A few broke away toward the east, but the smells from the camp would soon deter them. Others tried to escape into the broken rocks of the ravine to the west. Elk could see that direction quite clearly. Hunters rose up, yelling and shooting. The animals tried to turn back toward the open prairie but were met by the oncoming rush. There was a crash as the main portion of the herd smashed into those near the cliff's rim. Animals fell, to be trampled into the dust by those coming on. The herd was pushing, thrusting, running in panic. Elk saw the first cow, helplessly struggling, go over the edge. Another balanced for a moment, scrambling to survive, then toppled and fell. Yet another, and then the full force of the rush came, dozens of them, realizing their doom at the last moment but pushed by the relentless thrust from behind. It was like a gigantic brown waterfall, with death waiting at the bottom.

Then, suddenly, it was over. The survivors split into smaller groups and broke away, east or west, it did not matter now. People were rushing forward, laughing and cheering the success of the hunt. From the direction of the village, women and children began to straggle out to begin butchering and preparing the meat.

Small Elk stood up and began to untie the thongs of the calfskin. It was over. Finally, the drought and the threat of famine were at an end.

23

The thunder died, to be replaced by shouts of joy and cheers of triumph. But there was to be mourning too.

"Where is Antelope? I cannot find him!"

"He was in the ravine. Otter, did you see him?"

"There he is! What about those on the north end?"

"They are safe."

Confusing reports and rumors flew back and forth as relatives searched for missing hunters in the aftermath of the carnage. The men from the north end came straggling in. The scattered survivors of the herd, they reported, had fled out into the prairie where they were grouping together again. Barking Fox was dead, tossed and gored by an aggressive cow in her escape. The family of Fox began the Song of Mourning as they started out to retrieve the body. Short Bow went with the mourners to show them the way.

The task of skinning had already begun when Cat Woman, wife of the Southern band's leader, began to inquire as to his whereabouts. She had at first supposed him to be assisting others who might be in need of help.

"Small Elk, have you seen Broken Horn?" she inquired.

"Of course, Mother, he was directly opposite me, where the ravine meets the cliff, there."

"I mean now, since the rush of the herd."

"I . . . I am not sure. Maybe . . . come, we will ask Black Bear. He was on that side."

". . . not since the herd went over," Bear admitted. "He was on my left, and I saw him stand to shoot."

"*Aiee*, Broken Horn is too old to do these things," his worried spouse fretted. "He thinks he has to show the young men."

"He has shown us much, Mother," Black Bear said. "He gives us of his strength."

"He is a good leader," added Small Elk.

The two young men were still with Cat Woman when a wail of anguish came from below the cliff. The first of the People had made their way down to evaluate the extent of the kill.

Small Elk stepped to the edge and peered cautiously below. He could see a jumble of brown bodies. A few animals that had survived the fall were crippling away, and a few hunters pursued to finish them. Elk could not see the area from which the wailing came. There were trees that obscured the view of that sector, where the ravine opened below.

"What is it?" he called, dreading the answer.

"Broken Horn!" came the reply. "He is dead. He went over the edge with the buffalo!"

At Small Elk's elbow, Cat Woman gave a long shriek of grief and began to chant the mournful cadence of the Song of Mourning. She had feared the worst, and her fears had proved true.

The immediate family of Broken Horn quickly received the ill tidings, and began to chant the Mourning Song. Others joined in, for Broken Horn had been a good leader for a long time and would be missed. Close friends assisted in the retrieval of the body, and the traditional mourning continued.

But life goes on. Even as the mourners paused for their sad tasks, others began to skin and butcher the buffalo kill. The immensity of the food supply that had come to the People was beyond imagination. It was apparent that some of the meat would be wasted, even with the cooperation of every pair of hands, down to those of the smallest child. However, it was important to salvage as much as possible. Any dried meat, pemmican, and robes not immediately needed for the winter could be traded to the Growers for corn, beans, and pumpkins.

The work was beginning. Those most adept at skinning assisted others by slitting the hides up the belly and down the inside of each leg. Then the removal progressed, and the fresh skins were spread, flesh-side-up, on the ground. As meat was removed from the carcass it was piled on a skin to be transported, as time permitted, back to the village. In anticipation of a feast, some of the men hacked out chunks from the humps of some of the choicest animals. Fresh, crisply broiled hump-ribs, with their extra layer of flavorful suet, would be a treat that the People had not enjoyed for many moons.

"Small Elk!" someone called. "Over here. We need you to make the apology!"

Three men stood waiting with the severed head of the largest bull. This would be an important ceremony, the most important for generations, for this hunt had provided the kill that would enable the Southern band to survive. Small Elk walked over to the three.

"White Buffalo should do this," he explained. "I am only his assistant."

"We asked him," said Black Bear. "He said to find you, that your skill made the big kill possible."

"Is this true?" Elk asked the others. "White Buffalo said this?"

"Yes, of course, Elk. We would not say untruth about such a thing."

Elk stood for a moment in stunned astonishment. It was the greatest honor his father had ever granted him. He would have gone to White Buffalo to talk to him, but time was passing. The ceremony must be completed, and the hard work of preparing the meat must go on.

"It is good," said Small Elk. "Bring it over here."

There were those who said that this was the beginning of a new era in the history of the People, when Small Elk made the apology for this hunt. Others said no, it was at the dance ceremony later, and still others recalled the election of the new chief. But all agreed that this occasion, the most successful hunt at the end of the worst season in memory, was an important time. Small Elk faced the buffalo head, while those nearby watched reverently.

> We are sorry, my brother, to take your
> lives, but upon yours, ours depend. . . .

Even as the People worked, the smell of roasting hump-ribs began to drift across the area. Several fires were kept burning downwind of the butchering. Someone would pause in his or her task, step to a fire, and cut a piece of meat to chew, even while the work continued.

Necessarily, much of the heavier skinning and rolling of the carcasses was done by the men. Some of the men withdrew and stationed themselves as lookouts as soon as possible. There was every possibility that any Head Splitters in the area would also be aware of the presence of buffalo. This was no time to be attacked, when the winter's food supply depended on the tasks at hand.

As meat became available, women began the jerking of strips of muscle, to strip them away from the larger joints. These were sliced thinly and draped over willow racks to dry. Children were stationed with leafy branches to shoo away flies and an occasional enterprising bird.

The festoons of drying meat grew as the carcasses shrank to piles of stripped bones, but it was apparent that the hard work of salvaging the meat would go on. Before midday, most of the better-quality animals had been selected, bled, and gutted. Even the pile at the bottom of the cliff had, for the most part, been pulled apart and sorted for quality. A few animals had fallen into inaccessible places, in crevices or among the rocks. Some were in the water, in places too shallow to float but too deep to work in. These were abandoned as unsalvageable, at least for the present. One yearling cow hung grotesquely in the crotch of a tree above the stream. The unnatural posture suggested that it had died in the fall, probably from a broken neck or back.

Some of the People worked on by the light of the fires. Others slept for a little while, to rise and begin again. Out in the darkness, beyond the circle of the firelight, coyotes quarreled over the leavings of some of the butchered carcasses.

"Little Brother wants his share," a woman joked as she worked.

"Maybe he would come and help us," her friend suggested, laughing.

"Not likely. He is good at sharing the kills of others."

"Are not we all in time of hunger? *Aiee,* whose kill *is* this?"

She pointed to the fat cow they were butchering. Both laughed.

"You are right," the other agreed, turning to call into the darkness. "You are welcome, Little Brother. Take all you need, for we have plenty. We are fortunate this night."

She paused, and there was a chuckling chorus from the unseen guests in the darkness.

"Their cries sound like laughter," observed one of the women, who was heavy with child. "It is pleasant to hear. Maybe I will call my child that."

"What? 'One-Who-Laughs'?"

"No! 'The Coyote.' He is clever and cunning. Already, he runs a lot."

She pointed ruefully to her swollen belly, and the others laughed.

"*Aiee*, he will be hard to catch when he comes outside!" one suggested.

"No, I think not," said the expectant mother seriously. "He moves much, but quietly. He would rather not run if he can walk. So, I think he knows much, and saves his strength. Like the coyote."

"Does he also laugh, like the voices out there?"

The others laughed.

"I have not heard him yet," admitted the swollen one, "but I think he will!"

The work continued. There was good reason to hurry the preparation of their winter supplies. In only a few days, all the meat not processed would spoil. It was dangerous to eat tainted meat. Only two winters ago, a young hunter of the People had eaten a few bites from a dead elk that he found and had died before Sun Boy's appearance the next day.

Aside from that easily avoided danger, there were other problems. The buffalo killed in the fall from the cliff were upstream from the village. Their water supply would soon be fouled by the rotting carcasses, and a move would be necessary.

In addition to that, the nuisance of flies and the odor of rotting flesh would soon become intolerable. Already the sickly-sweet odor of blood and death was beginning to be noted. It was good that the nights were cool now, to retard the decay.

By the third day of hard work, it was decided to hold a celebration. The event that had been the turning point in the survival or death of the Southern band must be commemorated. The period of mourning for the dead would be past. There had indeed been mourning, despite the other demands. The songs had been sung, the bodies carefully wrapped in fresh buffalo-skins and placed in tree scaffolds. Cat Woman had mourned her husband by slashing her forearms and tossing handfuls of ashes on her head. Broken Horn had been a good leader.

Along with the ceremonial festivities, at some point the council would meet to select the new chief. There was, of course, much speculation. Some scurried around, promoting favorite candidates, but no clear choice had yet emerged. It should be one who had exhibited leadership qualities. Some men who had achieved a high degree of respect in the band were still not eligible for consideration. Small Elk was riding high on a swell of popularity because of the success of the buffalo hunt. But his area of expertise and knowledge, his priestly function, held a place of its own. The situation was much the same with Stone Breaker. Popular and successful, still his skills were not those of leadership, even without the handicap of his crippled leg.

A strong swell of opinion favored Short Bow, and this movement seemed to grow. He was renowned as a leader of the hunt. Short Bow was quiet and reliable, and had helped many youngsters perfect their skills through his teaching in the Rabbit Society. That alone would carry the weight of many votes.

Soon it appeared a foregone conclusion. Short Bow had few detractors. However, no one had consulted Short Bow. When someone finally mentioned the possibility to the candidate, he was astonished.

"No!" he said firmly.

"But you are a respected leader," his friend pleaded.

"In the hunt, yes. But not in politics. Besides, I am too old. There are many young men."

"But who? None stands above the others."

"*Aiee*, I cannot choose one. That is the task of the Warrior Society."

His gaze fell on a popular young man who sat a little distance away, avidly devouring a slab of broiled ribs. His ability to eat was legendary. It seemed to require huge quantities to fill this young hunter's large frame. It had earned him a nickname which by this time had become permanent.

"What about Hump Ribs, there?" asked Short Bow.

"None other is more capable at the hunt. He is respected by all. He would be a good leader."

"*Aiee*, maybe so," commented another, chuckling. "None is more skilled at eating, either."

In this way, almost by accident, the ground swell of opinion began to settle on this candidate. Mention of his name brought a smile, and there were none who had a bad thing to say. By the time of the meeting, most of the People were convinced that there was very little doubt. The new chief of the Southern band would quite likely be the likable young man with the voracious appetite, Hump Ribs.

24

» » »

As expected, the selection of a new leader for the Southern band was quickly accomplished. There was simply no opposition to the elevation of young Hump Ribs to the position. It was one of those fortuitous situations which seems so obvious once it has been accomplished. Everyone realized how appropriate the new leader was in this position and wondered that it had not been recognized earlier. Of course, there were those who claimed to have said so all along.

The new chief, quiet and mild-mannered, could be criticized by no one. He had simply never aroused any animosity in anyone. One possible danger, that he would not lend firm leadership, was quickly dispelled. The first public act of Chief Hump Ribs was to announce the day of departure, three days hence. Wise heads nodded. It was a good decision and met with the approval of the council. Some would grumble, feeling that there was not enough time to finish preparation of the bountiful provisions that had fallen to them. Most, however, realized that the move was urgent. There were an increasing number of flies, invading the lodges and clinging sleepily to the inside of the lodgecovers in the chill of the autumn nights.

The odor of rotting flesh was also becoming objectionable. Yes, it was time to move to winter camp, and the first pronouncement of the new leader was a good one.

Small Elk was pleased. Hump Ribs was a year or two younger than he but of the same generation. It was a bit startling to realize that the power and prestige of leadership was passing to this generation, but it was good. Elk resolved to seek out the new chief and offer him congratulation and support, but the evening was too busy and exciting at the moment. Fires were lighted, and the drums began to sound in preparation for the dance.

There is something in the beat of the drum that stirs a primeval spirit in the heart of mankind. It may be a racial memory of the pounding of the surf on beaches where life-forms that became our ancestors first crawled onto the land and breathed air. Or perhaps the echo of the beating mother-heart that sustained us in the womb. Maybe, even, the reassurance of the pulsing throb of the living planet that sustains all life. In answer to its rhythms, our feet become restless, our bodies begin to respond to the cadence of the drum. The pulse quickens. We find ourselves answering to the urge to join in the magnificent celebration of Creation, of Life.

In this case, the occasion was one of thanksgiving for the events that had provided survival. First, young men draped in buffalo robes enacted the role of the herd, moving slowly, swaying, mimicking the grazing motion of the animals. Then other dancers joined, reenacting their own parts in the drama, reliving deeds of valor. The dancers who represented the herd were crowded to one side of the arena and finally began to collapse. The front ranks first, simulating the spectacular rush of the buffalo over the rim of the cliff. Excitement reached a fever pitch, the drum cadence quickened, and more dancers joined in. The buffalo dancers cast aside their costumes and rejoined the others, now no longer buffalo but participants in the joyful thanksgiving.

The dance continued until everyone was near exhaustion. But there was yet one more event to occur, one unique not only to the People but to this band. The Southern band, more specifically its medicine man, was custodian of the White Robe. It had been handed down for generations. The exact story of its acquisition was by now indistinct with antiquity. It was known that a young medicine man of long ago had returned from a special fast carrying a magnificent buffalo-skin of pure white. He had tanned and prepared it as a ceremonial robe, complete with the horned headress that was part of the cape. The medicine man had, at the same time, taken the name White Buffalo. This name had been handed down through the generations, the cape with it.

There was thought to be something supernatural about

the cape. Around the story-fires, its origin had been told and retold, and had grown with the telling. It was popularly believed that the original White Buffalo had received it as a direct gift from heaven. Small Elk had once studied the story-skins to find out, but without success. The first record was a pictograph of many winters past. A man stood holding a white robe up to heaven. Nothing more, except this consecration.

Through the other pictographs, there was an occasional indication of someone with the White Buffalo name. That was handled differently. The figure of a man or woman would be depicted in whatever action was worthy of entry into the story-skin. The name was indicated by a small picture in a circle above, connected to the figure by a line. It was difficult to tell one generation from another in the story-skins. The White Buffalo name appeared, but there was no way to tell when it had been handed down. Small Elk had been frustrated, and his father had chuckled to himself in amusement.

The big dance-drum was quiet now, after the reenactment. Dove Woman began a slow, solemn cadence on the smaller medicine-drum, and the crowd quieted. Small Elk, who had been dancing with the others, now seated himself to watch the medicine dance of White Buffalo.

As the old man danced into the circle of firelight, the crowd parted to admit him to the arena. The change in the holy man was apparent immediately. A moon ago he had appeared old, feeble, and small. He was beaten, by the years and the Never-Rain summer. This did not appear to be the same man. He looked taller, confident, radiating his priestly authority. The white cape was as impressive as always as it swung and fluttered in the motion of White Buffalo's medicine dance. Onlookers were spellbound with the beauty of the ceremony.

Three times, White Buffalo circled the arena, his steps quick and precise, while the People watched in fascination. At the finale, he stopped, facing the fire, while the drum fluttered to a climactic rumble. White Buffalo lifted his arms to heaven and chanted thanks for the bountiful hunt.

Then the old medicine man did a thing which had never been seen before by anyone present. As the medicine-drum fell silent, White Buffalo called to his apprentice.

"Small Elk, come!"

Surprised, Elk scrambled to his feet and approached his father.

"Let it be known," the old man announced to the assembly, "that the success of this hunt was due to the medicine of Small Elk."

There was a murmur of approval.

"He has learned well," White Buffalo continued. "His medicine, that of the buffalo, has become strong and sure. His time has come."

There was a gasp as White Buffalo loosened the thongs at his throat and removed the headdress. With a dramatic flourish, he swung the cape and headdress and allowed it to fall across Small Elk's head and shoulders.

"My son, I give you my name," he intoned solemnly. "You are no longer Small Elk, but White Buffalo, medicine man to the People."

Elk stood numbly, caught completely by surprise. In his ears echoed the shouts of approval from the crowd. He was dimly aware that his mother's medicine-drum was beginning the cadence again. He turned to look, and Crow Woman was seated beside her, joining with her own drum in the celebration of the rite of passing the authority. Crow smiled at him, and he wondered if she had known.

"Let us begin the dance," his father said. The weathered old face was serious, but there was a gleam of pride and triumph in the medicine man's eyes.

Small Elk, now White Buffalo the Younger, moved out in the steps of the White Buffalo ceremony. It was a time of mixed feelings. For years, he had worked and studied toward this night, and it had come as a surprise. Now, with the handing down of the name and the office, he was perhaps the most influential medicine man in the entire tribe. It was the greatest triumph of his life, and it was a bittersweet accomplishment. For to achieve this honor, it was necessary that his father step down. It was a little frightening. Always before, he could refer to the older man's knowledge and skill with any question or problem. It would still be possible, of course, but now, he, Small . . . no, White Buffalo, would be the final authority. There was a moment of panic as he wondered whether he really wanted this responsibility.

On around the circle he danced, now followed by his

father. Past the two most important women in his life, as they kept his cadence on the medicine-drums. The faces of Dove Woman and Crow beamed with pride.

He spotted his boyhood friend, Stone Breaker, who waved proudly. They had come a long way since the day of the Head Splitter attack, when the boy fell from the cliff. And Hump Ribs, the new chief of the band. The young leader nodded as he passed, and Elk nodded in return. He would go tomorrow to pay his respects. The two young men would be working together for many years, it was to be hoped, and they must understand each other.

Slowly, he began to realize that this was a turning point in the future of the Southern band, a changing of the generations. Stone Breaker had already assumed his place in the new way of things. Now, in one night, the People had not only accepted a new band chief but a new holy man.

It was a time of triumph and looking to the future, but a time of sadness also. Things would never again be the same for the Southern band. Tears of emotion formed in the eyes of the young White Buffalo. He felt one trickle down his cheek and hoped that it would not be too apparent a streak in his facepaint.

25

With the great success of the buffalo kill that fall came a change in the fortunes of the Southern band. Hump Ribs proved an able leader. By the time the band was ready to strike the lodges and move to winter camp, he had announced their destination. They would move almost directly south through the Tallgrass Hills, to camp on one of the clear streams in the region where the grassland meets the oaks. There the climate would be milder through the moons of winter. They could also camp among the scrub-oak thickets, which would cut the bite of Cold Maker's icy breath.

The new chief's confidence was a thing of wonder to some. It was as if he had been planning for most of his life what he would do if he ever became the band's leader. The transition was accomplished far more smoothly than anyone could have foreseen, and without offense to any as far as could be seen. Of course, it is difficult to find fault when one is comfortable, well provisioned, and full-bellied, as the Southern band was.

Hump Ribs guided his band by a route past a village of Growers. They had traded there before. It was a great pleasure to have plenty of meat, pemmican, and robes to trade. Though the Growers had suffered from the poor season, they had an adequate crop of pumpkins and some corn. The People spent a few days there and moved on toward the oaks country. Weather continued to favor them. This was considered a good omen, and the new leader's prestige increased.

Small Elk, now White Buffalo, had paid a courtesy call on the morning after the celebration. He offered his help to Hump Ribs and congratulations on his selection as chief.

Hump Ribs modestly stated that he would welcome the help of the new holy man.

"I am pleased for you, too, Elk . . . or White Buffalo. It was a good plan, yours of the hunt. The Moon of Hunger will not be so bad this year."

"I was fortunate," the other answered. "It could have gone badly."

"Ah, but it did not, my friend. Your medicine is good, and you are skillful with it. I welcome your help. You will tell me, if you have things I should know?"

"Of course."

They had not known each other well before but were already developing a mutual respect that would stand them in good stead in the years ahead.

The band did winter well. There were few problems and very little of the winter sickness that usually came with Cold Maker's onslaught. One exception was White Buffalo the Elder. After giving his name away, it seemed that he also gave away his ambition. He was not as he had been earlier, during the deadly drought. Then he had seemed to shrink from lack of hope. Now it was as if he had completed a task. He was pleased and satisfied, and ready to relax with the pleasantries of a nap in the sun, a smoke with friends, and play with his granddaughter. He gave his son advice when asked but offered very little otherwise.

"I fear for him," White Buffalo the Younger told his wife. "He has decided that his life is over."

"Maybe," Crow agreed, "but he seems happy. His thoughts are good."

The old man continued to seem at peace with his world and pleased to give his responsibilities to others. They did not notice further deterioration as they had in the summer, but in the Moon of Long Nights, White Buffalo the Elder died quietly in his sleep. His passing was mourned by the entire band, for his medicine had been good. His burial scaffold was placed in a thicket of scrub oak, his head to the east, and his feet toward the grassland to the west, where the buffalo would pass in their spring migration.

"His work was finished," Dove Woman said simply, after the period of mourning. "He knew it was time to cross over."

There were many who admired the old medicine man's

ability to do so. Not everyone is so fortunate as to choose the time of one's crossing.

When White Buffalo unrolled the story-skin to record the events of the year, he was surprised to find new pictographs already there. In his father's familiar style, hordes of buffalo poured over the cliff like a waterfall. Standing over them was the figure of a man clad in a calfskin, his arms raised to heaven. It was with something of a shock that he saw the identity mark, a white buffalo in a circle, connected to the figure. Tears came to his eyes. His father had realized the reluctance that young White Buffalo would have to depict himself in this, the first pictograph of his new office. The old man had done it for him, and in a very flattering way.

"What is it, my husband?" Crow Woman asked.

Wordlessly, he turned the skin to show her the picture. She smiled, then came to sit by him and leaned her shoulder against his.

"His gift to you," she said. "Your father knew that you would not paint such a picture of yourself."

Slowly, White Buffalo rerolled the skin, wrapped it, and tied the bundle. Once more, he realized how deeply perceptive his father had been. It was, somehow, like a message of comfort from the Other Side.

Dove Woman moved into the lodge of White Buffalo and Crow.

"I do not wish to be a burden," she told her son's wife. "This is your lodge."

"Remember, Mother, I lived in your lodge at first, and you helped me much. I am proud to have you here."

It was noted that Dove Woman and her husband had always been extremely devoted and close. She had been like a partner in her husband's medicine. From time to time, he had seemed to confer part of his gift on Dove Woman, and she had performed many of the routine ceremonials. She was held in high regard in her own right. Now she seemed to have no direction. She was quiet and smiling, at peace with the world though obviously lonely. Early in the Moon of Awakening, she crossed over to rejoin her husband.

All of these events served to mark the beginning of a new era for the Southern band of the People. Supplies had been more than sufficient for the winter, but the taste for dried meat, even pemmican, becomes jaded. There comes a craving for fresh meat, the flow of the life-giving juices that will nourish both body and soul.

There was another urge, less well defined. The wild geese still feel it today, the restless call that stirs in the subconscious, an instinct that tells them, "Go north . . . *now!*" The quiet echo of this primitive migration urge still sounds in the souls of men and women today. We may stand on a hill in the pale sun of late March or early April, and watch the long lines of geese high overhead. Their distant call seems to reach out in harmony with the human instinct, calling, tempting us to come, follow the trail of the geese to the north, to the unknown adventure and excitement of the new season.

It was so that year, in the Moon of Greening, when Hump Ribs and White Buffalo stood on the hilltop and watched the sky, dotted with the graceful figures of the great birds—moving, shifting in ever-changing patterns against the blue but always moving north.

"Are the signs good?" Hump Ribs asked.

"For the move? Any time now," the medicine man answered.

"Then we move. We are a people of the grasslands. We should greet the return of the sun and the grass in the prairie, not here in the brushland."

There was a sense of excitement in the air, a spirit of expectation, as the band broke winter camp to start north. The start was early, but Hump Ribs wished to leave the scrub-oak country and range out into the grassland in expectation of the buffalo herds. The move would also allow them to cover part of the distance to the site of the Sun Dance.

The Real-chief, Spotted Elk of the Northern band, had sent word that the Sun Dance would be held at Walnut Creek. That site had been selected but not used last season, in that terrible Year-of-No-Rain. The runner also said that the other bands had survived. Hardest hit was the Red Rocks band, which had suffered heavy losses from starvation in the Moon of Hunger. A number of the old members of that band had walked out into the teeth of a blizzard during the Moon of Snows. They had gone, singing the Death Song, as warriors into a hopeless battle. They fought

Cold Maker to the death for the lives of the children. In this way, there had been enough food, though just barely, to keep the Red Rocks alive until spring.

In the autumn, the Southern band had reported their good fortune in the hunt and the loss of their chief. Now, they sent word by Spotted Elk's runner that they had wintered well and were en route to the Sun Dance and Big Council.

"We will stop to hunt, of course," Hump Ribs explained, "but we will be partway there."

The messenger laughed.

"You like the shelter of the scrub oak, but you miss the tallgrass prairie."

"Of course," Hump Ribs agreed. "That is why we wintered there."

Their leisurely migration continued. Each day, White Buffalo went out to read the progress of the greening. Small sprigs of grass were beginning to sprout among the dead stems of last year's disastrously short growth. He realized that as they traveled, the greening was moving north with them and at almost the same rate. There was little difference in the height of the sprigs of real-grass now, compared to that at the start of their journey. They would be able to choose the area of the spring hunt, *then* burn the grass and await the herds.

One bright spring morning as the band traveled, White Buffalo went out with one of the "wolves" to look for his signs of the season. It was an area of rolling hills, and they were out of sight of the moving column. The medicine man was kneeling to examine more closely a plant that was unfamiliar to him when he heard a startled exclamation from Woodpecker. He straightened to see three well-armed strangers only a short bowshot away. Their dress, hairstyle, and weapons marked them as Head Splitters.

White Buffalo had no weapon except for a knife, and the scout, though appropriately armed, was badly outnumbered. Nervously, he fitted an arrow to his bowstring. The enemy warriors seemed suspicious but approached in a circling fashion that gave a hint where their main party might be.

"Shall we fight or run?" young Woodpecker asked.

"Neither," suggested White Buffalo. "These are their

wolves. They do not know where our party is, either. Let us talk to them."

He made the sign of peace, right hand upraised with palm forward. The strangers seemed to relax a trifle, and one made the same signal in answer. They came a few steps closer, weapons still ready.

"Who are you?" the one who seemed to be the leader signed.

"I am White Buffalo, medicine man of the People."

There was a hurried conversation among the Head Splitters. The power of a strange holy man was not to be trusted and might be dangerous, but the strangers apparently wondered if White Buffalo spoke truth.

"We do not believe you," one signaled. "A medicine man would not be so stupid to be alone and unarmed, with only that one for protection."

He pointed derisively at the sweating Woodpecker.

White Buffalo was thinking rapidly. Why not take advantage of the other's doubt? He laughed aloud.

"You are the stupid one," he signed, while Woodpecker gave a little gasp of despair. "My medicine is strong enough to protect us. Would I dare be here otherwise?"

There was another discussion.

"You lie!" the Head Splitter accused.

White Buffalo laughed again, hoping he did not sound as nervous as he felt. Slowly, he reached a hand into the medicine pouch at his waist.

"Shall I show you?" he asked.

"No! It will not be necessary," the other replied quickly.

White Buffalo withdrew his hand from the pouch, empty. Now there was a slight exclamation of surprise from Woodpecker. Over the rise behind the Head Splitters strode a determined-looking warrior, then another. A couple of dogs ranged around them, sniffing curiously at new smells. Then came two women, leading a large dog that was harnessed to a poledrag. Immediately behind them straggled other people, dogs, and children. It was the main party of a traveling Head Splitter band.

For some reason, the three enemy scouts seemed not to notice. They were staring, absorbed by something behind White Buffalo and Woodpecker. The medicine man glanced over his shoulder. There, over the other ridge, came the People.

Both groups stopped and waited, discussing the situation among themselves. White Buffalo was greatly relieved, and it was obviously even more so with Woodpecker. Now two men detached themselves from the People's group and made their way down the hill. White Buffalo recognized Hump Ribs and Short Bow, who had participated in many such meetings.

From the other hill came a large, heavy-set man with an equally large ax in his hand. His demeanor plainly marked him as the leader of this band. With him was a young man of wiry athletic build whose dark and shifty eyes caused more anxiety than the size of his leader. Here was an unpredictable, hence dangerous man.

Each of the approaching groups joined their own wolves and paused for formal conversation. The People's representatives were still outnumbered, but it was no matter now; there would be no fight. Both groups on the opposing hilltops included women and children, the families of the envoys below. It would be too dangerous to fight.

"Greetings," the big man signed. "How are you called?"

This would be a formal discussion, carried out under strict protocol.

"I am Hump Ribs, of the People," the young man answered. "And you?"

"Bull's Tail. How is it that I do not talk to your chief?"

The young man drew himself up proudly.

"You do so," he signed. "Broken Horn is dead, killed in our most successful hunt, last autumn."

Bull's Tail laughed derisively.

"You lie. No one hunted well last season. I should not talk to you. I know that one, though."

He pointed to Short Bow.

"Our chief speaks truth," Short Bow signed. "The buffalo kill was great."

The astonishment in the eyes of the Head Splitters was apparent. They must believe Short Bow who was known to them, but it was obvious that their own winter had not been good. White Buffalo now began to notice that their buckskins were tattered, dark with the smoke of many lodgefires. They had had a difficult year.

Apparently, Hump Ribs was noticing the same thing.

"We have plenty of supplies," he signed. "May we give you some?"

White Buffalo nearly laughed aloud. Of course the Head Splitters would refuse rather than admit their poverty. More importantly, however, it allowed Hump Ribs to establish himself as a successful leader in the minds of the enemy. It was a triumph of diplomacy. The enemy had been faced down.

"No, we have plenty," Bull's Tail signed, though the lie was obvious.

"It is good," agreed Hump Ribs calmly, apparently not noticing the discrepancy.

He will make a great leader, White Buffalo thought to himself with amusement. The young chief had not only handled himself well but had embarrassed an older, experienced adversary.

There was one, however, who was obviously displeased. The dark wiry young man with the shifty look glared in anger. That would be one to watch for in the future.

"How are you called?" White Buffalo signed to him.

The young man stared angrily for a moment. White Buffalo realized that the man was very young, younger than he by several seasons. He must be well respected to be chosen to accompany the chief. This in turn implied again that this was a dangerous man.

"I am Gray Wolf. Remember it. You will hear it again!"

26

At the Sun Dance that year, the entire tribe buzzed with excitement over the doings of the Southern band. Even before the Big Council, where each chief related the events of the year to the assembly, the rumors made their rounds. The story flickered through the big encampment with the speed of real-fire in a thunderstorm, and the excitement rose. There was a new young chief in the Southern band, a nobody who had risen after the death of Broken Horn. Under his leadership the band had prospered. His decisions had been good. In a confrontation with the Head Splitters on the trail to this very gathering, he had publicly humiliated old Bull's Tail, one of the enemy's capable leaders. That story had grown, of course. In some versions, young Hump Ribs had heaped supplies on the ground before the hungry Head Splitters, forcing Bull's Tail to refuse the gift to save face.

Most of this, it was said, was due to the powerful medicine of a new holy man of the Southern band. In a time of starvation and drought, he had caused rain to fall and an immense herd of buffalo to appear from a hole in the ground.

"But is White Buffalo not their holy man?" someone asked.

"Yes, of course. White Buffalo gave away his name to this, his son, and then crossed over. His wife too, the medicine woman Dove, also crossed over. *Aiee,* my friends, this man is good! He has the medicine of both parents. Did you hear of the event with the calfskin, when he drew the buffalo over the cliff's edge?"

"Only a little part. How did he escape, himself?"

The teller of the story paused a moment, unsure. His

listeners were so intent . . . it would be a shame to admit that he did not know.

"I have heard," he half whispered, "that he leapt into the air and *flew*, while the herd passed under him."

"*Aiee!* The holy man can *fly?*"

"Well, maybe not. But the calfskin cape . . . it would let him float a little while, you know, with the help of his medicine."

"But I have heard that the death of their chief, Broken Horn, was caused by the buffalo. Is this a doing of the new holy man?"

That was an obvious suspicion which caused ugly rumors for a day or two. Could the young chief and the holy man have plotted to kill Broken Horn and take control of the band?

This was quickly proved untrue by the members of the Southern band themselves. First, the death of Broken Horn had occurred *before* the young medicine man had taken his father's name and prestige. White Buffalo the Elder was still powerful at the time. Next, young Hump Ribs did not seize the leadership. He was persuaded, after older and more experienced men had refused. He had been nominated, in fact, by the respected subchief Short Bow, after refusing the honor for himself. The final argument: Cat Woman, widow of the greatly respected Broken Horn, strongly supported the young chief and the holy man.

All in all, the members of the Southern band, when such questions were raised, became quite indignant. It was apparent that they would tolerate no suspicion over the events of the season. The rumors dissolved like wisps of fog on a sunny morning and were gone. They were rapidly replaced by admiration and even envy for the band that had most successfully weathered the Year-of-No-Rain. The Southern band had never been a great political power in the tribal council. Now, however, even the Real-chief spoke with respect. The Big Council sought the opinion of Hump Ribs when the time came to choose the site for next year's Sun Dance. Suddenly it was a matter of prestige to belong to the Southern band.

When the tribes separated after the events of the annual festival, the Southern band had grown by perhaps ten families. Of course, some of these were not the most desirable of members. Some people were constantly changing loyalties, looking for the reflected glory belonging to the most affluent band. However, it was still of some advantage to the Southern band. Sheer weight of numbers tips the balance of prestige, and the other bands noticed the swing of loyalty and were envious.

It was a good season. The grass grew lush and tall; the children were fat and the women happy. There were no more encounters with the Head Splitters. Hunting was good, and the Southern band settled in for the winter, quite comfortable and secure.

In fact, when White Buffalo unrolled the story-skin to record the year's events, there were few worthy of mention. It was somewhat frustrating to consider that in this season, his first of recording the pictographs, there was little to record. He decided on a successful hunting scene in tall grass, depicting several hunters of note killing buffalo. Above these, and slightly larger, was a figure identified as Hump Ribs, presiding over the scene. He was not pleased with it, but Crow assured him that he had done well.

"It is a good problem to have," she joked, "a season so successful that there is no event unusual enough to note."

Good omens continued, and the Southern band prospered. It was a mild winter, with little illness and practically no hunger. It seemed that the existence of the band was charmed, governed by the powerful medicine of White Buffalo and led by the skill and diplomacy of Hump Ribs.

White Buffalo knew that it was false. Things were going too well, and someday it must end. He was concerned that when it happened, there would be much dissatisfaction, and the people would begin to blame Hump Ribs.

This also put White Buffalo in an untenable position. It would be difficult to overcome the complacency of the People, whose existence was basically day-to-day, hand-to-mouth, anyway. In his position as a prophet and seer, he should warn that change would come. The problem was, when? If he issued warnings of dire misfortune and nothing happened, he would lose face, the People would chuckle behind his back, and his effectiveness would be impaired. On the other hand, if he did not voice a warning, when trouble came, he would be blamed for lack of vision. He wished that his father were here, so that they could consult. He tried casting the bones, but that was little help. The patterns that had seemed so clear when his father was the holy man never quite materialized.

Crow Woman sensed his unrest.

"What is it, my husband?"

There was little that he could keep from her or would wish to. He shared his concerns, and she nodded understandingly.

"The question is, when?" he finished. *"When* shall I try to tell them?"

"How do you know when to announce the coming of the rains or the buffalo?" Crow asked.

"That is simple. A change in the wind, the other signs. But in this, there are no signs!"

"There must be signs, sometimes."

"Yes, Crow, but I do not know what to look for because there is no way to know what form the changing omens will take."

"Could you warn that there will be misfortune someday?"

"Maybe. But I should be able to support that with a sign, and I have none. The casting of the bones . . . *aiee,* maybe their power is gone, with my father's passing."

"No, surely not," Crow said. "Have you asked Grandfather Buffalo?"

"No. That would be wise," he agreed.

He fasted, went out alone, and achieved contact with his spirit-guide, but he felt that it was little help. There were more questions than answers.

You will know, he was advised, *when the time comes, how to proceed. You cannot foresee everything. It is a gamble.*

How odd, White Buffalo thought, waking from the vision. His guide had seemed almost flippant about it. The comment about gambling . . . that seemed completely inappropriate. He tried to reason it through. It was true, of course. When the medicine man observed the signs and predicted rain or announced the time to burn, he was sometimes wrong. It was a matter of close observation, an attempt to be right more often than wrong. The holy man's skill and the power of his medicine were judged not by whether he was correct *every* time but *most* of the time. But in this case, he should have something to go on. This time it was important that he be right. There had been no major pronouncement since the Great Hunt. None had been necessary. His prestige still depended on the memory of that event. Prestige had a habit of fading, like the daylight when Sun Boy slips beyond the edge of the earth. White Buffalo needed something to reinforce his position, to solidify prestige.

And he must predict correctly. *Aiee,* if there were only some way, when he cast the bones, that he could know how they would fall. A gamble . . .

He was walking through the village one day, late in the Red Moon. Plums were ripening along the streams, and the People were gathering the fruit to dry or to eat. This always resulted in a seasonal gambling fever, with the plum-stone game. He paused to watch a group of young men, rolling the plum-stones on the smooth flesh-side of a robe spread on the ground.

The man who held the stones shook them between his cupped palms and with a triumphant flourish, cast them on the flat surface. The seeds skittered and bounced, and came to rest. There was a shout of glee from the man who had cast them. Of the five plum-stones, three displayed a red dot. The player swept them up to cast again. Three more times he tossed before the stones betrayed him, and he passed to the next player.

White Buffalo stood, deep in thought. The plum-stone game was an old one, highly favored among the gamblers. Any odd number of stones would be used, usually five or seven. All would be painted with a red dot on the side. The gambler's win or loss depended on whether there were more of the red dots exposed when the stones came to rest or the plain yellow of the natural stone.

What had caught White Buffalo's attention as he watched the game was one particular plum-stone. He could identify it at each throw because it was slightly larger than the others. It was considered best to have complete uniformity, of course, but sometimes a little variation occurred. The peculiar thing about this plum-stone was not its size but that it almost never came to rest with the red dot facing upward. He watched, fascinated. Apparently this plum-stone was flattened slightly on the one side,

which affected its tumbling motion. The players seemed
not to notice. They would probably lose these stones or
throw them away before the next game anyway. White
Buffalo watched a little longer to verify his impression,
then slipped away. His heart was good because he might
have found an answer.

For several days, well away from the camp, he studied
hundreds of plum-stones. Thousands of times he tossed his
selected specimens across a skin—choosing, discarding, se-
lecting again. The stones must have an asymmetry, flattened on one side but not enough to be noticeable. Yet he
must be certain that they would behave in a predictable
way most of the time. Finally, he selected nine plum-
stones which fit the requirements. It remained only to
paint them. Not red . . . that was too familiar to the gamblers. Black. Yes, that would do. And for this purpose, black
should be the favored side. Carefully he painted not just a
dot but one entire side of each plum-stone. He could
hardly wait for the pigment to dry, so that he could test his
theory.

Finally, he was able to toss the stones. On the first throw,
seven were black, two yellow. The second resulted in six
and three; the third, eight and one. White Buffalo was
delighted. Many times he cast the black stones, and only
once did they show more yellow than black, five to four.
That was no problem. The ceremony of Black Stones
which he intended could be based upon three throws.
Now he had his predictable ceremony. A thought occurred
to him. Could it be that the assortment of sticks and bones
he had inherited from his father was such a thing? No,
surely not. His father would have told him. But this new
ceremony . . . it must be used very seldom and very cautiously. It would be easy to misuse. Maybe, when the time
came to pass on his medicine to another, he would destroy
the black stones instead. He wondered for a moment who
that successor might be.

Now his task was to decide when to use his new skill, and
how. When the time came to move, perhaps. He conferred
with Hump Ribs, though he did not mention the black
stones.

When the chief announced the day of the move, White
Buffalo also announced his ceremony of prediction. It
would be held that evening, after dark. The flicker of fire-

light would make it more difficult to see the skittering plum-stones and determine how the thing was accomplished.

There was much interest. The ceremony began with a dance. Crow Woman, who knew only that it was a new ceremony, beat the cadence while her husband established the mystic mood with the dance. When the time came to cast the Black Stones, White Buffalo explained that three tosses were required. The stones would tell of good or ill, depending on the showing of dark or sunny sides of the plum-stones. Palms sweating, he rolled the first toss from a painted rawhide box that he had crafted for the purpose. There on the skin, plain for the onlookers to see, were seven black and two yellow stones. There was a gasp from the crowd. The next throw resulted in a score of eight and one; the third, in nine black stones.

Even White Buffalo was startled. He made a very formal ritual of gathering the plum-stones and storing them away in the little box. Then he spoke.

"There is danger on our trail," he predicted. "I cannot say what form it will take, but we must be ready when it comes. We have been blessed with good omens for many moons, but sometime it must end."

"When, holy man?" an old woman asked.

"Ah, Mother, I cannot tell that," White Buffalo answered seriously. "Even the Black Stones do not say."

27

Stone Breaker bent over the vein of blue-gray flint, pounding and prying at the block of material he wanted. It was loose, shifting a little with each pry of the stick but still not breaking free. It was much like picking the nut meat from a cracked shell, he thought to himself. Yes, the fragrant oily meat of the walnut was equally reluctant to come free. It must be teased out painstakingly with a sharp wooden awl. Some of the old women were highly skilled at such things. It had been good, in the time of No-Rain, to have such skills for survival.

The young man sitting near him gave a long sigh. Stone Breaker had taken a journey ahead of the band as they traveled, to secure some flint blocks. By moving a day ahead of the slower column, he would have an extra day to quarry the stone. The rest of the band would overtake him sometime today. One of the young warriors had agreed to accompany him for protection. He could also undertake any of the tasks that were difficult because of Stone Breaker's handicap. The young man, Turtle-Swims, had no particular interest in Stone Breaker's craft. This was only an opportunity to escape the boredom of the slow-moving band. Turtle had found the quarrying operation equally boring. He sat near the skin carriers on which were piled chunks and flakes of flint while Stone Breaker continued to work.

Stone Breaker was aware of his companion's disinterest, of course. His purpose was not to create an interest in the craft. Idly, he wondered if someday he should select a likely successor, as Stone Breaker the Elder had done. Ah, that should be a long time off. Maybe their child, now six winters old, would develop an interest. If not, so be it!

He was aroused from his thoughts by an exclamation of surprise from Turtle-Swims. Stone Breaker looked up to see three men standing on the canyon's opposite rim. They were scarcely twenty steps away, had the ground been level. But between them was a rough and rocky cleft of the little canyon's upper end. A man could, with no problem, walk down one rocky slope and up the other to the spot where Stone Breaker now worked in the quarry.

The situation looked desperate. These men were obviously Head Splitters, obviously confident. Their main force must be just behind the ridge.

Turtle had been negligent, Stone Breaker realized. It was his function to protect. Turtle should have been acting as a lookout instead of sitting in the canyon, bored with inactivity. He had depended too much on the approach of the rest of the band.

Now, as if to compensate for the mistake, Turtle-Swims leaped to his feet and started to fit an arrow to his bow. He was still looking down at the bowstring, fumbling to adjust the arrow, when he was struck from above. Stone Breaker heard the soft thud and turned his eyes from the Head Splitters back to his companion. Turtle looked upward for a moment toward the warriors above, a startled expression on his face. Then his knees bent, and his body collapsed limply, his hands still clutching the bow as he fell. Stone Breaker saw the feathered end of an arrowshaft sticking from Turtle's shoulder, near the neck. Horrified, Stone Breaker followed the estimated course of the shaft with his eyes and saw the head protruding half a handspan through Turtle's back on the other side.

He looked up in terror. The Head Splitters were chuckling. One was fitting a new arrow to his bow. Now the man raised his head to voice the yipping falsetto war cry that had struck such terror in the children so long ago. Stone Breaker felt for a moment that he was once again a helpless child, waiting for the death-dealing blow of the Head Splitter's arrow. He held up a hand in the sign for peace, and the others laughed.

"You, Lame One, what are you doing?" one signed.

"Digging flint," Stone Breaker signed back. "I do no harm!"

The Head Splitter, whom Stone Breaker now recognized as the evil-looking warrior they had seen last season, now laughed. What was he called? Ah, yes, Gray Wolf.

"*That* one does no harm!" announced Gray Wolf, pointing to the still body of Turtle-Swims. "*I* will decide who does harm."

Stone Breaker had given himself up for dead. The three men started across the gully, picking their way among the rocks. They paid little attention to Stone Breaker. What harm could he do? With a twist of the old hurt, he realized that he could not even run or try to escape. The enemy regarded him as harmless, a nothing. It was a long time since Stone Breaker had experienced bitterness over becoming a cripple, but now it returned. Along with it came the helpless feeling that he remembered from childhood, when he lay in the mud with the crippled leg under him, waiting for the Head Splitter to shoot.

Then his brain began to work again. These men were not a war party. There would be more of them. They must be wolves of a larger group of Head Splitters. Wolves of a war party? No, he thought not. Such scouts would not travel in threes, but singly, not openly like this. The other possibility that occurred to him was that these men were the advance unit, the wolves, of an entire band, traveling as the People were. If so, their families were vulnerable. Maybe he could plant that seed of anxiety, play for time. Possibly, he could even postpone the inevitable until the People arrived.

The Head Splitters approached now. Gray Wolf, who assumed the role of leader, walked up and slapped Stone Breaker across the face. Stone Breaker attempted not to show a reaction. This was a ritual, a counting of honors. It was a greater show of bravery to strike and thus insult a live enemy than to kill one. An idea struck Stone Breaker.

"You are a brave man," he signed, "to count honors on an unarmed cripple." He turned to the others. "Is he as brave with women and children?"

The other warriors laughed, and Gray Wolf's face was livid with rage. Stone Breaker thought for a moment that he had gone too far. However, his bold insult might have saved him. Now, if Gray Wolf harmed the prisoner, he would face the ridicule of his companions, who would also carry the story back to the tribe. In these few moments, Stone Breaker realized, he had achieved the upper hand.

Gray Wolf was now on the defensive. He must save face with his companions. The danger would be that the Head Splitter's fiery temper would flare into a destructive act. Stone Breaker must continue conversation, keep the man distracted.

"How are you called?" he asked. "Gray Wolf?"

"Yes," the other signed. "Remember it."

"You are the chief?" Stone Breaker signed innocently.

"The war chief," Gray Wolf answered.

"Ah, yes. Your chief, what is his name . . . Bull's Tail?" He had managed to remember.

"Bull's Tail was killed last season," signed one of the others. "He gave his name to his son, but that one is a child. White Bear is chief."

Stone Breaker had been thinking quickly, ". . . killed last season . . ." It must have been an accident in the fall hunt. He could take a guess, and . . .

"Bull's Tail was killed by a buffalo?" he inquired casually.

"How did you know?" came the astonished rejoinder.

Stone Breaker shrugged.

"Our buffalo medicine is strong," he signed. "Our new holy man has great skill."

An expression of wonder and doubt came over the faces of the Head Splitters. Then Gray Wolf reacted suddenly.

"Enough of this! That is nothing to me. Now, Lame One, is there any reason I should not kill you?"

Stone Breaker swallowed hard and tried to maintain his dignity. He hoped his captors would not notice his sweating palms and his near-panic.

"You wish to take the risk?" he asked in signtalk.

Gray Wolf reached for the stone war club at his waist. His swing had actually started when one of the others stepped in to seize his arm and stop the blow.

An argument broke out among the Head Splitters. Stone Breaker could not understand a word of their language, but the content was obvious. The others objected to killing the prisoner because of his boast about the People's medicine man. It was too great a risk. Gray Wolf was angry and destructive, and was arguing his right to kill the prisoner.

Stone Breaker edged away, out of the reach of the wildly swinging weapon. As he turned, he caught a glimpse of motion above him. He looked up and was astonished to see, on the rocky ledge overhead, the figures of Hump

Ribs, White Buffalo, Short Bow, and several others. The warriors were looking down on the squabbling Head Splitters, and Short Bow appeared ready to shoot if there was danger to Stone Breaker.

"*Ah-koh*, my friends! It is good to see you!" Stone Breaker said as calmly as he could.

His captors stopped squabbling and looked up. They had no way to escape, no place to run.

"Go ahead, kill us!" one of the Head Splitters signed arrogantly.

Another began to chant a mournful wail that was apparently their tribe's version of the Death Song.

Short Bow readied an arrow.

"Wait!" said Stone Breaker. "It is better to let them go."

"Let them go?" Short Bow was indignant.

Quickly, Stone Breaker explained his dialogue with the enemy. He had, without much thought, planted the seeds of doubt in the Head Splitters' minds. He had boasted of the medicine of White Buffalo, its strength and help to the People.

"If we let them go, they will carry this story to their tribe, and they will fear us," he explained. "Besides, I think their band is near."

"Yes," agreed White Buffalo. "We see them, over there. The People are near too."

"But they have killed Turtle, here," Short Bow protested. "Let us kill two and let one escape with the story."

"No, let them live," Hump Ribs interrupted. "But let us count honors first. There is time."

The young chief walked around and down into the gully. Solemnly and with dignity, he slapped Gray Wolf across the cheek, then repeated the gesture with each of the others. Gray Wolf looked as if, at any moment, he might burst into a mad suicidal rage, but he managed to keep his dignity.

One by one, the other warriors walked past and counted honors as the Head Splitters stood stoically.

"Go now," Hump Ribs signed. "No, leave your weapons."

The other warriors started up the canyon slope, but Gray Wolf held back a moment. He looked from one to the other of his captors with a dark, malevolent stare. It was as if he wished to fix in his mind the men who had shamed him, for future vengeance. The approach of the People could be heard now, the busy hum of conversation, the yipping of a dog, and the cries of children at play as they traveled.

Gray Wolf climbed the rocky slope and stood on the gully's rim to look back.

"You have made a great mistake," he signed insolently.

"You made the mistake," Hump Ribs answered. "You should not have killed our brother here."

He pointed to the still form of Turtle-Swims.

"No," Gray Wolf answered. "You should have killed *me*. You will mourn over that mistake."

With one final obscene gesture, he turned and was gone.

There were those who said that the medicine of the People was still strong. In an encounter with the Head Splitters, only one man had been lost. In addition, they had counted honors on the enemy and shamed him.

But some were uneasy. Among them at first was Short Bow, who favored genocide for Head Splitters when possible. Hump Ribs, White Buffalo, and Stone Breaker were uncomfortable with the results of the encounter but could not decide what would have been a better path of action.

Much later, it was agreed that this marked the turning point toward a period when good things did not happen to the People. Many times White Buffalo would remember the bitter remark of Short Bow at the camp that evening.

"That Head Splitter Gray Wolf was right."

"How do you mean, Uncle?" Hump Ribs asked.

The old warrior shrugged simply, as if the answer were apparent.

"We should have killed him."

» » »

28

It was not that there was so very much *bad* luck. The hunting was adequate. The winter was, if not mild, at least tolerable. But there seemed an absence of anything especially good. Maybe, after the extremes of the Year-of-No-Rain, followed by the great buffalo kill, an average year or two, either moderately good or bad, seemed uneventful.

But no, that was not the case. Beginning with the death of Turtle-Swims, things did seem to change. There were those who said that perhaps Turtle had caused it, that he had done something to displease the spirits. Stone Breaker, the only one of the People present at the young man's death, was certain that that was not it. Turtle-Swims had been careless and had lost his life as a result.

There were other things, however. A young couple, meeting outside the camp that summer for a romantic interlude, were standing under a giant cottonwood when it was struck by a spear of real-fire, the boom of Rain Maker's thunder-drum, and a spatter of rain. Then the storm was gone, leaving the two dead and their families to mourn.

An old woman was bitten by her own dog, which had been acting irrationally for a day or two. The dog was killed by her husband, but not before the woman became ill did the event take on ominous proportions. Then it was remembered that a smell-cat had walked boldly into the village about half a moon ago. It had been a source of much amusement, and the dogs had killed the animal. This dog, it was now remembered, had been scratched or bitten.

White Buffalo did his best with chants, ceremonies, and herbs, but he knew that it was useless. The old woman went mad, as her dog had done, and died in agony, convulsing and frothing at the mouth. There was no recovery from the Fears-Water Madness.

Hump Ribs announced a move, which was good. The madness might be restricted to this area. Meanwhile, children were instructed to avoid any animals, dogs or wild animals, which seemed to behave strangely. There were no more cases of the madness.

All of these things seemed to increase the prestige of the young medicine man. Had not White Buffalo foreseen these evils? He was, the People said, probably the most skillful of all holy men; his medicine was strong and his visions accurate.

White Buffalo saw all of this with misgivings. True, he had predicted evil things with the black stones, but now a gnawing doubt assailed him. He would dream at night of the skittering plum stones, dancing on the surface of the spread skin and coming up black, relentlessly, time after time. He would wake with a start and find it difficult to fall asleep again. The doubts grew larger. Could it be that his manipulation of the answer he sought in the stones was improper? Was it evil to try to *cause* a certain result as he had done? He considered burning the black stones, but could not bring himself to do so. He was afraid to use them again, so they remained in his medicine pouch. He confided in Crow Woman.

"You mean, you *caused* the plum-stones to behave that way?"

Her eyes were wide with amazement.

"Well, yes, in a way," he admitted. "I chose stones that would do that."

"That would all come up black?"

"Yes, they will most of the time. I painted them that way."

Crow Woman rocked with laughter.

"*Aiee*, my husband, you are clever. May I see them do it?"

"I . . . I think not, Crow. I have thought of burning them. Maybe they are evil. I am a little bit afraid of them."

"Afraid? I do not understand."

He was not certain that he could explain it, this question in his mind that he might be abusing his gift. He sighed deeply.

"Do you think, Crow, that I have *caused* these misfortunes with the Black Stones?"

"I think not, my husband," Crow answered thoughtfully. "They would only predict."

"Maybe I should have painted them the other way," he mused. "Make the yellow sides come up more often."

Crow thought a little while.

"No, that would not work. It would predict only good things, and bad things *do* happen. You wanted to tell the People that, and you did. They trust you more than ever."

"But if I had not cast the black stones, would the lovers have been struck by real-fire? Or old Bird Woman have gone mad?"

Crow put her arm around him.

"What did you wish to tell them, my husband?" She went on, without waiting for an answer. "That there will always be evil times ahead, that the good times we were having must not be expected to last. You have done that, done it well. They understand. Do you see bitterness? No. Mourning for the dead, but respect for your skill."

"Then you think I should not burn the plum-stones?"

Crow Woman laughed.

"Of course not! *Aiee,* it was clever, Elk."

She called him that, sometimes, when they were alone. It was a pet name, the name from their childhood.

"But it may not be wise, to try to control such things," he protested.

"You said you do not control them," she observed. "It is only that you know more about what they will do. Is that not also true of the grass, the storms, the buffalo? You do not question that knowledge."

"That is true," he agreed reluctantly.

"Then, your use of such things is not wrong. It is one part of your knowledge, your skill as a holy man."

Somehow, he always felt better after he had talked to Crow Woman.

It was that fall when a young hunter came running into camp, bleeding from a dozen minor wounds. His left ear was gone, and blood still gushed from the side of his head. He was almost hysterical as he related a horrifying story.

He and three others had been hunting, some distance from the village, when they were attacked by Head Splitters, some nine or ten in number. White Owl had been killed instantly in the first onslaught, struck down by an arrow. Red Dog had watched while the others, one at a time, were tortured, mutilated, and finally killed after many honors were counted. Then the skull of each had been crushed with a stone club, *after* their deaths. It appeared that this blow was symbolic, solely to identify this as the work of the Head Splitters.

Red Dog had cringed in terror when they approached him. He had expected the same torture and ignoble death, emasculated and mutilated. Instead, they had all counted honors, slapping him and pricking his skin with knifepoints. Then they freed his hands. As an afterthought, the Head Splitter who appeared to be the leader suddenly stepped forward and with a single sweeping motion, had slashed Red Dog's left ear from his head.

"The rest of your carcass belongs to me," the Head Splitter signed, as he waved the severed ear before his quaking prisoner's face. "Now, go!"

He struck the youth across the face again and pushed him to the ground. As Red Dog rose to his feet to run, his captor signed once more.

"Tell your people that Gray Wolf does not forget."

Red Dog finished his story and cried unashamedly, comforted by his family and friends.

Hump Ribs called an immediate council. There was much anger and not a little fear. It was apparent that this had been a war party, specifically for this purpose. The general area of the Head Splitter camp was known; it was three sleeps away. Thus, this could not be a hunting party, far from home. It appeared to be a vengeance raid by the young subchief Gray Wolf. They had marked him as a dangerous man before.

"He seeks vengeance for his loss of dignity at the flint quarry," White Buffalo suggested.

"But what of their principal chief, the one they called White Bear?" asked Stone Breaker. "Does he not keep the young men from such things? This is not usual, even for Head Splitters."

"*Aiee,* but sometimes the young do not listen," said an old man on the other side of the fire. "This is a bad one."

"We should have killed him when we had the chance," Short Bow offered.

There were murmurs and nods of agreement.

"That is behind us," Hump Ribs reminded them. "We cannot go back and do it now. But we must decide. What *will* we do?"

Some in the council favored immediate pursuit and reprisal. Calmer heads suggested that it was too risky. It was not known how many were actually involved in the enemy raiding party. Red Dog had seen nine, "maybe ten," but were there others nearby? Maybe this was only a small portion of the party, and the whole event a trap to entice the People out onto the prairie for ambush. It was a sobering thought. The few hotheads who argued for immediate retribution were quickly argued down. Besides, it was pointed out, to go out with a large war party would leave the village poorly defended. Maybe *that* was the Head Splitter plan, to attack undefended women and children while the men were gone.

"It is enough!" Hump Ribs announced finally. "We need to find a winter camp anyway. We move, in three days. We will go southeast, away from Head Splitter country."

There were a few voices of dissent, but not many. Hump Ribs's decision could be rejected by a vote, but it was apparent to most that the plan was a good one. Preparations began for departure.

The weather was uncommonly fine, with bright warm days and cool nights. It was the time of the Second Summer. They traveled into territory that was somewhat unfamiliar. There were fewer large expanses of grass and more trees. In some places, great groves of nut trees were prominent and oaks unfamiliar to the People. The world seemed brilliant as they traveled. The familiar clumps of scarlet sumac shone against the muted yellow-orange of the grasses. Large trees not familiar to the People produced a blaze of flaming red. It seemed that the whole world was aflame with beauty. Some became uneasy at the unfamiliarity of the terrain.

"We are people of the prairie," White Buffalo heard someone say. "We must not forget our beginnings."

"But the Eastern band camps in wooded areas," another responded. "It is good for them."

"*Aiee,* the Eastern band!" the first man responded. "Are we to become as *they* are?"

Everyone laughed.

"I wonder," observed a young woman, "if there might be worse enemies in the woodlands than Head Splitters."

"There *are* no worse enemies than Head Splitters," an older woman answered. She had just finished the mourning period for a favorite grandson.

That evening Hump Ribs sought out White Buffalo.

"Tell me," he asked, "what you can of this matter, my friend. Is there danger here?"

"There is danger anywhere," White Buffalo observed. "But here, I do not know. I have never been this far south and east."

"It is beautiful country," the chief observed. "I have never seen such colors in the trees. Yet I am made to feel that it is not for us. Can you seek a vision?"

"You know that some are uneasy over this?" White Buffalo asked.

"Yes. That is why I seek the help of a holy man."

"I could cast the bones."

"Good. A public ceremony?"

"No, I think not. Come to my lodge."

Shortly after dark, Hump Ribs came to the lodge of White Buffalo and Crow Woman. Even such a private ceremony was very formal, and White Buffalo began with a chanted prayer. He burned a handful of powdered plant material on the fire, filling the lodge with aromatic smoke. Then he drew out the container of small bones, wooden fetishes, and stones, and tossed them across the surface of the spread skin with a dramatic flourish.

"You do not use the black stones?" asked Hump Ribs.

"No, they are for another purpose," answered the medicine man.

Not even the chief, who was also his close friend, would share the full story of the Black Stones. He was absorbed in studying the scatter of small objects, and the position in which they had come to rest.

"There are good signs and bad," White Buffalo announced. "Nothing unusual. It is like all other things— light and dark, hot and cold."

"But what does it mean to us? Is it safe here for the winter camp?"

"No place is ever free of some danger, my friend. But I am made to think that we should seek a place to winter where there is some grassland, some woodland, some open prairie, and some woods, much like last season. And, as I said, I see both some good and some bad for the People."

Hump Ribs nodded, understandingly.

"It has always been so. Then tomorrow we stay here while the wolves search for a winter camp. So be it."

29

Despite the misgivings of some, the winter proved un eventful. There were some indications that other tribes shared the area, and this caused a certain uneasiness. A trace of smoke on the distant horizon, a footprint in the damp earth at a spring or stream, gave constant cause for concern. Constant vigil was maintained, except for the hardest part of the Moon of Snows. Then everyone huddled over the fires in the lodges and seldom went out. It was a mild winter, however. White Buffalo was unsure whether it was due to the different locale or simply a milder season than most. Maybe both.

Overall, though, it was apparent that the People were uneasy here. There was an unrest, a sense of not belonging. White Buffalo pondered at length about this feeling. Once again, the idea that the People are people of the open plain, the grassland, was a constant thought—in simplest form, *this is not our home.* He wondered how long it would take to become one with the land. The People considered the rolling Tallgrass Hills, the Sacred Hills, the source of their strength, the nourishment of their spirits. Yet they had not always lived there. The old legends told of their migration from the northeast, long ago. How long no one knew, but many generations. Surely, the People who first came to the Tallgrass Hills did not feel that land to be their source of life. How long had it taken? A generation? Two? Even three or more, maybe.

There was another possibility, of course, that came to White Buffalo as he considered. He knew the feel of strength, power, and spiritual uplift that came to him sometimes when he greeted the rising sun over the hills. Or when the moon was full, covering the grassland with its soft silver-blue light. At such times there was a feel of spiritual power, a Something, mystical and wonderful. It seemed to come from the earth and the sky, to be everywhere.

Maybe, White Buffalo thought, the People had been wandering since Creation, searching for this place of the spirit. When they found it, they stopped, realizing that their search was ended. From that time on, they had wandered only within the grassland areas that they had made their own. The spirit of the prairie had nourished the People ever since, and would forever. At least, he felt, if he had been with the first of the People to set foot in the Sacred Hills, *he* would have known.

As the Moon of Awakening came, everyone became more restless. White Buffalo recognized the symptom and approached Hump Ribs.

"*Ah-koh,*" said the chief. "Sun Boy renews his torch!"

"Yes. Its warmth is good," agreed White Buffalo.

They sat down to smoke in front of the chief's lodge. It was the first time that a social smoke outside the dwellings had been possible that season. White Buffalo looked at the swelling buds on a tree nearby.

"You wish to speak of moving?" asked Hump Ribs.

White Buffalo was a bit startled. Maybe he should not have been, he realized. Hump Ribs had shown remarkable perceptiveness as a leader. From a quiet, likable young man, in a very short time he had become a quiet, thoughtful leader. He anticipated well, and his judgement was good. The chief had already realized the concern of the holy man.

"Yes," White Buffalo said simply.

Hump Ribs nodded.

"The prairie will soon be greening," he noted. "We should be where our roots are. It has been a good winter, here in a strange land, but I am made to think it is time to go home."

It was a long speech for the soft-spoken Hump Ribs, but there remained little to be said. The announcement was made that day.

There were some, of course, who complained. It was always so, the wailing that there was no way that the People could be ready to move on three days' notice. As usual, the complaints were ignored, and those who complained were busy like everyone else, preparing to strike the lodges at the appointed time. It was merely part of the adjustment to the change. Maybe there was even less complaint this time, because there was a strong feeling that the People did not belong here, among wooded hills and strange plants—strange spirits, even. The feeling was even stronger when the wolves reported that they were being observed. Yes, the timing was good.

The travelers were observed from a distance for several sleeps, and a constant watch was maintained against possible attack, but none came. One morning the scouts reported no trace of those who had followed them. This resulted in one more day of extra caution. It might be a trick, to catch the travelers off-guard. Still nothing happened, and everyone began to relax.

The mood was cheerful and optimistic. The People were going home to an area they understood, one which gave them life. It was ironic, then, that the sickness began to appear. At first, it seemed only the usual cough and congestion of the springtime, though more severe. An old woman succumbed first, after coughing greenish phlegm flecked with blood for a few days. Then it was noticed that many children were ill and that they were recovering very slowly. Usually the illness of the small ones was rapid in onset but with equally rapid recovery. This time it was more prolonged.

"We must stop here," White Buffalo advised.

Hump Ribs agreed. During the days of travel, it was not usual to set up the lodges for each night's stay. Families slept in the open, and only in inclement weather did they build a temporary shelter. This was different. The lodges were needed for treatment. By closing the door and smokeflaps and sprinkling water on heated cooking stones, a sweatlodge was created. The steam filled the interior and soothed the tortured lungs of the afflicted.

White Buffalo was active day and night, performing his chants and prayers, moving from one dwelling to another, sprinkling his powdered plant materials over the heated stones in the lodges. This produced aromatic steam to liquefy the cloying congestion of sodden lungs.

It was a demanding, exhausting torture. There was even a time when White Buffalo wondered why he had ever consented to the responsibility of being a holy man. He had not eaten or slept for two days, except in short snatches. Finally, a time came when no one was pleading for his immediate attention, and he made his way to his own lodge, almost staggering from exhaustion.

As he approached, he noted that the doorskin was tightly closed, the smoke flaps too. *Aiee!* He hurried forward, calling out to Crow Woman. Her face was drawn with worry and lack of sleep as she held the skin aside for him to enter. She did not need to tell him.

"It is White Moon."

The child lay on a pallet of robes near the firepit, breathing heavily. A quick glance at the labored respiration, the sucking in of the small belly in a frantic effort to breathe, the anxious look of distress on the little face, made his heart sink. He had seen no child as sick as this, their own.

"I have kept the steam," Crow said, "and used the plants as you have taught me."

Mechanically, White Buffalo reached for his rattles and began the prayer-chant. Moon's eyes opened and focused in silent recognition. She smiled a wan little smile and closed her eyes again. All through the night they huddled together over her, hoping that the combined strength of their spirits would reach out to hers. For a time she seemed to improve a little, rousing enough to sip a mouthful of soup from a horn spoon. But this seemed to exhaust her. She sank back, unresponsive. Dawn was just breaking when she gave one last little sigh and was gone.

"She has crossed over," said Crow Woman simply, tears streaming down her face.

She gave a final caress to the now peaceful face, and began the wailing chant of the Song of Mourning.

When the People moved on, there were seven burial scaffolds in the trees where the sick-camp had been. Four were small scaffolds to accommodate the small bodies of children. The other three victims had been elderly, people of many winters whose bodies were simply tired of fighting.

Very few families had escaped the sickness entirely. The wife of Hump Ribs himself had been quite ill, having contracted the fever after caring for her own children. Slowly, she recovered. All of the children of Stone Breaker and Cattail had been ill, but they too had finally overcome the malady. Some of the People suffered for nearly a moon, and many had still not regained full strength when they moved on.

Everyone was loud in praise of White Buffalo's expertise in the emergency. His medicine had been strong, people reminded each other. He had predicted something of this sort, the bad luck. When it happened, he had been tireless in his efforts. Many gave his medicine credit for the recovery of their children, and his popularity and prestige soared. It was too bad, people told each other, about the holy man's own child. Her survival was not meant to be.

White Buffalo entered a period of deep depression. To him, it made little difference that he was held in high regard by the People. He felt that he was a failure. He had been unable to help his small daughter, their only child, who had been the joy of their lives, his and Crow's.

After the period of mourning, Crow Woman had seemed to recover and return to some sense of normality. She tried to comfort her husband, but his grief seemed unreachable. At one point, she tried to console him and was met with angry accusations that *she* did not feel the loss as he did. Wisely, she withdrew.

White Buffalo was nearly destroyed by his grief but also by guilt. He should have been able to do *something*, he thought. If not, what was the use of anything, of his entire profession and skill? He tried, through long and sleepless nights, to discover his exact source of error. Surely, he was being punished for some oversight or some misdeed. Could it be his neglect of some part of the ceremonial ritual? Or was it wrong that he had helped Hump Ribs with the decision to go to the new area? No, the family of Hump Ribs had survived. Yet . . . once more, the doubt over his creation of the Black Stones ceremony gnawed at his guilt-tormented mind. He felt useless and wondered if he might even be going mad. Usually he consulted Crow Woman with his problems, but with this he could not. Part of his guilt involved her. He had betrayed her, he felt, by not having the skill to save their only child. He was unable to approach her to share their grief together.

He must do something or go mad. He approached Crow Woman one evening after a period of absence when he had left the other travelers for an afternoon.

"Crow, I need to go away for a little while."

There was hurt in her eyes.

"I am sorry, my husband. How long?"

"A few days. I will catch up with the band, but I must be alone a little while."

"It is good. I will pack you some food."

"*Good?*" he blurted.

"Yes, my husband. Your heart is troubled. This will help you find peace."

She was already busy gathering dried meat and berry pemmican and placing it in a small rawhide pack.

"I may fast," he said.

"Then you will need this when your fast is over."

When White Buffalo rejoined the band a few days later, he said little about his quest. One does not ask about such private things, but it was apparent that whatever had happened, he had found himself. The People rejoiced for him.

With his wife, he was attentive, almost apologetic. Crow Woman assumed that he had talked to his spirit-guide, though he never said. There was a renewed interest, an inquiring quality about him, and he seemed older, more mature, with even more dignity than before. He was kinder, more thoughtful.

There was one other thing. From that time on, for the rest of his life, White Buffalo's hair was nearly as white as the sacred cape.

30

Suddenly, it seemed, they were old. White Buffalo, after the loss of their only child, had gone through a long period of mourning. For a while Crow had feared for his sanity, but finally he seemed to recover.

For many years they continued to hope for another child, but there was none. It was difficult to share the joy of Stone Breaker and Cattail at the progress of *their* children. Crow Woman never conceived again, and it was only gradually that she and White Buffalo began to realize that it was not to be. Nothing was said between them, but there was an understanding. Each knew that the other knew also, that the chances were ever more remote through the years. Finally, the hope was gone, and both settled in the knowledge that they would never again know the joy of a small child in their lodge.

The seasons passed, and the pictographs on the story-skins, painted each winter by White Buffalo, kept the record of the People. White Buffalo threw himself into the duties of his priestly calling, and his reputation grew. His influence and that of Hump Ribs, an able chief, gave the Southern band prestige among the people, and the band grew also. They migrated with the geese and more importantly, with the buffalo. Hump Ribs chose their wintering places well, and each summer they met the rest of the tribe for the Sun Dance and the Big Council.

There were losses in the band. One by one, the parents of the new generation crossed over. The parents of Crow Woman were gone and others of their contemporaries. Short Bow, who had seemed stolid and immortal to White Buffalo and Crow as children, grew bent and crippled by the aching-bones ailment, and finally he could no longer hunt. He lost the will to live and crossed over that winter, leaving two wives and a child of ten winters, a boy belonging to the younger wife.

This began a time when there was no clear warrior leadership in the band. The skill of Hump Ribs was in the area of diplomacy and in planning the seasonal moves. But no warrior rose up to lead the hunts or to lead the defense against the Head Splitters as Short Bow had done. The Southern band receded in numbers again.

They continued to encounter that dreaded enemy. There were few episodes of open warfare, but the enemy subchief Gray Wolf was a constant threat. At their chance meetings, he was boastful, insulting, and obscene. It was apparent that there could be no hostilities in such encounters, and secure in this knowledge, he had made open threats at each opportunity. This harangue was expected. It was irritating, sometimes infuriating, but no one ever made the mistake of starting open warfare, which would risk the lives of women and children.

Hump Ribs developed the knack of avoiding confrontation where possible. This brought scorn from the Head Splitters and a reputation for timidity on the part of the Southern band. There seemed little doubt, however, that it prevented bloodshed.

It did not, of course, prevent the sporadic raids which struck terror in the hearts of the People. At any opportunity, it seemed, Gray Wolf would swoop down on unsuspecting hunters or unsupervised children. He and his followers delighted in the opportunity to terrorize and kill and kidnap. Always, if possible, a mutilated survivor was left to tell the tale. The constant threat of kidnapped children revolved around the beauty of the women of the People. Small girls would soon be beautiful young women, to become slave-wives of their captors or sold to others. Boys were more trouble than gain to their captors, and their usual fate was a single blow with a war ax.

To avoid this danger to the children, Hump Ribs led his Southern band in new directions on unpredictable migrations. Some seasons they managed to avoid the depredations of the Head Splitters entirely. At other times, they blundered into frequent contact for a season. It was a dangerous game, this run-and-hide.

White Buffalo thought about it often. Short Bow, he

knew, would disapprove. He had always been one to stand and fight. But Short Bow was dead, and there were few warriors who demonstrated his type of leadership. It was not that Hump Ribs was a bad leader. On the contrary, he was very good. But sometimes White Buffalo thought that it would be good to have someone like Short Bow as a leader in the hunt and against the Head Splitters. Such a man could work well with Hump Ribs. But none came up through the Rabbit Society.

In truth, Gray Wolf and his followers killed so many young men over a few seasons that there were not enough husbands. Multiple marriages had always been known among the People, but were not common. Usually, a wife might take in a widowed relative as a second wife for her husband and to help in the lodge. More wives than two were rare. Now, however, several lodges had three or four wives. Something must be done for the women without husbands, and this had always been the way of the People.

"Maybe you should take another wife," suggested Crow Woman to her husband.

White Buffalo was astonished.

"Wh-what?" he blurted.

"A second wife. Maybe she could bear you a child. There is Gray Fox, who has lost her husband. She is pretty."

"No!" White Buffalo was firm. "No, I will not think of it. *Aiee*, woman, she would not know the chants and the drum cadence. What good would she be?"

Crow Woman smiled to herself. That was the answer she had sought. If he had wished it, she could have tolerated such an arrangement, but she was pleased with her husband's response.

As for White Buffalo, there was only one choice. What Crow suggested was unthinkable. Not the living arrangement—that could be made tolerable, except for the fact that a newcomer would be an outsider. She would be unskilled in the knowledge of the medicine that he and Crow shared. That was not the main obstacle. He could not tolerate the idea of what another child in the lodge would do to Crow. If it were their own, his and Crow Woman's, it might possibly take the place of the happy child that they had had for a few short seasons. But to watch Crow as she tried to accept the child of another woman, yet from the loins of her husband? He knew that he could never do that to her.

Meanwhile, as these things occurred among the People, the years fell behind, marked only by pictographs on the story-skins, lines in the faces, and graying hair. It had happened so quickly. One day, it seemed to White Buffalo, they were young, and their lives were ahead, the years full of expectation. Then one day he realized with some surprise that they were growing old, and their lives were no longer ahead, but behind. He could not say when it happened. There had been no middle years, it seemed. Even more puzzling was the discovery that there had been no dividing summit. Somehow, he thought, there should have been a sort of recognition of having crossed the hilltop and started down the slope. He was not ready for the Other Side, the crossing over of the spirit; even this life was such a mystery. There were young and old, and surely there had been a day when the change had happened. When had it been, and how had he missed it?

He knew that it was past because the aching of his joints on cold mornings reminded him. His step was not as quick and sure, though he could still perform the ceremonial dances. It was frustrating to have a young mind in a body that was beset by the ravages of time. Crow Woman, who was now past her child-bearing years, was still beautiful to him. The woman who had warmed his bed in their youth still did so. The sensation of shared warmth under the robes was still thrilling and exciting. For a little while they were young again, their blood racing faster and making them forget the tragedy and disappointment that life had brought.

White Buffalo thought sometimes about passing on the heritage of the buffalo medicine. The knowledge, the skills, the cape itself, as his father had done before him. It was easy to postpone such things. In the early years, he had expected to pass the calling to his son. Or, perhaps, to his daughter. There were respected holy women among the People. White Moon had shown promise . . . but that was gone now. White Buffalo wiped a tear from the corner of his eye. He was sitting alone on a hill near the camp, where he loved to go and meditate. He thought again of the years when he and Crow had thought, *Surely this year there will be another child.*

In that way, year after year, he had postponed the decision about his medicine and who would be the next holy man of the Southern band. Now it was time to face the question. There was no single event which had brought him to this way of thinking but a series of things. He had finally accepted that Crow could not bear another child. He refused to consider a child by a new wife. And now, while he still had some good years, he must find a successor. There was time to do so, but the seasons flew past much more swiftly now than in his youth. Yes, he must begin his search.

He told Crow Woman of his decision that night as they settled in, snuggled under the robes against the crisp autumn chill.

"I am made to think," he observed casually, "that I should find someone to learn my medicine."

She looked at him seriously in the flickering light from the fire.

"Are you not feeling well?"

"What? Oh, yes . . . I am well. But we are no longer young."

"We are not old, either." She cuddled against him suggestively. "I will show you."

He smiled at her.

"Sometimes my bones tell me otherwise."

Both chuckled.

"But, Crow," he went on, "it takes time to learn the dances, the ceremonies, the medicine of the plants."

"Yes, I well remember," she mused.

"So," he continued, "I must find an apprentice."

"What will you do?" she asked.

"I do not know. What do you think?"

"You could watch the Rabbit Society."

"Yes, that is good. You watch too. First, the child must have the gift of the spirit. But it is also necessary to have the interest. Also, most important, he must be willing to make the sacrifice . . . take the responsibility for the demands of such a life."

"He . . . or *she?*" Crow Woman asked mischievously.

"Well, yes. But a young woman would have even more sacrifices to make. She would have to take a vow of chastity or wait until her years of child bearing are over."

This was a delicate area, and he hated to go into it. Crow's fertile years were barely past, and he thought the subject might be painful to her. Then he saw the mischief in her eyes. He seized her and tickled her in places that he knew would provoke a response.

"Stop!" She giggled. "I only meant that—"

"Of course," he said more seriously as they settled back down. "I should look for women also who would make good apprentices."

"There is a girl I have seen," Crow said thoughtfully. "She seems wise beyond her years. She reminds me . . ." She paused a moment. "No! I know! Do you remember a young man called Mouse? I think he is a nephew of Stone Breaker, on Cattail's side."

"Maybe," White Buffalo answered. "A thin, muscular boy, big ears and a sharp nose."

"Yes," laughed Crow. "Mouse!"

"I remember him. A quiet young man. It is good, Crow. We will watch him."

"Could I ask Cattail about him?"

"Of course. But do not say why. No one must know what we are seeking."

"Not even Cattail? Stone Breaker?" Crow asked in wonder.

"No. It must not be. Would I try to choose an apprentice for Stone Breaker?"

"No, my husband. But, he already has one. Their oldest son."

"Oh? I did not know. Well, it is good. Stone Breaker too sees the need to choose an apprentice."

"Yes, I suppose so. But he is no older than you, and you can still warm my bed," Crow said seductively.

She cuddled against him, and White Buffalo forgot the urgency to select an apprentice. They were young again, and in love.

31

Mouse seemed a likely prospect. White Buffalo observed the youngster in the activities of the Rabbit Society. It was easy to do. There were always a few adults watching the instruction, cheering the children on. As they learned the skills of the hunt, the use of weapons, and the simple athletic skills of survival, it was possible to observe and estimate the potential of each.

And the potential of the one called Mouse did seem great. He was calm and mature in his approach, well liked but not an obvious leader. His range of skills was impressive, from his use of the bow to his well-coordinated speed in swimming. Yes, thought White Buffalo, this one will do to watch. Whenever opportunity offered, the holy man made his way to the activities of the day and sat to observe. Sometimes he chuckled to himself at a particularly clever triumph of someone, especially Mouse. Each day he was more certain.

There were also indications that the young man might have the gift of the spirit; at least, he seemed to have wisdom and insight beyond his years. It was something that could be nurtured, encouraged as it grew. If, of course, Mouse wished to do so. The youth appeared to be about fourteen or fifteen summers. There were few things that were notable about his appearance. He was neither tall nor burly in build but rather short and slender. His muscles were well defined, however, and his strength was deceptive. The large ears and pointed features made him appear rather comical, and the name he bore was quite descriptive. However, White Buffalo soon saw that here was a young man who would some day be taken quite seriously. There were leadership qualities behind that seriocomic face. While the appellation Mouse fit his description quite well, it had no correlation at all with the youth's spirit. Some day, thought White Buffalo, this one would outgrow that name and shed it as the snake does its skin. Little did the holy man realize that he would witness the event that caused such a change.

It was a warm day, early in the Moon of Falling Leaves. The word had been passed that soon the band would move to a wintering area, but a specific day had not been chosen. There was still good hunting, the weather was uncommonly fine, and the temptation to stay a little longer was great. There had been no contact with the Head Splitters this season, so it was a great surprise when the enemy came.

White Buffalo was sitting on the slope outside the camp, watching several young people practicing with the bow. Primarily, he was watching the quiet demeanor of the one he had begun to think of as his successor. The one called Mouse was active and skilled in this game. His arrows were usually in or near the white spot at the center of the grass-filled target-skin. Still he was quiet and unassuming, though confident. Of the six or eight others, two were young women. Naturally, there was some flirtatious courting going on, and White Buffalo smiled in amusement. He leaned back against a massive sycamore and closed his eyes, soaking in the comforting warmth of the sunlight. It seemed to help the stiffness in his joints to warm them in this way. He dozed off for a moment.

"You are next, Mouse!" someone called. "See if you can beat Red Hawk's shot!"

White Buffalo stirred and opened his eyes. He wanted to see this shot and to take a vicarious pride in the skill of his pupil. Of course, Mouse was hardly his pupil yet. He had not even approached the boy about such an apprenticeship. He must do so soon, maybe during the journey to winter camp. That would give Mouse a chance to consider as they traveled. Yes, he would speak to the young man soon.

Mouse loosed his arrow, and the cries of approval indicated another successful shot. Several ran toward the target to retrieve arrows while Mouse followed, pausing to fit another arrow to his bow.

At first, White Buffalo thought, in his sleepy state, that his eyes were deceiving him. But, no! There were shadowy figures flitting among the dogwood behind the target. He sat upright, wide awake now, ready to sound the alarm. Maybe it was only some of the dogs from the camp. Then he noticed the figure of a man crouching behind a bush only a few steps beyond the target. Even as his mind tried to interpret the message from his eyes, the man rose, part of a concerted rush. One of the girls screamed as a painted warrior sprinted toward her. Two other enemies were equally close, swinging the dreaded stone axes. More were visible among the bushes.

There was complete confusion. Some of the young men of the People had actually left their weapons behind when they ran to the target. One of the most arrogant braggarts, a popular youth called Red Hawk, turned with a squeal of terror and ran like a rabbit. An arrow came searching after him but missed.

Amid all of the terror and danger there was one who seemed to remain calm. Mouse dropped to one knee, took aim, and calmly drove an arrow into the chest of a charging Head Splitter. Surprise was evident on the man's face as he fell forward from his own momentum, driving the arrow on through, to jut upward from his lifeless back. Mouse roared a slightly high-pitched version of the gutteral war cry of the People and reached for another arrow. The Head Splitters paused. They had not expected resistance from these mere children.

"Fight!" yelled Mouse to his companions. "Shoot!"

He released another arrow, wounding a warrior who turned to cripple away, clutching at a bleeding arm.

A slim girl stepped forward to pick up the ax dropped by Mouse's first victim and turned to defend herself. The man who had almost reached to seize her now stopped, confused. His hesitation was his undoing. An arrow from the bow of one of the other youths struck him in the side. As he turned, trying to pluck away the offending shaft, the girl stepped forward and swung her captured ax.

"After them!" cried Mouse.

The fleeing youths turned to join the pursuit. Mouse sounded the war cry again. Now there were answering war cries from the camp, and warriors came pouring out to assist. The Head Splitters were in full retreat, leaving three dead and others carrying arrows in wounds of varying severity.

"Enough!" shouted Hump Ribs as he and the others caught up with the fight. "Do not go farther. It is too dangerous."

The young men began to withdraw, talking excitedly.

"We did it! We drove off the Head Splitters!"

"Is anyone hurt?" asked Hump Ribs.

Quickly, they looked from one to the other.

"No, we are all here," Red Hawk announced.

"Good," Hump Ribs answered. "What happened?"

"They came out of the bushes!"

"That one nearly grabbed Oak Leaf!"

Everyone was talking at once. White Buffalo had made his way down the slope in time to hear his impressions verified.

"Mouse killed that one," Oak Leaf said admiringly. "He turned the attack on them."

The others nodded.

"Who sounded the war cry?" asked Hump Ribs.

"Mouse," said several at once.

Hump Ribs looked over at White Buffalo, who nodded agreement.

"I was on the slope there," he told Hump Ribs later. "*Aiee,* that one is a fighter! He saved us from losses today. Our Mouse, it seems, speaks with a loud voice."

There was a celebration that evening in honor of the victory. The dances reenacted the events of the day—the first arrow from Mouse's bow, the turning of the fight, and the defeat of the Head Splitters. There was no immediate danger of counterattack. It was well known that Head Splitters avoided fighting at night. Their fear was that a spirit crossing over as it left a dying body would become lost in the darkness to wander forever. Thus there would be no attack tonight. Probably not at all. The attackers had been severely punished.

The hero of the day, of course, was Mouse, who was rather embarrassed by all the attention, though proud. Partway through the celebration, Hump Ribs stood by the fire to make a proclamation.

"We will move camp in two days. But for now, we celebrate."

He beckoned Mouse forward, and everyone shouted approval.

"Our young Mouse," Hump Ribs announced, "has done

well. He has shown bravery and gathered honors. Ours is not a timid mouse, but a Mouse That Roars!"

The crowd shouted with approving laughter.

"Mouse Roars!" someone cried.

The young man had acquired a new name, one that honored his bravery and would commemorate his deeds forever.

"It is good!" stated Hump Ribs. "You shall be Mouse Roars!"

The celebration continued, but White Buffalo and Crow Woman made their way back to their lodge.

"You were right about this young man," Crow said as they prepared for sleep. "He is a leader."

"That is true," acknowledged White Buffalo.

"Then why do you not seem more pleased, my husband?"

White Buffalo did not respond at once.

"Is something wrong?" Crow finally asked.

"No, not really," he answered wearily.

He was tired from the excitement of the day and the celebration. The throb of the dance-drums still sounded across the camp, and the chant of happy, triumphant songs echoed the cadence. He had been excited, but now in the aftermath he felt old and tired again. There was a disappointment that he did not quite understand in the thrill of victory.

Crow Woman snuggled close to him under the robes.

"Elk, is there something that the others do not know?"

"Maybe. Gray Wolf was one of those I saw. He tried to get his warriors to turn and fight."

"But that is nothing new."

"Yes, I know. But, today was not the end, only another fight."

"Yes, my husband. It has always been so."

"That is a bad one, that Gray Wolf," he said, almost to himself.

"But what . . ."

"I do not know, Crow. I am made to think he will become more of a problem than ever, and for a long time."

"Is there something we must do?"

"I think not. This is ours to live with."

"But what of Mouse? Mouse Roars." She chuckled in the flickering firelight. "*Aiee*, he has proved himself!"

Suddenly, White Buffalo realized what it was that was bothering him, causing his depression.

"Yes," he said slowly. "He has proved himself. But now I cannot ask him to be my apprentice."

"Why not?" asked the astonished Crow Woman.

"I saw him today, when he 'roared.' *Aiee*, that was something to see! The others were running in fear, and he turned it into victory."

"But then—" Crow interrupted, but he waved her to silence.

"That is it, Crow. He is a leader. But that sort of leader. He might make a great medicine man, but the People need him as a warrior, a chief who can stand and fight the Head Splitters. Mouse Roars can do that."

He fell silent, and Crow was silent too for a little while. Finally she spoke.

"Then we look some more."

"Yes."

Mouse Roars never knew that he had been considered, and the dejected White Buffalo continued to search in the Rabbit Society for the next holy man.

32

The girl was tall and well formed, and moved with a confident grace. Her walk reminded White Buffalo of the gentle sway of willows in a summer breeze or perhaps the nodding of heavy seedheads on the real-grass in the Moon of Ripening. It was not a seductive walk. At least, not intentionally, he thought, as he watched her at the games and contests. But it would be difficult for any man to watch her and not see the beauty of her body. Part of that beauty was that she appeared unaware of its effect on men. She used her long legs well in the contests of running, jumping, and swimming. She handled the bow with equal skill.

White Buffalo found it necessary to overlook her grace and beauty, and concentrate on her spirit. That, after all, was the thing which had caused Crow to notice the girl and to suggest that she would be one to observe.

Crow seemed determined to see that a woman would at least be considered. Certainly White Buffalo had no objection. His only reservation was that it would be a greater sacrifice for a woman.

He was impressed immediately with this young woman. Big-Footed Woman, she was called. Not that her feet were exceptionally large. True, they were ample, but a tall woman must have long feet to carry her longer frame. The reason for such a name, it appeared, was her skill in the athletic contests. Her strides, her accomplishments, were great, bigger than most. Her feet carried her well. As a thinker might be said to have large thoughts, so were this young woman's feet in deeds of speed and skill. Yet her deeds were also those of spirit and thought, White Buffalo noted. He recalled that it had been Big-Footed Woman who had grasped the fallen Head Splitter's ax and helped to repulse the invaders. A cool head. And confidence. Not *over* confident but secure in the knowledge of her own skills. *Mature*, that was it. The girl seemed to have wisdom beyond her years.

"She reminds me of you at that age," he told Crow Woman.

"Aiee!" Crow laughed. "I was not so pretty or so athletic. Besides, that was when you did not like me, so how would you know?"

"I was talking of her spirit," he began.

Then he saw that she was teasing him. There was no way that he could win this discussion.

"Woman," he snarled with a terrible grimace, "you test my patience!"

He threatened to tickle her, and she retreated, still laughing. Finally they tired of the game, and she turned to the fire where a stew of corn, beans, and dried meat bubbled in the pit. Crow removed a cooking stone with her willow tongs and deposited it in the coals, replacing it with a freshly heated one. The stew hissed and subsided to quiet bubbling again.

"Elk," she said thoughtfully as she came to sit beside him, "it is good that you see good things in this girl's spirit. I think she has the gift."

"This may be," he agreed. "Let us observe her a little longer, and then I will talk to her. Your feel for the spirit is good, Crow. You could have done this."

She leaned her head on his shoulder.

"Yes," she said thoughtfully, "I think so. I knew it then, but I would rather have borne your children."

A tear formed at the corner of her eye, and she brushed it away.

"You knew," White Buffalo said sadly, "and you rejected the gift, for me. Now you have neither."

"No, no, Elk. I have you. I have helped with *your* gift. I would do so again, to be with you."

They sat, leaning together, enjoying the warm comfort of touching, until suddenly Crow sat upright.

"Aiee!" she said, "I am neglecting my cooking. The stew will be cold."

She began bustling around, busily attending the cooking pit which needed little attention.

* * *

The Southern band had settled into winter camp now. Crow and White Buffalo had continued to observe Big-Footed Woman and continued to be pleased. The girl was quick and observant, thoughtful of others. Already she was assisting with teaching the first dance-steps to the tiny beginners in the Rabbit Society. She was popular, but in a different way. Friends seemed to come to her for advice and counsel. There were others who appeared destined for leadership, but this one's role seemed different. Perhaps her maturity lent itself well to helpful friendship, and her warm wisdom was appreciated by her peers.

"It is good," White Buffalo observed to Crow. "This one will learn well and has the spirit to use her gifts wisely."

Still, it was a long time before they approached her. White Buffalo must be very sure, certain that his choice was a good one. Eventually, Crow Woman issued the invitation.

"The holy man, my husband, wishes to talk to you. Will you come to our lodge?"

The girl seemed surprised but quickly regained her composure.

"Of course, Mother. But what could he want of me?"

"He will tell you."

"When? Now?"

"As you wish, child. There is nothing urgent in this."

The sunny smile that they had noticed lighted the girl's face.

"Then let us go now," Big-Footed Woman suggested. "I would not keep the holy man waiting."

Pleased, Crow led the way to their lodge.

The girl's eyes were wide with wonder as White Buffalo questioned her about her thoughts and feelings about the matter at hand.

"You mean, Uncle," she finally blurted in astonishment, "that *I* might have such a gift, a gift of the spirit?"

"Why not, my child? You are wise beyond your years, and you know many things. I am made to think that you *do* have the gift of vision, of the spirit."

"*Aiee!* What must I do, Uncle?"

"That is your choice," he said simply. "One may refuse the gift. Some do, for the trail is hard. There is much to learn, much responsibility. It is quite permissible to say no."

"Must I say, now?"

"No, no. Think on these things. Then come back and tell me."

The girl nodded.

"Uncle, another question. I . . . you see, I know no holy woman. Are there some among the People?"

"Oh, yes, my child. Only one now, I think. She is of the Mountain band. But, there have always been medicine women of the People as well as men."

"Their position is much the same?"

"Yes. There are always differences from one holy one to another, men or women. But much the same. You would develop your own medicine and follow where it takes you."

"I see . . . maybe . . . might I start to learn and *then* see where it leads?"

"Of course. But do not think too hard about it now. Go, think carefully; you will be guided in the right way."

Big-Footed Woman left the lodge of the holy man, still full of wonder. White Buffalo was pleased with her reaction. The girl had shown humility yet was pleased to think that she might be chosen for so special a vocation. Her every reaction was good.

"Yes," White Buffalo told his wife, "this one has the gift. I am made to think that she will be back quickly."

It was only two days when young Big-Footed Woman returned, humbly and in earnest.

"I am ready, Uncle," she announced. "I am ready to learn."

Her instruction started that very day. White Buffalo was delighted with her quickness of thought, her eagerness to learn. Crow Woman too welcomed the young woman's presence and helped with her instruction. Very quickly, Big-Footed Woman was learning the drum cadences of the ritual chants, and White Buffalo acknowledged that her drumstrokes spoke with much authority. Very quickly, she also became a part of their lodge. Both Crow and White Buffalo felt pleased and happy in her presence. Crow said nothing but did not fail to notice that her husband was showing more interest in life. She had not heard him chuckle so much since . . . well, not since the loss of their own White Moon. This young woman, it seemed, was tak-

ing the place of the daughter they had lost. The surprising
thing was that it seemed right. Through all the years, both
the holy man and his wife had assumed that no one could
possibly take their daughter's place. Now it appeared that
they need not have been concerned. The years that White
Moon had been with them were still fresh in their memory, they found, now that there was someone to help them
forget the sadness. It was a pleasant thing to have the
bright cheeriness of the young woman in their lodge. It
was a winter of happiness that had not been theirs since
their loss.

Big-Footed Woman continued to learn rapidly, and
White Buffalo was ever more pleased with her progress. In
the Moon of Awakening, he suggested to Crow that they
ask the girl to move into their lodge.

"It is good," agreed Crow Woman. "The time is at hand
when you will have much to show her, many lessons. I will
ask her tomorrow."

When Big-Footed Woman arrived the next morning,
cheeks flushed from the wind, Crow was ready to make the
offer. It was exciting—the thought of a daughter in her
lodge again. The girl had become so much a part of their
lives that this seemed a completely natural step.

"I have something to speak of with you," Crow began.

Big-Footed Woman's eyes were sparkling with excitement.

"I too, Mother! Let me tell you first. I am going to
marry!"

"*What?*" White Buffalo exclaimed. "Child, you cannot
. . . I mean, you must think on this. You would cast aside
your gift?"

Crow sat dumbly, unbelieving.

"Not cast it aside, Uncle! I would only postpone it. You
have said some women do so, until after their child-bearing years."

"Yes, but girl, that is a long time from now. I need—"

He had started to say that he must have someone *now* to
whom he could impart his skills. But that would be unfair.
Frustrated, he lapsed into silence.

Crow Woman regained her composure.

"Who is your young man, child?" she asked pleasantly,
trying to keep her voice from trembling.

"His name is Coyote. May I bring him in?"

"Of course! Bring him!" Crow said.

Big-Footed Woman gave Crow a quick hug and slipped through the doorskin.

"*Aiee!*" exclaimed White Buffalo. "*Coyote?* How can she do this?"

Coyote, who had been a child at the time of his father's death, was often a source of amusement to the band. The youngster was adept at practically nothing. He was a bit fat, a bit lazy, and seemed to take nothing seriously. From the time he was small, he had been a buffoon, more interested in jokes, pranks, and laughter than in learning.

"I will not allow it!" White Buffalo sputtered.

"It is not yours to say," said Crow. "You must accept her choice."

"But I do not have to approve!" he snapped.

"No. You must respect it, though."

"Do *you* approve?"

"I did not say that, my husband. Only that the choice is hers. My heart is heavy too!"

By the time Big-Footed Woman returned with her self-conscious young man, White Buffalo had at least recovered his composure.

"Coyote," the girl said proudly, "my almost-parents, Crow and White Buffalo."

The young man nodded, embarrassed, and giggled nervously. White Buffalo recalled now that this chuckling little laugh, like the chortling cry of the coyote in the night, was the origin of the boy's name. He took a deep breath and determined not to show his repugnance if he could help it.

"I knew your father well," he ventured. "Short Bow . . . a man to admire."

"Yes, Uncle. He was such a man. It is good that you speak well of him. Thank you."

Well, thought White Buffalo, the boy is polite at least.

"He gave his name away, did he not?" White Buffalo asked.

He knew that to be true, or the words *short* and *bow* would not be in use. It was actually a cruel thing to say, a reminder to Coyote that *he* was not the recipient. But the youth only smiled, unperturbed.

"Yes, Uncle. To my oldest brother, before I was born."

Somehow, White Buffalo felt that he was losing control

of this conversation. At every turn, the young man spoke quickly and appropriately, even with what seemed a degree of wisdom and maturity. This was disconcerting to White Buffalo, who was prepared to be critical.

"Mother," the girl was saying to Crow, "you wanted to speak of something before?"

"What? Oh, yes, I have forgotten now, in the excitement. It was nothing," Crow said.

The conversation continued a little while, and then Big-Footed Woman rose.

"We must go," she apologized. "I will bring him again."

The two young people ducked out the door, and then the girl turned to poke her head back inside for a moment.

"I am so glad you like him!" she whispered, eyes glowing with excitement. Then she was gone.

"Like him?" sputtered White Buffalo. "I cannot tolerate him!"

"Now, Elk—" his wife warned.

"Yes, I know. I will try. But Crow, he has spoiled it all!"

His heart was very heavy.

33

White Buffalo did not know which he resented most. Young Coyote was preventing Big-Footed Woman from carrying out her calling, and that was bad enough. But to make matters worse, the medicine man found that he resented the girl's choice. This Coyote was a buffoon, a lazy nobody without a serious thought in his head. Why, why would a beautiful, intelligent young woman choose to burden herself with such a man? He recalled that this was not uncommon. Such a young woman, with such potential, would sometimes choose such a nobody. It was a thing of wonder, of resentment and envy to all other men.

There was another odd thing here, however. White Buffalo felt a sense of rejection. It irritated him, embarrassed him a little, and it was something that he did not feel free to discuss with Crow. It was actually much like the feeling of rejection that had obsessed him long ago when he thought that Crow had married their friend Stone Breaker. It was ridiculous, of course. He had never wanted this young woman in that way. She was more like a daughter to him. To them both. Yet it bothered him, the thought of this beautiful girl and the short, fat little Coyote in bed together. The girl's long, graceful legs . . . *aiee!* In a completely illogical way, he was jealous. He would not have been so, he told himself, had Big-Footed Woman chosen one of the handsome, capable young men of the band. But *Coyote? Aiee,* life is strange.

Crow Woman, wise in the ways of such things and even wiser in the ways of her husband, had some idea of his frustration. She felt much the same, as a mother does who feels that her daughter has not chosen well. She brought up the subject one evening as White Buffalo sat silent and sullen.

"You are thinking of Big-Footed Woman."

It was a statement, not a question.

"What? Oh, yes. Maybe. My heart is heavy for her, Crow."

She came and sat beside him.

"Elk, we know this young woman well, do we not?"

He gave a deep sigh.

"I thought so, but . . ."

"Now, think, my husband. Has not she shown good judgement?"

"Yes, always. That is why—"

Crow held up a hand to silence him.

"Yes," she agreed, "she has. So, my husband, let us see it this way: Either she sees something fine in this young man that we do not see, or . . . ," she paused a moment for effect, "or she will soon see her mistake."

Crow was always so logical. She could make things seem astonishingly simple. White Buffalo could not argue with her reasoning. He was still frustrated, but the course of action that Crow's statement suggested was the only one available to them—waiting.

Probably the most difficult thing was that Big-Footed Woman continued to spend much time at their lodge. They were glad for her presence, of course. She had become closer than family in many respects. Only the instruction had ceased. The problem, an irritation that grated on the already stressed emotions of White Buffalo, was that the girl usually brought Coyote along. The young man was jovial and pleasant, and his chuckling giggle was not so obnoxious as his nervousness began to decrease. He was even helpful sometimes, bringing firewood for Crow Woman or assisting in some minor way around the lodge.

Gradually, Crow began to appreciate the quiet helper— the gentle understanding, the hidden maturity of Coyote. He still made jokes and soon began to tease Crow in a mischievous, flattering way. By the end of a moon, Crow was completely won over.

"She is right, my husband. This is a kind, gentle, and very intelligent young man."

"But he has no ambition!" White Buffalo snapped irritably. "And he does not do well at the hunt."

"Maybe that is not his skill," Crow suggested. "For some,

another way is better. Stonebreaker does not hunt, nor do you."

"That is not the same, Crow. He does *nothing*. He is lazy."

"He has many friends," Crow observed. "Big-Footed Woman says his counsel is sought after."

"And I do not understand that, either," White Buffalo sputtered. "Everything is a joke to him."

"But his jokes *teach*, Elk. They are wise."

Even though these two women, most important in the life of White Buffalo, understood and admired Coyote, the holy man was slow to accept it. Coyote seemed not to notice, casually coming and going, apparently taking nothing seriously. Sometimes he asked questions, which irritated White Buffalo at first.

"Uncle, it is said that the Head Splitters do not fight at night."

The holy man nodded but said nothing.

"Why is this? I have heard they are afraid that spirits of the dying, crossing over, will become lost in the darkness."

"So it is said."

"But, Uncle, *our* spirits sometimes cross over during darkness."

"Yes, that is true."

"Yet they do not become lost?"

"That is our belief."

"Then, Uncle, if we have to fight Head Splitters, we should do so at night? It would give us advantage."

White Buffalo sat silent a moment. No one had suggested this before.

"Maybe," he admitted. "Of course, one does not fight Head Splitters by choice."

Coyote chuckled.

"Of course. Uncle, do you believe the thing about spirits crossing over in the dark?"

"It does not matter what I think but what Head Splitters think."

Coyote chuckled again.

"That is *their* problem then, Uncle?"

White Buffalo smiled, a little reluctantly. This young man had far deeper insight than he had imagined. Maybe, as Crow Woman had suggested, there were qualities in the young man seen only by Big-Footed Woman.

Gradually, White Buffalo was convinced. The fact that Coyote could carry his own end of an interesting conversation helped greatly. So did his thirst for knowledge. The young man asked about everything, from uses of the herbs and plants to how the geese know when it is time to fly south.

"The buffalo see that the grass is drying, I suppose," he said one day, "but how do the geese know? They start before it is cold."

There were other questions, about things of the spirit. Over a period of time, White Buffalo came to look forward to Coyote's visits. Then came a day when the holy man reached a startling conclusion. He was actually covering information in these sessions that he had taught before. These were the things he had been teaching to Big-Footed Woman. Ah, he thought, of course! Here is a young couple who can work together, as Crow and I do. The spirit-force is strong in both. *Aiee*, what a wonder that he had not seen it before! This Coyote, who was already beginning to learn, could be his apprentice. Yes, of course! He, White Buffalo, would begin at once to teach them. The only thing that still stood in the way was Coyote's agreement. He could be asked at his next visit.

Crow Woman was not so certain.

"He may not wish to do so," she warned.

"Of course he will," White Buffalo scoffed. "Look at him, the questions he asks. Already, he understands many things. Things of the spirit. Crow, this is the one! Big-Footed Woman came to bring him to us. It is meant to be!"

When the two young people next came to the lodge, White Buffalo could scarcely contain his enthusiasm. As soon as possible, he contrived to draw Coyote aside.

"Let us walk," he suggested.

The two men strolled out of the camp toward the crest of a low rise a little distance away. Coyote asked his usual questions, his casual manner concealing his depth of thought and the solemn character of the inquiries.

"Uncle, the People do not eat bears, but some others do. Why?"

"Because . . . well, that is our way."

"Yes, Uncle. But *why* is it our way?"

"It has always been so, since Creation."

Coyote walked in silence a little way. He appeared to realize that questions like this could irritate the holy man.

"Some were told to eat bears at Creation, but we were told *not* to do so?" he asked cautiously.

"Yes," White Buffalo stated crisply. "It is the way of things."

"What would happen if one of the People *did* eat bear meat, Uncle?"

"That would bring very bad happenings."

"On the eater, or on the People?"

"Both, maybe. *Aiee*, Coyote, you ask questions that are too serious. Only after much instruction—"

White Buffalo paused, aware that he was about to imply too much. He tried to relax and remain calm.

"But let us not speak of bears, my son," he said in a kindly voice. "Your questions do, however, remind me of why I asked you to walk with me."

Coyote interrupted briefly to point to a pair of young foxes a bowshot away, rolling and playing like puppies in the sun.

"Yes," White Buffalo nodded, smiling in spite of himself. He was slightly irritated by the distraction. But, this very character of young Coyote, the inquisitive observation, was the very thing that made him a likely apprentice.

"Coyote, let me speak with you of a serious matter. Here, sit."

He pointed to a ledge of white stone near the rim of the hill, and the two men sat down. White Buffalo hurried into his subject, before some other sight or sound could distract young Coyote.

"I am made to think," he began cautiously, "that you have the gift of the spirit. I could teach you my medicine, you and Big-Footed Woman, to use for the People, after me."

Coyote was silent for a little while and looked unusually serious.

"You would allow *me* to learn your medicine, Uncle?"

"Of course. That is what I am suggesting."

"I thought you did not even like me."

White Buffalo brushed this aside.

"I was offended when you stole my apprentice. But now you bring me another. Yourself. You have the gift. Now, when do you plan your marriage?"

"I . . . I do not know, Uncle."

"Well, no matter. We will continue instruction, and when that happens, so be it!"

Coyote appeared troubled.

"Uncle . . . I am pleased that you think well of me and would take me as apprentice, but . . ."

"Wait!" White Buffalo said quickly. "You do not need to give an answer now. Think about it; talk with your wife-to-be."

"I have thought already, Uncle. I cannot do this."

"But . . ." the holy man sputtered, "you have the gift; you love the learning . . . you could be a great holy man."

"That is true," Coyote stated, with no modesty whatever, "but the task is too hard. No, I do not want to take the responsibility. I must refuse the gift."

White Buffalo stared at him in amazement. Slowly, the realization dawned.

"You *knew*," he said in astonishment.

"Of course. I have known for a long time," Coyote said calmly. "And I knew that I must refuse. My way is not to work that hard. Maybe it is like bearmeat, Uncle. Some eat it, some do not. And I am made to think that I should not do this."

White Buffalo stared at the younger man. He felt a strange mixture of emotions. Surprise, anger, disappointment. He argued, cajoled, almost pleaded, but Coyote was firm.

How ironic, thought White Buffalo. He had searched for years, almost but never quite finding an apprentice worthy to become his successor. Now he had found one who seemed already to have the gift of the spirit and to recognize it. How tragic to have him then reject it.

Coyote rose and stretched.

"No, Uncle," he said. "I am honored, but it is not to be. I am not a White Buffalo. I am only Coyote, the laugher on the hills and the teller of small jokes."

Part III

Two Medicines

White Buffalo sat in the sun in front of his lodge and leaned against the willow backrest. The years had continued to pass more swiftly, and he had still found no successor to whom he could teach his medicine. It was still a worry to him, but he had nearly decided that this was meant to be. Through the passing of the seasons, year after year, he had searched, but no suitable apprentice had been found. The likeliest would have been Coyote, although his wife, Big-Footed Woman, could easily have been the one. But both had rejected the gift, and they had married.

Aiee, that seemed only a short while ago, but it was many years. Their lodge had several children, and the eldest were now of fifteen or sixteen winters. That seemed hardly possible. How could it be, when he, White Buffalo felt no different? He had sometimes felt old then, and he did now, sometimes. At these times he worried more about a successor, but the years had numbed his anxiety about it. Maybe the Southern band was simply destined not to have a holy man . . . or woman. That would be unfortunate, but in the long view, it probably made no difference. If the Southern band died out entirely, time would go on. One band had been destroyed many generations ago and was now remembered only by the empty space in the council circle.

At first, when Coyote had rejected the gift of the spirit, White Buffalo had been furious, then hurt. It was some time before the holy man had been able to converse with Coyote without becoming angry all over again. Slowly, however, he had been able to realize that the decision had been Coyote's to make. He was helped greatly in this by the wisdom of Crow and Big-Footed Woman.

Slowly, he came to tolerate, even appreciate, the presence of Coyote. In a year or so, the two men had become close friends. There was a great difference in their ages, but this was more than overcome by the communication of their spirits. Coyote continued to have a vast respect for the knowledge and skill of the holy man. White Buffalo, in turn, increasingly appreciated the whimsical wisdom of Coyote. The young man had an uncanny knack of cutting cleanly through to the heart of any matter. But it was done in an unassuming, jocular way. No one could take offense.

White Buffalo noticed this especially when Coyote would speak in council. These occasions were rare, because the young man was not inclined to venture opinions. Usually, his comments were phrased in the form of questions, allowing others to think that they had thought of the solution themselves. It was a strange but quite effective form of leadership.

One incident was fixed in White Buffalo's memory. There had been a heated discussion over the move to winter camp. The weather had remained warm and pleasant, and the hunting was good. There was much reluctance to move yet, though it should have been time to go. Hump Ribs, unwilling to risk an unpopular decision, had called a council. The discussion was going poorly, popular opinion leaning against the wisdom of an immediate move. Finally Hump Ribs, frustrated by the opposition, had looked around the circle.

"Coyote," he said, "you have not spoken."

Coyote looked startled, as if he had been roused from half-sleep.

"What?" he stammered. "Oh, I was listening to the geese."

He pointed overhead, and in the sudden silence could be heard the honking cries of southbound flocks.

"How do they know," Coyote asked, as if to himself, "when Cold Maker is coming?"

There was a murmur, and the discussion was resumed, but the tone was different. Coyote's simple question, actually a diversion, had put the problem into its proper place. White Buffalo chuckled to himself. Soon the vote had turned, and the question was not whether to move but how soon. No one seemed to realize that the tide of opinion had been turned by Coyote's simple ploy. *But Hump Ribs knows,* thought the holy man. *He did this intention-*

ally. This observation pleased White Buffalo greatly. It showed the skill and wisdom of the chief, and of young Coyote.

Through the years, this odd combination of leadership and wisdom had worked well. Probably, few people were aware of the process. Coyote was content *not* to be a leader but to help quietly to bring about that which was for the good of the band. People laughed at his droll remarks but valued his counsel and appreciated it. Their appreciation was shown by gifts of meager value. A shared haunch of meat, an extra skin. The lodge of Coyote and Big-Footed Woman was never hungry, and the mention of the name of Coyote always brought a smile.

Under the leadership of Hump Ribs, the Southern band had remained stable, neither gaining nor losing lodges. It was respected by the other bands, though others were larger and carried more prestige.

The Southern band, however, continued to be a favorite target of Head Splitter raids. The run-and-hide tactics of Hump Rib's chieftainship had been only moderately effective. Gray Wolf had mellowed not at all and led an attack whenever opportunity offered. The enemy chief, it seemed, still held a grudge, a bitterness from long ago, when he had been shamed by Hump Ribs and the other warriors of the People.

When White Buffalo saw Coyote approaching on this pleasant summer afternoon, he perceived immediately that something was wrong. The usually placid face of Coyote was drawn with care. He approached the seated holy man and sat down, puffing just a bit from his exertion.

"*Ah-koh,* Uncle," he said.

"*Ah-koh,* Coyote," the holy man answered.

He assumed that there was a matter of some concern—probably the Head Splitters, though no one else seemed to know of it.

"There is some difficulty, my friend?" he asked.

Coyote looked at him sharply.

"Do you know of something, Uncle?"

"No. You seem concerned."

"Oh. I do not know, Uncle. It is something to talk of. You may know some meaning."

"Coyote, what are you talking about?"

"Strangers, Uncle. From the south. A man from one of

the Caddo tribes stopped with us this morning. I talked with him at length."

"Are these strangers Caddo?"

"No. They are like gods, it is said. They come from far away, no one knows where. Their skins are bright and shiny, and they are many. Too many to count."

"*Aiee!* What is their purpose?"

"No one knows that either. But this Caddo said that some of his people were tortured and killed. That is why he came north."

"To escape?"

"Yes, and to warn."

"But why should Caddo warn people of the Tallgrass country?"

Coyote shrugged.

"They felt it important. There is more, Uncle."

"*More?*"

"Yes. It is said that these strangers have with them many dogs of great size."

"Dogs?"

"Yes, Uncle. They carry burdens, and some of the gods ride on their backs."

"Nonsense! The Caddo tells tales."

"Yes, that was my thought. But he seems sincere. He says that some of those who first saw this thought that they were all one—a large body like a dog's, but with the upper part of a man on the front."

"Surely that cannot be," White Buffalo pondered. But his resolve was weakening. He was remembering some of the strange things he had seen on his vision quest long ago.

"Probably that was only talk," Coyote said, "and this man agrees. It is now known that it is a dog, ridden by these gods with shiny skins."

"Where were they seen?" asked White Buffalo.

"They come from the southwest. Now they travel nearly straight north."

"And they still come? *This* way?"

He had not quite understood the immediacy of the problem.

"Yes, Uncle. They are maybe only six or seven sleeps away."

"*Aiee!* Does Hump Ribs know?"

"I sent the Caddo to him."

Somehow, it seemed that Coyote always knew what was happening more quickly than anyone else. Of all the men in the band, how appropriate that the visitor had encountered Coyote.

"It is good," White Buffalo stated. "Now, my friend, there are things we must do."

He rose quickly, almost forgetting the little jab of pain that went through his knees when he moved quickly.

"Come, I will go to Hump Ribs. You wait for me by the stream, there."

The Caddo visitor had already departed when White Buffalo tapped on the lodgeskin of the chief. He was beckoned inside, and for a little while talked earnestly with Hump Ribs. The story was much the same, that of the advancing party of gods. Hump Ribs was inclined to doubt the story of the traveler, but there was much that seemed convincing. Unless the Caddo was completely crazy, he must have a story of much importance. And the man had not in any way seemed crazy, Hump Ribs admitted.

"So Coyote says also," White Buffalo commented.

"He talked to Coyote?"

"Yes, Coyote sent him here."

"Ah, I see. That makes sense."

"What will you do?"

"Nothing, for now. Send wolves, of course."

The holy man pondered a moment.

"Yes," he said slowly. "That is good. But my friend, I am made to think that this is a very unusual occurrence."

"You have had visions?"

"No, I have not tried yet. I will, of course, but meanwhile, our wolves should leave to begin their journey."

"Yes, that is true."

"Now, we must have their discoveries quickly. We may have to move the camp out of the gods' path."

"Yes. I will have wolves waiting at places a sleep or two apart, to carry the word."

"Ah, that is good," White Buffalo agreed. "One more thing . . . I would have Coyote go with the wolves."

"*Coyote?*" asked Hump Ribs in astonishment. "He is . . . well, my friend, he is not one of our ablest warriors."

"True," agreed the holy man, "but he *is* one of our ablest *thinkers.*"

Hump Ribs considered a moment.

"Yes," he said. "That is true."

"Just as you need warrior information, I need things of the spirit, and Coyote can observe those."

"Yes, it is good," replied the chief. "Coyote does have that ability. Did you not once consider him as an assistant?"

"Once, long ago," White Buffalo said sadly. "He refused."

Hump Ribs laughed.

"He is lazy," he commented.

"A little, maybe. But he is useful as he is. He does not want to lead but is a keen observer. We both use that to our advantage, my friend."

Both men chuckled.

"Do you think this mission is too dangerous to send such a man as Coyote?" Hump Ribs asked.

"I do not know. Maybe I will have more thoughts on this later. But for now, my chief, I am made to think that this event of the gods' advance into our territory is too dangerous *not* to have a man like Coyote with the observers. Now I must go."

He rose and made his way to the river where Coyote waited. Quickly, he outlined the plan.

"Anything you see, or even *think*, I want to know," he said. "If it is important enough, you come back yourself. If it is only about their location and direction, Hump Ribs's wolves will tell us."

White Buffalo felt that he was not expressing well what he wished to say, but Coyote nodded in apparent understanding.

"I will do so, Uncle."

Coyote moved toward his lodge to gather a few supplies, and White Buffalo watched him go. The little man's casual gait belied the importance of his mission. The holy man could not have explained it, but he somehow felt that these events were a most important turning point in the history of the People. Whether for good or bad, he did not know.

35

It was much as the Caddo had told it, Coyote reflected, watching the moving column in the distance. There was a very large number of the big dogs the man had described. Some were indeed ridden. Not only that, they could be ridden at great speed, much faster than a man could run. For this reason, the wolves of the People had elected to stay some distance away and watch only the column as a whole.

The gods were very dangerous according to a group of wolves whom they had encountered from another tribe. These warriors told, in sign talk, of capture and torture. None survived capture, it seemed. And the gods moved on, northward, relentlessly, day after day. Their purpose was still not known.

Coyote viewed this entire venture with a confusion of emotion. His curiosity told him to get closer, to learn of these strange beings. His natural reluctance to expose himself to danger, or even much exertion, told him to stay away. He wondered sometimes what he would do if suddenly confronted by one of the gods astride his great dog and carrying the long spear that the wolves had noted. Coyote would prefer to run in such a situation, but he was not very good at running. The thought crossed his mind that he could leave the wolves to return to the band and report his impressions to White Buffalo. He was only two sleeps away. But his natural curiosity won out, and Coyote stayed.

It had been decided not to move the camp. The path of the gods would bypass the area if they continued on their present course. That was the situation as told to the Southern band by word of mouth. Coyote, however, hearing the news from the messengers who shuttled back and forth, read a deeper meaning into such a decision. He knew that White Buffalo and Hump Ribs would be in constant communication. They would know from the messengers that an attempt to move would be useless. The Southern band, with lodges and baggage, would be more conspicuous, and more vulnerable, on the move. With the speed of travel that the gods possessed, the People could not escape anyway. Coyote knew this, but it was reassuring to most of the People if their leaders merely announced that they would not move. It would be a narrow miss at best, Coyote realized, if the column continued as it was, and he was concerned for the safety of his wife and family. Well, another day, and he could go to them. And, of course, to the holy man, to tell him of the amazing things he had seen.

White Buffalo waited, restless and impatient. He had not heard from Coyote. The chief's messengers had reported daily on the progress of the gods, and the holy man had talked in turn with Hump Ribs about their observations. The approaching column of gods was traveling rapidly, now only two days away. It had become apparent that it would be futile to break camp and run. The People would be even more vulnerable while traveling. Besides, they might remain unnoticed if they remained quietly where they were now camped. Hump Ribs and White Buffalo discussed the situation, and the chief announced that they would stay, remain alert, and avoid all contact if possible.

"Could your medicine be used to stop them?" asked Hump Ribs.

"I do not know," White Buffalo answered thoughtfully. "Maybe. I must think on this."

It was a truly important decision that White Buffalo found thrust upon him. At first he had been startled that Hump Ribs would even suggest such a thing. Then he realized that the chief did not fully understand what he was asking. In the scheme of things, a holy man was given powers of the spirit to use as he saw fit. Sometimes his ceremonies and visions were successful, sometimes not. But one basic premise remained true. The medicine of the holy man must be used only to help, not harm. Medicine used for evil, even against an enemy, was very dangerous, possibly fatal, to the holy man who invoked it.

In the present situation, if White Buffalo attempted

spells to harm the invading column, even to save the People . . . *aiee*, he had no desire to die, unless that seemed the only way. To complicate his narrowing choices further, the nature of the invading gods was quite unclear. They tortured and killed, it was said, so maybe they were bad gods. Still, the torture was, so far, merely rumor. If these were indeed gods and *not* evil, any attempt to injure them would surely be fatal.

If only he had more information! Why did Coyote not return? Coyote's keen insight might easily provide the information he needed.

Meanwhile, White Buffalo sought solitude to commune with his spirit-guide. In anticipation of such a need, he had begun his fast earlier. Now he prayed and chanted, and waited for his guide to join him. He had great difficulty falling asleep, and even then, he woke several times, having had no visions.

It was nearly morning before he reached the strange mystical state between sleep and awakening and found himself approaching his spirit-guide.

Ah-koh, *Grandfather*, he greeted.

The great bull rolled an inquisitive eye at him, but there was no answering thought.

Grandfather, I have come for help. I am in great need.
Yes?

Ah, at least there was an acknowledgement of his presence.

There is a large number of godlike persons approaching my people. It seems that they mean us harm.

This may be true, came the answer.

Ah, so the gods *are* dangerous, White Buffalo thought.

It has been suggested that I use my medicine to try to stop them.

There was no response for a little while, and White Buffalo began to be afraid that he would get no answer. Finally the bull rolled an eye at him, and the mind-talk continued.

That is yours to decide.

The vision started to fade, and White Buffalo felt the grip of panic.

Wait! Don't go . . . Grandfather, I need you!

The bull was moving away now, but paused to look back.

It is yours to decide, came the spirit-message. *Maybe they will turn back.*

White Buffalo awoke, shaking and in a cold sweat. He had never before totally lost his composure in the presence of his spirit-guide. And he felt that he had never received less help in time of need. This was probably the greatest danger to the People in White Buffalo's lifetime. He had been able to serve them well, but now he had grave doubts. He was angry that he had received little help. Yes, angry at his spirit-guide.

In desperation, he was ready to use his gift to do harm to the approaching gods. If, of course, it was possible. But what else could he do? There was so little time. Tomorrow might be too late. He hurried back to the village, already planning his ceremony to invoke harm to the gods.

Crow's face was anxious and drawn.

"How is it, my husband?" she asked.

"Not good, Crow," he said as he began to search among his herbs and medicine things.

"You did not find your spirit-guide?" she asked in astonishment.

"Yes, but it was no help."

"No help? How can this be?"

"Crow, I have no time to explain. I will perform a ceremony to try to stop these strange god-beings."

Crow's eyes were wide with wonder.

"But, Elk, is that not dangerous?"

He hesitated, wondering if his wife knew how dangerous this could become.

"Elk," she persisted, "is this good use of your gift? You have said that if a holy man uses his power for evil, it will kill him."

"That is true," White Buffalo agreed, "but is this evil, to try to save the People? Maybe these gods are bad gods."

"And maybe not," retorted Crow. "My husband, you could be in great danger. I wish you to think carefully about this."

"I know. I have thought, Crow. I must try to use my medicine to stop them."

"As you must," Crow Woman said sadly. "I do not understand, though, why your spirit-guide would not help."

"Nor do I. The only message was that maybe the gods will turn back."

They looked at each other, and a great light began to dawn on both.

"Elk!" gasped Crow Woman excitedly, "that is it! They do not *have* to be defeated!"

"Only to turn aside, to pass our camp, without discovering it. I can use my medicine for such a purpose, Crow, because it would not be evil!"

"How can I help?" she asked.

"The drum cadence. Let me prepare my ceremony, and we will begin. Bring my facepaint."

"Will it work against gods?" Crow asked.

"I do not know, but it is all we have. Anyway"—he paused long enough to smile at her—"we do not know that these are gods. That is only the word of the Caddo."

Inwardly, he wished that he knew more about these strange beings with shiny skins and dogs that could carry a man. He wished that he was younger, so that he could have gone with the wolves instead of sending Coyote. *Aiee,* what had happened to that one? Why did he not return or send word?

White Buffalo busied himself with preparations for his ceremony, now with greater confidence. He still might offend the gods with his attempts to turn them aside, but at least he would not run the risk of death from his own medicine.

The drumbeat began just after sunset. The dances, prayers, and chants, with intermittent ceremonial incense burning, continued throughout the night. It was a private ceremony, carried out within or just in front of the holy man's lodge. The People knew that something was going on, possibly something important. It was assumed that it had to do with the advancing column that was being observed by the wolves of the People. Consequently, there was a curious scatter of onlookers who came and went during the night, discussing quietly these events.

Sun Boy was lifting his torch above earth's rim when White Buffalo finished the last chanted prayer of supplication, and the drum fell silent. Half-stumbling, he made his way to the lodge and almost fell into his sleeping-robes. Crow Woman covered him with a robe and lay down near him, watching with concern as the holy man fell into the deep sleep of complete exhaustion.

It was nearly evening when White Buffalo awoke. He lay there a moment, becoming oriented to the day. Crow Woman lay sleeping. He knew that she too must have been exhausted. Quietly he rose and slipped outside.

He was just relieving his bladder behind the lodge when he heard a shout. One of the wolves was returning. White Buffalo hurried to the lodge of Hump Ribs, arriving at almost the same time as the messenger.

"Come in," the chief beckoned to the holy man, as he held the doorskin aside for the messenger.

It was apparent that the scout had news of great importance. He had the appearance of one who had been running, striving to reach the village before dark. But was his news good or bad?

"My chief," the runner panted, "the gods have turned back. This morning, they broke camp and moved away to the west, or southwest."

A broad smile broke the stern countenance of Hump Ribs. The crisis, the threat to the Southern band, appeared to be over. He nodded approvingly.

White Buffalo sat numbly, listening to the more detailed description of the messenger. His prayers and ceremonial chants had been successful, but he found that he had mixed feelings about it. It was over, and he had not had the opportunity to see the gods, to try to fathom their secret powers. And it was too late. He had been born at the wrong time. If only this had happened when he was young, so that he could have been with the wolves, could have seen for himself the wondrous god-beings. His mind wandered for a moment and then was sharply jerked back to reality by the words of the scout.

"One god was left behind," the man was saying. "He appears to be lost. He rides one of the elk-dogs."

"Elk-dogs?" asked Hump Ribs.

"Yes, my chief," the messenger chuckled. "Coyote calls them that. These dogs are as big as an elk. We have not seen one closely. Oh, yes, holy man, I have a message for you. Coyote says to tell you he will watch this lost god today and come to you tonight."

"They are that close?" asked White Buffalo in amazement.

"Oh, yes. The lost one has continued this way. I do not know, since I left, but they should be very close tonight."

"It is good," said Hump Ribs. "I will go back out with you."

36

"Uncle, I am made to feel that this is very important," Coyote said wearily.

His fat round body was not well suited to hurried travel.

"Yes, yes, go on!" White Buffalo urged impatiently.

"Well, they told you that the gods have turned back?" White Buffalo nodded.

"But there was this one who appeared lost," Coyote continued. "We followed him. Uncle, the shiny skins that we have heard of . . . I do not think they are skins. A garment, maybe . . ."

White Buffalo exhaled a sigh audibly and impatiently.

"Forgive me, Uncle." Coyote hurried on. "There is so much. . . .This lost one is apparently abandoned by the others. Maybe they expected him to rejoin them, but he is injured."

"Injured? How?"

"He fell from his elk-dog."

"Wait. It is true, then, that they ride on the backs of these animals?"

"Yes, Uncle, and some carry burdens. But this one was startled by a real-snake. When it rattled, the elk-dog jumped, and the shiny god fell. We thought he was dead and came near to see. A long time he was dead, but then he rolled over and woke up."

Ah, thought White Buffalo. A god is immortal. He cannot die.

"But then," Coyote continued, "the god vomited. Uncle, would a god crawl on all fours, and grovel in his own puke?"

Before the holy man could answer, Coyote hurried on.

"Forgive me, Uncle, there is so much . . . the god then sat and seemed to remove his head."

"His head?"

Coyote giggled at his little joke and continued.

"So it seemed to some. There was a headdress, round and shiny. He removed it and appeared to take his head off. Some of us had seen that it appeared to be fastened with a leather strap or thong, so it was not really his head, but . . ."

"Go on, Coyote," White Buffalo urged.

"Yes . . . well, he is called Heads Off because of this and how it appeared. Hump Ribs called a council to decide what to do."

"Hump Ribs is still out there?"

"Yes, Uncle."

Coyote paused, seeming reluctant to relate his own part in these events.

"There were those," he said slowly, "who wished to kill the god and his elk-dog to remove the danger. But Uncle, I am made to think we must know more of this."

"What do you mean, Coyote?"

"Well, there are many things. Could a god be injured in this way? His head is bloody, and the shiny headdress probably saved it from being burst when he struck. Then he was sick. Several times. I do not think . . . Uncle, I do not believe these are gods at all. They are *men*, from a far tribe, much different than ours."

White Buffalo had begun to suspect something of the sort.

"How, different?" he asked.

"He has fur," Coyote said.

"*Fur?*"

"Yes. Black fur, which grows from his face. Not like ours, which we pluck with the clam-shells. This is black and curly, like that of the buffalo."

"Could it be a mask or a garment?"

"No, Uncle. It grows directly from his face."

"*Aiee,* that is strange."

"Yes, and the shiny skins—as I said, I do not think it is their skin. It is of the same material as the headdress."

"You think the fur covers his whole body, like the bear?"

"Maybe. I do not think so. His hands are not hairy."

"Did he speak?"

"Nothing we understood. He moaned a lot and said words strange to us. Oh, and he does not know handsigns. They meant nothing to him."

"You have been close to him. It did not seem dangerous?"

"Not really. He is sick and weak. My fear was that somebody would kill him before we could learn of his tribe. But they are not thinking so much of that now."

"Why?"

"Well, he seems harmless. And I . . ."—Coyote paused to chuckle at his own cleverness—"I gave him a name."

"A name?"

"Yes, Heads Off, as I said." He giggled again. "It is harder to kill someone if you know his name."

Yes, that is true, thought White Buffalo. *Coyote is clever, as always.*

"What is happening now?" the holy man asked.

"Nothing. He has bedded for the night. We are watching him. The elk-dog stays near."

"The elk-dog? It did not run away?" White Buffalo asked in amazement.

"What? Oh, no. It stays with him and eats grass."

"This 'elk-dog' eats *grass*?"

Coyote giggled.

"Yes, Uncle. Now it seems more elk than dog. But it has no horns."

"Tell me more of this elk-dog."

"Well, some wanted to kill it. It looks good to eat. But I thought it must, for some reason, be better to ride it than eat it. Otherwise, Heads Off would have eaten it already!"

Coyote sat back, smiling, pleased with his reasoning.

"So they will *not* kill it, you think?"

"No. I talked to Hump Ribs, and he told them not to. We could kill it later if we really need the meat."

"Tell me more of this elk-dog."

"Well, it has a beautiful skin. Gray in color, like a gray wolf, but shorthaired, like an antelope. It eats grass, and its eyes look at us without fear. It is proud . . . a look of eagles is in the eyes . . . oh, yes, I nearly forgot—its hooves are not split like other animals'."

"What?"

Coyote held up a hand, fingers apart, to demonstrate.

"There is no cleft. The foot is solid, Uncle." He paused to

chuckle. "When we first saw it, it seemed to wear a turtle on each foot."

White Buffalo's head whirled. He had been so preoccupied with the invading god-beings and his ceremony . . . but now . . . he had completely forgotten his vision of so long ago. A lifetime ago, it seemed. The strange creature of his vision, the one that had seemed so important but was never seen again. Was he now to learn of it, in this strange way? His heart was pounding, and his palms were sweating.

"A turtle?" he asked in a hoarse whisper.

"Yes," laughed Coyote. "Of course it only looked that way. The hoof was solid, not split."

"Yes," said White Buffalo absently. "Coyote, I must see this animal. I will go back with you."

"There is no need, Uncle. It is just over the hill. You can see it in the morning."

"It is *here?* That close?"

"Yes. Heads Off, too. Hump Ribs said we will watch him but not bother him, until we see what he will do."

"But, he is sick with a broken head?"

"Yes, but it seems he will recover. We will see."

Coyote wandered off. White Buffalo was not certain whether he meant to return to the watch or to spend the rest of the night at home. The holy man turned back to his own bed.

"Elk," Crow Woman whispered, "did I hear right? Coyote spoke of the creature of your visions, the turtle-footed elk?"

"Yes," White Buffalo said thoughtfully. "Crow, I have never told anyone but you, and my father before his death. No one knew of this creature, that I had *seen* it long ago. *Aiee*, what can this mean?"

Crow shook her head.

"I do not know, but it must be very important."

"Coyote said that, too. *Why* is it important?"

"Do you not feel that?" asked Crow.

"Of course. But I do not understand it."

"Maybe it is not *meant* to be understood, my husband."

"That is true. We will go and look at this creature, the elk-dog, in the morning."

There was to be more than one startling development that next day. The People awoke to find that buffalo had come. For most, this news of immediate importance overshadowed any speculation about elk-dogs and gods who remove their heads. Here was food for the coming winter. Times had not been hard, and there was food, but at the Moon of Falling Leaves it is wise to make preparations. There may be very little hunting for the next few moons, and every lodge should have a season's supply of dried meat and pemmican stored in the space behind the lodge-lining. Therefore, the arrival of the buffalo was an important marker in the trail of the seasons.

It was immediately apparent that this was not the main fall migration. Only a few hundred animals, the forefront of the great herds to come. They were sleek and fat from grazing on lush grasses in the Sacred Hills and farther north. Now, like the People, they were moving south for the winter season. The move was early, even before the seasonal change in the wind. White Buffalo wondered if this was an omen, a sign of a coming hard winter. He would cast the bones later.

But for now, his greatest desire was to go and see the elk-dog and its strange rider. With Crow Woman, he started in the direction indicated by Coyote.

He was interrupted by a group of hunters who asked him for a prediction for the coming hunt. Impatiently, he performed the ceremony and sent them on their way. Of course they would have a good hunt, he thought to himself. The season, the fat herd—everything was right.

Again, he and Crow started for the hill from which they could see the god and his elk-dog. As they topped the rise, it was like a dream in which one can see everything at once. The gently rolling valley spread before them, the buffalo just moving into the northern end. And there, scarcely a long bowshot away, was the elk-dog. It was calmly grazing. White Buffalo gasped in wonder. He had already known but still it was a shock to see the creature, warm and alive, in all its graceful beauty. It raised its head and seemed to look at him. Even at such a distance, he caught a hint of the intelligence in the dark, wideset eyes.

"Aiee," he said softly.

"It is beautiful," Crow Woman whispered at his side. "This is the turtle-footed creature of your vision?"

"Yes," he answered simply. What more was there to say?

Now their attention turned to the figure near the elk-dog. Yes, thought White Buffalo, it was as Coyote suspected. This was a man, not a god. The man moved stiffly, as if from injury, even limping a little. He picked up something from the ground, something not seen well at this distance, and approached the elk-dog. It was difficult to see, but the man appeared to wrap some thongs around the creature's head and place something in its mouth. *Ah,* he thought. *This is his secret, the way he controls the elk-dog, his elk-dog medicine.* White Buffalo longed for a closer look, to determine the nature of this powerful spell over so large and strong a creature. He could see a shining sparkle, a reflection of sunlight, around the elk-dog's nose and mouth. It reminded him of the flash of silvery minnows in the stream, when they turn as one, and their sides glint in the sun. This must be part of the powerful medicine.

Even though he was beginning to understand, he did not quite know how—ah, now the man picked up a small robe or pad with thongs and straps attached and carelessly tossed it on the animal's back. He tightened the straps, placed his foot in a dangling loop of some sort, and stepped up, to sit astride the creature's back.

They saw now that the man carried a long spear. Its point, too, sparkled like the medicine around the mouth of the elk-dog.

"Should we run?" whispered Crow.

"I think not," White Buffalo answered, his voice hushed in awe. "He does not even see us. Look, he rides toward the buffalo."

Fascinated, they watched while the elk-dog trotted calmly toward the grazing animals. The man seemed to select one, and moved toward it, a fat cow. It was over in a moment—a sudden rush, a thrust of the long spear. The elk-dog slid to a stop, withdrawing the weapon, and the running cow took a few more frantic leaps, stumbled, and fell to lie kicking in the grass. White Buffalo was astounded at the efficiency of the procedure.

"Ah, so *this* is the real value of the elk-dog! To hunt!"

It was the voice of Coyote, who had joined them, unnoticed.

White Buffalo nodded, still entranced by the scene below.

"Maybe," he said slowly. "Maybe there are even more things that this elk-dog can do. But do you see how his medicine controls the animal? *Aiee,* he is powerful, Coyote."

The man had dismounted now and was rather clumsily hacking a chunk of meat from the hind quarter of the cow with a knife. He succeeded and withdrew to some distance away, to build a cooking fire, using sticks from a packrat's nest in a scrubby tree on the hillside. He appeared to have no use for the rest of the carcass.

It was not long before some of the hunters had sent word back to camp. A butchering party approached, cautiously at first. When it appeared that the elk-dog's rider, who owned the kill, did not object, they fell to the work of butchering with enthusiasm. In a short while, only stripped bones remained.

By evening, the word had been passed from Hump Ribs and the council. Heads Off, the outsider, and his elk-dog, were not to be bothered in any way. There was a strong feeling that it would be good to have him in the area. It was apparent that he could easily kill more buffalo than he could use, and someone might as well benefit from his kills.

White Buffalo had grave doubts, however. He saw too ready an acceptance of this strange foreign medicine. He would remain cautious until he knew more. Of one thing he was certain—things would never be the same again. It was a time of change, and in his declining years, he had come to dread change.

37

There was change in the wind. It had been some time since Heads Off's first kill when White Buffalo saw the signs of the seasonal shift. From the gentle breezes that blew from the south all summer came the change to a new direction. A cutting northwest wind whipped across the prairie, chilling the bones of the elderly and nipping the noses and ears of the young. Cold Maker was coming.

That was not the only change observed by White Buffalo. The People had developed a new attitude toward Heads Off, the outsider. With the help of his elk-dog, the newcomer could kill a buffalo, almost at will, whenever he was hungry. The People watched closely because Heads Off never used more than enough meat for a day or two. The remainder of the kill was always utilized by the women. Winter stores were filling with much more ease than ever before. Increasingly, there seemed to be a dependency developing. The People were relying on the skills of Heads Off and the elk-dog. This worried the holy man. The People, he feared, would be unprepared when the visitor moved on, leaving them to fend for themselves in the old ways.

He wished that the man would do so and went so far as to carry out, quite in secret, a ceremony with prayers that Heads Off would go, to rejoin his own tribe. Of course, at first the head injury prevented it. It was apparent that any activity caused much head pain. Heads Off would lie on the ground for some time after a kill, holding his injured skull in his hands.

White Buffalo was somewhat offended by the attitude of Coyote. Coyote seemed fascinated by the stranger and had assumed the role of protector. He had given Heads Off a buffalo robe to protect him from the weather and was

teaching him the hand-sign talk. Coyote reported faithfully to the holy man, however, so there was a certain
advantage to the tenuous arrangement. White Buffalo
could remain well informed without seeming to do so.

It was some time before the holy man realized what he
found so worrisome. Everyone in the band was talking
about Heads Off, his activities, his skills. White Buffalo was
threatened with a loss of prestige. Yes, that was it. He could
hardly admit to jealousy, but it must come to that. In final
form, the outsider presented a threat to the professional
skill of the holy man. His elk-dog medicine was becoming
more important daily, eclipsing the traditional buffalo
medicine of the People. Again and again, White Buffalo
found himself wishing that the man would go and take the
cursed elk-dog with him. He wondered if his own position
in the tribe would become obsolete. No one seemed to
need him anymore. He performed small ceremonies designed to move the intruder on his way, though he was
careful not to use his medicine for harm. It was more of an
attempt to persuade, he told himself.

The young men, too, were fascinated by the novelty of
the outsider and his elk-dog. There were two especially,
youths not quite grown, who followed him and pulled
grass to feed the elk-dog. *Aiee*, that was a bad sign, White
Buffalo thought. It was unlikely that any gifted youth
would be interested in apprenticing to the medicine man
when they had the elk-dog to follow. To make matters
worse, one of the favorites of the outsider was Coyote's
son, Long Elk. The other was Standing Bird, son of Mouse
Roars.

Meanwhile, Heads Off had been invited to live in the
lodge of Coyote. It was now understood that "Heads Off
hunts for the lodge of Coyote." Of course, Big-Footed
Woman was generous with the kills, and the arrangement
continued to benefit all.

All except White Buffalo, of course. He was increasingly
frustrated. It was becoming extremely irritating to have
Coyote popping in, every day or two, to relate the wonderful events that had occurred. Coyote seemed as completely charmed by Heads Off as the boys.

Something must happen soon, White Buffalo reflected as
he strolled through the camp. They had made the move to
winter camp shortly after Heads Off joined them, and he

had accompanied them. According to Coyote, the stranger was staying with them to find water, since the People knew its location. Their southward migration was the proper direction for Heads Off too, so it seemed logical. Except, of course, that White Buffalo did not like it. Heads Off had stayed so long now that with the change in the weather, it would soon be too late to travel. He was looking for Coyote, to ask him about it.

His eye caught a group of children at play. One boy rode on the back of another and struck a third with a long stick. Even without an explanation, it was easy to tell what the game represented, but he stopped to ask.

"We are playing Heads Off, Uncle," a child replied. "He strikes the buffalo with the real-spear, and the buffalo falls down."

"Yes, I see," the holy man said, half to himself.

He saw only too well. The young of the People were being corrupted by the influence of the stranger. Something must be done to stop the spread of this evil. But what? He was certain that Heads Off was using his medicine to invade the minds of the children, but what to do? It must be done quickly, for when even the children's play was affected, how long before they would lose their time-honored heritage?

Reluctantly, he began to think that to remove the threat, the stranger must be destroyed. The most powerful medicine of the People must be their own, the medicine of the buffalo. He told himself that this was not just a threat to his own prestige but to the People's way of life. A test of power between the two medicines. He was uneasy, because in a clash of power, he was not certain that his own medicine was strong enough to triumph. Maybe, if he could not use his medicine against the intruder for fear of defeat or the risks of misuse . . . maybe he could kill Heads Off himself. No, that would not be good. That would surely sacrifice all his prestige. Maybe someone would be willing to assassinate him. . . .

"*Ah-koh*, holy man, are you looking for something?" asked Mouse Roars.

Mouse Roars was seated in front of his lodge, smoking comfortably against his backrest.

"I . . . ah . . . yes, have you seen Coyote?" White Buffalo stammered.

"Yes, Uncle, Coyote and Heads Off are in the lodge of Hump Ribs." He pointed at the chief's dwelling. "Shall I tell him when he comes out?"

"No . . . no, Mouse. It is nothing. I will see him later."

He turned and stalked off toward his own lodge, angry and even more frustrated. *Aiee,* for Coyote to take Heads Off to visit the chief . . . were they all in a plot to discredit him?

It was later that day when Coyote appeared at the lodge of the holy man.

"*Ah-koh,* Uncle," he began pleasantly.

White Buffalo merely grunted a greeting. He was still angry.

"I have come this time at the bidding of Hump Ribs," Coyote said formally. "He wishes me to bring Heads Off to see you."

Ah, then the test of medicines was to be at the request of the chief. The thought was like ashes in his mouth. After all his years of faithful service, of selflessness and sacrifice for the People, such ingratitude was beyond belief. Yet to refuse the contest would admit weakness. All his prestige would be gone and his medicine weakened.

"I think his medicine is very powerful," Coyote was saying, "but Heads Off has used it only to help with the hunt. Maybe I can persuade him to bring his medicine, so that you can examine it."

"This is not a contest?" White Buffalo asked.

"What? Oh, no, Uncle. Hump Ribs wishes you both to use your medicine to help the People."

That was not quite Hump Ribs's interpretation but Coyote's. He was carefully manipulating the shifting power structure as skillfully as any diplomat of other cultures.

White Buffalo set the scene carefully—his paints, fragrant-scented herbs and powders to toss on the fire, ready for use. He shook out the white cape and brushed it with a hawk's wing, smoothing and grooming the thick white fur.

"*Ah-koh,* Uncle, we are here," called Coyote, outside.

Crow Woman welcomed the visitors into the lodge. White Buffalo noticed at once that Heads Off was wearing the strange shiny garment once thought to be his skin. It was also apparent, however, that the young outsider had adopted the garment of the People to some extent. His

eet were now covered by soft moccasins, which showed
he unmistakable patterns and craftsmanship of Big-
Footed Woman. He also wore new leggings and breechclout, undoubtedly from the same source. White Buffalo
found himself somewhat irritated by this easy acceptance
of the interloper. Big-Footed Woman was treating him like
family.

The customary small talk ensued, and the holy man was
surprised at how rapidly the newcomer had learned to
communicate. There was some hesitancy, but between his
knowledge of some words and some hand signs, a conversation was possible. White Buffalo did not fail to notice,
however, that it was constantly assisted by Coyote. At
times he was not certain whether the ideas being expressed were those of the visitor or of Coyote.

The holy man found, however, that he was powerfully
intrigued. Rarely, once in a lifetime, perhaps never, would
this opportunity happen to understand the medicine of
another. Especially a medicine so powerful and so different from his own.

As he began his dance, imitating the dance of the buffalo, his mind was occupied with these thoughts. He concentrated on perfection of the ritual, giving meaning to
each shake of the head, each pawing motion of a hoof. As
he began to feel each swaying motion, once again to get
"inside the head" of the great animal he represented, he
felt at home, confident. This was a medicine that the
stranger did not have, *could* not have.

There remained the doubt, however, the silent fear of
being displaced. If the stranger and his medicine remained
with the People, there would be no need for the medicine
of the buffalo. White Buffalo's usefulness was over. So he
must do something. He could wait a little while. Maybe for
the winter, even. But then, if the stranger did not leave
. . how should it be done? By use of his medicine? Simply kill him? Or maybe someone could be found who
would act as an assassin. Kill the elk-dog, maybe? That was
a possibility that had not previously occurred to him. With
no elk-dog, could there be elk-dog medicine?

White Buffalo finished the ceremony, and the drum fell
silent.

"Now," said Coyote. "Come, we will show you the elk-
dog medicine."

Coyote led the way outside to the place where the elk
dog waited. The shiny medicine-thing was in the crea
ture's mouth, and the pad was strapped to its back. White
Buffalo had not seen the creature up close before and was
impressed by its size. It did not appear too threatening
however. It turned its head to gaze curiously at him with
large gentle eyes. There was little that was frightening
And this was plainly the creature of his vision quest.

Now Coyote was talking.

". . . this circle, I think, Uncle, the ring around the jaw
That is the medicine that lets him control it."

Maybe, White Buffalo thought to himself. *That is not too
complicated.*

"What is the purpose of the elk-dog?" he asked. "Besides
hunting buffalo?"

"Heads Off says, to ride long distances, for war, or to
hunt."

"Do his people eat elk-dogs?"

"No. Hump Ribs asked that. Sometimes if they are starving, but not usually, Heads Off says."

The little man cleared his throat, a trifle embarrassed
and went on.

"I am made to think, Uncle, that the medicine of Heads
Off is greatly different from yours."

"Of course!" snapped the holy man.

"No, no," Coyote said quickly, "I meant no harm, Uncle
It is only that the medicines seem to work well together.'

"What do you mean?"

"Well, Uncle, your medicine makes for easier kills. One
medicine helps the other!"

Of course. Coyote, the thinker, had found the answer to
the dilemma. It was only necessary to acknowledge the
new medicine to remove its threat—to point out its differences.

"Yes," White Buffalo said slowly, "they are quite different, these medicines. Mine brings the buffalo, to be killed
with the aid of the elk-dog. It is good. They will help each
other."

White Buffalo was quite pleased with the outcome of the
meeting. This was a situation that he could now manage
But he was no more pleased than Coyote, who smiled to
himself as he turned away. It had gone quite well.

38

Once he had decided in his own heart and mind that the two medicines were not in conflict, White Buffalo settled into a more comfortable existence. He still did not feel, somehow, that his position allowed him to associate closely with the stranger and his medicine. He was content to observe, to let Coyote relate to the new elk-dog medicine.

He sometimes felt pangs of jealousy that Coyote's interest lay there, instead of in his own, the medicine of the buffalo. It was different, however. It became apparent that the medicine of the elk-dog was a very physical thing. Agility and active use of the body were required, while Coyote was a bit clumsy and at best, lazy. Coyote's relationship to the medicine of the elk-dog was that of a thoughtful observer rather than a participant. That pleased White Buffalo. It also kept him informed, as Coyote continued to share his observations. But the stranger seemed less threatening now. No longer semisupernatural, he could be observed as a man. A strange complicated man from a far tribe, it was true, but that was only a matter of interest now. It was discovered that the black fur did not cover the entire body of Heads Off. Coyote had seen him remove his garment to empty his bowels.

"His butt is as shiny as mine," Coyote reported with glee.

Heads Off proved quick to learn. By the time Cold Maker arrived in earnest, the hair-faced outsider could use sign-talk well and converse in the tongue of the People. He still spoke with an accent but was understandable. Coyote continued to instruct and inform the visitor.

It was known that Heads Off wished to return to his own

tribe. It was simply too foolhardy to attempt in the winter moons, noted on the plains for unpredictable weather. So Heads Off waited, a little impatiently at times. When the band moved north in the Moon of Roses, White Buffalo supposed, Heads Off would move south, the direction from which he had come. That would be a time of mixed feelings. The People would regret the loss of easy procurement of meat when Heads Off was no longer there to kill buffalo. To White Buffalo's way of thinking, however, that would be an opportunity to return to the traditional ways. He would no longer need to be concerned by any possible threat to his own prestige. Yes, it would be good to see the visitor go when the time came.

Meanwhile, the moons passed in winter camp, with gambling and smokes and storytelling. Heads Off participated, and his communication skills continued to improve. Coyote related that they had exchanged Creation stories and that Heads Off had reacted much as anyone else would in the telling.

"Is the Creation story of his tribe a good one?" asked White Buffalo.

"I have heard worse," Coyote observed. "Their Great Father made First Man out of mud and breathed life into him. Then he gave the man a woman to live with."

White Buffalo nodded.

"I must listen to it sometime."

"He liked our story also," Coyote went on. "I told him how we crawled out of the earth through the log."

That had always been a favorite story of the People. They had lived in darkness, it was said, until they were summoned by a deity who seated himself astride a hollow cottonwood log. With a drumstick, he tapped on the log, and with each tap, another of the People crawled out into the sunshine. There was a joke involved in the telling. It was customary when a stranger was present to stop at that point in the story, hoping that the listener would ask the obvious question: Are they *still* coming out? No, said the standard reply. Alas, a fat woman got stuck in the log, and none has come through since. That is why we are a small tribe.

"Did you tell him about the Fat Woman?" asked White Buffalo.

"Yes," chuckled Coyote, "but he did not understand it.

Uncle, I am made to think that the tribe of Heads Off does not enjoy its religion very much."

"Perhaps that is their way," suggested the holy man.

"Maybe so," Coyote pondered "Maybe he would like to hear the Creation stories of the Growers. Did some of them not come up out of a great river?"

"I think so. Someone to the north of us . . . Mandans, maybe, crawled out much as we did, by climbing the roots of a large grapevine."

"Ah, yes, I remember that one. A good story."

It was still assumed that in the spring, when the People moved north to the Sun Dance, Heads Off would return to his own tribe. Despite the interesting contact for a few moons, White Buffalo continued to look forward to that event. It would be the time of returning to the old ways. The confusion of the strange medicine from outside would be finished, and it would be good.

There was still a question in White Buffalo's mind, however, that refused to go away. *Why?* Why had he been given the vision of the elk-dog so long ago? When he first saw the animal in the flesh, he had known that it was the creature of his vision, and it seemed that all was complete. Yet there was something missing, something not quite right. Soon the hair-faced outsider would leave, and the great episode would be at an end. The holy man had already painted the event on the story skin. It was a figure of Heads Off, removing his headdress in the incident which had provided his name.

Still, something was missing, and White Buffalo could not think what it might be. There seemed, in the events of the past year, not enough importance to give meaning to the vision of his youth. Ah well, maybe he was only showing his age, the holy man pondered. The visions of youth are always bright with the promise of the future and become less important with the reality of the passing years. But he did not believe it. There *was* something, a purpose of some sort, he was sure. He had simply not seen it yet. Maybe he never would . . . Heads Off and the elk-dog would be gone soon, and he, White Buffalo, would have missed the entire significance of this important event in the lives of the People.

He worried, prayed, and even discussed the matter with

Crow. That was unsatisfactory because even with her keen insight and intuition, Crow had not seen the *vision* of the elk-dog. She could not understand.

It was now common knowledge, as the Moon of Greening changed the prairie almost before one's eyes, that soon the People would start their move. Not everyone realized, probably, that Heads Off would be traveling in the other direction, but it was foremost in the mind of White Buffalo. He was wondering when Hump Ribs would announce . . . maybe he should go and talk to the chief.

These thoughts were interrupted by the approach of Coyote. The little man was laughing.

"Heads Off cannot leave us!" he announced with glee. "His elk-dog is pregnant!"

A mixture of emotion washed over the holy man. Regret that the incident of Heads Off's stay would *not* be over. Relief that he might have the opportunity to solve the mystery. And many questions came to mind about elk-dog reproduction.

"What . . . how? . . ." he mumbled in surprise.

Coyote laughed again, the high-pitched animal chuckle of his namesake.

"I do not know all, Uncle," he admitted. "Heads Off was very angry. I think the elk-dog may not travel well when it is near to birthing."

More confusion whirled in the thoughts of White Buffalo. The elk-dog at first had been an almost supernatural creature in his mind. Now it was almost commonplace. Even the earthy process of reproduction marked it as a quite ordinary creature, though one with special talents. Why, then, *why* had he been subjected to the startling vision of the elk-dog so many summers ago? It must be something to do with the *medicine* of the elk-dog. Yet he had satisfied himself that the elk-dog medicine was not *his* medicine but that of Heads Off.

Aiee, every time he thought he had solved the mystery, there was a new twist to the path he was following. And such a ridiculous twist. *Aiee!* A pregnant elk-dog!

It was only half a moon later when the elk-dog gave birth to a black, furry creature with knobby legs and large curious eyes. Long Elk and Standing Bird were enthralled and in a short while were handling and stroking the small elk-dog. It was a source of much amazement to all. In a remarkably short time, the foal could lope alongside the mother.

According to Coyote, this event led to much indecision. Heads Off was undecided whether he could travel with the small elk-dog. Apparently there was some thought of killing or abandoning the foal to spare the mother the stress of nursing. In the end, Heads Off decided that such a thing would be unwise. This pleased Coyote greatly.

The visitor had still not chosen his path of action when the word came that the time to move was at hand. White Buffalo waited, with the old confusion of mixed feelings, to see what Heads Off would decide. In the end, with apparent reluctance, Heads Off mounted the elk-dog and followed the People, the small elk-dog scampering playfully alongside.

"Why does he do this?" the holy man asked Coyote as they walked.

"I am not certain. Maybe the elk-dog would not travel well with her young. It is a far journey that Heads Off must go."

"But he goes with us?"

Coyote spread his palms, perplexed.

"We travel more slowly . . . *aiee*, Uncle, I do not know. Who knows what a Hairface is thinking?"

So the confusion continued for the holy man. He still felt, somehow, that he was overlooking something. He would have been more comfortable if Heads Off had gone home to wherever his own tribe lived. But again, that would not solve the question that still burned below the surface like hot coals deep in the ashes of an almost-dead campfire. *Why* was the elk-dog so important to the life of White Buffalo? He was a holy man of a small band of hunters belonging to a tribe that was not a great power on the plains.

A hundred times he almost convinced himself that the coming of the stranger, riding on an elk-dog, was an isolated incident. Heads Off would be gone as soon as the small elk-dog was able to travel well. The entire season of the elk-dog would be only a memory and a picture on the story-skin. Then why, he asked himself, was he given the vision, and the sense of the elk-dog's importance? Once more, he would arrive at the same point with no apparent answer.

One further incident occurred which confused White Buffalo even more. The band was traveling without incident when one of the wolves trotted in to report that there were Head Splitters over the next ridge.

"They are traveling too," he told Hump Ribs. "Women and children . . . it is as usual."

Still, there was a thrill of excitement and potential danger that swept through the band like a chill wind. Children clung closely to their mothers, and men checked their weapons, all the while hoping they would not be used. Hump Ribs, Mouse Roars, and another warrior moved forward to the low ridge to meet the delegation from the enemy column. Coyote and White Buffalo followed closely, and the rest of the People grouped closely together some distance behind, protected by the rest of the warriors.

There were the usual greetings, small talk, and comments on the weather, carried on in hand-signs between the chiefs. Then an apparently meaningless observation by the enemy leader seized the holy man's attention.

"I see," signed the Head Splitter, "that you have an elk-dog."

There was a moment of confusion, there being no standard hand-sign for "elk-dog," but there was little doubt of meaning as the Head Splitter pointed to the animal. The mare was grazing calmly while Heads Off had dismounted to hold the rein.

"Yes," Hump Ribs replied calmly, as if elk-dogs were an everyday sight, "it belongs to an ally who is spending the season with us."

White Buffalo smiled to himself. Hump Ribs was certainly handling the situation well. Then a slight doubt arose in the back of the holy man's mind. It concerned the Head Splitter's attitude. The enemy chief had also tried to act as if elk-dogs were commonplace. This implied that the animal was not unfamiliar to him. As far as could be observed, this band of Head Splitters had no elk-dog, but they had *seen* them. This indicated, in turn, that there were more elk-dogs on the plains. The implications of this idea made the holy man's thoughts whirl. What if the Head Splitters too could hunt as easily as the hair-faced outsider?

They would become wealthy and powerful. And dangerous, more dangerous than before. The People might easily be driven from the Tallgrass Hills that had been their home for many generations.

Now White Buffalo was more confused than ever. This, perhaps, was the importance of the elk-dog vision. But how did the office of the holy man fit into this? He still did not understand.

39

The Sun Dance that year was memorable. The Southern band had much news to report at the Big Council, and Hump Ribs was equal to the task. He told the council in glowing terms of the elk-dog and of the powers of Heads Off with the lance. It was obvious that the Southern band was well fed and well dressed, and that the reason was the outsider and his hunting skill. Of course, each member of that band took pride in telling of their collective good fortune.

White Buffalo was quick to note the difference in the condition of the Southern band from the others'. The Red Rocks band, for instance, looked thin and ragged by comparison. They had eaten many of their dogs. The Eastern band had also seen better winters. Maybe, thought the holy man, the elk-dog was even more important than he had thought.

All of the People were fascinated by the elk-dog and her foal. All the bands had heard of these creatures, but none had seen them except the Red Rocks. They sometimes ranged far to the southwest and had encountered a band of strangers, they said, who possessed such an animal. It was used as a dog to carry packs, but they had not seen it ridden.

Because of the great interest, Hump Ribs, through Coyote, arranged for a demonstration of the hunt as carried out by the outsider. Heads Off was willing, and the wolves began to scout for buffalo. A small herd was located and arrangements made for an appropriate site where the spectacle could be well seen. White Buffalo took an active part in the preparation. How could he do otherwise? He must strengthen his own position by pointing out the effectiveness of his medicine in attracting the buffalo. Heads Off also seemed to take an interest in the preparations, as one should who wishes to show his medicine well, thought the holy man.

The meadow which had been selected was relatively long and narrow, bordered along one side by the stream, and on the other by the ridge where the People sat. From generations of hunting buffalo, the People understood the importance of quiet and concealment. Even so, there was a tension in the air as the first of the herd entered the meadow from the far end. White Buffalo found his palms sweating. The wary old cow in the lead paused, sniffed the air, and finally seemed to decide that the meadow was safe. She led the way, the other animals scattering to feed in the grassy flat.

Now Heads Off nudged his elk-dog forward from behind the shoulder of the hill. He chose a fat yearling bull and carefully moved toward it. A good choice, thought White Buffalo. That one will be excellent eating. It was a distinctive animal also, an odd mouse-colored hue, different enough to attract attention. Yes, a good choice.

The demonstration went extremely well. Heads Off pursued, and managed to drop his quarry directly in front of the party of warriors who sat on the ridge with the real-chief. A cheer of victory went up, a yell of triumph, led by the voices of the proud Southern band. Heads Off turned the elk-dog and rode slowly up the slope to face the assembled council. He lifted his lance.

"I give this kill," he shouted, "to Many Robes, chief of the People!"

Aiee, what a clever thing, White Buffalo thought. This outsider understands the use of medicine. Possibly Coyote had suggested such a dedication, but no matter—it was good. That distinctive skin . . . no matter where Many Robes chose to use it, the robe would always recall Heads Off and the strength of his elk-dog medicine.

The rest of the annual celebration—the Sun Dance, with its prayers, sacrifices, and ceremonies—seemed almost an anticlimax now. The days were completed, and the People began to disperse to their separate areas for the season.

None could fail to note, however, as they went their separate ways, that the Southern band had grown. Seven lodges, with possibly ten hunters, counting young men still in their parents' homes. Of course, White Buffalo observed, some were the opportunists, always ready to switch allegiance for some gain in social status. Everyone knew who these were.

But there were others whose reputations were above reproach. He noted Two Pines, of the Red Rocks, with his family. Another lodge appeared to be that of Two Pines's daughter and her husband. Well, the Red Rocks had suffered. Not from lack of leadership, perhaps, but from the whims of fortune. They would be in a time of change, some seeking a band with a stronger chief. Such was the shifting of political prestige. These changes did take place, and White Buffalo was pleased that it was to the Southern band that the discontented were shifting. Sheer numbers would strengthen the band's reputation.

Of course, he knew that it was largely the novelty of the stranger and the elk-dog that created the attraction. No matter. Once the newcomers became members of the band, even for a season, they would see the leadership of Hump Ribs. At least, the more desirable individuals would. It was a good feeling to see others wishing to join the Southern band. It had long been one of the weaker bands of the People. Now the prestige was moving their way, and it was good. Possibly, when Heads Off went to rejoin his own tribe, the numbers would shift away again. That was to be expected. Meanwhile, let the Southern band enjoy the honor.

The hunting was good that season. Every lodge was able to store an adequate supply of food for the winter with the help of Heads Off. The young outsider seemed to enjoy using his skills for this purpose. But the time came when Heads Off announced that he must leave. The small elk-dog was growing rapidly, and Heads Off thought that it should travel well now.

There were many who were sad to see Heads Off go. Especially disappointed were the two young men who had spent so much time learning of the elk-dog. Strangely, though, the holy man found himself reluctant too. After the threat to his authority had been set aside, he had rather enjoyed the novelty of the elk-dog, as well as its efficiency. White Buffalo actually found himself wishing for Heads Off to stay. There would be great benefits from the elk-dog's continued presence, not only to the Southern band but to the whole tribe. It was apparent that if Heads Off remained, there were now not one, but *two* elk-dogs. That would make the hunt even easier as the younger animal grew to maturity. Possibly Long Elk or Standing Bird could learn to ride and use the long spear. Already, Heads Off had allowed them to sit on the larger animal.

White Buffalo did not share these thoughts, even with Crow. A few moons ago he had actually considered killing the stranger, and now—*aiee!* It was a good joke on himself; unfortunately, one he could not share. Now he wondered if there might be some way he could prevent Heads Off's departure.

As the season drew to a close, the preparations of Heads Off to depart neared completion. Finally, the actual day was decided. There were many who regretted this loss. Life had been much easier when the difficult part of the hunt had been carried out by the hair-faced newcomer.

"One more hunt, Heads Off," some of the young men requested. "Let us go into the winter with plenty."

"It is good," Heads Off agreed. "Tomorrow, a last hunt, and then I must go."

White Buffalo rose early and watched the hunters go out. He wished them well and performed the ceremony for success in the hunt. But then, after their departure, the holy man performed a private ceremony outside the camp, unknown even to Crow. He burned fragrant herbs, chanted, and prayed that the stranger who had become one of them *not* depart. He wondered if this complete reversal of position might displease the spirits but decided that he must risk it.

It was later in the day that White Buffalo saw Heads Off ride in, jerking the elk-dog savagely to a stop. He was puzzled. Word had been sent back that the kill had been made, and the butchering parties had already gone out. Why, then, was Heads Off so furious? The young man stripped saddle and bridle from the horse, released it to graze, and stalked away to be alone. In his present mood, no one dared speak to him. Curious, White Buffalo waited.

Sun Boy had passed the top of his run before people started to trickle back to the camp, laden with meat. Impatiently, White Buffalo waited, wondering what event had provoked the rage he had seen in Heads Off. Finally, Coyote approached and came straight to the lodge of the holy man.

"What is it?" White Buffalo demanded. "Heads Off came back, and—"

"*Aiee,* Uncle, he was mad with rage! He broke his spearpoint."

"*Broke* it? But it is made of the shiny metal . . . it can be broken?"

"Yes! It struck a bone and snapped. It was maybe this long, you know, and broke near the middle." Coyote indicated with his hands. "My wife found the broken point as she butchered and gave it to him, but it appears that it is useless."

"But spearpoints do break," White Buffalo observed.

"Yes, but he has no other."

White Buffalo began to understand. The weapon had been part of the medicine of the elk-dog. It was different from any other weapon and essential to the hunt as Heads Off performed it. Without it, he could not hunt, and . . . *aiee,* without it, Heads Off was virtually unarmed!

"I will talk to Stone Breaker," Coyote said. "Maybe he can make a new point."

During the next days, it was quite unpleasant to be around Heads Off. It was a little while before the others realized the gravity of the loss. Stone Breaker did indeed craft a magnificent spearpoint of the finest blue-gray stone. Some said that it may have been his finest work yet. However, when Stone Breaker and Coyote took the point to give to Heads Off, the young man's reaction was quite irrational. He shouted angrily at them in his own tongue and seized the carefully crafted spearpoint in a rage. He threw it into the river, accidently cutting his finger on its sharp edge as he did so. This, of course, further angered him, and they felt it best to let him alone.

In a few days, when his rage quieted, Heads Off did seem apologetic. Stone Breaker managed to recover the spear point from the crystal-clear stream, but he and Coyote decided to wait awhile before approaching the subject again.

Heads Off made several attempts to repair the broken point. Coyote faithfully reported to White Buffalo on these occasions. The metal could be heated in a fire until it

glowed red, like hot coals in the ashes. Heads Off then tried
to make the broken parts stick together by pounding them
with a rock. Coyote had assisted him in this, but each effort
was a failure.

"Once, I thought it would work," Coyote related. "It did
stick together until he tapped it on the ground, and then it
snapped again."

Finally, Heads Off gave up the effort at repair. He remained withdrawn and depressed, and no one had summoned courage to suggest the stone point again.

"Has he said what he will do?" asked White Buffalo.

"No," Coyote answered, "but what can he do? He cannot travel without a weapon, so he must stay another winter with us."

White Buffalo said nothing. He was a bit apprehensive as
he thought of his secret ceremony. He had attempted to
cause Heads Off to remain with the People and had succeeded. At least, it appeared so; yet something had gone
wrong. The thing that had made Heads Off stay was the
loss of his spearpoint, part of his elk-dog medicine.

White Buffalo's heart was heavy because the possibility
that he had caused this dilemma nagged him. His prayer
had been granted, that Heads Off remain with them. But
there was this cruel twist. The medicine, the reason they
desired Heads Off to stay, was gone. Now he could not
leave, but there was no longer a purpose for wishing him to
do so. The secret ceremony had been too risky, White
Buffalo decided. He had overstepped his authority, had
misused his medicine.

40

It was spring before Coyote managed to coax Heads Off into testing a spear with the stone point. Stone Breaker flatly refused to offer *anything* to Heads Off again but agreed to cooperate with Coyote. With the skill of a weapons expert, he assembled a spear, using the broken weapon as a pattern. Coyote had quietly borrowed it for the purpose. The new weapon was tipped with the recovered stone point, carefully scraped and smoothed for balance.

"Its heft is as good as his own," insisted Stone Breaker, still somewhat disgruntled by the rejection of the past autumn. "He should appreciate this, but *I* will not offer it to him."

"No, no," Coyote agreed. "I will do that. You have done your part well."

So it was that Heads Off, convinced by Coyote that he had nothing to lose, agreed to try the new lance. He made his kill flawlessly and seemed a new man. He was almost jovial and made a great show of thanking Stone Breaker for his efforts.

But now, White Buffalo observed, the same dilemma had returned. Now, with a weapon, the rearmed Heads Off was ready to depart. The solution came about in a very frightening and unexpected way.

The holy man was relaxing in the warm sun of the Growing Moon when it happened. He heard a cry of alarm and looked up to see a dozen Head Splitters mounted on elk-dogs, charging into the village. It was terrifying, happening so rapidly that no one had time to think. The total surprise and the unfamiliar appearance of attackers on elk-dogs caused complete and utter confusion. Very few even tried to resist as the enemy swept through, clubbing and spearing, riding boldly through the camp, yelling their bloodcurdling falsetto war cry.

There were some exceptions. He saw one aged warrior, Black Dog, step calmly into the path of the charging horsemen, singing the death song:

> The grass and the sky go on
> forever,
> But today is a good day
> to die.

Black Dog loosed his first arrow, which knocked one of the leading warriors from his horse as if swatted by a giant hand. The old man managed to shoot again, but White Buffalo could not see whether the arrow struck. Black Dog was overrun and trampled beneath drumming hooves.

The People were running in terror, fleeing for the questionable safety of the river and its fringe of timber. Resistance was still thin. He saw Heads Off running toward the fight, pausing to grab the lance. Mouse Roars emerged from his lodge and began shooting calmly at the invaders. A warrior came swooping down on Heads Off, club swinging, and an arrow from the bow of Mouse Roars struck the rider down. Heads Off turned.

Both he and White Buffalo saw the young chief on the spotted horse at the same moment. Horsemen were riding among the lodges, striking or thrusting at targets of opportunity. As Mouse Roars readied his arrow for another shot, the horse came stepping quietly from behind his lodge. It was a beautiful creature, white with reddish rosettes over the entire body, spots no larger than a man's palm. The rider urged the animal toward the unsuspecting back of Mouse Roars. White Buffalo tried to yell a warning but could not make himself heard amid the screams and war cries. Heads Off was running forward, but too late. The Head Splitter's club swung, and Mouse Roars slumped forward, his weapon under him.

The attacker turned, and as the wife of Mouse Roars rushed from the lodge to kneel beside him, the horseman circled, looking at the mourning wife. He seemed to consider, to decide that the woman was not young enough, or perhaps not pretty enough, to be worth abducting. The great stone club swung again, and she fell across the body of her husband.

Now Heads Off rushed forward and charged at the horseman, screaming a challenge. The young chief reined toward him and kicked the horse into a run, his club whirling for a death blow. In the space of a heartbeat, it was over. White Buffalo had expected to see the form of Heads Off fall to join those of the others, but it was not so. Heads Off had dodged the swing of the club and had thrust his buffalo lance up over the elk-dog's shoulders into the belly of the attacker. He had grabbed the elk-dog's rein, and was hanging on as the animal reared and plunged, bucking frantically to dislodge the flopping corpse on its back.

The horse quieted, and now Heads Off was shouting to the others to catch the loose elk-dogs. A few warriors were still shooting, but the battle was over. The Head Splitters were retreating after the death of their leader but leaving a village strewn with the dead. White Buffalo saw a small girl, thrown across the shoulders of a Head Splitter's elk-dog, screaming and struggling as she was carried off. A riderless horse thundered past and clattered across the gravel bar at the river.

People were returning or emerging from lodges where they had hidden, and the wailing dirge of the Song of Mourning began to rise here and there. Standing Bird stood, numbly staring at the bodies of his parents. Others were frantically calling names of missing loved ones.

A hastily called count indicated that there were three Head Splitters dead but seven of the People. In addition, it appeared that four were missing and presumed abducted. One was a boy of about ten summers; two were small girls. The fourth was Tall One, the oldest daughter of Coyote. She had run forward to stop the abduction of one of the younger children, and the abductor, probably pleased with his good fortune, had taken her instead.

Tall One had recently developed into a strikingly beautiful young woman with the intelligence and poise of her mother. It had seemed only natural to those who observed that Heads Off had been attracted to her, living in the same lodge. Still, nothing had come of it. Perhaps Heads Off himself had not realized it until now, when the girl was taken. But it did explain his active participation in the hastily held council.

The discussion was loud and argumentative, largely about what should be done, which direction to flee. Into this argument, head-on, came the hair-faced outsider. At first he shouted in his own tongue. Then, in the moment of calm that resulted from the shocked surprise, he seemed to realize his mistake and calmed somewhat. He proposed pursuit of the Head Splitters, pointing out that there were no more than ten and that their leader was dead. Instantly, several youths volunteered to go with him, led by Standing Bird and Long Elk. It was a touchy moment, but Hump Ribs rose to the challenge.

"Wait," said the chief firmly. "If there is to be a war party, *I* will lead it, with the help of Heads Off."

Clever, thought White Buffalo. Hump Ribs enlists the help of Heads Off without giving up his own authority.

It was quickly decided. A war party of fifteen would proceed on foot and would probably overtake the Head Splitters in the darkness. That in itself would give the People an advantage. White Buffalo performed a ceremony for success, and they were gone, following the trail left by the horses.

They were back shortly after daylight, and Coyote came to relate the events of the night.

"Hump Ribs let Heads Off direct part of the attack," he explained. "Part of the plan was to steal elk-dogs. That would create a diversion, and when the Head Splitters stood up against the sky, Hump Ribs' bowmen . . . *aiee*, my friend, it was a great victory."

The little man chuckled, still excited.

"You recovered the children then? Your daughter?"

"Yes, yes. And elk-dogs too!"

"Elk-dogs? How many?" asked the astonished holy man.

"I do not know, Uncle. We caught two or three after the battle. Maybe six more. All they had."

"You captured *all* their elk-dogs, Coyote?"

"Of course! Well, not I, but those who were with Heads Off."

"But how?"

"Long Elk said they took thongs, like those they had been using on the small elk-dog, and tied them around the lower jaw . . . you remember, the medicine-circle, the ring?"

White Buffalo nodded, still amazed.

"Well, they rode on some of the elk-dogs and led the others."

"Were the Head Splitters all killed?"

"No, a few got away. Some wanted to chase them, but Hump Ribs said to spare them. They could tell their tribe that the People are to be reckoned with!"

Coyote danced a joyful little step or two, then stopped suddenly.

"Uncle," he said seriously, "something else! He asked me for Tall One!"

"What . . . *who* did?"

"Heads Off! She rode on the elk-dog with him on the way back. You have not seen how they look at each other?"

"I . . . ah . . . well, yes. Will you let her marry him?"

"Why not, Uncle, if she and her mother agree? Which they will. We will be proud to have him in the family. And it may prevent him from leaving."

White Buffalo looked at him sharply. Was Coyote aware of the holy man's changing feeling about this? Did he even suspect the part White Buffalo had played, or attempted to play, in keeping Heads Off with the People? There was just a hint of a cunning smile on the little man's face. Maybe . . .

"Well, I must go and rest, Uncle," Coyote continued. "It has been a long night. But I wanted you to know."

He turned and started away, then turned back.

"Uncle," he said seriously, "I am made to think that this man brings important things to the People. Beyond what we have talked of before. It is good, this feeling, to beat the Head Splitters."

This was a far more serious conversation than one could usually have with Coyote.

"You think this is because of Heads Off, Coyote?"

"Yes. Or, because of his medicine. Maybe . . . did you see, yesterday, Uncle, how great an advantage they had when they attacked on elk-dogs? But now *we* have elk-dogs."

"What are you saying?"

"I am not sure, Uncle. But, all my life, the People have feared the Head Splitters. We always run and hide. Now

. . . this feels different. Uncle, you and I have talked of the two medicines, yours of the buffalo and his of the elk-dog."

"Yes."

"But we have thought more of the elk-dog for use in the hunt. Maybe this other use, to defend ourselves, is more important even. And, when we move, think of all an elk-dog can carry. Uncle, there is a change in the wind."

There were, it turned out, eleven elk-dogs in all, not counting Heads Off's gray "First Elk-dog" and her foal. Within a day or two, several of the young men had asked for the help of Heads Off in learning to use the animals. The Rabbit Society gave way, among the older boys, to instruction by Heads Off. Long Elk and Standing Bird, already well along in the skills of handling, progressed rapidly. One of the other boys inquired about the use of the real-spear. Wooden lances were contrived for practice until Stone Breaker could produce the special spearpoints necessary. Day after day they practiced, charging a willow hoop tied loosely to a bush until they could thread it neatly on the spear shaft most of the time.

Meanwhile, some of the young men had begun to experiment with the use of a bow from horseback. This was foreign to the experience of Heads Off but appeared useful.

"Look, Heads Off," one called. "To use the real-spear, you approach the target from the left. For the bow, it is better from the right."

It was true, and in a combat situation or in a buffalo hunt, this could be significant. In addition, it was soon noted that some horses preferred to approach the target from the left, some from the right. Quickly the bowmen capitalized on this fact, trading for horses with the tendency to run to the right side. Heads Off was pleased and proud over their progress. He could hardly wait to let them try their skills at the hunt before they started north to meet the rest of the People at the Big Council.

In a very short while, the group of young men were being called the Elk-dog Society, at first as a joke suggested by Coyote. But they wore it with pride.

41

It was with great pride that the Southern band arrived at the Big Council that season. A dozen warriors rode elk-dogs, and made a great show of doing so. By day's end the others were referring to the Southern as the Elk-dog band. It was in a joking, tongue-in-cheek way, but their envy was plain.

The Elk-dog Society had progressed rapidly. Already they had staged a buffalo hunt, killing nearly a dozen animals at a single sweep. Hump Ribs, a natural storyteller anyway, managed to extract every bit of attention with his report to the Big Council on the night after their arrival. By custom, the chiefs, seated around the circle in their assigned places, told in turn of their band's doings during the year just past.

On this occasion, though most of the bands had little news, it was obvious that there had been much change in the Southern band. The news had spread like a prairie fire in a high wind when the Elk-dog Society arrived. But still it remained for Hump Ribs to relate the tale formally in the Council. And Hump Ribs, aware that this occasion was coming, had rehearsed carefully. The listeners were spell-bound as the deep voice of the Southern band's chief related the details of the attack by Head Splitters, the bravery of Black Dog, of Mouse Roars, and of Heads Off. And the pursuit and capture of the elk-dogs, the rescue of the prisoners, all lent suspense and interest to the story.

By the end of the seven days of the Sun Dance, there was much talk of the rising prominence of the Southern band. This band's unique characteristic, of course, was the possession of elk-dogs. That much was plain, and there was surely prestige and honor involved. But there was more, a vaguely defined something, an attitude. There was a change in the Southern band's approach to the world. Of all the bands, perhaps this one had traditionally been the most conservative. Maybe *timid* would be a better term. It was, in the end, a run-and-hide mentality, resulting from generations of persecution by the Head Splitters.

But now the winds of change had swept across the prairie. It was strange that fate had chosen this band, which seemed least likely of all the People to lead the change. But whether it was by chance or that the gods of the grassland had so decreed, it was happening. There was a difference in the posture of the young men, a straight-backed pride that had not been evident before. The others of the People saw the change, and although they may not have realized what they were seeing, they spoke with respect.

Possibly no one was more affected by this than Hump Ribs. When he had become chief, he was unassuming and quiet, not a well-known warrior. Circumstances had beckoned to Hump Ribs as they had to the Southern band. This had provided the opportunity for his leadership qualities to emerge and grow. In the years since his election, Hump Ribs had changed. Formerly the reluctant leader of a small band, almost embarrassed when he spoke to the Council, he had risen in confidence and in prestige. He was considered a statesman, one of the finest leaders to emerge from the warrior ranks of the People in many generations. There was talk of his fitness for real-chief when the time came to elect. After all, old Many Robes had weathered many winters. Someday, death would end his tenure, and the People would elect a new leader. For several generations the real-chief had been selected from the Northern band, but it was not a requirement. It might easily be that with the rising respect accorded the Southern band, this would be a manner of recognizing an existing shift in political power.

Of course the reflected glory fell on others of the band also. White Buffalo found that there was greater respect for the strength of *his* medicine. Heads Off, who had been regarded largely with curiosity last season, received a measure of respect, acceptance, and even honor now. He was regarded as one of the subchiefs of the Southern band. Coyote, the amusing buffoon, pretended to be unaffected by all this but secretly reveled in the greater attention to his droll stories and antics. These were exciting times.

The term "Elk-dog Society" seemed to catch on rapidly, and the handful of young warriors who were fortunate enough to ride elk-dogs considered themselves an elite guard. The name, started in jest, was worn proudly by the Elk-dog Society. Quickly it became apparent that there were now two societies in the Southern band, the old Warrior Society and the youthful Elk-dog warriors.

Of course, there was some shaking of heads and clucking of tongues among the elders. Could there be two warrior societies? No one seemed to know. There was an uneasiness in some of the older warriors, yet so far, the elk-dogs had brought only benefits. It was already apparent that elk-dog medicine and buffalo medicine worked well together in the hunt. That had been proven and was already well accepted. But this was a new and different question. In armed conflict, how would elk-dog medicine combine with the old ways? There were many misgivings, yet the effectiveness of the charge into the village by mounted Head Splitters had been awesome.

"But they could have been stopped," stated Two Pines. "We were caught by surprise. Black Dog and Mouse Roars killed two of them!"

"Ah, but where is Black Dog? Mouse Roars? Dead!" argued another. "Men on foot cannot stop men on elk-dogs!"

"If they had had help," Two Pines insisted, "it could be done. We were taken by surprise, and that must not happen. Our wolves must be alert."

"But the elk-dogs move too rapidly!"

"Ah, but *we* have elk-dogs too!"

The arguments raged on, hindered not at all by the inexperience of the participants. Coyote watched and listened quietly and without comment. Finally, when the opportunity offered, he approached Heads Off.

"Heads Off, your warriors use elk-dogs in battle?"

"Yes. We have talked of this, Uncle. What is it?"

"Yes, I know. What I wish to know, is this . . . not *all* your warriors ride elk-dogs and carry spears?"

"Oh, no. We talked of the bowmen, who fight on foot. Then there are those who use"—he paused, searching for a word—"a . . . sort of long knife."

"On an elk-dog?"

"Well, sometimes. Sometimes on foot. Others use a very long spear, on foot."

"I see . . . then there are several warrior societies?"

"I . . . I guess so. Yes, warrior societies. Why?"

"Ah, the men talk. About the Elk-dog Society, you know. It seems like a new warrior society. But there is still the old one. So, can there be *two?*" He chuckled.

Heads Off laughed.

"Why not? My tribe calls them lancers, bowmen, pikemen, swordsmen."

"It is good," decided Coyote. "We have Warrior Society and Elk-dog Society."

Coyote giggled again, and Heads Off nodded.

"Yes, they are already called that," he agreed.

The entire concept of elk-dogs for the hunt and for battle was so broad, so far-reaching, that it was hard for the mind to grasp. White Buffalo was only now beginning to understand the importance, the *why* of his elk-dog vision so long ago. The use of the elk-dog, he now realized, was to be the greatest change in the ways of the People in his entire lifetime. Maybe even, the holy man was beginning to see, the greatest change since the People came through the log. It had been difficult for him to accept at first, and it was still a thing of wonder. White Buffalo had thought that he had reached the height of his powers, his medicine-gift. He had even thought himself on the way down, but now, *aiee*, this might be only the beginning. These were exciting times as the winds of change swept the grassland, opening a new way of life—and perhaps of death.

When the Sun Dance finished this season, the Southern or Elk-dog band, had grown again, by ten more lodges.

The marriage of Tall One to Heads Off took place in the autumn of that year, in the Moon of Falling Leaves. The holy man noticed that since the Sun Dance—no, even before that—there had been no talk of Heads Off's departure.

"He speaks no more of it," Coyote explained. "*I* will not ask him. He talks only of marriage."

It was apparent to everyone that this was a devoted couple. They spent much time together, walking beside a clear stream or sitting on a hilltop. They watched the hawks circling high above on fixed wings, riding the invisible currents of the wind. This special courtship was a source of pride and pleasure to the band. It was romantic, the manner in which Heads Off had helped to rescue his intended bride from the Head Splitters. The story grew with the telling, becoming even more romantic. In an odd way, this courtship increased the prestige of the outsider. Heads Off, largely due to circumstances, was following custom. By example, then, he was becoming one of the group, the People—even more specifically, a respected member of the Southern band.

Normally, when a young couple decided to marry, they would first live in the lodge of the bride's mother until they could set up their own lodge. However, the women had decided, possibly at the suggestion of Coyote, that an honored warrior such as Heads Off should have a lodge. After all, it was due to his elk-dog medicine that materials were available. The summer was spent in dressing and sewing skins for a lodge cover befitting the dwelling of an important couple.

It was also in this season that the People realized that a lodge could be much larger than before. Prior to the elk-dog, the size of a dwelling was limited to how many skins could be handled and moved by three or four people. Transportation of a lodge on a pole-drag was likewise limited to the strength of people and dogs.

Now the limiting factor was the strength of the elk-dog. Many skins were available, and with materials and the ability to transport . . . *aiee!* How large could a lodge be? There was a joke that the limit would be found in the availability of lodge poles. Long poles were at a premium and were traded as a precious commodity. The size of one's lodge, of course, reflected the hunting skill of the owner, his ability to obtain larger numbers of skins.

All of this influenced the construction of the lodge of Heads Off and Tall One. Possibly he was unaware of it to some extent. Finally, in time for the ceremonial nuptials, the lodge was finished and was set up for the first time. The band was already in winter camp, in one of their favorite areas where the grassland meets the scrub oak.

The ceremony was carried out in front of the lodge of Tall One's parents, with many friends, relatives, and well-wishers in attendance. Coyote, trying his best to retain his dignity, performed the ceremonial prayers for the happiness of the couple. The two knelt side-by-side before the symbolic fire of their union, and Coyote dramatically drew a robe around the shoulders of the two.

They rose, the robe still covering the new couple as they made their way past smiling faces to their own lodge. Inside, the first fire of their new home was burning; there was food and the bed of soft robes opposite the doorway. The doorskin fell silently into place behind them, and the People dispersed to their own lodges. Their hearts were good, for the happiness of these two.

42

It was no surprise to the Southern band when the news spread that Tall One, daughter of Coyote and wife of Heads Off, was pregnant. In fact, it had become something of a joke, the preoccupation of this young couple with each other and with their privacy.

The young elk-dog men, during the warm days of late fall and early winter, would have some question about the elk-dogs but could not find Heads Off to ask.

"Let him alone," advised Long Elk. "They are in their lodge."

"*Aiee,*" one answered, "he has not been *out* of that lodge since the Moon of Falling Leaves!"

"Think about it," suggested Standing Bird. "Would *you* have left that lodge?"

There was general laughter, the ribald amusement that reflected a certain envy. Tall One was certainly one of the most beautiful women. Her lithe grace and shapely form could be expected to arouse the imagination of young men. Fantasies could not even begin to approach the reality of a winter in the warm and loving lodge of Tall One.

"It is true," agreed the questioner. "Let him alone."

There was laughter again.

By the Moon of Greening, Tall One was showing her enlarging belly. Her buckskin dress now appeared smooth and taut around the waist. There was much speculation among the People. What would be the appearance of the child? Would it bear fur upon the face, like that of Heads Off?

The newcomer had by this time settled into the ways of the People quite comfortably for the most part. His dress, the trim and plait of his hair—everything indicated that he belonged, except for the facial fur. That remained the mark of an outsider. The men of the People, of course, possessed some facial hair. It was thin and scanty, and at the onset of puberty, the emerging hairs were plucked as a part of increased interest in one's appearance. Heads Off had actually considered such grooming and with Coyote's help had experimented. However, one session with the clam-shell tweezers proved adequate to dissuade the continuance of such a project. In half an afternoon, only a patchy bare spot resulted on one cheek.

"This is not good, my friend," Heads Off had protested. "I know now why this custom is not found among my people."

Coyote giggled.

"It would be a great test of manhood," he teased.

"There are other ways to test manhood, Uncle," Heads Off protested again. "Follow your customs in most things I will, but *aiee*, my face is sore!"

"It is true," Coyote had concluded. "The face-plucking is not for those with heavy fur."

So it was decided. The hair-faced outsider did not attempt to pluck his face, and this was easily accepted. He was respected for his willingness to follow the customs of the People in most other ways. The current situation provided an amusing diversion with many jokes and questions. Some of the inveterate gamblers were already quietly betting on whether the upcoming offspring would bear facial fur.

However, first things must come first. The birth was expected no sooner than the Moon of Ripening. First the band must travel to the Sun Dance, which would be held on the Walnut River this season. But even before that, an odd incident occurred which cast a suspicious shadow over events to come.

The spring hunt was excellent, and every lodge was well supplied. Perhaps the outstanding successes of the year for the Southern band influenced the chief's decision about the day of the move. Surely, any leader would anticipate the honor and prestige that would go with such a year. Therefore, it may have been that Hump Ribs called for the move a bit early.

The usual protest arose from the women. They couldn't possibly be ready in three days. The meat from the recent kill was not yet prepared. Even while they protested, they started preparations for the move.

Big-Footed Woman was among the most vocal of the protesters. It was foolish, she scolded, to think that all the fat from the recent kills could possibly be cooked down properly in so short a time. Mere men, even chiefs, could not understand such a problem. Just because times were now improved was no cause to become wasteful. Good food had never been wasted by the People, even in times of plenty. She, for one, would never leave meat on the prairie to rot. She had no intention, she continued, of leaving this campsite until her work was done. The men wisely refrained from argument.

In fact, it was noted that both Coyote and Heads Off scrupulously avoided their wives after the striking and packing of the lodges. It seemed advisable to avoid contact, where possible, with the sharp tongue of the irate Big-Footed Woman. Let her vent her wrath, and perhaps by day's end her temper would be cooled somewhat.

By noon, the column was on the move, but it was time to stop for the evening camp before Coyote and Heads Off noticed anything amiss.

"Where is your mother?" Coyote asked Long Elk.

"She stayed behind to finish cooking the fat," Long Elk answered. "You did not know? She said they would catch up later. Tall One is with her."

It was immediately apparent that Heads Off was quite upset at this turn of events. He seemed to blame himself, fidgeted and paced, and finally spoke to his father-in-law.

"I go to look for them," he explained, as he swung up onto the gray mare.

"I go with you," Long Elk said quickly.

Shadows were growing long over the abandoned campsite, but one fire still burned.

"Mother, we *must* leave! Please forget the rest of the fat!" Tall One entreated. She had stayed behind to help finish the cooking and to help with the carrying. She had had no idea that her mother would stay this long over her silly grudge.

Actually, Big-Footed Woman hadn't intended it this way. She would, she thought, let them leave without her. She was certain that the men would come back as soon as their absence was discovered. She would then grudgingly consent to leave, having proved her argument.

But the men had not come. Her anger was rekindled, and her stubborn streak began to manifest itself even more strongly. She would stay here until they did come, she decided.

But that was while the sun still shone. Now the darkness was falling, and the whole thing began to seem a little foolish. Maybe they should pack up and travel, she thought. They could follow the trail of the entire band, even in complete darkness. She was about to capitulate and in fact had drawn in her breath to speak when Tall One held up a hand to listen.

Unmistakably, there was a sound of hoofbeats. Three or four elk-dogs were approaching at a walk. Both women brightened considerably, and Big-Footed Woman began to plan her scathing remarks for the men. She turned her back and began paying utmost attention to skimming melted grease and spooning it out to cool.

"Here they come," she murmured, savoring her moment. The horses came closer, to the very edge of the firelight, and stopped. She heard a chuckle, but not until a gasp of surprise and fear came from Tall One did she turn.

There were four men, each sitting on his horse in a relaxed, amused posture. They made no immediate move, merely sat smiling and chuckling. It took a long moment for the significance of the situation to make itself felt to Big-Footed Woman. Somehow her mind was slow to grasp so unexpected a scene. She had been certain that when she turned, she would see her husband and Heads Off.

But these men were complete strangers. And by their ornaments and weapons, Big-Footed Woman could see that her bull-headed escapade had backfired. These men were not even of the People.

They were Head Splitters.

"Hello, Mother," signed the oldest of the Head Splitters, apparently the leader. "Is our supper ready?"

Foolishly though she had acted that day, Big-Footed Woman was wise enough not to do anything foolish at that moment. If either of the women rocked the delicately balanced situation, the result might be instant tragedy. As it was, the Head Splitters seemed to be enjoying the game.

Their only chance, both women realized, was to play along and stall for time.

"Get down and sit," signed Big-Footed Woman. "You are early. My husband will be back soon."

Laughter from the Head Splitters. They could see that the camp was abandoned. They slid from the horses and wandered around the fire, poking at the strips of fat.

"Get away from my cooking," the woman said irritably, reinforcing her demand with sign language and a gentle shove. "I will say when it is ready!"

More laughter.

It's working, she thought. We will be safe as long as I can keep them laughing. Maybe the men will come.

Of course, both women knew that their cause was hopeless. They could feed the strangers and for some time possibly dissuade them. Eventually, the Head Splitters would tire of the game and would kill them, probably after raping them. Already the small one with teeth like those of a squirrel was letting his glances rove over the long body of Tall One. The best that might happen would be that they would take her with them instead of killing her outright. Too bad, thought Big-Footed Woman. I did want her to bear the child of Heads Off.

Even while her mind was busy with such morose thoughts, her hands were busy with the cooking fire. She chattered on in a combination of talk and sign.

"Stay back, you'll kick dirt in my cooking!" she ordered.

The Head Splitters were enjoying this scene immensely. One of them made an exaggerated move to escape her scolding, and the others rocked with laughter. Big-Footed Woman began to cook some small strips of meat and hand the morsels to the men. She wondered how long she could continue this process. She cooked small portions, only a few at a time, assisted by Tall One, who had thus far been silent.

Full darkness fell, and the process of cooking and feeding the strangers continued. Tall One kindled a torch and propped it nearby for light. Once the older man impatiently demanded that they cook bigger portions.

"Mother," said Tall One finally, "don't you think that little one looks like a squirrel?"

Tall One glanced at the little man. Complete absence of

any understanding shone on all four faces as they chewed pieces of meat or joked among themselves.

Her mother nodded. "And the big one is the ugliest I ever saw."

The big one in question smiled and nodded.

"I thought so," concluded Tall One. "None of them understands a word of the talk of the People. Now I will tell you my idea. I do not intend to go to bed with Squirrel Tooth over there."

She smiled at the man again, and he responded with a toothy grin.

Rapidly, Tall One sketched her plan.

Her mother nodded. "It is good. Even if it does not work, we may escape in the darkness."

Finally it seemed that the nearly insatiable appetites were becoming satisfied. Squirrel Tooth was looking hungrily at Tall One. It was time to make a move. Tall One strolled over to replace the sputtering torch with a fresh one. Instead of propping it for light, she suddenly lifted it high and dashed off into the darkness, the flame bobbing and dancing over her head.

The Head Splitters leapt to their feet and ran after her, shouting to each other as they ran. Big-Footed Woman quickly picked up a heavy stone war club and slipped into the darkness.

Tall One ran down the familiar path, counting on her pursuers' unfamiliarity with the terrain. She looked back, slowing her pace slightly. It was important that the pursuit be as close as possible. The line of flight led straight across a level area with no obstructions, and her long legs kept her barely ahead of the running warriors. She wondered if they thought her stupid to be carrying the torch.

A hundred paces behind the abandoned lodge site, the level meadow dropped off sharply to the river. The edge was a shelf of stone, jutting out of the earth and ending abruptly. Below lay a tangled pile of jagged pieces broken from the shelf through the centuries and dropped into the stream's bed.

Straight for the edge ran Tall One. As she neared the drop, she sprinted faster, pulling slightly away from the runners behind. She waved the torch high, then suddenly flung it ahead of her and dodged quickly to the left, slipping quietly into a clump of bushes. The plan worked perfectly. The men, in full stride, continued to pursue the bobbing, flashing torch as it bounced over the rocks. The two in the lead did not even break stride as they plunged over the edge. It seemed a long time before the dull sounds of their bodies striking rock was heard. The third man, Squirrel Tooth, realized something was wrong just as he reached the ledge. He attempted to save himself but overbalanced and fell, a short exclamation of surprise choked off by the dull thud.

The fourth man was warned and managed to stop at the edge. He called into the dark, but there was only a low moan in answer. The torch lay far below, flickering in a crevice near the water. He turned to look for the girl, shouting angrily. Tall One hugged the earth and tried not to breathe too heavily.

"Tall One!" a voice called from the darkness. "Bring the big ugly one back to the fire and let him catch you, almost!"

The big man turned toward the voice, but the girl jumped up with a frightened squeal and ran back toward the fire, the warrior in hot pursuit. She dodged around, barely staying out of his reach, until she saw from the corner of her vision where her mother was located. Twisting, turning, the agile young woman maneuvered her pursuer into proper position and finally stumbled, sprawling with a little scream.

The man loomed over her in rage, and his hands reached for the girl. She was glad that he had no weapon. At the last moment, there was a dull *thunk,* and the Head Splitter slumped forward, falling almost on top of her. Big-Footed Woman brushed the hair back from her face as she hefted the borrowed war club in case another blow was needed. It was not.

The exhausted women made their way back to the fire. As they built up the blaze, they suddenly heard hoofbeats again, and both slipped warily into the darkness.

Heads Off and Long Elk rode into the circle of the firelight and paused, calling their names. Big-Footed Woman stepped quickly from hiding.

"Heads Off! Long Elk! Over here," she called.

They returned to the fire.

"Mother!" shouted Long Elk. "We were very worried!"

"Oh, we are all right," she managed to say calmly. "We traded meat to some travelers for four elk-dogs."

She pointed to the animals, tied in the shadows.

Heads Off was irritated. He had been nearly frantic with worry and did not appreciate the light treatment of a near-tragedy.

"Come on," he snapped gruffly. "Let us join the rest."

"Of course, Heads Off," answered his wife meekly, "as soon as we finish skimming out the fat."

43

What had shown every promise of being a triumphant, prestigious Sun Dance full of celebration was almost a disaster. It became quickly apparent that with the exception of the Southern band, no one had fared well.

The Eastern band, of course, rarely fared well. That was assumed to be due to their own foolishness. But the others had suffered too. The Red Rocks, especially, were at a low point in their entire history. They had been attacked more than once by the Head Splitters. The enemy now appeared to be usually mounted, and the frightening impact of an attack by well-armed horsemen was demoralizing.

Additionally, there had been encounters during travel. These noncombative confrontations, where protocol prevented open hostilities because of danger to families, were quite useful sometimes. It was possible to see whether the enemy had fared well and to observe changes in customs and attitudes. The reports were all the same. The Head Splitters, who were probably of several different bands, had all behaved similarly. They were arrogant, even more than usual. They had many elk-dogs, and they were insolent and threatening.

One fact stood out above all others, however. At each contact, the Head Splitters had mentioned the same theme. Gray Wolf, who now appeared to be their principal war chief, was looking for blood. The young chief killed by Heads Off in the skirmish the previous year had been the son of Gray Wolf, who had now declared an oath of vengeance against "Hair Face."

"I will decorate my shield with that fur," Gray Wolf had vowed.

Repeatedly, this message had been relayed to the bands of the People at any encounter. It was causing much consternation and fear. Coyote attempted to put the threat in proper perspective.

"I have heard it said," he observed whimsically, "that to use a cat's fur, it is first necessary to skin the cat."

This attempt to lighten the burden of worry fell largely on deaf ears. There was, in fact, some animosity, both toward elk-dogs and toward Heads Off, bringer of the elk-dog.

"It was not so before the strange beasts," one old woman babbled. "We should drive them away!"

"Yes, and the hair-face too," a man of the Mountain band said quietly. "It is against this outsider that the Head Splitters vow revenge."

"Stupid ones!" Big-Footed Woman replied indignantly, "Look for yourselves. Which band among us is strong? Whose children are fat, and their women happy? The Southern band, who have elk-dogs!"

"But the Head Splitters . . ." the old woman insisted.

"Mother," said Big Footed Woman gently but firmly, "All your life the People have feared the Head Splitters. That has nothing to do with elk-dogs!"

It appeared that a complete rift in the tribal structure was a distinct possibility. White Buffalo was alarmed and was pleased when Many Robes called the Big Council at the earliest possible opportunity. This friction must be resolved.

The Council opened in a confused jumble of misunderstanding and resentment. The smug attitude of some of the Southern band was creating much friction.

"Even our women can defeat Head Splitters!" boasted one man.

The episode of the capture and clever escape of the two women had been told and retold, but some had begun to resent even that.

"It is not for you to boast!" snapped an old warrior of the Red Rocks. "Wait until you are attacked again!"

"The Head Splitters have elk-dogs, many of them!" another burst out. "They move fast, strike, and are gone!"

Several suggestions were introduced. Some favored merging two or more bands, to gain strength in numbers. To others, the answer was to move out of the traditional territory of the People, away from the Head Splitters. The wrangling continued.

Finally, Many Robes held up his hands for silence, and the noisy argument quieted. The real-chief looked around the circle for a moment as if searching, and his eyes lighted on Coyote.

"Coyote, my brother," he said, "you have not spoken. Tell us, what do you think?"

Coyote paused a moment, and once again White Buffalo marveled at the man's skill. He could recall no one who could manipulate a group of people as Coyote could, achieving what he wished but able to make others think it had been their own idea. White Buffalo had long been aware of this, but now he wondered . . . yes, surely, the Real-chief must realize it too. That was why he had waited until the proper moment to ask Coyote's opinion.

The crowd was quiet, waiting to hear Coyote's remarks. This might be quite humorous, and the interest mounted, a relief from the heat and anger that had held the Council in its grip. Coyote waited, like a performer skilled in the use of the long pause, waiting for the right moment. He giggled nervously, and the crowd smiled and relaxed.

"My chief," Coyote began, "there is much that I do not understand. But it is a question to me . . . I hear the People say 'aiee, the Head Splitters have elk-dogs.' Why do the Head Splitters not say 'aiee, the *People* have elk-dogs'?"

There was a moment of silence, and argument broke out again.

"But they have more!"

"*We* have *none!*" shouted a man from the Mountain band.

Many Robes held up a hand, and the crowd quieted.

"Hump Ribs, your Elk-dog band has not been attacked?"

"No, my chief, except for the women."

The crowd chuckled.

"Then they are attacking only those of us who have no elk-dogs," observed the real-chief.

"This is true, my chief," spoke Black Beaver of the Red Rocks. "But it seems their quarrel is with Heads Off and the Southern band, who now have elk-dogs."

There was a murmur of assent.

"But they do not attack that band yet," Coyote said whimsically. "Maybe they fear *our* elk-dog soldiers."

Again, there was a moment of silence as the crowd reflected on the truth of Coyote's remark.

"Yes!" exclaimed Two Pines. "If *all* bands had elk-dog warriors—"

"We need more elk-dogs!" stated young Standing Bird, who was already gaining recognition as a skilled rider and hunter.

"But where can we get elk-dogs?" one of the dissenters asked scornfully.

"Where did *ours* come from?" Coyote asked with a bland smile.

"The Head Splitters?" someone asked in astonishment.

"Maybe we could . . ."

"Aiee! I don't know . . ."

"We *could!"*

"No, it is too dangerous!"

Many Robes gestured for silence again.

"Black Beaver," he addressed, "your band is in closest contact with the Head Splitters. Where do *they* get elk-dogs?"

The chief of the Red Rocks shrugged.

"We do not know. But they have many. They seem to bring them from the south or southwest. It is said that there are tribes of hairfaces living there."

Glances turned toward Heads Off, who seemed embarrassed by the attention. Coyote intervened. "My brothers," he began jovially, "let us ask my daughter's husband. Heads Off, is your tribe living in that area?"

Heads Off, still embarrassed by this turn of events, hesitated for a moment and then managed to speak.

"I do not know, Uncle. They have villages farther south. Has anyone seen other hairfaces?"

There was silence.

"No, only stories," said Black Beaver finally.

White Buffalo wondered if the outsider still longed to return to his people. But now Many Robes was speaking again.

"Then more elk-dogs . . . for the People . . . must come from the Head Splitters, it seems."

"Can we trade with them?" asked someone.

It was not unheard-of to trade with the enemy, and such commerce was often useful. Any tribe might easily have more robes or meat than they needed, and, enemy or not, one must be practical.

"Our women traded with them this season," Coyote observed with a chuckle.

There was general laughter. Big-Footed Woman's exchange of bits of meat for the weapons and horses of her captors was the joke of the year.

"Maybe," Coyote went on, "we could trade for more in this way."

"What do you mean?" someone demanded.

"Wait!" Many Robes held up a hand. "What Coyote suggests is this: If we are to have elk-dogs, we must get them from the Head Splitters. They will not wish to trade, so we must take them."

"*Aiee!* Did I say that?" Coyote asked softly. Everyone laughed again.

"Could this be done?" Many Robes asked.

Again, there was the murmur of discussion. Though there was some dissent, the general tone was now *how* to effect the proposed course of action. Gradually, a plan emerged. The Southern band would accompany the Red Rocks for the season, along with warriors from any of the other bands whose interest leaned toward elk-dogs. Raids would be attempted to acquire more horses from the enemy, and the Southern band would teach the others the use of the medicine of the elk-dog.

Quickly the excitement grew. Each band could see itself becoming as successful and wealthy as the Southern band after the coming of the elk-dog. Young men rushed to state their wish to participate.

In the aftermath of this council, the excitement of the Sun Dance was almost anticlimactic. Yet there were many prayers, sacrifices, and vows made in the ensuing days. When the People struck the lodges to move out in separate columns for the season, it was with greater excitement than ever before. There were many good-byes that held greater importance than before. Relatives who were separated each year now realized that this season would be different. There would be different dangers, but also adventure and the promise of reward if the proposed scheme proved successful.

Hump Ribs sought out Heads Off after the council.

"Can this thing be done, Heads Off?"

"The elk-dogs? I think so, Uncle. If they are there, we can get some. And our young men are becoming skilled."

Hump Ribs nodded, pleased—not only at the prediction of success but at another thing that Heads Off had not even noticed. "Our young men," he had said. Yes, the chief thought, Heads Off is really becoming one of the People.

Meanwhile, White Buffalo was doing much thinking of his own. This entire concept, the idea of absorbing and using the medicine of the elk-dog, was so large, so far-reaching. He could see it working, helping the People. Yet it was happening so quickly. He found doubts forming again. Could it really be done, this grand plan for the season? He must go and think—and pray, and cast the bones. . . .

These were exciting times. The People seemed ready for this major change, but sometimes White Buffalo wondered if *he* could still handle the excitement.

44

The two men cautiously worked their way up the slope toward the crest of the ridge. Both were aware that today was the culmination of the season's effort, but for the moment, that was forgotten. More important now was the danger of their position. Sees Far carefully crept alongside a large rock, hoping that its broken outline against the sky would make his own silhouette less conspicuous. The rising sun was behind them. This too was calculated to make observation more difficult for the enemy.

The raiding party had worked its way deep into enemy territory, carefully avoiding all contact. Now it had become apparent that a large band of Head Splitters was camped ahead. Tracks had suggested that they had many horses. This appeared to be a summer camp, much like that of the People, though in somewhat different terrain. Now they were scouting to plan the attack.

Sees Far peered over the rim and suppressed a gasp of amazement. He motioned to his companion, and Heads Off wriggled forward to join him. Below lay a large camp of scattered lodges, possibly as many as those of the Southern band and the Red Rocks combined. There was little activity at this sunrise hour. Here and there among the lodges were tied horses—only a few, probably favorite mounts of warriors who would rather not risk pasturing them with the herd.

And the herd! *Aiee!* Heads Off immediately saw the reason for the gasp from his companion. Quickly they estimated. There must be at least a hundred animals. The two remained a little while, studying the terrain and the best route of approach and retreat. Then they quietly withdrew.

"*Aiee,* so many elk-dogs!" Sees Far exclaimed when they were at a safe distance. "Where did they all come from?"

"I do not know," Heads Off admitted, "but they have young, as ours do. It would not take long to have many elk-dogs."

"How old must a cow elk-dog be to have young?"

"Three years, maybe. It would not be called a cow elk-dog . . . *aiee,* Sees Far, I do not know! We can talk of this later. Now let us plan."

They returned to the rest of the party and related what they had seen. Hump Ribs was willing to relinquish the planning to Heads Off.

"There is a small stream," Heads Off explained. "We can cross there, in the dark, and move them across, to come this way. Those who are riders will take ropes and catch an elk-dog to ride. Others can stop any pursuit."

It was decided that if any problem arose, a long yell would signal everyone to escape as best he could.

The day seemed long, the waiting interminable. Men slept, talked, gambled, or checked their weapons. The attempt would be made just before dawn, to take advantage of the Head Splitters' well-known reluctance to fight at night. But by moving out just before dawn, they would have good light for traveling rapidly. Pursuit was likely, but if most of the enemy's elk-dogs could be stolen, the numbers of mounted pursuers would be few.

It was a bold and risky plan, but expectations were high. White Buffalo had promised to strive to the utmost of his ability and the power of his medicine for the success of the raid. His signs, it was said, had been good. Every man knew that at this very time, back at the summer camp several sleeps away, the holy man would be actively helping. There would be chants, fasting, ceremonial dances, and prayers. Probably White Buffalo would not even sleep during the night or two of importance to the raid.

By the time of the late rise of the half-moon, men were beginning to stir in the camp. One by one, they began to rise. They wakened the few sound sleepers and quietly moved out, led by Sees Far and Heads Off.

The yellow smudge of false dawn was barely showing in the east when the young men of the Elk-dog Society began to move among the grazing animals, knotting thongs around lower jaws and choosing animals to ride. So far, there had been no evidence of any sentry or wolf. Apparently the Head Splitters, deep in their own country, felt completely secure. The word was passed quietly, and the horsemen began to urge the herd toward the creek. Still there was no alarm. It was not until the splash and clatter of many hooves stirred the gravel of the ford that some early riser in the enemy camp noticed anything amiss.

A warrior, awakening, rose to attend to the urge of his aging bladder. It was no longer efficient enough to maintain capacity completely through the night. He yawned and stretched and stumbled sleepily out of the lodge and around to the rear to urinate. It was only then that he heard the rattle of gravel at the stream. He paused a moment and realized that the herd was crossing at the shallow ford. What a nuisance, he thought. The creatures wander. A bear, maybe, like the last time. Or possibly one of the great long-tailed cats that sometimes came down from the foothills. He raised his voice in a long yell to rouse the others. He noted even as he did so that this seemed to startle the herd. Startled the stalking bear probably, he thought, and that in turn had panicked the elk-dogs. Now, from the sound, the entire herd was in full flight. It would take some of the young men most of the day to round them up. Well, it was no concern of his. This whole elk-dog thing was for younger men. Having done his duty by raising the alarm, he turned to a more important matter, loosening his breechclout to relieve the now urgent pressure of his swollen bladder.

The Elk-dog men of the People, meanwhile, assumed that the long yell was a signal that they were discovered. Quietly, they swung up to the backs of their horses and quickened the pace, urging slower animals across the ford. As the herd began to move as a unit, the men rode back and forth, circling, keeping the animals together, continuously pushing ahead. They passed half-hidden bowmen, stationed to delay pursuit, but so far there was none.

It was well past daylight when Heads Off suggested a stop to evaluate the success of the raid.

"Aiee!" someone cried, "this must be every elk-dog the Head Splitters had!"

"There were a few more in their camp," Sees Far said, "but most of those we saw are here."

"They may have others somewhere else," warned Heads Off. "But is there no pursuit?"

The bowmen were now rejoining the main party.

"We saw no one," Two Pines said, puzzled. "We left wolves to watch."

Sometime later, the wolves reported that they were indeed followed.

"Only two riders. They ride slowly and do not seem alarmed."

"Could it be," asked Sees Far, "that they do not *know* their elk-dogs are stolen? That they believe the herd only wandered off?"

That seemed the likeliest explanation. Perhaps this had happened before.

"Or," suggested someone, "the medicine of White Buffalo is very powerful, to close the enemy's eyes."

"They will not stay closed," warned Hump Ribs. "Soon they will see our tracks."

"Those who follow must be stopped," Standing Bird said firmly. "I will go."

"Wait!" called Heads Off, "you—"

"Let him go," advised Hump Ribs. "He is thinking of his parents."

Standing Bird had picked up his bow and now started back on foot, jogging.

"Let us move on," Hump Ribs decided. "He will catch up."

It was much later, when they had paused for a rest stop, that someone pointed to moving figures in the far distance.

"We are still followed!"

"But by only one," Sees Far noted.

They watched as the rider made his way down the opposite slope and crossed the valley toward them. He was riding one horse and leading another, it appeared. And there was something familiar about the way he sat—his posture and balance.

"It is Standing Bird!" exclaimed Sees Far.

Standing Bird rode toward them, unhurried, and finally swung down. He removed the rawhide war bridle from one of the animals, and released it.

"We are no longer followed," he said simply.

* * *

Back at the camp of the People, the days passed slowly. White Buffalo was certain that the raid was over. He had *felt* the time of decision and was optimistic that the raid had gone well but was hesitant to say so. After all, he could be wrong. It was possible that his urgent wish for success could make him misinterpret his feelings and the signs that he now saw.

Aiee, he would be glad when this was over! It was not unpleasant, this slightly different country of the Red Rocks band. Different, with a variety of plants not found in his own Tallgrass region, or in the Sacred Hills. But not unpleasant. However, he would be glad to move back to a more traditional locale. The season was still fairly early, and White Buffalo hoped that they could survive winter in a more familiar site. He would urge such a move, perhaps.

But his feeling for the season was good. Elk-dogs had made the Southern band strong and prosperous, and could do the same for all the People. His signs had been good for this raid, and he was sure of the success of the raiders. Well, almost sure. There were always factors which might interfere with all the good signs that might be present. Some unknown things even, of which he might be completely unaware in a strange country.

He tried to maintain his composure, to radiate confidence that he only partly felt. That was important in his position, not to reveal any doubts. Not that he had any real doubts, of course, but . . .

Crow was hurrying toward him from across the camp. He half rose from the backrest, a little flare of alarm rising in his throat. Then he saw the smile on her face.

"It is her time," Crow said happily. "Tall One! She is ready for birthing!"

White Buffalo sank back on his rest, relieved that there was no emergency.

"It will go well, I know," Crow Woman was saying. "Her family has always had easy birthing. *Aiee,* Elk, I can hardly wait to see this child! A child of Heads Off!"

She entered the lodge, and he could hear her singing happily to herself as she went about her work. *Aiee,* she should have had a child.

A man trotted into the camp from the west, and his voice rose in a long hail.

"Ah-koh!" he shouted. "Hear me, my brothers! The raid-

ers return! More than a hundred elk-dogs, and we have lost no one!"

White Buffalo smiled to himself as he settled back once more to lean on the willow rest. It was good. Yes, his medicine was strong, even in this strange country, and his instincts were still good.

45

As it happened, the son of Tall One and Heads Off did not have fur upon his face. Tall One and Big-Footed Woman were quite disappointed at first. They had hoped that the child would show the mark of his heritage. Heads Off, startled initially by their disappointment, assumed that there was something wrong with the child. He was almost frantic with worry.

"But what is it? The child is deformed?" he asked anxiously.

"He has no fur," Tall One said sadly, stroking the ruddy cheek.

"*Aiee,*" Heads Off cried, laughing. "Newborn babes do not have facehair!"

Gently, he unwrapped the infant.

"Look, there is no hair on the private parts either. That comes later."

"Will he have facehair later, Heads Off?" Big-Footed Woman asked.

"Maybe. Probably some. He will have to decide whether to pluck it."

Now it became a matter for joking and laughter, that Tall One had anticipated a fully furred infant. The entire band laughed about the hairless babe for most of the winter with new jokes constantly. Tall One named the child Many Elk-dogs, in commemoration of the day the raiding party returned in triumph. But the name did not stick. The People immediately began calling the infant Bald Eagle. After all, were his head and face not bare and white like those of the eagle?

Both names, of course, were nicknames. They would be used only until his second year, at the time of the youngster's First Dance. Then he would receive his name from the oldest male relative, in this case, Coyote. While it was customary for this ceremonial Uncle to bestow his own name, it was not always so. Somehow, White Buffalo had the idea that when the time came, Coyote would surprise everyone with a name other than his own.

But that was in the future. For now, the most important thing before the People was to learn the use of the newly acquired elk-dogs. Heads Off had thrown himself whole-heartedly into the teaching of his skills. It was little short of amazing how rapidly the young men learned. Standing Bird and Long Elk, already experts, assisted in the instruction. The young men were learning the use of the long spear and the bow on horseback as well as care and feeding of the animals.

In addition, Heads Off seemed obsessed with trying to get the elk-dog men to ride in unison, working together. He took a dozen or more willow hoops and fastened them to bushes a hundred paces or so away. Then the fledgling lancers were formed into a line and led into a full charge by Standing Bird. Each man would attempt to thread a willow hoop, a handspan across, on the shaft of his lance as he swept past. Accuracy was rare at first, but soon nearly every target dangled on someone's lance after the charge.

Heads Off came over to where White Buffalo and Coyote sat on the slope to watch.

"Ah-koh," he said as he sat down to join them.

"Your young men do well," observed White Buffalo.

"Thank you, Uncle. They learn quickly."

"Heads Off," Coyote asked, "why do they learn this . . . the running at targets all at once?"

"Uncle," Heads Off said seriously, "these warriors will have to fight Head Splitters on elk-dogs. It is done so in my tribe, the learning to strike at the same time. This brings fear to the heart of an enemy, all charging at once."

"I see. But what protects them from arrows of men on foot?"

"Well, I . . . they move quickly. Our warriors wear a metal shirt."

Coyote nodded. "We have no metal shirts. Could they carry a shield?"

"A shield? Like a man with a war ax would use?"

"Yes, maybe. One a little smaller, but of good rawhide, from the back of a bull."

"It might work, Uncle. Would it turn an arrow?"

"Unless it strikes straight on. A spear too, unless it is a direct blow. Will you try it?"

A shield was brought, of the heaviest of bull's backskin, stretched and dried to rocklike hardness. Coyote fastened it to one of the dogwood bushes, and the young riders galloped past in turn, loosing an arrow or thrusting with a lance. Incredibly, only one arrow caught the shield just right and penetrated to half its length. All others were turned aside, glancing from the flint-hard surface of the rawhide, like a flat pebble skipped on the surface of a still pool.

"It is good!" shouted Heads Off in delight. "Let each warrior carry a shield. A little smaller maybe."

White Buffalo, too, was impressed. *Aiee*, there was much to learn about this elk-dog medicine. He and Crow had been given an elk-dog by the returning raiders. They would not ride it but used its great strength to drag the lodge poles and cover during a move. It was good, and it made him and Crow happy to use this method of transport.

"Oh, yes," Crow explained to an acquaintance, "we have an elk-dog. The raiders gave it to us in thanks for my husband's help."

On every fair day during that winter, the elk-dog warriors practiced. On inclement days, they repaired weapons or worked on their new shields.

There were no Head Splitter attacks on anyone that spring. At first, this was difficult to understand. Finally, after much discussion, it was decided that the loss of elk-dogs the previous fall had been an even harder blow to the enemy than they had realized. The stolen horses must have been the major concentration of all elk-dogs held by the Head Splitters.

"But they are angry," reported Black Beaver as the People gathered for the Sun Dance. "We encountered a traveling band only a moon ago. They blame Heads Off . . . Hair Face, they call him. Ah, that Gray Wolf is a bad one! He threatens again to use the face hair on his shield."

Heads Off approached Coyote about these repeated threats.

"Tell me, Uncle, what do you know of this man? He has long threatened my life. What do you know of him?"

Coyote giggled, a little nervously perhaps.

"Who knows anything about a Head Splitter? But this one . . . well, you have seen him. You might not remember . . . your first season with us. A big man, one of their subchiefs then. Probably a little crazy."

"What will happen, Coyote? How will this thing come about?"

Coyote shrugged.

"They will attack us sometime."

"This season?"

"Probably. We must be ready."

The first inkling that hostilities were being resumed came shortly after the Sun Dance. Four youths, confident in the glory of their manhood and the strength of their elk-dog medicine, had boldly left the Sun Dance before the others.

As the Southern band traveled the next day, White Buffalo had been watching a pair of buzzards circling high on fixed wings above the prairie. Suddenly, first one and then the other broke the perfect symmetry of the circles to drop away to the plain below. Another and yet another of the creatures appeared in the distance, each dropping as it neared the same spot.

The four bodies had been placed side by side, almost ceremonially, where the travelers would be sure to find them. The skull of each was split by a blow from a war ax. There was no sign of their elk-dogs.

Two of the four had apparently been already dead from arrow wounds when they had been placed here. The shattering of their heads was purely symbolic, a message to the People. Travel was delayed for a day to allow for mourning and for scaffold burial of the corpses. Then Hump Ribs called a council.

"We must be very careful, my brothers. We must have wolves out at all times."

There was some discussion but basic agreement. This season, it seemed, would be a time of decision. A summer campsite was selected largely on the basis of defensibility.

And the attractive stream with its tree-lined banks and clear pools over white gravel received a new name. No longer would it be known as Sycamore Creek, but as Head-Split Creek.

* * *

Despite the expectations of conflict, there was none that summer. Impatient, the young men suggested a campaign against the enemy, but Hump Ribs objected, and the council firmly backed him. There must be no unauthorized forays. Mention of the fate of the four who had met the enemy at Head Split Creek quieted the discussion.

White Buffalo was pleased with Hump Ribs's handling of the matter. Quiet, firm, and sensible, the band chief seemed to grow in stature as he held the office. Again White Buffalo recalled that some men seem to grow when a position of leadership is thrust upon them. It had been so with Hump Ribs. Part of his leadership was a matter of circumstance, of course. The Southern band had been the one to acquire the First Elk-dog and had the advantage of Heads Off to teach the young Elk-dog men. But even that might not have been, had not the insight and quiet leadership of Hump Ribs allowed for it.

Now the Southern band, increasingly called the Elk-dog band, was easily the most prestigious band of the People. Its leader, in turn, was respected above any other of the band chiefs. It seemed certain that when the time came, Hump Ribs would be the new real-chief.

At the appropriate season the band moved into winter camp. Again, the chosen site was for the best defense against attack by mounted warriors. It was an excellent site, a long narrow meadow several hundred paces in width, protected on the south by the river. On the north was a rocky slope, gradually curving down to meet the river at the east end. The only access to a mounted attack was from the west.

No winter attack was anticipated, but a close watch was kept. With the Moon of Awakening the wolves began to range farther across the prairie. The reason was twofold. This was the time of year favored for forays by Head Splitters. In addition, the buffalo herds would be migrating northward, following the lead of the restless geese.

Long Elk and Standing Bird, ranging to the west by two days' journey, first observed the Head Splitters. At least fifty mounted warriors, well armed, traveling eastward with their wolves well deployed. This was no hunting party. Long Elk stayed to observe their progress, while Standing Bird hurried to report the approach of the enemy.

It must be assumed that the Head Splitters knew their location, so it also followed that the camp might be under observation. A carefully contrived charade was carried out to make everything appear normal. Women scraped skins and chattered to each other at their work. Men lounged against their backrests and visited, and children played happily among the lodges. To the enemy they must appear totally unsuspecting.

The horse herd had been carefully divided. Mares, foals, and immature animals were herded into the meadow behind the lodges, openly watched over by youths too young for combat. The best of the hunting horses, meanwhile, were kept hidden in the heavy timber along the creek, each under the care of its owner. White Buffalo's vision promised success in the venture.

Part of the strategy involved enticing the enemy to attack at the proper moment. A decoy hunting party set out next morning in an innocent manner. Four young men, mounted on the fastest and most surefooted of horses, set out casually, wandering as if looking for game. They were sure to be observed and avoided any opportunity for surprise or ambush by using the terrain. Finally, at the proper location, they showed themselves at the top of the hill, and pretended panic at the discovery of the enemy.

They turned and urged their horses in frantic escape. The Head Splitters, scenting blood, raced in hot pursuit. The four youths pounded across the valley, down the long strip of meadow, and in among the lodges, screaming the warning.

Behind them came the rolling thunder of dozens of hooves. Women screamed, children scurried, and there was a general exodus from the village as the People fled in panic before the charge. Echoing down the valley and reechoing from the rocky hillside, came the chilling war cry of the Head Splitters.

46

To the charging Head Splitters, this must have seemed
an ideal raid. To be able to pursue four terrified youths
directly into the unprotected camp of the enemy was beyond all expectations. People were screaming and running
frantically away from the attack, toward the timber beyond the horse meadow.

White Buffalo and Crow ran with them, but stopped in a
rocky outcrop and settled down to watch. Nervously, the
holy man began to chant, while his wife beat the cadence
on the drum.

The first of the riders had almost reached the nearest of
the lodges when the unexpected happened. From behind
and within the front row of scattered lodges, suddenly
appeared well-armed warriors. The seasoned bowmen of
the band, led by Hump Ribs himself, loosed a flight of
arrows at almost point-blank range. The effect was devas-
tating. Several riders were swept from their mounts, and
horses in the front ranks went down before the withering
fire. The charge faltered, then reformed for another approach, just in time to be met with another barrage of
arrows. Casualties were heavy again.

The horsemen milled in confusion, attempting to reor-
ganize under the shouted commands of their chief. Just at
that moment came a long yell from the timber. Dozens of
young warriors of the Elk-dog Society poured out of the
trees with lances ready, cutting off the avenue of retreat. A
few of the Head Splitters fled in panic into the broken
rocks of the hillside. Others turned to meet the new attack,
and in the space of a few heartbeats, the two groups of
horsemen were mixed in a dusty, bloody melee.

The Head Splitters were traditionally fierce fighters,
skilled in the use of weapons. In addition, they were fight-

ing for survival, trapped between the foot soldiers of Hump Ribs and the mounted lancers of Heads Off. There was no retreat, and the invading force fought with the ferocity of a trapped cougar at bay.

The men of the People, although backed by a tradition of defensive combat only, had readied for this day. The pent-up resentment of years, perhaps centuries of abuse by the Head Splitters was reaching its climax today. Lances found human torsos as vulnerable as the rib cages of buffalo, and warriors tumbled into the dust.

Heads Off kneed his mare through the milling, fighting crowd, searching for the Head Splitter chief. He made a run with the lance at a youth scarcely older than Long Elk. The young warrior initially made a firm stand, readying his shield and club. At the last moment, his resolve faltered, and he threw himself backward from his horse to avoid the lance thrust. Heads Off swept past, unable to stop his charge, and as he glanced down, saw the young Head Splitter's face contort in agony. His own horse, stepping backward to avoid the impact, had crushed the boy's chest.

Heads Off dodged the swing of a club and thrust out in answer with his lance. The point drew blood, but he knew that it was only a flesh wound. The next moment the tide of battle had swept the two apart, and he lost sight of his adversary in the dust and confusion.

Still, he must find and challenge the Head Splitter chief, Gray Wolf. The other would be looking for him also. The reports of personal revenge had continued. Now was the time to resolve this conflict once and for all.

Across the meadow, White Buffalo saw two of the elk-dog soldiers charge at a tall, burly Head Splitter on one of the largest horses he had ever seen. The two made an excellent run. One or the other would certainly strike home. To his amazement, the Head Splitter was as quick as he was large. He parried the lance of one attacker with his rawhide shield and almost simultaneously swung his war club at the other lancer. The club was longer and heavier than most, and even the glancing blow to the shoulder bowled the young rider from his horse. The youth rolled, regained his feet, and ran, his left arm hanging useless as he dodged the pursuing Head Splitter.

Heads Off reined his horse around and kneed her in that direction. The boys were clearly outclassed by a veteran combatant. As he moved closer, the young man gained the shelter of the broken rimrock. The pursuer abandoned the chase and reined his huge bay around to rejoin the battle. As he turned, the symbol on his painted shield became visible to Heads Off for the first time. A geometrically styled design of an animal, with erect ears and a drooping tail—a wolf! This must be Gray Wolf, the mighty warrior, real-chief of the Head Splitters.

At almost the same instant, the other seemed to recognize his sworn enemy. He roared a challenging war cry that was more of a bellow and kneed the bay forward in a charge. The heavy war club whistled in a deadly circle as the two horses approached each other at full speed. Heads Off directed the lance point at the soft midriff just below the ribs and confidently braced himself for the shock of contact.

To White Buffalo's complete surprise, at the last instant the other swung his shield into position. The parried lance-thrust slid on past, and the shoulder of the larger horse crashed into the gray mare's. The little mare rolled, but her rider had kicked free and managed to get out of her way. He was dazed and somewhat disoriented as he floundered around in the dust, trying to avoid the finishing blow that must be coming.

Momentum had carried the Head Splitter's horse beyond the fallen Heads Off, and now they whirled for another run. Heads Off was on hands and knees in the dust. The whirling war club began to gain momentum in circles designed to finish the fight at the end of the charge. Dimly through the dusty haze, White Buffalo saw the big horse thundering down and saw the deadly swinging club.

The next action of Heads Off was more instinct than reason. He dove directly under the front feet of the galloping bay. His reasoning, if he had any at all, was simply to put something between himself and the deadly club. The Head Splitter would be unable to strike directly beneath his own horse. The horse unwittingly assisted too. A horse instinctively jumps to avoid obstacles under its feet, and the big bay tucked up his forefeet neatly and cleared the rolling body. Momentum carried the charge beyond, while Heads Off floundered around looking for his weapon.

White Buffalo gasped as the pounding hooves thundered down on the unhorsed Heads Off, who was at a definite disadvantage. He was on foot. The other's mobility and the length of the club made the lance less effective. He could throw the weapon, but if he missed, he would be unarmed.

The great horse approached, the rider swinging his ax. Then, to White Buffalo's astonishment, Heads Off leaped aside and turned to thrust his lance deep into the soft flank of the elk-dog. Instantly the holy man understood. Now they must fight on foot.

The bay screamed and reared, nearly falling backward, then bucking convulsively until it fell headlong. Heads Off was already running forward. The impact had torn the lance from his grasp, and he snatched the knife from his belt. Gray Wolf was rising from his knees when Heads Off dived headlong over the dying horse to prevent his finding the war club.

The two rolled in the dirt—kicking, biting, gouging. Gray Wolf kneed at the other's groin, grasped his knife wrist, and rolled on top, striving to turn the blade toward its owner.

In desperation, Heads Off swung a long sweeping blow with his left fist. It collided with Gray Wolf's ear, startling and confusing him. The use of fists in combat was entirely unfamiliar to the Head Splitter. Heads Off struck again, and the grip loosened on his wrist. Another blow and he wrenched the knife free and thrust upward with all his strength in a last desperate effort of survival. The point entered the other's throat between the jawbones and sank deep. Blood spurted over Heads Off's face, as the massive weight of the warrior's body sank heavily on his chest. He lay his head back, unable to move.

The sounds of battle were farther away now. Someone pulled the dead Head Splitter's body away, and Heads Off rolled over and filled his lungs. Weakly he crawled over and sat on the dead horse, still breathing heavily.

The Head Splitters were on the run, leaving their dead behind them. A number of warriors of the People rode in hot pursuit or loosed arrows after the fleeing remnants of the attacking force.

Coyote came over, leading Heads Off's gray mare. He handed Heads Off a heavy, blood-spattered club.

"Here, Heads Off. You will want to keep this."

Heads Off looked at the dead chief and shook his head, still unable to speak.

"No matter, I will keep it for you. You may want it later."

Coyote stood quietly, his presence comforting. A loose horse clopped past, reins trailing, nickering in bewilderment. Women were returning from the timber, looking for loved ones. Here and there a sudden cry, a wail of grief, and the rising notes of the Mourning Song.

The heaviest fighting had been in the meadow, where the horsemen had clashed, and the heaviest casualties were there. The wounded were being assisted by their friends and relatives.

Tall One glided gracefully through the carnage and embraced Heads Off.

"I am proud, my husband."

"I want to go home," he gasped. "To lie down."

They moved in that direction.

Near the first of the lodges, a cluster of people, both men and women, crowded together in a knot. There was a sense of urgency, of extra tragedy, in the keening wails arising from this group. Some simply stood, numbly staring. Attracted by the dread fascination of the unknown, Heads Off motioned, and the three altered their course. They elbowed their way into the crowd toward the motionless figure in the center of the circle. White Buffalo, too, hurried over.

The dead warrior was Hump Ribs. The People of the Southern band were without a leader.

47

In the aftermath of the Great Battle, a feeling a numbness settled over the Southern band, like the heavy pall of a gray cloudbank. There was mourning and the duties attendant upon those who cared for the dead. The People went about their daily tasks of living like sleepwalkers, numb from all the death and destruction. The weather was warm, and very quickly the stench of rotting horseflesh became overbearing. The level meadow along the stream was no longer pleasant, but a place of death. There were still bodies of Head Splitters rotting among those of their elk-dogs. It was time to move.

It would have been time anyway, because the gathering of the People for the Sun Dance and Big Council was imminent. The travel time would be no more than sufficient to reach the appointed place. But, there was no one to say the day, to announce that now or three days from now we will move. There was no leader. Despite this, the need to move quickly became apparent, and the People seemed to move by instinct. The packing, preparation, and striking of the lodges happened. One family began to take down its lodge, and someone else, seeing it, followed suit. A great deal of organization was not needed. The purpose and direction were plain. It remained only to do it, and the People did.

They straggled out of the campsite, still numb, bedraggled, and mourning. Behind them, the trees along the river held burial scaffolds, stark against the sky. They were easily visible, even at last view, amid the budding twigs of new spring growth. Death gives way to new life, thought White Buffalo. He stood a moment, looking back, thinking that the scene looked very much like a heron rookery, with its dozens, sometimes hundreds, of heron lodges. Scaffolds of sticks, built by the herons to hold new life, as these scaffolds held death. He sighed and turned to follow the procession, wending its way to join the rest of the People. The Southern band was confused. They had won a great victory over the traditional enemy. Yet there was still death and mourning, destroying the taste of that victory.

Coyote waited beside the trail and fell in beside White Buffalo. The two walked in silence for a time, and it was Coyote who finally spoke.

"The People need a leader."

Yes, thought White Buffalo. A leader. Someone to inspire, to point a direction. Just now, the People were floundering. They were moving toward the Sun Dance because there was nothing else that was solid and lasting. They would seek that celebration because its time and place had already been set. But beyond that, the future was indefinite. There should be a council within the band to select a new chief. None had been called in the numb confusion that had followed the battle. Why? White Buffalo wondered for a moment. Who should have called such a council? The Southern band had enjoyed good leadership for many summers, but now, who?

Mouse Roars had been a leader and teacher, respected and followed by the young men. But Mouse Roars was dead. His son Standing Bird had shown leadership talents but was still too young. Two Pines? No, he still bore the stigma of having changed loyalties when he left the Red Rocks. Sees Far? His skills lay in other directions, as a scout and tracker.

White Buffalo himself could, and probably should, call a council to make the selection. He had been avoiding it, he decided, because he saw no clear candidate for leadership. *Aiee,* nothing was ever simple, even in victory. He studied Coyote as they walked along. Why had the little man brought up the subject? He thought about Coyote's ways, how Coyote had no desire to lead but managed to manipulate situations without seeming to do so.

"Yes, we should call a council," White Buffalo said tentatively.

"A good thought," Coyote answered and walked on in silence.

Ah, the holy man thought, I am right. He *does* have an idea.

"Who will they select?" White Buffalo wondered aloud.

"Who knows?" Coyote shrugged. "Who is a leader?"

"Two Pines is well thought of," ventured the holy man.

"Yes, that is true. But will the young men follow an outsider?" Coyote asked.

"My thoughts also. *Aiee*, we need someone like Mouse Roars."

"Or Hump Ribs," said Coyote. "That is the problem."

"Coyote, who do the young men follow?"

The little man giggled.

"Heads Off, of course."

"No, I mean . . ."

Suddenly, Coyote's purpose became clear. White Buffalo had been racking his brain to think of a leader but had found none. He had been thinking, however, of the traditional warrior-hunter, the bowman, fighting on foot and teaching others to do so. The interests of the young men did not lie in that direction but in the skills of the elk-dog. They were following the one who could teach *those* skills, those of the elk-dog medicine. The idea of two warrior societies came back again. It was a fact of life now. What was more, the Elk-dog Society was assuming the stronger position.

And that, the holy man now realized at last, was the basis of the present problem. There was no clear leader emerging because he would be expected to come from the old traditional warrior-hunter society, now called the Bowstrings. There was no leader there, because the young men were following the call of the elk-dog and of another leader.

White Buffalo doubted that Heads Off was even aware of the political implications here. There would probably be young men who would choose the more traditional ways, but just now . . . *aiee*, the chief *must* be an elk-dog leader, and there was none except . . . It was unthinkable, the thing that kept repeatedly intruding itself into his mind. If Two Pines was unacceptable because of changed loyalty, then how could a complete outsider hope to lead? The answer came back to him: Heads Off leads because of his special medicine, which Two Pines does not have. Which *no one else* has.

White Buffalo stopped in his tracks and stared at Coyote in amazement.

"Heads Off?"

Coyote giggled nervously.

"Why not, Uncle? The young men follow him already. They followed him into battle. He is respected by the elders, even though they do not understand him."

"But, he . . . I . . . Coyote, this is not done."

"It has not been, Uncle," said Coyote almost gently, "because until now there has been no elk-dog medicine. But there is change in the wind."

Yes, change, thought the holy man. Once again, he wondered if he was ready. But he must. It was not possible to go back.

"Would he do this, Coyote?"

Coyote shrugged.

"Who knows? Let us ask him."

It was late in the day before they contrived to walk with Heads Off while he led his horse for a little while. White Buffalo, after some small talk, came straight to the point.

"Heads Off, the men want you to become the new chief."

"What? Oh, no, Uncle, I could never do that."

"But the young men follow you already," Coyote pointed out.

"No! I only teach them. No, Uncle, both of you . . . I could not do this. I do not know the customs of the People . . . I . . ."

"But you have learned much, my son," White Buffalo reminded him. "You speak the tongue. You have married here, sired a son. No one knows *all* of the customs, and we will help you, Coyote and I. Your wife too."

The three argued for a long time, Heads Off resisting.

"Could this really be done? You would advise me closely?" he asked finally.

They nodded eagerly.

"How is this done, the choosing of the chief?"

"We call a council."

"When?"

"Tonight."

"Aiee!"

"No, wait!" Coyote suggested. "Talk to Tall One. Ask what she thinks."

Yes, of course, thought White Buffalo. *An excellent plan!* The girl could present the situation in a proper light.

"Of course! Speak to her," he urged. "We will talk later."

When the council of the Southern band was held two days later, there was little discussion and no argument. The journey continued, but now there was a sense of direction, of pride in belonging. The People began to look forward to the Big Council, to the telling and retelling of the story of their victory in the Great Battle. Their entire mood had changed. They had a new leader. He might be a good leader or not—only time would tell. But he was a leader, and the band responded with purpose.

Meanwhile, White Buffalo, Coyote, and the women worked to prepare Heads Off for his appearance at the Big Council. Tall One and Big-Footed Woman worked tirelessly to create new buckskin garments with embroidered quillwork. Heads Off's hair was trimmed and replaited.

"He needs something around his neck," Coyote observed.

"His medicine?" White Buffalo asked.

Without a word, Tall One took down the bit, the marvelous artistry in metal, whose medicine controlled the elk-dog. She hung it on a thong around the neck of the confused Heads Off, where it dangled and bumped gently against the white buckskin of his shirt.

It was worn so a few days later when the Southern band proudly followed Heads Off to his seat in the circle of the Big Council. There was pride in their eyes when he in his turn rose to address the Council.

"I am Heads Off," he announced in a ringing voice, "chief of the Elk-dog band of the People. My brothers, this has been a very big year for us."

48

White Buffalo shifted comfortably, scratching his shoulder against the backrest as he lounged in the sun. Life had been good the past few summers. Fourteen in all, he counted, since Heads Off had become band chief, and much had happened.

The entire tribe had prospered with the expansion of the use of the elk-dog. In these few years, the People had become a major power on the plains. Other tribes, even, sometimes referred to this tribe as the Elk-dog People. There had almost been a split in the tribe as everyone became more affluent through greater ease in hunting. A small, militant splinter group of young elk-dog men who called themselves the Blood Society had withdrawn from the tribe entirely. At least for a time. They had returned to assist in another battle with the Head Splitters and were now welcome again. This had resulted in not two but three Warrior Societies with slightly differing interests and motives but mutual respect.

The People, able to kill and skin more buffalo and to transport heavier lodge covers, now made their dwellings larger and finer. Some were constructed of thirty skins. Wealth was expressed in this way and in horses. Children learned to ride before they could walk. It was common to see a toddler, tied to the back of a trustworthy old mare while she was turned loose to graze. The sons of Heads Off and Tall One had been raised so and were fine riders. Especially Eagle, the older boy. Coyote, in a surprise move at the First Dance, had given the child the nickname he had borne all along. It had seemed to fit, as the boy matured and soft fur appeared on his upper lip only a few seasons ago. The young man remained Eagle, and as Coyote said, the youth's eye carried such a look, the look of eagles. This one would earn fame.

The other child was called Owl. Two years younger, he had never seemed quite as aggressive or as popular a child as his brother Eagle. But his name fit well. This child had arrived in the world wide-eyed, as some infants do, eager to see and to learn. His large dark eyes, much like his mother's, seemed to glow with an inner curiosity as well as wisdom. Yes, Owl was well named.

There had been other changes as the People adapted to the new affluence that the elk-dog provided. Time formerly spent in the quest of food for survival could now be devoted to things of the spirit. More elaborate decoration of simple garments and household things, more songs and ceremonies. There was a surge of interest in the throaty melodies of the courting flute, which in turn led to seasons of romance.

And, all in all, it was good. White Buffalo could hardly believe that at one time he had resisted such change, had even considered destroying Heads Off to stop it. Heads Off had been a good leader. He had made mistakes, as all leaders do. But people forgive their leaders for honest mistakes. Only one thing people find unforgivable in a leader, White Buffalo observed—indecisiveness. A wrong decision is forgiven more easily than no decision. And Heads Off had never been guilty of that. True, he could never, as an outsider, be more than a band chief, a subchief in the structure of tribal politics. But, the Elk-dog band was still the strongest and most prestigious of the bands of the People. That had been the function of Heads Off.

White Buffalo filled his nose and mouth with the fragrant smoke from his pipe and blew it out gently, savoring the mixture of tastes. Tobacco, sumac, the roasted bark of the red willow, and other favorite substances lent their fragrance. Everything, he now believed, had its function, its place in the world. As Heads Off did. As every person does, maybe. His own position, that of interpreter of the change for the People. Only after the fact had he known. His entire career as holy man had been shaped by forces of the spirit-world, to help the People take this great leap forward as they changed to accept the medicine of the elk-dog.

He thought of Coyote, who had changed not one bit in

the past seasons. A little grayer, a little fatter, maybe, but the same likable buffoon. White Buffalo had been irritated, angry even, when Coyote had refused the gift of the spirit and had taken another path. Now he realized that that too had been part of the entire plan. Coyote had been used as a go-between, to help bring together the medicines of the buffalo and the elk-dog. As he looked back, White Buffalo could see many things that had not been apparent. All the events that had taken place in his lifetime had come to rest in proper perspective. From his earliest feelings of the spirit, his strange visions on his vision quest, the dreams of the elk-dog as a youth . . . Now it all was seen as a part of his mission, his life's work.

It was satisfying, this feeling that he had been permitted to be a part of so great a change. But there seemed to be one thing that still did *not* fit. It had begun to bother him many years ago that no young person had come forth to become his apprentice, to learn the medicine of the buffalo. He had realized, in light of the sweeping changes brought about by the elk-dog, that there had been a reason. The lives of Coyote, Big-Footed Woman, the other possible holy ones, had all held other purposes. Parts of the pattern, which had been fitted together like the multicolored quills of decorative embroidery on a ceremonial shirt. But there was still a flaw. Somehow, the purpose of his own life seemed incomplete. So far, it was full, satisfying, overwhelming almost in its scope, but what now? There was an emptiness, a regret, in this, the autumn of his career. It was not difficult to identify, of course. It was a feeling of concern, of failure almost. Disappointment. There had still never been a young person to accept the gift of the spirit, one to whom he could teach his skills, his medicine.

He had tried to put it away, to crowd it back in his thoughts, but it was difficult. It was much like the disappointment that he and Crow had never had another child. That had been pushed aside, accepted, but was still a deep hurt sometimes. He did not understand it, any more than he understood the lack of someone to carry on the medicine of the buffalo. Was he to die with no successor? Was that too part of the plan?

His reverie was interrupted by the approach of Coyote, who had with him his grandson Owl.

"*Ah-koh,* Uncle," Coyote greeted him, "we would speak with you."

Coyote's tone was serious. This then was no idle visit. What was it? The holy man motioned for them to sit.

The youngster, of maybe twelve summers it seemed, appeared uneasy and a little frightened. Coyote was quick to assist, explaining that Owl had questions about his background and why his father, the band chief, was considered an outsider. The boy had been teased and bullied, it seemed, by a couple of ne'er-do-wells.

White Buffalo thought it over. He could see the young man's dilemma. At twelve summers, one does not wish to be different. He had seen the older boy, Eagle, successfully adjust to the fact, but this child seemed to have more misgivings.

Well, why not start at the beginning? A trifle bored by the entire thing, the holy man nevertheless wished to help the grandson of his friend Coyote. He brought out the story-skins, and spent some time showing the pictographs of Heads Off on First Elk-dog, the buffalo hunts on horseback, the Great Battle with Heads Off defeating the Head Splitter Gray Wolf. The boy had heard the story before, but now seemed to be searching for new meaning.

"Your father is now one of us," the holy man concluded. "Heads Off is well honored by the People."

"But what of his own tribe, Uncle?" the boy asked. "Their medicine?"

An odd question, White Buffalo thought.

"His medicine is very powerful," the holy man said. "As strong as my own, in a different way."

He warmed to this, a favorite topic.

"Mine is the medicine of the buffalo. My visions tell the People where to hunt, how to find the herds. Your father's medicine is that of the elk-dog. With this medicine, he controls the elk-dogs, so that men ride upon them to hunt or fight."

He pointed to some of the pictures with the metal bit worn as an ornament on the chest of Heads Off. The boy nodded. He knew that talisman well. All his life it had hung in the place of honor over his parents' bed.

"Tell me, Uncle," said the boy suddenly. "How do you know where to find the buffalo?"

White Buffalo almost gasped. This was a much more

complicated question than it appeared. It involved the very heart of the holy man's expertise and was not a question to be taken lightly. It implied deep soul-searching questions by the young man. White Buffalo shrugged.

"The visions, of course."

He could tell that the youngster was deep in thought, but he was completely unprepared for the next question.

"Uncle, how does one become a holy man?"

Like a wave of water moving down a dry wash in the time of flash flooding, the answers came flowing over White Buffalo. Of course! Why had he not seen this before? A sensitive young man who carried the blood of two gifted ones, Coyote and Big-Footed Woman, besides that of Heads Off himself. Of course this one might receive the gift of the spirits.

The holy man looked across, over the boy's head, and his glance met that of Coyote. The little man's face was squinted in his good-natured half-smile, but his eyes reflected more. Coyote understood what was happening. How long had he known?

The pieces were falling together too rapidly, though they seemed to fit so well . . . he must have time . . . to pray and think, and seek visions.

White Buffalo tried to assume an expression of serious dignity, though he wanted to leap and sing for joy.

At last he was finding the answer he had sought so long. He turned back to the boy, trying not to speak too gruffly.

"Come back tomorrow. We will talk."

There was satisfaction in the boy's face, and in Coyote's. And White Buffalo's heart was very good.

ABOUT THE AUTHOR

Don Coldsmith was born in Iola, Kansas, in 1926. He served as a World War II combat medic in the South Pacific and returned to his native state, where he graduated from Baker University in 1949 and received his M.D. from the University of Kansas in 1958. He worked at several jobs before entering medical school: He was YMCA Youth Director, a gunsmith, a taxidermist, and for a short time a Congregational preacher. In addition to his private medical practice, Dr. Coldsmith has been a staff physician at the Health Center of Emporia State University, where he also teaches in the English Department. He discontinued medical pursuits in 1990 to devote more time to his writing. He and his wife of thirty-two years, Edna, operate a small cattle ranch. They have raised five daughters.

Dr. Coldsmith produced the first ten novels in the Spanish Bit Saga in a five-year period; he writes and revises the stories first in his head, then in longhand. From this manuscript the final version is skillfully created by his longtime assistant, Ann Bowman.

Of his decision to create, or re-create, the world of the Plains Indians in the early centuries of European contact, the author says: "There has been very little written about this time period. I wanted also to portray these Native Americans as human beings, rather than as stereotyped 'Indians.' As I have researched the time and place, the indigenous cultures, it's been a truly inspiring experience for me. I am not attempting to tell anyone else's story. My only goal is to tell a story and tell it fairly."

Look for Don Coldsmith's novel, RUNESTONE, available in paperback from Bantam Books.

Set in the first years of the eleventh century, RUNESTONE tells the story of two sturdy, swift-moving longships that have set sail from Norway with their handpicked crews, and are venturing across the great sea to Vinland and the colony of Straumfjord. But the real journey will only begin when a group of sailors pushes on into the waterways of the vast, uncharted continent itself—and into a historic rendezvous with a native culture unlike anything they have ever seen.

Combining the grandeur of Norse adventure with the lush, lyrical atmosphere of Coldsmith's tales of the People that form his towering Spanish Bit Saga ("Devastatingly assured writing, commented *The New York Times Book Review)*, RUNESTONE is Don Coldsmith's *magnum opus:* a novel with unsurpassed reach and range, one of the most satisfying reading experiences of the year.

Turn the page for a preview of RUNESTONE by Spur Award-winner Don Coldsmith.

Runestone

1

Nils Thorsson stood in the foredecks, watching the other ship cleave her way through gray-green water. A white curl of foam spewed out of each side of the prow as she ran before the wind. Running with a bone in her teeth, the old men called it. It was a glorious feeling, the free-flying run of a well-built ship, looking alive as a bird in flight.

It was easy, as he watched the *Norsemaiden*'s trim lines and the nodding of the tall dragon's head on her prow, to see her as a living thing. The red-and-white sail bulged full-curving, filled with the wind's push.

The two sister ships raced forward, running parallel courses. The *Snowbird*, on whose deck he now stood, was slightly ahead.

It had been a good voyage so far. Only once since they left Greenland's south coast had the men been forced to turn to the oars. Even then, Nils thought, it might have been unnecessary. He suspected that the commander, Helge Landsverk, had ordered the stint at rowing only to test the mettle of his crews. Thirty-two oarsmen the ships each boasted, all handpicked for the voyage. They had done well, and soon a freshening breeze had made it possible to unfurl the sails again to run with the wind.

He could sense the shudder of resilient timbers under his feet when they struck a slightly larger wave. The ship seemed to raise her head for a moment, and then plunged back to her task. Again he felt the life within her sleek hull. She was a living, breathing creature with a spirit of her own that seemed to communicate with his. Nils wondered if everyone felt this affinity for a good ship. Probably not. Some did, though. He could tell by the glow in the eyes of the old men when they told their sea tales of long ago.

Why, too, did one ship have a different spirit, somehow, than another? These two, for instance. The *Snowbird* and the *Norsemaiden* were as nearly alike as the shipbuilder's skills could make them, yet everyone knew they were different. Neither was better nor worse than the other, only different.

As two women may be different, perhaps, he thought. Both beautiful and desirable, yet different.

The *Snowbird* always breasted the swells as if she challenged the sea, asking for the contest, daring the legions of the sea-god Aegir to do their worst. She savagely reveled in the struggle. Perhaps it was only something in the painted eye of the dragon's head above the prow. There was definitely a proud, aloof expression. But no, it was more than that. She *did* have such a spirit.

Norsemaiden, on the other hand, was more sedate. Perhaps her responsibility as the flagship of the commander gave her a more mature dignity.

Nils could see the arrow-straight figure of Helge standing in the bows. He had known Landsverk since they were boys. It was because of this friendship, in fact, that Nils now commanded the *Snowbird*.

It was a great adventure that his friend had sketched out for him. Helge Landsverk, skilled as he was at navigation, had been eclipsed by the dazzling exploits of an older relative, Leif Ericsson. Leif had already led an expedition on the course they were now following, and had founded a colony on the new land. Vinland, Leif had called it, for the myriad of grapevines he found growing there.

There were some who thought it a new continent, as large as Europe, perhaps. It was on this precept that Helge based his ambition. Let Leif explore the seas, establish colonies in the islands and extend the new religion that so obsessed him. He, Helge Landsverk, would push into the western continent itself, this Vinland that seemed so exciting. If grapes could grow, so could other crops. He spoke with admiration of Thorwald Ericsson, Leif's younger brother, who espoused similar ideas.

Nils had once met the young Ericsson, a bombastic, hard-driving youth of about his own age. It was easy to see, in the enthusiastic demeanor of Thorwald Ericsson, the influence of the old Viking blood that coursed in his veins. It was said, Nils recalled, that Thorwald was much like his father, the irrepressible Eric the Red. Perhaps even *old* Thorwald, Eric's father, who had fled to Iceland to escape prosecution for murder.

Yes, there was little doubt that a generation or two ago, young Thorwald Ericsson would have been in the forefront of those who went a-viking, raiding and pillaging mercilessly along the coast and into the Isles.

It was exciting to hear Helge's stories of the sea, to see his eyes glitter in the light of the smoky oil lamp on the table.

"Thorwald is somewhere over there now," Helge had told him.

"Where? Vinland?"

"Yes!"

Landsverk's face was ruddy with excitement and wine as he described the deep fjords and clean cold water of the coasts. Nils was confused.

"You have been there?" he asked.

"No, no. Only as far as Greenland. But, Nils, Vinland is better. I have talked to Thorwald. There are bold headlands, sheltered harbors, all just waiting for settlement."

"There are no people there?"

"No. None civilized. A few Skraelings."

"Skraelings?"

"Yes. Primitives. Barbarians. They are no problem against civilized weapons."

Nils ignored the faint warning deep in his consciousness, the hint that his friend was actually anticipating such an opportunity for combat. He was excited at the possibilities, too.

He became more so as Helge unfolded the plan, an exploring expedition paid for by Helge's father. It was hoped to establish trade. In his semi-inebriated condition, it did not occur to Nils that the goal of trade was moderately incompatible with that of invasion and combat, leading to colonization.

After much further drinking of wine and recalling of childhood memories, Nils had accepted Landsverk's offer to command the *Snowbird*. He did protest, though not too strenuously, that he was not skilled in navigation. It was no matter, Helge had insisted; "I will be navigating anyway, and you will have a skilled crew."

They had embarked from Stadt in late May. Now, here he was, far from Norway, gaining experience as sailor and navigator, setting forth on another leg of their journey. And he had found it good.

Thus far, they had made brief stops at Iceland and again on the southern tip of Greenland, where a vigorous colony flourished. Each time, the sailors spent a few days recovering from the pitching roll of the Atlantic and loading supplies for the next leg of the journey. To be light and fast, yet sturdy, a ship had little room for supplies and cargo. The crew was cramped for space. Even the larger ships, such as these two, carried little beyond necessities and a few items for trading.

Water, of course, was one of the biggest problems on a long sea voyage. Casks were stowed amidships and refilled at every opportunity.

Across the waves, Landsverk waved and pointed ahead. A waterspout spewed into the air as a whale breached the surface and rolled. The creature was close enough for the men to see the great eye, fixed for a moment on the intruders before the monster slipped beneath the sea again.

They had seen whales before, east of Greenland. It was a frightening thing, a feeling of vulnerability, to watch the creatures calmly approach. There had been a moment of terror while the mind tried to comprehend the enormity of the creatures. Longer than the ship, they could have destroyed the entire expedition with a flick of the tail. It was only slight consolation to recall that there had never been an instance of one of these giants attacking a ship.

The shiny gray bulk slipped out of sight and they were alone on the sea again. Svenson, the steersman, had relinquished his task to a relief man and was making his way forward.

"You see him?" Nils asked.

"Aye, a big one!" Svenson grinned.

"It always surprises me. I'm never expecting it."

"Right. Ye never get used to it."

The men stood at the prow, studying the sea, but the whale did not reappear. Svenson was pulling his cloak around him more snugly.

"By the hammer of Thor, there's a bite to the wind. It will be a cold one tonight."

Nils nodded, amused. Svenson wore a crucifix around his neck, symbol of his conversion. Still, in matters like the sea and the weather, he swore on the names of the old gods. Such habits die hard.

"Sven," he asked, "you have been to Vinland before?"

"Yes, of course."

"How many days yet?"

The old sailor chuckled.

"You grow impatient, lad."

He looked at the sky, the horizon, and the gently nodding sea, as if for a sign.

"Maybe two, three days."

Nils nodded again.

"There is a harbor?"

"Yes. It is much like the coast at home. Fjords, deep inlets. They were building a dock when I was there."

"That is good."

"Yes. It will be much easier."

Abruptly, Svenson turned and made his way back to the stern to take the steering oar again. Only for a short while was he ever willing to relinquish the responsibility. That, Nils supposed, was one of the qualities that made Sven a good steersman.

Nils shivered a little against the wind, and pulled his wolf-skin cloak up around his ears. Even the setting sun looked cold and watery. Svenson was right. This would be a chill night.

2

The colony nestled in a meadow that sloped down to the sea on the north shore. Nils wondered at the exposed location, but soon realized its advantages. The little harbor opened on a deep channel, with plenty of room for maneuvering. In the distance to the north lay a massive headland, tall enough, it appeared, to provide some degree of shelter from the winter's blasts.

The land mass where the colony stood stretched southward as far as eye could see, green with vegetation during this summer season. There were trees and meadows and rolling hills, much more hospitable in appearance than the barren slopes of Iceland, or even Greenland.

Of course, they were now farther south. For the past several days, it had been apparent that the Polestar was lower in the sky at night than in the more northern regions. Svenson had demonstrated an old sailor's method of reckoning position. He lay on his back on the deck with his head pointing south, knees raised and feet near his rump. Then he placed a fist on his right knee with the thumb sticking straight up.

"See?" he invited. "When ye're this far south, the Polestar is not far from the thumb. Farther north, she's farther away, higher in the sky."

It was reasonable, and so simple that Nils was surprised

that he had never heard of this trick. Of course, he had never had to reckon his position north and south to any extent. Most of his sailing experience had been along the coast, seldom out of sight of land.

More important in the open sea was identification of direction, rather than position. In clear weather it was no problem, by the position of the sun. At noon a shadow, cast by a stick, pointed due north. At night, the Polestar provided orientation. It was more difficult in overcast weather, especially in the absence of prevailing wind. Then the whole world became a faceless, unfeeling gray. Nils could well remember the first time he had felt the terror of the *hafvilla*, the panicky feel of being lost at sea. It was all he could do to maintain his composure until the sky cleared enough for him to see the red stripe of the sunset far to the west along the horizon.

On this expedition, however, they had been relatively free of such difficulty. The weather had been cooperative, and except for a chilly night or two, it had been a comfortable crossing. Nils was gaining confidence, aided by the sage advice of Svenson, who had taken a liking to the young shipmaster.

They steered into the channel from the northeast under full sail, tacked toward the distant harbor, and then furled the sails to approach the dock with the oars.

Three cargo ships wallowed at anchor near the docks, potbellied *knarrs*, heavy and slow compared to the trim dragon ships. They reminded Nils of three fat sows nosing around a trough. He looked again with a seaman's eye. They were well built, their massive holds designed to carry livestock and cargo amidships. Fore and aft there would be living quarters. Thorfinn Karlsefni had brought his settlers in these ships, some hundred and sixty men and women, to sink their roots into the soil that Leif Ericsson had called Vinland.

At the dock rode a sleek ship with slender lines. It was a thrill to look at her, bright paint glistening in the sunlight. Men moved along her decks, performing the constant tasks required for the maintenance of an ocean-going ship. Nils turned to ask Svenson about her, but the old sailor anticipated his question.

"Ericsson's here," he grunted.

"Leif Ericsson?"

It would be an honor to meet the famous explorer.

"No, Thorwald. You know him?"

"Not really. I met him once."

"A little crazy," Svenson commented as he turned his attention to the steering oar.

Crazy or not, Nils told himself, the man is exciting. The very thought of charting unknown coasts made his heart race, and sent a tingle up his spine to prickle the hairs at the back of his neck.

Ahead of them, *Norsemaiden* completed her turn and headed for an area near the landing. Svenson heaved on his oar and *Snowbird* followed. People were coming down to the docks, to stand waving as the ships approached. The arrival of ships from home would be a major event for people in such isolation.

Beyond the landing area, he could see the several buildings of the village of Straumfjord. Three of them appeared to be of the common Norse longhouse style, dwellings for a number of families each. These would be temporary, until the colony became better established, he knew. Then each couple would be drawing apart to build their own houses. He wondered in passing if living with fifty or more people in one house inhibited romance. He could hardly imagine making love with the knowledge that dozens of other couples were listening in the darkness. Of course, they would have the same problem.

A familiar sound struck his ears, the ring of a smith's hammer on an anvil. He spotted the smith's forge, to one side of the settlement, by the occasional puff of smoke and sparks that rose when someone pumped the bellows. He wondered if they were mining iron here, or bringing it from home. Well, he would find out later.

Sheep gazed on the meadow behind the village, in the care of a handful of young men. Nils noted that they seemed to be herding rather closely. Somewhat more than would be expected, he thought. He wondered if this was because of fear of attack, or threat of wild animals. He knew nothing of what sort of beasts might be found here. Wolves? Probably. Perhaps bears, even some type of the great cats reported elsewhere. Very little was actually known about this new land.

Possibly, even, there was a threat from the natives. What had Helge called them? Skraelings, that was it. Helge had referred to them as barbarians. Further suggestive evidence was seen in a high palisade of poles that encircled the compound. Nils wondered how they compared to the natives in southern Europe, or in the islands of Britannia. Some of them could be quite formidable. Would there be different tribes, as the Scots seemed to have? Ah, well, that too could wait.

Norsemaiden slid smoothly alongside the dock, her sails now furled. Men standing there caught thrown lines fore and aft, dallying expertly around the pilings that formed the support of the structure. There was a cheer from the shore as the ship settled to, rocking slightly and tugging gently at her tethers.

Nils saw that there was no room for the *Snowbird* at the dock. He turned to call to the steersman, but once more Svenson anticipated him. A pull on the steering oar, and the ship responded eagerly with a slight change in direction. Nils had his doubts about this maneuver, but Sven had, after all, been here before. He should know . . . ah, yes, there on shore were pillars made of stones piled carefully to indicate the landing area. They must have used this stretch of shore before the dock was built.

Knowing what was needed, Svenson altered his stroke and *Snowbird* curved forward, running at an angle toward the sandy beach. She turned, easing in parallel to the shore. There was a sliding sound, then a soft hiss as the underbelly of the hull gently brushed on the sandy bottom. The incessant rocking of the sea had ceased, and the heaving deck was still. Nils stood, still swaying. It would take a little while to regain his land legs.

Nils jumped down and splashed ashore, helping drag the bowline, and ran up the beach to a piling to secure the ship. He looked back to check the *Snowbird*'s position. Yes, good, his eye quickly estimated. Secure now, but at high tide she'd be afloat. He dreaded this maneuver on a strange beach. A hidden rock, even a relatively small one, could disembowel the light dragon ship, ripping the thin shell of her belly from stem to stern. There had probably been no cause for concern. This landing had been used by Karlsefni's ships since they arrived. The colonists would know every stone. Still, he was glad the mooring was over.

People from the colony swarmed down to the beach, laughing, jostling, and shouting. Nils turned and waved to the crowd. Strange, the affinity of these people for adventure. He had thought of *them* as the adventurers, carving a colony out of the rugged wilderness. They, in turn, regarded him, as master of an exploring ship, a person of excitement and daring.

Men waded into the surf to examine the lines of the *Snowbird*, and run hands along the planks of her sleek hull. There was something about a ship or boat that stirred Norse blood. Maybe that was it. He remembered his grandfather, who had told him endless stories of the sea.

As a small child, Nils had been fascinated by his grandfather's stories. The old man had been well educated, and had contributed much to Nils's general knowledge. His lifetime had spanned many changes. The new religion, the change from the old runic alphabet to the new . . . he had attempted to teach both to Nils . . . and the change in philosophy from Viking raiding and plunder to exploration, settlement, and trade. But most of all, his love of the sea came through to the eager ears of his young listener.

"A man without a boat is a man in chains," the old man had once said.

Nils recalled his grandfather for a moment as he saw the light of excitement in the eyes of the men who affectionately caressed the flanks of the *Snowbird*.

He was jolted back to reality by a pair of blue eyes. The girl was standing quietly on the beach, not running excitedly or shouting with the others. She only stood and looked at him, coolly and confidently. She was tall and well formed, almost manly in appearance. There was a suggestion of motion, however, in the way she stood. It was like the energy one feels in a cat, waiting tensely to spring at any moment. The girl moved a step or two, out of the way of someone carrying a burden. Her willowy motion extended his impression of latent agility. He could visualize the lithe body, now concealed by the rough cloak that hung from her well-formed shoulders. Her hair, the color of ripe wheat, curled around her neck and fell across those shoulders in a shining sheaf.

The strongest impression of all, however, was that of her spirit. It reached out to him, through the sky blue of those striking eyes. It was easy for him to believe, at least for the moment, that this woman had come to the beach for the sole purpose of welcoming him, Nils Thorsson.

He pulled his gaze away, realizing that he had been ogling the girl. *Thorsson*, he told himself, *you have been at sea too long*.

Still, he answered his own thought, the girl did not seem to object. Perhaps he would encounter her later.

3

There was a celebration that night, with feasting and revelry. The feasting was necessarily restrained because of the obvious shortage of supplies, but the spirit of merriment was apparent. A moderate quantity of wine was consumed, partly from the stores of the travelers. The wine that the colony had fermented from wild grapes harvested the first season was appreciated, even though young. The newcomers pronounced it a success, and admired the musty, robust flavor of the native fruit, not quite like any European grapes.

Dancing continued until far into the night. The women were eager to dance with the visitors, to entertain them royally, and sailors were not hesitant in their participation. Nils noted a few jealous stares from husbands. Even so, there was so little opportunity to stray, in the close confines of the colony, that there seemed to be little danger. Everyone was having a good time, dancing until physically exhausted, which would itself help to preclude any unacceptable trysts.

Additionally, Nils was sure that such a colony would contain mostly, if not entirely, married couples. At least, if he planned it, he would declare it so. It would avoid much trouble. It seemed he had heard, back in Stadt, of two women who had returned with Leif Ericsson's ship. Their husbands had been killed in a fight with the natives, as he recalled.

He finished a dance with a toothsome redheaded wench, who then moved on to another partner. He sat on a bench, breathing hard, warm from the wine and the exertion, and sexually aroused from the fleeting touch of the girl's soft body. His thoughts and his vision were a trifle blurred, dreamlike, when he saw the blue-eyed girl. She was whirling in the arms of one of the sailors, laughing and showing even white teeth. She tossed her head and the sheen of her hair in the flickering firelight was a glimpse of loveliness.

His first thought was one of jealousy toward the man who held her. The next was that she must have a husband here in the colony, and close on the heels of that, resentment that *anyone* should share the bed of this beautiful creature. It was a strange emotion, that of resentment and jealousy toward a man he had never seen. To make matters even more confusing, that jealous feeling was over a woman he had never met, with whom he had never even spoken. Ridiculous, he told himself.

Still, as he watched the whirl of the dancers, he could not control his fantasies. He kept visualizing the motion of that lithe young creature in bed. He shook his head to clear it of thoughts that might lead him into trouble. They *had* been a long time at sea. Human nature could sometimes become quite animal. Some of the sailors manage a romantic interlude with some of the colonists' wives, unless Nils missed his estimate of men and women.

What was he thinking? A little disgusted with himself, and more than a little frustrated, he rose to leave the party. He was a bit unsteady on his feet, tired and pleasantly drunk, and went to seek his blankets. Nils had always been something of a loner, and periodically found it pleasant to be alone to think. He took his blankets and his wolfskin cloak, and sought a secluded spot near the log palisade.

Nils was almost asleep, dimly aware of the distant sounds of revelry, when he heard someone approaching. Some other sailor was searching for a place to spread his robes, and he resented the intrusion on his privacy. He turned his back, and drew his cloak up around his ears.

Almost immediately, however, he felt the warming touch of a soft body, as someone lay down next to him. Startled, he turned to face the newcomer. The starlight was dim, but he could see, as well as feel, that it was a woman. Then realization dawned. Not only a woman, but the incredibly beautiful blue-eyed woman he had seen at the shore and again at the dancing. Smoothly, she lifted the edge of his blanket and slid in beside him. Almost simultaneously, she bestowed a kiss squarely on his lips.

Perhaps it was the surprise, the wine, or the long weeks at sea, but this was a kiss like no other. It was warm, moist, urgent yet yielding, lingering on his lips, with just a tantalizing hint of an exploring tongue before she pulled away.

"Nils Thorsson," she said.

It was not a question, merely a statement of fact. Her voice was deep and seductively husky.

"Yes," he blurted, his breath coming in excited gasps. "What?"

"Would you do something for me?" she whispered in his ear.

He wanted to shout "Anything!" but managed to control himself.

"What is it?"

She snuggled against him, rubbing her knee against his

thighs, encircling his chest with her arm. She breathed tantalizing into his ear.

"Will you take me with you?"

She kissed him again, before he could answer. A longer, deeper kiss, filled with promise of things to come. His hands were caressing her body, pulling her closer to him, but she gently pushed him away.

"Will you?"

He paused, confused. The girl was giving him mixed messages, enticing him while she held him off. This helped to bring him back to reality.

"You have no husband?" he asked pointedly.

The girl shrugged.

"He is nothing. As interesting as a sack of flour."

She snuggled closer to him again.

"He does not know how to treat a woman."

Resentment flared at Nils. He could not imagine a man who would fail to treat this woman like a goddess. He cradled her in his arms and rocked her gently.

"I would leave him for you!" she whispered.

Tears were wet on her cheeks.

"But," Nils protested, "I am just starting on this exploration."

"Then take me with you!"

"No, no, it would not be possible."

"You do not like me," she pouted, pretending to turn away from him. "If you really loved me, you would take me away."

"But I hardly know you!"

She cuddled closer and kissed him again, making his heart race and his breath come in short, excited gasps once more. This girl could turn hot and cold as quickly as . . . She was nibbling on his earlobe now, driving him crazy with desire.

"You *could* know me better," she whispered. "Better than my clod of a husband. Please help me."

Nils was beside himself with a mixture of sympathy and desire. He genuinely wanted to help this desperate young woman, who appeared to be trapped in an unfortunate marriage. Why did she not simply leave her husband, he wondered. It was quite permissible under Norse custom.

Except, he reminded himself, there would be nowhere for her to go, unless she left the colony. And, of course, there was no way to do that, except on one of the infrequent ships that stopped at Straumfjord. And what could she offer in exchange for help? She had nothing. Nothing, that is, except herself. Her body. The exquisite, desirable body that now snuggled against him under the wolfskin cloak.

Nils was of sympathetic nature anyway, and the plight of this woman tugged at his heartstrings. Of all the men here at Straumfjord tonight, she had chosen him to ask for assistance. It was a tremendously uplifting, flattering thing to be the one she felt she could approach. He felt that he *must* help her. Besides, the promised rewards were so desirable. He gathered her to him and kissed her, trying hard to control his breathing.

"I cannot take you with me now," he whispered, "but when I come back—"

She pushed him away.

"You will never come back!" she sobbed, tears starting again.

"Yes, yes, I will. When we finish the exploration, we will stop here on the way home.'

"Really? You will come for me?"

She was happy in an instant.

"Yes," Nils promised.

He was trying to ignore the faint warnings in the back of his mind, to go slow, be careful. He kissed her again, long and passionately, and she responded with equal fervor. Gently, he stroked her body, reaching down for the hem of her skirt. He had just succeeded in touching the smooth skin of a shapely leg when she suddenly pushed his hand away and sat up.

"No!" she said huskily. "Not now. The risk is too great. Later, it will be better."

She kissed him, warmly but briefly, and sprang to her feet, smoothing her skirt as she turned.

"Later," she promised.

She blew him a kiss and was gone.

Nils lay in the dim starlight, staring after her gracefully retreating figure. He was completely frustrated, still breathing heavily, and with the dull ache of unfulfilled desire in his groin. An even worse ache was that of doubt. Had she been only toying with him? Was it a game with her, to see how far she could go with her torment and then give nothing? He was angry, disappointed.

As his anger cooled, he began to rationalize. He wanted badly to justify the girl's behavior. She was desperate, he assumed, or she would never have approached a stranger with this sort of proposition. And, since she had only one thing to offer, it must be held in reserve until she was certain of the bargain. Seen in this light, her behavior was at least understandable, if not totally acceptable to him. His sympathy for her plight began to return. He hoped he could prove worthy of her trust.

The ache of frustrated desire still remained, and he thought for some time of her promise. "Later." How much later, and under what circumstances, he wondered. There were many unanswered questions here. He thought again of the warmth of her kiss, the feel of her body against his, and the seductive thrill of her breath in his ear.

Restless, he rose and went back to the area near the fires, where the thinning crowd still laughed and sang, and wine still flowed. He did not see the girl, and the revelry was not the same. Even the wine had lost its savor. Disappointed, he turned away.

Back in his blankets, he was almost asleep when an odd thought struck him. He did not even know her name, the name of the blue-eyed goddess who had offered to share his bed.